at dawn

at dawn

JOBIE HUGHES

SOFT SKULL PRESS
BERKELEY, CALIFORNIA

Library of Congress Cataloging-in-Publication Data is available

ISBN: 978-1-59376-449-4

Interior Design by Neuwirth & Associates, Inc.
Cover Design by Michael Kellner

Soft Skull Press
An imprint of Counterpoint
1919 Fifth Street
Berkeley, CA 94710
www.softskull.com

Distributed by Publishers Group West
Printed in the United States of America

10 9 8 7 6 5 4 3 2 1

For my mother

prologue

I AM TEN THE first time we leave. The summer after fifth grade, early June, a month before my eleventh birthday. I walk in the door after the last day of school. My mother is at the dining room table with a duffel bag at her feet. She's smoking. Her eyes are red and puffy.

"Hi, Bubby," she says, using the nickname by which she has always called me. "How was your last day?"

"It was good," I say.

"That's great. Listen, you need to go pack a bag for at least a week. We're gonna go camping."

"Is Dad coming?"

"No. And we need to be outta here 'fore he gets home."

I look at the clock. It's three thirty. He'll be home from work in a half hour.

"You need to hurry."

I walk into my bedroom and flip the switch but the light doesn't come on. The electricity has been off for a few days now. I empty my backpack and fill it with clothes and anything else I can think to bring. I'm nervous because my father has been back to work for only two weeks now and he sometimes comes home early. But at a quarter of four we're out the door unnoticed. We drive for a half hour and enter a town I've never been to before.

"Are you leaving Dad?" I ask.

"I don't know what I'm doin', Stratton. I just need a break."

I nod. "It's okay if you are."

She looks over and smiles, places her hand on my leg, and squeezes reassuringly. "Thanks, Bubby."

She turns back to the road, and for the first time, I see that she has unsuccessfully tried covering a bruise on her right cheek.

"Did he hit you?" I ask.

"Yes."

"I hate him."

"No you don't," she says. "He's yer dad."

"Yes I do."

A mile outside of town, we pull onto a paved road beneath an overhead sign that reads SHADY LAKE CAMPGROUND. We enter a thick forest of sylvan charm and on each side of the road there are trails entering and exiting the woods. I can see people walking and biking on them. I grow excited. It's been a very long time since we last went camping. I enjoyed it then and know I'll enjoy it now.

"Is there a lake here?"

"A big one," she says.

"Can we swim in it?"

"Yep. We can rent boats, too."

Signs lead us to the lodge. I wait in the car while she checks us in, and five minutes later she returns with papers in hand. She gives me the map, tells me the lot number, and asks me to navigate the way. There are over two hundred numbered lots but we find ours without trouble. It's a circular clearing tucked within a thicket of trees some twenty yards off the road. A fire pit sits in the very center, and beside that stands a metal charcoal grill.

In the trunk I find a packed cooler, a four-man tent, four pillows, two sleeping bags, a grocery bag full of dry goods. I pull it all out and set it beside the flattest spot of land I've judged to be the best place for the tent. As I'm doing so, my mom sits on a log with her legs crossed, staring past the campground and into the far trees on the opposite side of the road. She looks as though she's pondering the fate she's created for us. Just the two of us, alone, sleeping in a tent because there's no other place for us to go. I've come to think of my mother as a fighter, a drinker, a lover, a nurturer. She's short and thin but has the biggest heart of any person I've known. But now she looks lost, and the pain in her eyes makes me wish I had something I could offer to take it away. But I have no soothing words, no money, no home in which we could hide. Nothing more than a son's love, and even though I know she'd say that is all she wants, to me it seems terribly insufficient. I walk to her and hug her tightly. Because she's sitting, her head only comes to my chest. When I pull away she says thank you.

Together we build the tent. It's the domed kind with fiberglass poles that slide into polyester sleeves. When it's up I hammer the stakes into the ground while my mother starts dinner, dumping charcoal bricks into the grill. She douses them with fluid and lets me light it with a match. Fire sweeps across the bricks with a whoosh. We grill hamburgers and eat potato salad scooped with our fingers from a grocery store container.

"I like it here," I say.

She nods. "It sure is peaceful, isn't it?"

❧ 2 ❧

I wake in the middle of the night, sweating, out of breath. I reach over, terrified that my mother isn't there, but my hand brushes her shoulder. I go to the front of the tent and poke my head out. Silence, the lot numbers bathed in soft light at the front of each plot.

"What's the matter?" she asks behind me.

What is the matter, I think? It's too juvenile to tell her that I had dreamt my father showed up drunk and angry. That in my dream he had every intention of harming us both. That I was the only one who could prevent it, me and all my sixty pounds and what others have called buggy-whip arms.

She sits up, her tired face puffy with sleep.

"Nothing," I say. "I have to use the bathroom."

I exit the tent and urinate on the side of a tree twenty feet away. When I finish I tiptoe to the road and look in both directions. No cars, though in the diagonal lot, I notice the burning embers of a cigarette. An old man with a pinched, wrinkled face and gray hair. He lifts his hand. I wave back, then return to the tent. My mother is already asleep. I lie on my back staring at the top of the tent. It takes a very long time to fall back to sleep.

When I wake, my mother is gone. Judging by the heat and the light I assume that it's close to noon. I find her sitting on the same log as the day before, drinking a cup of coffee, her dark haired pulled back. The bruise on her cheek has darkened and she's again staring blankly at the woods across the road as though waiting for an answer. She looks my way and smiles.

"It's going to be hot today," she says. "I was thinking we could go swimming."

"That'd be awesome."

"You hungry?"

"Starving."

I build the fire and she cooks bacon and eggs on a cast-iron skillet. Bicyclers pass and most wave while we eat in silence. A lazy wind pushes through the trees causing dapples of sunlight to dance at our feet.

"Do you want to shower?" she asks.

I shake my head. I'm camping in the middle of a forest; I have dirt beneath my fingernails; my hair is a mess. Today we'll hike trails and swim and row a boat into the middle of a lake. I'm living a kid's dream. The dirtier I become the better.

My mom wears a swimsuit beneath a pair of white shorts and a tube top. We walk a wide trail until it opens onto the lake, which is large; thick algae floats out fifteen feet from its muddy shore. I count five frogs. There's a floating log where three turtles are perched, their long, extended necks soaking up the sun. The beach is a five-minute walk away, the place to rent boats and set them ashore another ten minutes beyond that. I skip rocks across the water while we walk. The rowboats have all been rented, and all that's left is a pedal boat, which we rent for the next three hours.

It's blue and white, two seats for the pedalers, two seats for riders. There'll be no riders except for us. My mother sets a bag of snacks and drinks in the built-in cooler and then we're off.

It takes a half hour to reach the lake's center and I can tell my mother's legs are tired once we're there. Nonetheless, we strip to our swimwear and dive in headfirst. We're not sure if swimming is even permitted but neither of us cares. The water is cold. We swim awhile before we rest beside one another with our arms perched over the side of the boat. She pushes me off and I swim below and pull her under by her ankles.

We laugh the entire time.

When we climb back aboard we eat the sandwiches she has made, explore other areas of the lake, and return the boat when the third hour is up. We're both exhausted. We walk to the beach and my mother falls asleep on her towel. I swim for a while, play Frisbee and volleyball with a few other kids and their fathers, then return. She's still asleep, on her stomach, and after a while I fall asleep beside her.

⊱ 3 ⊰

On Saturday, our fourth day in the campground, I go for a hike along the winding trails while my mother takes a nap, which is how she's spent a good majority of the trip. When she isn't sleeping she walks aimlessly around the site, picking up sticks or kicking stones like a bored child. For the most part she's quiet, and when she catches me watching her, she merely smiles politely.

The trails are crowded. I venture off them, climbing trees, chasing squirrels. The forest floor is blanketed with twigs and leaves, the leaves above a ceiling of green with the occasional stain of blue coming through. I get lost, find my way again, end up on trails I haven't yet explored, but quickly return to the wilderness for areas left untouched. The park seems to stretch for miles. There are pines, oaks, elms. Bushes with berries, bushes with thorns. I find a branch as tall as I am and tear away its limbs and use it as a hiking stick. The only sounds are the ones I make, everything fresh and organic, like the smell a thunderstorm leaves behind. I hike beneath a perched hawk that looks down on me with fierce orange eyes. How long have I been gone? Two hours, maybe three. I end back on a trail and navigate up it until a spot of pale light shows ahead, which can only mean a clearing.

I exit the trail onto the road my mother and I had entered the campground on. I have no idea how to get back to our site from here. I look to the right. The road disappears into the trees a hundred feet away. To the left, five hundred feet from where I stand, I can see the arched sign heralding the park's main entryway. Cars speed by. And then, just as I'm looking at it, a red truck coasts by, hits its brakes, then squeals in reverse until it's able to make the turn. My heart sinks and blood rushes to my face. The back of my neck turns cold. I know immediately that it's my father.

I recede into the trail and peer from behind a tree and wait for him to pass. Then I see him, his right hand on the top of the steering wheel, his left arm hanging out the door. The truck rolls by and I stare at it in awe until it disappears. Panic sweeps through me. I drop the stick and make a mad dash down the trail. Has my mother told him where we are, or has he guessed by noticing the missing sleeping bags, the tent, the cooler? It wouldn't take much to figure it out.

I sprint as fast as my legs will carry me. Nothing looks familiar. I turn down one trail and second-guess myself and go flying down another. Out of breath, heart racing. But I keep sprinting and my pace doesn't waver. What will I do if he beats me there, if he's drunk and angry?

I race by others. They stare. One man tells me to slow down and I have the urge to turn around and tell him to go screw himself but instead I drop my head and run faster. I make another turn and pass through an unexpected dip that causes me to lose my balance and fall. I scrape both knees and the palm of my right hand. I rush up and carry on but stop when I reach a circular clearing. I bend over to catch my breath. A slight trickle of blood leaks from my palm. I lick it away. All I can think about is my mom sleeping in the four-man tent, not having a clue as to my father's sudden appearance.

I'm a goddamn moron for being lost. Six trails head in opposite directions. I haven't the slightest idea of which, if any, will lead me to my mother. Only one of them has a sign. It reads LODGE. The lodge won't help me, so I follow the trail that leads in the opposite direction. As each minute passes I grow more certain that he's come to hurt her. The thought terrifies me. Another fork in the path. I don't stop to ponder it, instead pick a direction and go. It's been at least ten minutes, maybe fifteen. I'm covered in sweat. Surely he would have spotted her car by now, parked right out in the open for anyone to see.

Up ahead I finally catch sight of another opening. My eyes now sting with sweat and my shirt is soaked. Both knees hurt. My hand throbs, still bleeding. My legs and lungs burn fiercely but I push the pain away and sprint even harder. The trail opens onto a road. There are signs pointing in the direction of certain numbered lots. Ours is 134. I follow the arrow. Finally the road looks familiar, and when I make the turn, I immediately see the back of my father's truck.

When I reach the campsite they're sitting on opposite logs facing one another, talking in hushed voices. My father smiles as though I should be thrilled to see him, fully expecting me to walk over and hug him, which I don't, and instead I look at my mom, who also smiles. And in that smile I realize that she has told him where to find us. I feel betrayed. I bend over, hands on knees, trying to catch my breath.

"Hey, bud," my father says. "How are you?"

"Good."

"Been havin' fun campin'?"

"Yes," I say, then to my mother, "Are you okay?"

"Of course, Stratton," she replies, as though the question is absurd.

"Got paid yesterday," he tells me. It's his first paycheck in a year and a half. "Finally got the electric turned back on," he continues, as though this bit of news is meant to impress me. It doesn't. Over the winter the gas was shut off and I had to take cold showers, which is one thing in the summer, but an altogether different thing on the coldest days of December. When he works he is short with both my mother and me and sometimes even hits her. He's only ever happy when he's able to drink late and sleep later. If a man is made by his ability to provide for his family, or his knack for discipline, or even his willingness to sacrifice, then my father is no more a man than the log on which he now sits.

"Does this mean we're leaving?" I ask.

"Why don't you go grab us some snacks from the lodge," my father says. He reaches into his back pocket and pulls out a few dollar bills and holds them out to me. I don't reach for them. I look to my mother and she nods.

"I don't want to."

"Well go anyway," he says, his voice firm and adamant.

I turn around without taking his money. I stay gone for twenty minutes, slowly walking along a familiar trail to kill time. When I return, our tent has been taken down and, along with everything else, loaded into the back of my mother's car.

at dawn

one

❦ 1 ❧

I LEFT NEW YORK on a cold November day of dark skies and sideways rain, but I don't care to say why other than the city itself had changed and I no longer felt I could sustain a living there. Gone was the New York I had idealized in the years before I finally arrived, the city of milk and honey, a place where dreams were achieved. But I'd been without a job for six months, my unemployment benefits had run dry, and work, once plentiful, had become as scarce as a street free of litter; the perpetually high rents were now higher, even in the outer reaches of Queens, Brooklyn, and Jersey, all of which once served as safe havens for the less-than-affluent; each day brought new demonstrations, sign-wielding protests and marches in the streets. The fight against inequality. Wall Street versus Main Street. Even the homeless seemed to have multiplied and, truth be told, I feared becoming one of them. Living in perpetual fear for the future. Each day more rife with anxiety than the day that had come before it.

I was headed for Chicago. I wasn't sure I expected things to be different there, but I had to give it a try if for no other reason than to hope a little longer. Or, failing that, to at least reach the endlessly evasive mind-set in which I could stop making shitty, self-involved quips like "hope a little longer."

I had an old friend there who said I could stay with him until I found a job and place of my own. I hadn't seen him since high school and was hesitant since he was precisely the type of person I wanted away from—a deep family pedigree, pretentious, uptight, and, above all, successful where I had failed. But he was a familiar face when the whole world felt unfamiliar and just about the only option I had, so I took it.

I'd hoped to leave New York by plane but the cost of airfare would have left only lint in my pockets. I considered taking the train, renting a car, even hitching my way across the Midwest, but in the end I bought a bus ticket and left it at that. I didn't care how I got out. I just knew I had to, and fast.

I boarded the bus on a Wednesday afternoon, soaking wet, out of breath, carrying a green canvas rucksack full of everything I owned. I had three hundred bucks and knew it wouldn't last long. The bus was half full. I sat adjacent to the only halfway decent-looking girl—modestly pretty with shoulder-length dark hair, brown eyes and pale skin, the feral brows of a twelve-year-old who'd yet to discover tweezers. She wore low-rise jeans and leaned forward as I took my seat and I could see the waistband of her panties. They were black. I closed my eyes and leaned back, took a deep breath, affixed on my face the grin of a man sure of his own luck, and suddenly looked forward to the fifteen-hour trip.

⚙ 2 ⚙

I was terribly hung over, freezing, still in the clothes I'd worn the night before, which were now sopping wet. A ragged, thin jacket. Cold wind coming in through several cracked windows. The bus wound its way off Manhattan, sped through Jersey. After a half hour the rain stopped and my clothes dried and I finally quit shivering. A movie showed on dropdown screens but the girl beside me busied herself with a paperback I wasn't familiar with. I watched from the corner of my eye. She didn't seem to notice so I kept leering, hoping for an introduction to conversation, at the very least another peek at her panties. I'm horrible with women, always have been aside from a quixotic confidence that sometimes finds me both fleeting and unpredictable. I was lucky enough to have been born with blue eyes and what others have called good looks. Or, as a girl

I briefly dated once said: "You're a very handsome guy. Maybe someday you'll actually realize it."

The tires of the bus sliced through puddles of standing water that had yet to drain. Cold and gray pressed against the windows, the landscape paling away into a sunless murk, misty and somewhat eerie looking. I was exhausted. I'd gone out the night before after convincing myself I was celebrating new beginnings, but really I was trying to drink away the emptiness my decision to leave had left me with. It was the right decision, but not a single thing about it felt right; I didn't really want to leave, but the sad truth was that I'd grown desperate for some semblance of direction. I'm a firm believer that things rarely change with a simple change of scenery, but something had to give and it sure as hell wasn't giving in New York.

I'd gone out in the East Village. I'm fond of the dingier bars there, the kind where your feet stick to the floor and a jukebox plays songs for a quarter and quarters line the only pool table, the whole interior redolent of flat beer and cigarette smoke and regardless of where you stand the urine-soaked sanitary cube still finds you from the bathroom—which is to say, the kind of bar in which I was raised.

I entered the first at six o'clock. It was empty. I had three beers and left. A few people were at the second but I drank in the corner away from them. I wasn't in the mood for talk and instead pondered what I'd do in Chicago and how my life would be different. I would make friends, not always linger alone in the quiet interiors of bars and cafés; I wouldn't try to sleep with every girl I met; I would read as many books as I could, and try finishing the one I'd already started; and even if it killed me, I'd find a meaningful job to keep from undermining my always modest solvency so that things might return to the way they were in the beginning, when I first arrived, freshly printed college degree in hand. A hotshot ready to take on the world.

I walked into the fifth bar after eleven and my luck turned for the first time in months. The bar was half full. Loud music, laughter, intermittent smells of perfume hanging in the air. It took ten seconds to spot Natalie, a petite NYU grad student with dark hair and eyes who, for some reason still unclear to me today, allowed a onetime *unification* four or five months back. We'd met at a party on the Lower East Side. We were partners in beer pong and we kept winning, which meant we kept drinking. We ended the night at her place and, after undressing one another piece by piece until, carefully and with an elated grin I hoped she couldn't see in the weak light, I slipped her lacy panties from her toned thighs and fell into her with nothing short of drunken chaos, most of which I could barely recall in the morning. She was the last person I had slept with. I was lucky then and, having found her, felt lucky again, a feeling undoubtedly bolstered by the eight or so beers I already had in me.

She stood talking to a tall man who wore a dark blazer and pressed jeans, polished shoes, a watch that looked expensive even from as far away as I was, and upon his face there resided the arrogant sneer and sharp eyes of a privileged life. I wasn't sure how to intervene.

I strutted into the bathroom and strutted back out, took a stool, twirled my beer and tried emitting a level of self-assurance I knew I'd never possess, eyes slightly slanted while feigning indifference to everything around me. Quiet confidence, I've heard it called. Natalie was being flirtatious, laughing beyond politeness, touching the man's arm or shoulder and blushing at all the appropriate times. Her ass perfectly framed in dark pinstripe pants, shiny hair past her shoulders gathering the light around her. I burned for her as I sat and stared and tried recalling what she had looked like naked that night and, when I couldn't remember, I wondered if I'd even seen her in the first place, that perhaps she was the shy type who refused to undress until beneath the covers with the lights off. I knew damn well she wasn't the shy type.

The bar quickly filled. Two servers worked the floor and it was clear that if I didn't do something soon, then the opportunity would be lost. I panicked. I couldn't very well walk over and interrupt; a stronger, more confident man could have, but not me, that wasn't me anymore, and when the server passed I impulsively reached for her and nearly knocked the drinks off the tray she carried.

"I want to send a drink across the bar."

"Tell one of the bartenders," she said with a curt nod.

"I don't mean the bar, to the woman in the corner."

She looked to the corner, sighed, rolled her eyes.

"What do you want?"

Laid was the first thing that came to mind. Maybe a thousand bucks. Hell, I'd settle for a blow job. But then said, "A vodka and tonic."

It was a ten-dollar drink and I tossed fifteen on her tray, which of course was stupid of me, but I was drunk and in possession of the carelessness that typically comes with it. She walked away. I shook my head in disgust. What did I really expect to happen, that Natalie would accept the drink and rush over and fall headlong into me while claiming unbridled love and asking herself how she'd survived these past five months without me? No, of course not. It was a weak ploy and I was burning through cash and still in New York.

I counted what money I had left but was too drunk and arrived at three different numbers, none of which I found very encouraging. I put my wallet away and spied the server marching toward the corner. A rush of nerves. Why didn't I walk by and casually bump into her, act just as surprised to see her as she'd be to see me, make small talk until I could weasel my way into the conversation? I was being a reckless idiot and upon this realization my face grew flush.

The server handed Natalie the drink. She pointed at me and I smiled and toasted the air, for what else could I do? Natalie squinted, looking confused until it finally occurred to her who I was. She lifted her glass in mere politeness, nothing more. She didn't return the smile and instead turned around and resumed talking to Moneybags, who grinned my way, a grin that said he knew precisely what I was trying to do and that I had no chance whatsoever of doing it. And he was right, of course, and though I was already in a glum mood, it was at that very moment that the incredible despair of my situation fully settled in. That was what my life had come to in New York: barhopping, alone, the few people I had once called friends all unsurprisingly busy for my going-away bar crawl, and yet I still went along with it, equipped with the lone goal of running into someone I'd slept with in the past so that I might sleep with her again with none of the effort typically required—the arduous task I've always called "punching the clock." The futility depressed me, and the smart thing would have been for me to save what money I still had and return to the place I'd been staying to get a good night's sleep and catch the bus clearheaded and feeling good. But of course I didn't. Instead I took the man's grin, his obvious success, as a personal affront, as a challenge, for within it there was the unmistakable element of condescension, and the last thing I needed was to be kicked in the gut when I was already down.

I waved to the same server and sent over another drink.

"You sure?" she asked, eyeing me with pity as though it was obvious how this whole farce would end and the only person who didn't know it was me. But I did know. I simply chose not to care.

"Absolutely. And a Greyhound for me."

I winked and threw a twenty on her tray. A few minutes later she brought my drink and took Natalie hers. Hell, I wasn't even sure her name was Natalie.

She rejected the drink outright and shook her head while, just behind her, Diamond Jim Brady stared, poised and intrigued. I flipped him off and mouthed *fuck you*. He raised a brow and stepped forward and I thought he was going to walk over. Instead he stopped short and, with an air of authority, whispered in the ear of a large man wearing a staff shirt I hadn't noticed before, and in that moment it became clear that Daddy Warbucks either owned the bar or had some stake in it. The bouncer started my way, which in turn forced me into a furious race to finish my drinks. I slammed the Greyhound, made it halfway through the beer, when a hand slapped firmly down upon my shoulder.

"It's time for you to say goodnight," he said in a gruff, adamant voice.

"Fine," I said.

I stood and turned. Through the endless clatter of voices and laughter, I raised my arm and launched the half-empty bottle across the room. I watched it sail through the air with ease, a thing of beauty if there ever was one. That is, until it missed Moneybags by a good six feet and exploded like a mortar shell against the exposed brick behind him.

I made to swing but another bouncer jerked me backward from behind. I hit the floor. Somebody's drink fell into my lap. My hands were pinned behind me but I forced them free and threw errant punches that struck only the air while catching no less than four to the back of my head as they dragged me out. Just before we made it to the door I gazed back toward the corner, and there stood Daddy Warbucks, flashing teeth with a raised brow and his arm around Natalie, amused as though the whole charade had been staged for his enjoyment.

I was launched through the air in the way of cartoons. I hit the pavement and felt my phone break in my pocket. I rolled over onto my back and stayed down for a full minute, staring up at the night sky, surprised at how many stars I could see. A crowd gathered around me. A few asked if I was okay. I didn't answer because I wasn't sure. Some offered hands but I didn't take them.

And then who do I see? Why, Mr. Cashman himself, standing tall among the crowd, smiling his perfect smile down at me. He opened his jacket and removed his wallet, plucked from within it a fifty-dollar bill, and ever so casually let it slip from the tips of his manicured fingers. It twisted and fluttered in the air like a butterfly and landed directly in the center of my chest.

"Thanks for the drinks," he said. "Now have a good night." He turned and walked back inside. I reached up and clutched the crisp fifty in my right hand, thankful as hell to have it.

❧ 3 ❧

I fell asleep, woke outside Cleveland, the bus parked at a gas station off the highway in Twinsburg. I wouldn't have known it was Twinsburg—or Ohio, for that matter—had the driver not announced it loud and clear, which is what woke me. It was dark outside. Most of the others were off the bus, walking around, stretching for the final push to Chicago. A prickly chill shot up my spine. I didn't want to leave the bus, felt if I didn't literally put my feet on the ground, then it was like I was never there.

The station lights threw shadows across the naked trees, white in the darkness like skeletons of bombshelled buildings after World War II. A grainy haze over everything. I sighed deeply while the past smothered over me. A pair of trembling hands and a pounding heart to go with them. I could feel it, hear it, see it through the threadbare shirt I wore. The image of my mother. Young. Cross-legged on the couch with her hair wet and smiling her crooked smile with the soft light upon her freshly scrubbed face. My old man in a beer-stained shirt with red-rimmed eyes, a thick line of drool down his stubbly chin. *No*, I thought, shaking my head.

I reached down and tore through my bag until my hand brushed the bottle of Xanax, a testament to better days when I actually had a job and health insurance and I was able to stockpile the pills when the economy first dipped and the rumors of layoffs began. I usually needed one. I took three, washed them down with stale water from a silver flask given to me as a birthday gift from an ex-girlfriend. I had to be patient, had to let the pills find their way and work their magic. They always did.

I counted backward from a hundred and kept my head covered as the people took their seats. I slouched in mine as the bus pulled away ten minutes later.

We were forty miles from where I grew up.

I peeked out the window and watched the landscape race by, the pills taking their dear ol' time. I counted the highway mile markers. 179. 178. 177. Too far till Indiana. The pills started working. My lips numbed. My eyes tingled and I kept blinking as the world began to blur. We passed the Cleveland exit, 173, then Strongsville, 161. Closer to home. If I stayed awake long enough we'd pass Amherst, then what, fifteen miles away?

The modest streets of my youth, Spencer, Ohio, little more than a tiny dot on a state map. With a population just shy of a thousand, the town once bore my name at its four borders and, as far as I know, still does to this day. In my mind I could see it, the single traffic light that hung in the town's center at the intersection of two state roads, the only ones by which to come and go. A general store, a gas station, a bar, a bank. Fields and farms on the outskirts, and opposite our simple home, behind the bank, there stood a hitching post where the Amish tethered their buggies. A quiet place of porch sitters, unlocked doors, and secrets never kept, a haven of gossip as all small towns are. Hours could pass without a single car on those wintry nights when the ice froze on the insides of our rickety windows, the fierce winds howling like coyotes creating statues of us in our beds. And in the summer the feedlots of the surrounding farms were cleaned and the manure spread in the fields and left to bake beneath the August sun. It was always then that a wind blew in from the west and the smell entered every home and stayed firmly rooted for weeks, so strong that it penetrated our dreams.

August, that month I can never escape.

My teeth began to itch and in that seat I could smell the manure from that August all those years ago. I shook my head free of it and clutched tightly to my bag. No more looking out the window. In time my breathing slowed. My eyelids grew heavy. I squeezed them shut against the darkness. Eventually I fell asleep.

two

THE BUS WAS PARKED. My head throbbed and I needed to piss something fierce. I don't know if I was shaken awake or whether I had felt the driver standing over me. He had wiry hair and bloodshot eyes, supporting his weight with his elbows on the back of the seat in front of me. Within his pale, downcast face he possessed the look of madness most commonly derived from pulling a double shift, functioning on too little sleep and too much caffeine, and thus appeared as though he was liable to fight or to cry (maybe both) at a moment's notice.

"What the hell's the matter with you?" he asked.

I sat up and wiped the sleep from my eyes. The bus was empty. I was groggy. I was always groggy after too much Xanax and not enough sleep.

"We in Chicago?"

"We've been in Chicago for twenty minutes now."

My first thought was that I had slept thirteen of the last fifteen hours and still felt like hell. My second was that I had made the entire trip without talking to the black-pantied girl, that she was gone forever now. I lumbered up. With both hands I tried smoothing the wrinkles from my shirt. The driver shook his head.

"You have any Aleve?" I asked.

"Get off the damn bus."

I grabbed my bag and walked off. I went around the first corner and relieved myself. I didn't know where I was or where I needed to go. I couldn't call my friend, Jeff, because of my broken phone. I had his address and phone number in an email but that created another problem of finding a computer with Internet.

It wasn't as windy as I'd thought it'd be, but it was pretty damn cold, midthirties by my guess. Morning, just after eight. I didn't own gloves. My jacket was nothing more than a black fleece windbreaker ill-equipped for Northern winters. My hand kept going through a hole in the right pocket. I'd have to find something heavier soon.

I made my way to the inner Loop and entered an Argo Tea on State and Randolph. I bought a large coffee and a muffin, sat in the corner, wrapped my hands around the steaming cup to warm them. There was a long line of people waiting to order. Businessmen and women headed to work. Students and professors headed to class. And there I was, alone and a little scared in a city I'd never been in, feeling apart from the rest of the world while headed to the couch of an old friend I hadn't seen in eight and a half years, a friend I was nervous to see again. A friend who, for better or worse, knew who I was and where I had come from, and with that I couldn't dispel the feeling that somehow my personal fortunes (or what there was of them, anyhow) had taken a turn for the worse.

I sighed and again tried figuring out how I'd ended up here, what concatenation of events had pushed me from New York. There wasn't any single earth-shattering incident that served as the impetus, but more like a series of mishaps beyond my control, missed opportunities, being one of many casualties of a defective economy, and a few small fuckups along the way that in the end were tantamount to the same thing. And besides, did the reason really matter? My situation wasn't going to change regardless of how well I understood it. Somehow I had lost my way. That's all that really mattered.

I people-watched until I was warm. I finished the coffee, washed my face and hands and changed clothes in the downstairs bathroom, then left. Outside, the sky was covered with low, gray clouds. There were few trees, seemed to be far more leaves swirling than there were trees to shed them. The wind had kicked up and howled with steady sibilance. The city quickly passing into winter.

Jeff's place was near the lake, a five-minute walk off the Armitage stop, in Lincoln Park, just north of downtown. The neighborhood was nice, the air imbued with a crispness I found somewhat welcoming, cars parked along each side of the tree-lined street. He owned the second floor of a well-kept three-story brownstone. I had spent all morning bumming around downtown and it was four o'clock when I got there. He said he'd arrive at six. Instead of waiting I propped my bag against his door and found a nearby deli. I spent six dollars on a sandwich and ate it as I watched the shadows lengthen. The longer I sat the more nervous I grew, and my heart was pounding by the time I walked back. I found Jeff on the porch, bent over my bag with his back to me.

"Hey asshole, why don't you rummage through your own shit?" I said.

He turned around and grinned. The overhead light cast down a pillar of yellow that illuminated only his face, and the second I saw it, something shifted inside of me. His eyes took me in. What did I see in them? Was it pity at my obvious indigence based on the clothes I wore and the bag I carried, or was it because of my past, the look of conceit that comes with being privy to secrets unknown to others? I guessed the latter, for it was the same look I endured from others my last two years in Ohio that had made me flee the first chance I got. I felt self-conscious, the years weighing heavily in the empty space between us.

There was no doubting just how successful Jeff had become. He had maintained the same good looks he'd had in high school, the same dark, bushy brows, except now they looked trimmed, maybe waxed. He wore a full suit beneath a black wool coat that fell to his calves—the kind almost exclusively worn by businessmen and attorneys—while exuding hints of academic dignity from the red plaid scarf around his neck. Leather gloves covered his hands and he slowly rubbed them together as though in contemplation. Clean-shaven, hair slicked back with pomade. I remembered now just how much I'd always hated him.

"Stratton Brown, you bastard. How the hell are you?"

"Still livin'. That's something, right?"

"Sure, sure."

We shook hands and hugged awkwardly with our free arms, giving the obligatory manly pat on the back. I grabbed my bag and followed him up the stairs, at the top of which a second door opened into his sprawling apartment that occupied the entire floor. Along the hallway were the doors for the bedrooms, bathrooms, and closets, and across from them Jeff took me into the large, open area that contained the living and dining rooms, the kitchen, an office made up of a desk, computer, and two bookcases tucked away in the back corner. The space was meticulously clean and organized and obviously professionally decorated to create a cold, modern feel; it looked like some display at a fancy furniture store shopped at exclusively by the supergentry of Manhattan. Various paintings surrounded us; matching bronze statues of provocative Greek nymphs stood on each side of the black leather sofa; lush plants dangled in the windows. The coffee table was curved glass atop shiny metal. A flat-screen television neatly adhered to the far wall and tiny, almost indiscernible speakers hung around the room.

"Just got that last week," he said as I stood in front of the TV. "Sixty-four inches."

He turned it on, flipped through the channels until he found a college basketball game. He cranked the surround sound. I stared at the screen and he stared at me, seeking the very approval I was averse to giving. I could feel my clothes ruffle from the deep bass, and the picture itself was pretty damn impressive. I told him as much, and in reply I was given a smile and a wink.

From there we toured the rest of the 2,300-square-foot space, each room more of the same. Everything pristine and in its place, not a speck of dust anywhere. A far nicer place than any I'd lived in or stayed at before. We were both twenty-seven and it pained me to see how much he had already accomplished.

In the larger of the two guest rooms, I unpacked my bag into a tall oak dresser while creating a pile of dirty clothes on the floor. Jeff carried in a bottle of Scotch and two glasses full of ice. He handed me one and filled it halfway while remaining mindful that his hand wasn't covering the bottle's label, which he kept aimed at my face.

"Nothing wrong with a quick celebratory drink, right?" he said.

We clinked glasses and drank. It was rich and smooth, far easier to drink than any whiskey I'd ever had before. Jeff watched my reaction in much the same way as he had with the TV, smiling widely when I nodded approval.

"Johnnie Walker Blue Label, my friend. Two hundred bucks a bottle. The finest Scotch in the world," he said with pride. It was almost as though he had invited me inside for the sole purpose of admiring his possessions.

"It's pretty damn good," I replied, though I felt I was somehow compromising myself by admitting it.

"I'm meeting a few friends at a bar down the street at eight. You want to come?"

I hesitated, knowing that a night of drinking was the last thing I needed or could afford.

Jeff, picking up on my hesitation, said, "Come on, first night in Chicago. My treat."

I shrugged then, and said sure, why not, though I didn't really feel like going out at all, nor did I trust myself not to have a similar meltdown as I'd had two nights before. I was still tired and groggy from the trip and knew a full night's sleep was the thing needed to restore my sanity to a manageable level, and perhaps assuage a bit of the anxiety derived from living within society's frayed edges, the result of barely getting by for the past six months. But it was Jeff's apartment, and there was something about staying there alone when he had offered to pay that didn't sit right.

I finished unpacking while Jeff watched the day's financial news at an absurd volume in the living room. We had two glasses of Scotch each. When I poured myself the second he stared through narrow eyes as I filled it to the top. I carried the glass into the shower. When I came out the bottle of Johnnie Walker had been replaced with a plastic jug full of bad whiskey. I poured myself some and gave it the obligatory swirl. The color was slightly darker, seemed thicker. It smelled like turpentine and tasted like piss. Jeff went to the bathroom and I switched his glass with mine. He came back, took a drink, and cringed.

"Damn," he said and looked at me.

"What?"

He shook his head but said nothing, politely drinking my glass while I finished his. It was, I later realized, one of the few victories I'd earn while staying there.

❦ 3 ❧

The bar was ten minutes away. As we walked, the tail of Jeff's long coat fluttered in the wind behind him like some kind of superhero's cape; his hair didn't move at all. Lights lined the street and painted the mist that escaped with each taken breath. A cold night, quiet in the same Midwestern way I remembered from Ohio.

"So what did you do with all your stuff?" he asked.

I glanced over without the slightest idea of what he was asking.

"Didn't you have furniture?"

"Nope, only what I brought with me. Mostly just clothes, a few books, notepads. Stuff like that."

"No shit?"

"No shit."

"You're a brave man."

I snorted. "I'm something. Don't know if I'd call it brave."

Jeff continually glanced over at me.

"Man, it's really been a long time, hasn't it?" he finally said. "Seems like only yesterday I hip-tossed you straight to your back in the field house."

"That happened only once, dick," I said laughing. "And only because I was staring at Kristin Palmer's ass as she was doing lunges across the weight room wearing white spandex," I went on, which was true. Jeff was the quarterback of the football team, and as a junior I had just finished second in the state in wrestling. There were no off-season workouts for wrestlers and I often lifted with the football players to keep up my strength. Jeff and I were horsing around one day when the girls' track team was lifting, and when I was distracted, he had stepped into me, rotated his hips, and threw me straight to the hard, black mats of the weight room floor. Everybody had heard it and looked our way. I caught shit for it for months after.

"Excuses, excuses," Jeff said. "I still got to say I hip-tossed the state runner-up."

I chuckled. "True, but you have to admit, Kristin Palmer had a nice ass. Almost worth being hip-tossed for."

Jeff nodded. "Her ass was incredible."

We incurred a moment of silence, then I asked, "You make it back much?"

"To Spencer?"

"Yeah."

"Usually twice a year, sometimes three. I'm actually flying back for Thanksgiving in two weeks. Do you?"

"Not once since graduating. The bus here took me through Ohio, though. It was the first time I'd even been in the state since."

"You're kidding me?"

"Nope."

He crinkled his brows in thought and nodded. "Yeah, I think I always expected you to do that."

A heavy silence passed. We walked a full block before I asked, "You ever see Jason anymore?"

"Jason Daniels?"

"Yeah."

"It's been a long time. I lost track of most everyone when I left for college. Hard to keep in touch with people when in California, and then I moved here right after I graduated. I think the last time I saw him was Christmas break my sophomore year. I can't remember what he was doing in regard to work, but I think he's still around."

"Yeah," I said, not at all surprised he was still there, in or around our small hometown and, like most of the others, probably hunting, attending Sunday Mass, and voting Republican, three practices that never suited me very well. He was my best friend growing up and I lived with him and his family my last two years there.

Jeff and I passed the rest of the walk in silence. I studied the wares displayed in the storefront windows while feigning deep concentration to keep from feeling uneasy. I was growing tired, somewhat down, a little uncomfortable at the prospect of socializing with a group of guys I didn't know, of impersonating a friendship with Jeff whom I hardly knew any better in the years that had passed since we were kids; it was obvious that we had become two different people.

It was on a whim that I had searched for him online. After finding him on Facebook and seeing that he was in Chicago, I wrote and explained my wanting to move, that I was thinking of the Windy City based on the fact that I had never been before while being mostly honest about just how dire my situation had become. He said it was a great place and that I should come and could even stay with him on a short-term basis if I needed to. I attributed his offering the place so willingly to pure nostalgia for the simpler days of youth, the friendship between the kids we once were back in Ohio, for who doesn't occasionally crave those times and connections? Needing a fresh start in the worst way and unable to afford any other alternative, I didn't think twice about taking him up on it.

⊰ 4 ⊱

The bar was a chic place full of suits and skirts and knee-high boots. Everything silver and black, shiny, the bartenders rouged and powdered. The dance floor at the rear was empty though the tables at the front and sides were filled. It had been a long time since I'd been in a place like this, and I never liked them much to begin with. I immediately felt underdressed, wearing sneakers, jeans, and a black thermal with the sleeves pulled to my elbows. Jeff's friends were in a booth against the left wall. There were three of them, all men around the age of thirty, and each still wore his workday suit with loosened tie, and for some reason this presented them in a far greater light of formality than had the ties been tight around their collars. Before the introductions were made, I could tell I was going to have a rough go of it by the air of superiority with which they eyed me. I immediately felt like a kid at a table full of adults, and I only remember the name of the guy across from me, Frank, a strikingly handsome man who oozed confidence and possessed the toned, slender look of a movie star.

Jeff ordered a round of shots for everyone and two martinis for us. If he was buying, then I didn't care what he ordered. They immediately started talking business and I gleaned that each was employed in finance. They bitched about the long hours and the low pay and made empty threats about how the bonuses had better be big or they'd quit after Christmas. I could contribute nothing of worth to the conversation despite my having worked in the same field for slightly over a year after college, for who can talk money when broke and out of work and whose most recent weeks were spent bouncing from couch to couch to avoid sleeping on the streets following an eviction?

Our martinis came, a shot of Scotch placed in front of each man. They clinked glasses and drank. I sniffed at mine first, shivered, then followed suit. I had a buzz already from the two Scotches at the apartment, and since I'd only eaten a muffin and a deli sandwich all day, I knew the liquor would hit me quick. The olive-soaked martini tasted awful and I had to muscle it down with big gulps. Eating the olives was out of the question. I dropped them on a napkin. One of the guys eyed me with dismay so I picked them back up and returned them to the drink.

I tuned out their conversation and in no time I felt a bit numb and I noticed my foot tapping to the music. I spied the rest of the bar. As many women as men. My chance of bedding any of them, however, was a whole other issue. But what did I care? I was in a new city full of new people and nobody knew who I was or the struggles I was going through. That's the great appeal behind fresh starts, the luxury of pretending we're somebody we're not. Sometimes we even believe it. Sometimes we can convince others to believe it, too.

"So how do you two know each other, anyhow?" the guy beside Frank asked me. The inflection in his voice made him sound like some old-time gangster from the prohibition era, or as though he'd been raised in the Bronx.

"We grew up together," I answered.

"Another Ohio boy, eh?"

Jeff nodded and threw his arm around me. "This guy right here," he said, meaning me. "State champion in wrestling and national All-American."

"No shit?" Frank asked.

"I kid you not," Jeff said. "Was an animal on the mat. Used to beat the shit out of guys."

I cracked a smile. "Back in the glory days, anyhow," I said.

"Very cool," Frank said, and then changed the subject by asking, "And you just came from New York?" I nodded. "Never did like the city much myself," he went on. "Kind of snobbish. The people always seem rude and standoffish to me."

I shrugged. "I think you'll find people like that anywhere," I said in a voice I hardly recognized.

"A hell of a lot of money there, though, that's for sure," he said, and then apropos of nothing he began telling me of his penniless beginnings, of how he got to where he was because of hard work and determination, detailing step by step how he had paid his way through both undergraduate and graduate school on his way to becoming a self-made man. He was very proud of it, and his story reeked of the obvious self-aggrandizing desire to smoke his own ham in front of the new guy and, furthermore, to trump my story of being a state champion, which he somehow felt diminished his own accomplishments. Nobody asked a single question when he finished; it was very obvious by their reactions that the other guys had heard this story before, and probably more than once. As for me, I didn't care that he had paid for his own education. I had, too, aside from a small athletic scholarship, and I still had the loans to prove it, but what better was I because of it? It didn't make me study any harder or strive for better grades. I wasn't richer for the experience. All it did was create a hell of a lot of unneeded stress during an already stressful time, which hindered my grades, not helped them. I would have gladly let somebody else foot the bill.

I looked down. The martini glass was filled with only the olives. Another round of shots and drinks was ordered. More Scotch. I was surprised to see these guys drinking as hard as they were, considering they all had to work the next day.

Frank's story had left a bitter taste in my mouth. I tried shrugging off the fact that the guy across from me was far better looking and had a hell of a lot more money, all of which he had made on his own, had a better education, and would go on to marry a far more beautiful woman with whom he'd live in a huge house filled with well-behaved children. And there I sat across from him, able to carry on my back everything I owned, with less than three hundred bucks in my wallet. And now I could add the word *vagabond* to my description. I shook my head. I had drunk enough to be susceptible to sadness, still two drinks away from being immune. I would have four to be on the safe side.

The server brought our drinks. I had a Scotch on ice to chase a shot of Scotch. There was no escaping it. Everyone at the table had a limited dictionary of drinks with a single entry: Scotch. I had had enough Scotch already. I now hated the word.

The guys reverted back to business and when a group of skimpily dressed girls walked by they became quiet and stared. I stared as well. There were four of them, and despite the wintry weather, each wore a short skirt that left little to the imagination. They were blonde-haired, tan, big-breasted, tight-bodied.

"Wow," Frank said, and without another word, he stood from the booth and walked straight up to the prettiest in the group, a girl with bright blue eyes who didn't look a day over twenty-one and, who, in the breathless way she held herself, still radiated the vibrant sheen of youth that rarely sticks with one past their twenties. She smiled at Frank and it was obvious she reciprocated his interest, and was maybe even impressed he had the nerve to approach. I would have given anything to hear what he was saying; he talked and laughed with her as though there were nothing to it, and while I watched I burned with agonizing jealousy at his effortless self-confidence, the exhibited aplomb that I had spent a lifetime trying to learn. I had to look away, and in direct retaliation I freely ogled the rest of the girls in the bar, staring at their crotches without caring that the evidence of my eyes revealed everything one needed to know about the thoughts in my mind.

I became antsy after ten minutes. I couldn't take sitting there any longer and excused myself from the table. I took my drink with me. The bar was stuffy, hot, loud. We'd been there an hour. The crowd had doubled. I weaved through it to the bathroom at the rear and slammed my drink while I urinated. I walked to the bar and bought a beer, spending what little money I had for the simple fact that I couldn't stand one more sip of Scotch. Not once did any of them ask if I preferred to drink something else. The bartender dropped off my change and I ordered a shot of Jameson. I paid again, took the shot, drank half of the beer in three large gulps. I figured there were three or four drinks in my gut that had yet to hit me. It didn't bode well that I was already dizzy.

Everyone talking, flirting, laughing around me. I leaned against the bar and watched the world move at its own pace. My first night, spent at the bar, the very place I promised I'd stop going, the place I'd stay away from to get my life back on track. And I had just blown fifteen dollars on a shot and a beer. It wasn't the start I had hoped for.

A dry, ticklish sensation spread behind my face and all ten fingers tingled. I was finally able to smile. As I had guessed, Jeff was now standing beside Frank talking to one of the other girls. He had always had a way with women. I turned to the dance floor. Several girls danced in groups and clusters of men were scattered around them. I looked back and forth from the floor to the table. My first crossroad. I could do the responsible thing and go back to the table, drink for free and leave at a decent time to get an early start in the morning, or I could stay right where I was and dance. I glanced between the two a final time, then turned towards the smoky dance floor and bobbed my head to the music.

three

I OPENED MY EYES to a pounding headache, throbbing bladder, a hazy recollection of the night before. I remembered walking to the dance floor, remembered dancing. Everything after was a blur. A slight whisper of anger, of frustration and sadness. Did I dream it?

The apartment was silent. The air was cool and gray and shapeless; watery sunlight broke through the two treated windows and threw jagged shadows across the floor. Friday morning, slightly after ten. I was crazed with thirst but hurt too badly to move. It took five minutes of deep breathing to finally gather the strength to nudge the covers aside. I hobbled to the bathroom and downed three Advil with sink water before crawling back beneath the blankets. I shivered violently though I wasn't cold. I lay there twenty minutes feeling sorry for myself. I tried fighting down the inevitable vomit but it was futile. I made a mad dash to the toilet, vomiting first the water and then only air and the occasional string of bile. I couldn't stop shivering.

I flushed the toilet with my cheek against the seat and stood with a helpless sigh. I took three more Advil. The water sloshed in my stomach as I walked back to the bedroom. I hoped I could keep it down this time. I curled into a ball and buried my head beneath the pillow. I closed my eyes. When I next reopened them the clock on the wall read two. I rolled to my side and looked at the slivers of light coming in the room where the blinds pulled away from the nearest window, beside which hung a painting of a man and a boy climbing into a small boat with a pole and tackle box in each hand, both smiling, the dawn of a new day, the surface of the lake a calming sheet of glass. On the adjacent wall hung a second painting, this of a white-haired old man with his hand pressed to the side of his unshaven and deeply wrinkled face, hard eyes staring out at the world contemptuous of everything they saw.

I went to the kitchen, made a bowl of raisin bran, sat at Jeff's desk to eat and check my email. I could hear the soft hum of his iMac. I jiggled the mouse and the screen popped up asking for a password. I shook my head and sighed, then finished eating and placed the bowl in the sink and took a long hot shower.

❦ 2 ❧

I left the apartment at three. I passed a Verizon store, and upon being informed that my contract was up, I renewed it for another two years and received a basic flip phone for free. I had been without one for two and a half days. I had no new messages.

I found the library the man at the Verizon store had told me about and settled into a terminal while dreading what I had to do. I've always hated the monotonous task of applying for jobs, filling out the same forms, answering the same questions or, even worse, new questions, for they required time and well-thought-out answers I was certain wouldn't be read, anyway. Submitting my résumé and writing cover letters and if I was lucky I'd receive a response from one out of every ten positions for which I applied, and sometimes less than that. Such was the state of the economy. A surplus of workers competing for a shortage of jobs. The laws of supply and demand.

It was three thirty. I promised myself I wouldn't spend a second under a half hour reworking my résumé, which I had already done several times over the past few weeks. I inserted the flash drive containing everything of electronic importance to me and began making myself glow. My GPA increased a few points; I made the dean's list a few more semesters, volunteered to help the homeless, stayed at my first job, which was by far my most meaningful one, a few extra months. I must have looked at the clock every minute until my time was up, but when it was, even I had to admit that I finally shined on paper, which seemed to have eluded me up until then for the simple fact that I had adhered to the facts. But I was desperate, and the truth had no place in my job search. Not then.

I stood, stretched my arms to the ceiling, and convinced myself that the time would pass regardless of how it was spent so I might as well make the most of it. I took another deep breath, sat back down, and committed myself to an hour and a half of submitting my résumé to open positions, promising that God himself couldn't tear me from the seat before that hour and a half was up.

It didn't take long to settle into the routine and I applied for everything I was halfway qualified for—a few technical writing positions, a few editorial, one in a factory in a suburb I'd never heard of, part-time jobs of varying duties from loading trucks to cleaning kennels. I didn't really care what kind of work I did as long as it paid a wage. I felt an accomplished giddiness because of the effort and was smiling stupidly by the time I was done. I knew I'd do the same thing the next day, and every day after if that's what it took.

❧ 3 ❧

I strode back to Jeff's and found him standing on the porch in much the same way as I had the day before.

"What's going on?" I asked with cheerfulness. He glanced over his shoulder and inserted the key into the lock.

"How are you?" he asked in a strained voice that gave me pause.

"I'm okay. You?"

"Remember much of last night?" He unlocked the door and flung it behind him, then trod heavily up the stairs. I followed.

"No, not really. Why?"

"Don't remember the fight you almost got into, don't remember calling Frank a rich, pretentious fuck?"

I smiled, at first thinking he was shitting me, but when I noticed the mechanical way in which he unlocked the second door without turning around to look at me, I knew that he wasn't.

"I said that?"

"Yes."

"Please tell me you're kidding."

He shook his head.

"Shit, man, I'm really sorry," I said. "I don't remember any of that. Why did I say it?"

"How the hell should I know? They were kicking you out after you dropped your beer on the floor. You could hardly stand. Frank made an offhand comment about you being a lush and you flipped your shit."

A sickness in the pit of my stomach, embarrassment, a miserable weariness weighing heavily down upon my shoulders. Jeff walked into his room, his back straight and rigid, the same implicit disappointment in me that I remembered from our freshman year of high school. I went on my first date with him and two pretty girls, one of whom I had a terrible crush on, the other being so far out of my league that I could only look at her with indifference. They were also freshmen, and I've never felt entirely comfortable around girls my own age. I didn't know what to say and deferred to Jeff to keep the conversation going, laughing a canned laughter at everything he said. We ended the night at his house. We always did. It was large, clean, inviting. His parents had modified the place by adding an indoor pool and Jacuzzi that we often used year round; they never minded when their son had others over. The girls went to the bathroom together the minute we walked through the door.

"Stratton, you have to get your shit together and talk to this girl. I'm running out of things to say, man," he said once the door closed behind them. My face warmed and no matter how hard I tried I couldn't pull it together after that, feeling even more awkward than before because of the added pressure. Too much for my fourteen-year-old self to handle. That's what I remembered as I watched him walk into his bedroom, and I again didn't know what to say or do. He dropped his bag on his bedroom floor.

"He wasn't happy."

"Shit," I said again, shaking my head. "Are things okay now?"

"It took a lot of calming him down to keep him from kicking your ass."

I tensed and dropped my own bag on the floor, the madness of pride rushing to the surface. I've always hated that about myself, my tendency to flare up the second I feel threatened or disparaged.

"You think he can kick my ass?"

Jeff guffawed. "You're not Mr. State Champion these days."

"Oh, I imagine I have a bit left in the tank," I said.

"Stratton, Christ, this isn't a pissing contest," he said. He clenched his jaw, pinched the bridge of his nose, closed his eyes. Then, with his hand out in front of him for emphasis, he said, "If you want to stay here you can't treat my friends that way. I don't give a shit what you've been through. We're not in high school anymore."

I took a deep breath to calm myself, then counted backward from five. "I'm sorry. I can't speak for what happened last night because I don't remember it. I know that's not really an excuse, but it's the truth."

He made no response and instead walked into the living room and repositioned the television remote to the left side of the coffee table, then walked to the side of the couch and moved a lamp on the end table I had bumped earlier. As he was doing this I tried wiping away the ring of milk I had spilled on his desk while eating breakfast.

"How long do you need to stay here?" he finally asked, and the obvious insinuation from his shitty tone was that the sooner I left the better off we'd all be.

"Not long. I spent all day applying for jobs. Going to do the same tomorrow. I'm guessing a week, maybe two," I said, which was about half the time I actually believed I'd need.

The milk had dried. I couldn't wipe it away. I swept into the kitchen and wetted a paper towel. When I came back out Jeff was already chipping it away with his thumbnail.

"I was just about to clean that," I said.

He turned on the computer and said nothing further as I wiped up the milk. It was as though I wasn't there. I tried looking over his shoulder as he entered his password but he typed too fast. I tossed the paper towel into the wastebasket, picked up my bag off the floor, walked into the bedroom. I lay on top of the covers and stared at the ceiling. I wasn't sure what I should do. I took out my wallet and counted how much money I had left. Two hundred and sixty-three dollars, which was a little less than what I thought there'd be. I took two hundred and buried it at the bottom of my underwear drawer, put the rest back into my wallet. From the living room where Jeff sat a pervasive tension penetrated the walls. I was uncomfortable, and there wasn't a chance in hell I was going to spend all night holed up in his room.

I tiptoed out of the apartment as quiet as a mouse with my smaller bag, inside of which I had a legal pad, a few pencils, and a book. Outside I walked until I found a coffeehouse on Clark. I sat near the window and removed the legal pad and started writing figures. If I busted ass the following week searching for a job, I could potentially start work the following Monday. Scratch that, I *had* to start the following Monday. When I started—ten days from this exact day—I could expect a paycheck two weeks later, three at the most. I could assume that I'd be paid for one week of work two weeks after starting. It would take luck, and if it worked out that way, then the soonest I'd be paid was in twenty-four days. After buying a cup of coffee, I had $260. Divided by twenty-four, that left me with $10.83 per day. How could I have three meals a day on that alone? Or even two meals, for that matter?

I closed my eyes, ran my fingers through my hair. I double-checked the figures. They were correct. I wasn't sure what I could do. The only person in Chicago I knew was Jeff. I had nothing left to sell. I realistically needed another hundred to make it, maybe a little less if I really pinched. Perhaps I could find some short-term work in the meantime?

I crumpled up the sheet of paper to keep from looking at it and walked outside. A cold rain began to fall and I stood beneath the awning to keep from getting wet. The blurred streetlamps looked bleak and desolate standing alone in the dripping mist. People ran for cover into bars and restaurants. And where was I? At a coffeehouse because coffee was the only damn thing I could afford, and even that was a stretch. One coffee, two dollars and some change, nearly a quarter of my daily budget. I couldn't make it on what little I had.

In a feeble attempt to reestablish my wits, I stood outside until I was shivering. Then I walked back in and gathered my things and left. The rain had stopped and the air smelled of wet pavement. I walked for an hour along the streets glistening in the November cold. I mostly kept my head down and hands pocketed. When I returned, the lights were on in the apartment and Jeff's silhouette passed by the front window.

I found a playground and sat on the swing waiting for him to leave, feeling the cold burn the tips of my ears and fingers while wondering how I could survive the next two or three weeks. I couldn't make it any longer than that. I'd have to keep a low profile, make myself invisible, do my best to be out of the apartment when he was there. I doubted it'd be enough. Jeff was precisely as I remembered: uptight, patronizing, someone who'd cut and run at the first hint of trouble, someone who couldn't care less about those less fortunate than he. We were a group of five back then, and I don't think any of us were ever great friends with Jeff, though at times we might have parodied a great friendship. His father was the president of the bank. Our parents sweated at the forge or worked construction. Though it wasn't fair, I think we all hated him for that, the way everything was simply handed to him while the rest of us wore hand-me-downs and ate microwavable dinners. He was confident and in his eyes there was always that glint of intelligence we hoped was in our own. He was a person we secretly tried to mirror, a novelty, one who'd move on to great things and forget the rest of us in the process. There was never any doubt about that. And we all hated him, even while desperately seeking his approval. Now, this many years later, I can't figure out why in the hell we wanted it in the first place.

four

ON MONDAY MORNING, AFTER I'd spent much of Saturday and all of Sunday applying for more jobs, my phone rang requesting an interview in Evanston later that day. My eyes shot open. I gripped the phone tightly, so excited at the prospect of a job that I had only a foggy notion of what the position actually was—something editorial—but had I understood completely I wouldn't have cared. I'd shovel shit if it paid (and had even applied to do so).

I unrolled my only suit. It was wrinkled, imbued with stale cigarette smoke that I could smell even before it was out of its vinyl bag; I had last worn it eleven months earlier to a New Year's Eve party. I walked through Jeff's bedroom, entered his bathroom, and sifted through the ten or so bottles of cologne I'd noticed when he gave me the tour. I found one I liked. I plugged in his iron and set up the board. I laid out the pants first, which smelled considerably worse since I'd taken off the jacket early in the night. I used five sprays of the cologne, ironed the slacks, sprayed them five more times, ironed them again. The smoke was reasonably masked, but there was no denying it was still there.

I tore through my clothes looking for my white dress shirt, but after ten minutes I conceded that I'd lost it somewhere along the way. I went into Jeff's walk-in closet. Everything was hung by type—shirts grouped together, jackets, pants, vests, belts, silk ties neatly folded and delicately placed upon a mahogany shelf—and further sorted by color and style, everything perfectly aligned and evenly spaced. There were no less than

thirty shirts covered with dry-cleaner plastic, though the standard wire
hangers had been replaced with the sturdier plastic kind. The smallest
white button-up was still two or three sizes too large, and I took the hanger
with me, certain that, fastidious as he was, Jeff would notice the missing
shirt immediately. Then I sat around waiting for the interview, growing
increasingly nervous as the time ticked by.

❧ 2 ❧

I jumped on the purple line at Armitage and took it all the way up to
its second-to-last stop on Central Street, and from there walked a half
mile west to a drab one-story brick building that looked terribly out of
place beside Northwestern University's overbearing football stadium.
The company was called Manufacturing Directories, Inc.—MDI for
short—and they published annual yellow-pages-type directories that listed
every company that did some form of manufacturing. They released fifty-
one books a year, one for each state except for Illinois, which got two. I
understood this much when my name was called. I stood, buttoned the
jacket to keep from showing the shirt pocket centered on my stomach
instead of my chest, and followed the receptionist through the door with
my hand covering my crotch; I had broken my pants zipper while rushing to get dressed and couldn't find a safety pin in Jeff's apartment to
close the gaping fly.

Worn, ratty carpet, frayed at its edges where it touched the walls, led
to beige cubicles housing employees who peered at me with despairing
eyes. Fluorescent lights lined the ceiling, casting the interior in a gloomy
pall. The smell of age was unsuccessfully masked with Pine-Sol in much
the same way that the scent of smoke was still redolent on my suit despite
my best efforts to cover it. I reached the office of the manager with
whom I had spoken, and I immediately felt the blood rush to the back
of my neck, a product of nerves and pressure. Her name was Cathy. She
sprang from her leather chair with her hand extended. I shook it. Then
she motioned me into one of two open seats while she went back around

her L-shaped desk, the entirety of which was covered with uneven stacks of paper. She lifted my own résumé from a large pile of them and gave it a quick once-over while I did the same to her. Mid- to late thirties, plain-looking with pale skin and flaxen hair that fell to just below her shoulders, wire-rimmed glasses. She could have been attractive had she tried, but she didn't and therefore was, at best, average.

"Stratton, that's a very interesting name. I've never heard it before," she said and looked at me for validation. I wasn't sure what she expected me to say, so I said nothing. "So, tell me about yourself."

I crossed my legs, placed both hands over my crotch, and smiled. Somewhere along the way I had gotten good at interviews, a product of having been through so many of them while possessing the right balance of vanity and lack of regard for the truth in the way of politicians, pretending to be a far better person than I really was—harder working, more ambitious, sometimes telling downright lies. Most of the time I wasn't even nervous. Except for today. My only hope was that my extreme desperation wouldn't shine through.

"First off, let me start by saying thank you for taking the time to talk with me," I said. "I'm assuming from the stack of résumés on your desk that there's no shortage of applicants for the position, so I very much appreciate the opportunity to interview for it."

She nodded. "Thank you for coming in on such short notice."

It was my turn to nod. "I'm brand new to Chicago—I just moved here on Thursday, actually—and prior to that, I spent the last five years in New York, though I'm originally from a small town in Ohio. I attended college in Pennsylvania on an athletic scholarship and my undergraduate degree is in finance, which was a field chosen not because I was highly passionate about it, but rather I didn't know what I wanted to do when I was nineteen other than make money and understand how to make it grow. And now I'm here."

"I can understand that. Did you enjoy New York?"

"I loved New York for the first few years I was there, and then it began to wear on me. I'm sure you've noticed the recent news; there's quite a lot going on there now. Living there got very tiring toward the end."

"So I've heard," she said with a nod. "And now you're giving Chicago a try. If you don't mind my asking, what brings you here?"

"An old friend I grew up with, mostly. Plus I had always heard great things about the city."

"It is a great city," she agreed. "So, now that you're here, what do you want to do with yourself?"

"I want to edit MDI directories," I said with a smile.

She laughed. "Let's be candid. I'm not so naive as to believe that MDI is a career path, though for some I suppose it is. We're a small company, family owned, and we pride ourselves on choosing people who fit well into the culture here, even if only for a short amount of time," she said, then looked from me to my résumé. "So tell me, how does a man—and excuse me if I'm being repetitive—with an undergraduate degree in finance, a sixteen-month stint at a brokerage house called Horne, Barnes, and Mueller, a year working for a wine importer, and who spent the past year up until May as a driver for a beverage distributor come to want to be an editor at a small company in Evanston, Illinois? And that's not to mention the several gaps in employment I've noticed."

I looked down. "There were a lot of things I enjoyed about working in finance. And of course, there were things I didn't. When I was there, before the recession, the only thing that mattered was making money. I don't know," I said and shrugged. "I grew up very poor. Money intrigued me, as though I didn't really believe some people actually had it, which is part of what led me to choosing the major I did." I shifted in the seat. "When the recession hit, I lost my job along with almost everyone else at the company. I received a small severance package and collected unemployment until I found a job with a family selling imported wines from Italy, France, and Greece. It was about as far from finance as I could have gotten. It wasn't a career and I didn't make much money there, but it was kind of fun organizing wine tastings and selling our imports to stores and shops, which was challenging in its own way. But then the market got even worse and the family fell into trouble with the IRS because of tax evasion. I stayed with them until they went out of business a few months later. Through the contacts I made there, I was able to drive a truck for a beverage distributor, which is what I did."

"With the succession of jobs you've held, it kind of seems as though you're heading in a somewhat antithetical direction, don't you think?"

I shrugged. "It's been a tough economy. I did what I had to do."

"For us as well. The position we're trying to fill was originally done by five people. Now there'll be just two of you."

"I'm up for the challenge if you are," I said and again smiled, trying to put the glint in my eye that I had practiced many times in the mirror, the very glint that said I was a hardworking, honest man who could be trusted in good times and bad.

Cathy returned my smile and made a note on my résumé. "So you haven't worked since May. Though I think I already know the answer, what have you done since then?"

"I mostly looked for work. Trying to find a job in New York right now is like trying to find the Holy Grail, or so it was for me. When I wasn't looking for work I was writing a book. I love reading and writing, which is why I want to be an editor now."

"Well, that certainly makes sense," she said and scribbled something else. As before, I couldn't see what it was. "Here's just a silly question I like to ask sometimes. What is it that you're most proud of?"

"In which regard? What am I most proud of at this moment, or overall what is the thing I've done in my life that makes me the most proud?"

"Answer it any way you like."

I paused, not because it was a tough question, but because it was an easy one that required little thought.

"I was a state champion in wrestling my senior year of high school, then went on to become an All-American, placing third in the nation," I said, and had the urge to continue, wanting her to understand just how much wrestling had meant to me in the wake of everything that had happened, how it was the one thing to which I had clung to make sense of the world. My mind went blank for a time, lost in reminiscence, and when it returned, Cathy was watching me closely with the same look shrinks sometimes give you when you're close to a breakthrough, when you've dug deeper than your comfort zone normally allows.

"Nothing in this world has taught me discipline more than wrestling has," I said. "You have to factor in dieting and weight loss, which don't exist in other sports, but in wrestling they are just as much a part of the sport as practice is. If you want to wrestle in the tournament on Saturday, you'd better have the discipline to watch what you eat during the week leading up to it. Otherwise you're sitting in the stands watching with the spectators. It's because of wrestling that I'm every bit as disciplined in my approach to life and work today as I was back then. I learned that hard work does in fact pay off."

"I can understand that," Cathy said. "And third in the nation? That's very impressive."

"Thank you," I said. "But I should have taken first."

Cathy smiled, and from there the interview segued to a friendly conversation as I'd hoped it would, both of us laughing like old pals who hadn't seen one another in ages. I had no trouble answering her questions and I asked plenty of my own as well. When we finally finished I was certain I had the job.

"Well, that's all I have for you," she said. "Do you have anything else you'd like to add before we end?"

"Only that I want this job," I said. "I really do. I'll work hard for you. You have my word on that."

"I don't doubt that," she said. "It's been a pleasure, Stratton."

"For me as well."

"Can I offer just a small bit of advice for the future?"

"Yes, of course."

"Go easy on the aftershave for interviews."

I smiled, stood, and shook her hand.

The call came at noon the next day. The second I heard the levity in Cathy's voice I knew I had the job. Relief swept over me. I was so ecstatic—to have a job in hand and to know that a good majority of my troubles were on their way to being over—that it took a moment to realize just how little they were offering. I never made much money—even when I was in finance—because I never had the confidence to ask for it. But what little I had made then was still far greater than the $10.50 an hour Cathy was offering. I wasn't even sure I could make it on that alone. But when she asked if I accepted, I bit my tongue and said yes.

"Great! When can you start?"

"Would tomorrow be too soon?"

She thought about it a moment, then said yes, tomorrow would be fine. "Let's say nine thirty then."

She spent two minutes filling me in on what to expect before the call ended, and when it did, I could have wept at the mountain of stress that had just been lifted; I was starting five days sooner than what I had projected in my budget, which meant I was now seventeen days away from my first paycheck. Even though it'd only include six days of work (three days this week, three days the next, shortened because of Thanksgiving), I was ecstatic; it'd be my first paycheck in well over six months. My first stroke of good luck in the Windy City.

"I have a job," I kept repeating to myself, pacing the apartment, pumping my fist in the air. "I have a job." And I still had about two hundred dollars left. Perhaps I'd be able to find my own place on that alone. Or maybe not, but at the very least I was well on my way to getting out of Jeff's.

five

THE JOB WAS BORING, so mindless that an invalid could perform its tasks, which justified—barely—the low pay. I was to *edit* new companies being published for the first time in one of MDI's directories. Even when there was just one employee—which more often than not meant a retired old man whittling figurines in his basement (more for pleasure than for profit)—I was to call and confirm the facts we had (i.e., the correct address, the correct spelling of the owner or company officer, the proper description of the product being made). I spent most of the day on the telephone, asking questions and writing the answers I was told onto printouts. I'd create a stack of them and then, at day's end, I'd hand them all to Cathy so she could enter the new information into the database. Apparently I'd get to enter the information myself after the first month. From there, the advertising department took over and tried selling ad space in the directories.

Aside from telling Jeff that I had found a job, that first week passed silently between us; not a word was spoken otherwise. That is, until I walked into the apartment on Saturday morning and found him sitting at his computer.

"How are you?" I asked, the first words I had spoken to him since Tuesday. I had been coming and going quietly, trying to keep out of his way to buy myself as much time as possible.

"Good," he said, his eyes remaining locked on the screen.

"I get my first paycheck on Friday, the first. At the very latest I'll be out by then, but hopefully sooner. I've already been looking for a place."

"Good," he said, still without so much as glancing my way, and I was amazed at how quickly he had turned this cold. And why? Because I had gotten too drunk off of Scotch he himself had bought and then called his friend a rich asshole? I had felt bad about it and even apologized. So why the prolonged hostility? In our little hometown we were friends out of necessity—we had to take what we could get. He was the cool kid in the grade, the rich one who owned ATVs and dirt bikes, of which the rest of us were envious. He was the quarterback of the football team, but with wrestling I was the one in the papers, and for me a tacit competitiveness had always existed between us. In my desperation I had been honest in my emails, telling him my exact situation, my indigence and lack of options. It was something I never did, knowing that any vulnerability I revealed would be later used against me like a trump card; when rational thought flees and anger takes the reins, people will employ any means necessary to destroy you. I'd been guilty of it myself. I wondered if that was the true reason Jeff had extended the invite so freely, not out of youthful nostalgia as I had believed, but so I could witness firsthand just how well he was doing in light of my own struggle to get by.

"Have you been drinking my liquor?" he asked.

"I had a few drinks," I said, and I had, but not enough to where I thought he would notice. When I later looked, I found, on the side of each bottle, an almost indiscernible spot of black made by the tip of a marker that tracked the various alcohol levels. That's another thing I remembered about the Midwest, the inherent passive aggression.

He slowly turned his head and looked me in the eye. "Why?" he asked, the same irritation in his voice that was now in every part of me. I was inclined to argue, but sound reasoning prevailed; I knew he was the type to turn me out onto the street even though I had no other place to go. There was nothing to do but swallow my anger and pride. Both went down like a razor blade.

"I'm sorry, I didn't realize it was a big deal. I'll buy you another bottle when I get paid," I said, though I had no intention of doing so.

"Fine, don't drink anymore," he said, which was all he had needed to say in the first place.

He turned back to the computer and didn't acknowledge me further. I took a deep breath, walked into the bedroom, and closed the door behind me. I dropped my bag on the floor. I gently placed one of his plush and very comfortable pillows in the middle of the bed, and when I had positioned it just right, I proceeded to repeatedly punch the damn thing as hard as I could. I felt better after about ten times. I hit it ten more times just to be sure.

I went for a long walk that lasted three hours and ended up at the library before it closed. I rented a few books with a card I'd gotten earlier in the week. When I returned to the apartment, several of Jeff's friends, Frank among them, were in the living room drinking beer and watching the Bulls game on television. They all looked up and a hush of silence descended as though they'd been talking about me up until the very point of my materializing. I nodded, tried emitting a smile I'm sure looked every bit as fake as it felt, then hurried away and locked the bedroom door behind me. My face felt warm. I had to go to the bathroom but didn't want to face the crowd again, so instead I pissed in a cup and dumped it out the window, and did so numerous times that night to keep from leaving the room.

❦ 2 ❧

Jeff left the apartment on the following Wednesday to spend Thanksgiving in Ohio. I was on the sofa in the living room, and before he walked out he histrionically charged into the kitchen and removed all the liquor from the cabinets and, with his arms full of the bottles, he carried them into his bedroom while keeping his body angled in such a way so that I could see. When he came back out he slammed the bedroom door and carefully locked it, jiggling the knob several times so that the unmistakable sound of it reached my ears. I found the gesture quite funny, and he was in such a huff that I knew it had nothing to do whatsoever with his fear of me drinking his booze, but rather with his desire to deprive me of something he felt certain I deemed important. The irony was that I had no desire to drink, and instead planned to post myself on that very sofa and watch football and sappy movies on his flat screen the entire time he'd be gone. But it didn't end there. Right before he left—actually, he went as far as to walk out the door only to come rushing back in as though he'd forgotten his keys—he swept into the living room and informed me for the third or fourth time that he was going *home* for the holiday and would return on Saturday. Then he left without waiting for a reply, which was fine with me for I had no intention of giving him one. But it was the way that he'd said "home" that got me, as though the place was reserved for him only and that I had no right of entitlement myself, goading me, going so far as to smirk as the word left his mouth. Aside from a flash of anger that quickly passed, the incident didn't upset me as it might normally have, and instead got me thinking about my own past and the Thanksgiving that first brought my parents and me to Spencer, Ohio. I wonder now whether I can tell their story exactly as it had happened. I'm not sure, but whether the truth is bored into every last detail is irrelevant; our memories, after all, have their own story to tell, and I stand by mine.

My parents were both born and raised in West Virginia, though they didn't meet there and instead found each other in a bar outside of Cleveland when my mother had just turned fifteen; her best friend's father owned the bar and allowed them to drink there once they possessed the desire to. My birth came nine months later.

When I was born my parents were unwed, but not for lack of trying. The legal age to be married in Ohio then was sixteen, that is, unless a parent consented. My grandmother despised my father, and the hatred between the two was instant and mutual. No matter how hard my mother lobbied, my grandmother refused to sign off on it.

"It'll turn out shit," she had said (as recanted by my mother many years later). "I'll be damned if I'll allow myself to be the one responsible for it."

"You don't know that."

"The hell I don't."

She turned sixteen a few weeks after I was born, but they didn't wed until six months after that. Though he didn't come right out and say it, my father wanted my mother thin in a wedding dress, and by the time she finally won the battle against pregnancy weight, there wasn't enough money for a proper ceremony. Instead they married at the local courthouse minus the white dress my mom had romanticized. It was a victory for my grandmother.

He was twenty-nine when he met my mother, making him fourteen years older. She was an only child; my father was not, having two older brothers and a younger sister, none of whom he ever mentioned. I didn't learn any of their names until I, myself, was sixteen. That should have been an early indication of the type of man my father was, that he had no contact with his own family—whether it was because of him or because of them, I don't think it matters—but if my mother had her doubts, she never let on.

I was much closer to my mother, always grasped her legs during the early years we lived in Cleveland. She was a small woman with a big heart, fiercely loyal in regard to family, and even with the hatred that existed between my father and grandmother, it was still hard for my mother to be away from her. She hated Cleveland, hated the dilapidated one-bedroom apartment we lived in on West 65th Street, and when I was three and my grandmother had her first stroke, it wasn't an opportunity for my mother to move, but a necessity. Spencer was nearly an hour southwest of us and my grandmother lived alone. My father said no. When my mother said she was going regardless, the three of us moved together a few weeks later on the day before Thanksgiving, and on the next day my grandmother laid out a spread. It was one of the few days deprived of strain, the bottles of wine being poured without judgment.

After that welcoming dinner, however, the tension was immediate. My grandmother saw my father as a lazy, manipulative man. My father believed my grandmother meddled, and in her eyes he saw a vision of himself he couldn't bear to witness, which is to say, she saw the parts of him he had hoped to keep hidden, and there are few things as threatening to us as individuals as a person who perceives our worst flaws, especially when those flaws are all they see. I think my father was frightfully conscious of this every step of the way, and it made him defensive, then angry, and finally, after many months, he resigned himself to the fact that he'd never convince her otherwise, at which point he simply gave up. They would never trust each other, and they rarely ever talked, but at least there was some harmony to that.

My mother was nineteen when we moved, which was the legal drinking age at the end of 1986, and my parents took advantage of this at the local bar where my mother would later work, the bar in which I was raised. Before she had her stroke, my grandmother had still earned a modest salary, still controlled the savings left behind by my grandfather, who was killed in an automobile accident in West Virginia when my mother was ten years old. His death is what prompted the move north to Ohio. My grandmother wasn't wealthy, but coming from an apartment where the gas or electric was often turned off, where I was without a room and slept on the couch, it seemed like we were suddenly rich. My parents used her for this, neither in a rush to find a job, spending most nights at the bar a two-minute walk away while the parenting duties fell to my grandmother. And when she had her final stroke when I was six, my parents had spent nearly everything she had saved. The only way to pay for the funeral was to refinance the house that, until then, was halfway paid off.

It was Jeff's father who granted my parents the loan that would gnaw at them for the rest of their days, and in an indirect way, it would gnaw at me as well. And while I concede that Jeff's dad was a decent man who helped my parents out of a serious bind, I recall a time—years later when I was in the fifth or sixth grade—when Jeff asked me in front of a group of kids if my parents were ever going to stop being hillbilly lowlifes and pay their mortgage on time, or if they always planned on being a month behind. Everybody laughed and my face burned with embarrassment. That was the first time I wanted to hit him, but I didn't, and merely shrugged and feigned laughter with everyone else, trying to show levity in light of my parents' inability to manage money, regardless of how little of it they had.

Remembering back to my parents' indigence led me to count all of the money I had left, which came to eighty-one dollars, an amount I had to make last for the next eight days. I felt confident doing so for the simple reason that I had no other choice.

For Thanksgiving dinner I made two peanut-butter-and-jelly sandwiches and washed them down with a glass of milk. I was feeling lonely and a little down and tried opening Jeff's bedroom door with a butter knife to get to his liquor. It wouldn't budge. I gave up and went back to the sofa and resumed watching football in high definition with the surround sound cranked up, both of which were luxuries I'd always done without. Yet one more example of something Jeff had that I did not.

❦ 3 ❦

Before Jeff returned, to ease the tension between us, I spent three hours cleaning every nook and corner of his apartment. Dusting every surface. Polishing every object. Though the place was in perpetual sheen already, after I was done it looked even cleaner, smelling as fresh as springtime tulips. A sparkling gem that even the most obdurate obsessive compulsive would be happy to come home to.

I had just stepped out of the shower and stood in the hallway when he walked in. I was in jeans and an old wrestling T-shirt. It was black, and on it our high school's name written in gold lettering encircled a pirate's head with a sword clenched between its teeth. Jeff looked at me, lowered his gaze until it fell on the pirate in the center, and snickered. He then shook his head and walked into his bedroom and shut the door. I had the urge to kick through it and ask him what the hell was so funny. Instead I left the apartment.

At the library I scanned craigslist ads, which is what I'd been doing for an hour or so every day at work, but I had yet to find anything promising. Most were apartment shares. I yearned to live alone but the reality was that it'd be too expensive on my modest wage. Though they were far from New York prices, Chicago rents were anything but cheap. I searched for a half hour and responded to five ads before stumbling across the following:

Lakeview studio—400 sq. ft.—2nd floor—
Between Belmont and Addison El stops—$550/month

It was small but I didn't care; I could afford $550. Was there a catch? Probably, but what expectations did I have to begin with? The ad was only ten minutes old and I entered the number into my phone and rushed outside. A man's gruff voice answered on the second ring.

"Hi, I'm calling about the apartment. Is it still available?"

"Sure is," he said, then cleared the phlegm from his throat. "Would you like to see it?"

"I can come right now," I said, already huffing it to the train.

It was an old three-story building covered with beige siding discolored and cracked from the seasons. It seemed to lean at a slight angle as if it were a drunkard tired of standing upright, and the kicker—the reason for the cheap rent, I was sure—was that the back of the building was mere feet from the El. If the empty apartment was the second-floor rear-facing unit—which I was confident it was—the trains would pass by the windows so close I could probably reach out and touch them.

The man's name was Gene. In defiance of his gravelly voice, he was clean-shaven and fit and looked to be around sixty, tall and slender and sharp featured with close-cropped graying hair. He was nicely dressed in a black polo tucked into khaki slacks that made the half-smoked cigarette dangling from his lips look amiss. He squinted his blue eyes to keep the rising smoke from burning them. He shook my hand firmly, and the way he pumped it hard one time caused me to like him immediately.

"Come on up," he said.

The building contained four units, and of course the studio was in fact where I had guessed. It was small, perfectly square save for two side-by-side doors to the left of the main entryway, one the bathroom, the other the closet. The kitchen, which contained a two-burner oven, a fridge, and a 1½-foot-long counter with sink, was situated to the right. The walls and floor were covered with dust and cobwebs.

"So how bad are the trains?"

"You get used to them."

There were two windows at the rear, both of which were wooden and warped with age and contained a single pane of glass similar to those in the home I'd grown up in, which is a way of saying that they'd do little to keep out the cold. The left wouldn't budge when I tried forcing it open; I was able to muscle the right one up just enough to stick my head out. A view looking east, cold winter mornings with the first light of day as the sun reached over the lake. The tracks were just a few feet away, almost close enough to jump across to, and beyond those was the blank rear of the building opposite. I looked to the left and could see a train stationed at Addison coming our way. I pulled myself in and walked into the bathroom. One person could fit in it, two people could not; so small that I could literally shower, shit, and shave at the same time if I felt so inclined. The sink jutted away from the wall and over the toilet so that I'd have to piss while standing at a slight angle.

"Not exactly a generous bathroom," Gene said.

I opened my mouth to respond but was interrupted by the train. It started as a low rumble, like the engine of a classic car, and quickly grew from there. The windows shook so violently I feared they might break. Gene stood smiling and it was pointless to talk; there was no way he'd hear me. I could see the tops of the steel wheels and the train's bottom half flying by. Even the floor quivered and I thought the whole building might collapse. And just as it had slowly started, it just as slowly faded away. There'd be no silence here, chaotic quarters that'd offer security without any warmth.

"I recommend putting your bed away from the wall," he said. "And earplugs aren't a bad investment."

"Wow, I think you might be full of shit saying one gets used to it."

He grinned. "This is a tough apartment to rent," he said, and a small bit of excitement bubbled up within me.

On the back wall between the two windows stood a hole a foot in diameter. The drywall had been smashed in, exposing the interior studs, plaster, and brick.

"What happened there?" I asked.

"No idea. Left over from the last tenant. He lost his job and just disappeared. Took me a few weeks to even realize he was gone. But it'll be fixed if you take the place. And obviously everything will be scrubbed down and painted," he said, and I wondered why he hadn't done so already if he was truly serious about renting it.

Gene's own apartment took up the entire third floor. It was warm and inviting, large but simple. The floor was carpeted and the windows were updated vinyl, triple-paned, which I'm sure diminished or solved entirely the train dilemma. The only extravagance was the living room, which was hardly a living room at all aside from the sofa, recliner, and coffee table in the center of the room, but rather a compact and densely populated library; all four walls were shelf-lined and stuffed with books.

"Now we're talking," I said. There had to be thousands of them—Lost Generation, Beat Generation, English writers, American, books that looked brand new, books that had to be a hundred years old.

"Do you read much?" Gene asked, removing a hand-rolled cigarette from a silver case. He snapped it shut and slipped it back in his breast pocket, lit the cigarette, and exhaled a puff of smoke that dissipated in the air around him.

"Yes. Trying to be a writer, actually."

"Oh yeah?" he said, a trail of smoke following him into the kitchen while I continued scanning the books. I lifted *The Sun Also Rises* from a middle shelf, opened it at random, and buried my nose in the binding and inhaled deeply. A yellowed copy that smelled of dust and age. My nose was still in the binding when Gene returned carrying in each hand a highball glass filled with ice, liquor, and a floating lime wheel.

"I do that very same thing," he said.

"No better smell in the world."

"You haven't been with the right women then," he said with a grin, handing me the drink. I took a sip.

"It's a Gin Rickey," he said. "Fitzgerald's favorite. Any aspiring writer can appreciate that, right?"

"Sold," I replied.

He motioned me into the dining room. It was mostly bare except for the large formal table in its center and family photographs adorning the walls. I sat across from Gene. I could see the bottom of a faded tattoo peaking from the shirtsleeve on his right bicep, which appeared to have lost none of the toned rigidity of its youthful shape.

"The apartment has been empty for about five months now. It's not the best unit but I'm sure you know it's a great neighborhood, a lot of people your age, a lot of energy, a five-minute walk from Wrigley Field while passing no less than thirty bars and restaurants along the way. Are you interested?"

I nodded. "Yes, absolutely. The trains are going to take some getting used to, but I just moved here a week and a half ago and I need something I can afford and would prefer to live alone. So yes, I'm interested. More than interested, actually. I want the place."

"Good, good. What are you doing for work here?"

I explained my situation, going as far as to tell Gene the money I had in my wallet, the estimated amount of the first check I'd receive the following Friday, and the amount I expected from each check thereafter. I held nothing back, hoping that the truth and all its vulnerabilities would speak volumes about my character. When I finished he crossed his arms and eyed me cautiously until the phone rang. It was an old rotary an arm's reach away and he snatched it up from its cradle, looking at me as the person spoke, and then he said, "I'm sorry, I just rented it actually, but thanks for calling." He hung up. I couldn't stop my facial features from doing precisely what they wanted to do, which was break out into a smirk of excitement.

"I listed the apartment at five fifty because I was hoping to rent it for an even five hundred, which I'll be happy to give it to you for," he said. "But my terms are fifty dollars now to hold it. Another two fifty when you're paid on Friday and you can move in. The paycheck after that you pay the remaining balance—two hundred—and then I expect the rent to be paid in full on the first of every month. You can pay early if you want, but not late. You've seen the place and know its condition, so there isn't much point in asking for a deposit, nor will I make you sign a contract. All I do ask is that you give me a month's notice if you decide to leave. Do we have a deal?"

Had I not noticed the picture on the wall of a much younger version of Gene wearing army fatigues, or the one beside that in which he looked fifteen years older wearing the same uniform, the methodical way in which he spoke would have still led me to assume a life in the military. He sat straight and kept one hand over the other. His words seemed carefully weighed before he spoke them and his eyes never left mine. I believed his terms were done for the sake of order, and not because he believed I would slight him in any way. He was testing me, my commitment, my will, by leaving me with only eleven dollars for the next six days. I felt I needed to prove it to him. Call it pride. Going without was nothing new for me; I'd had twenty-seven years' worth of training to become inured to the rigors of hard living.

"You bet," I said and shook his hand. I removed a fifty from my wallet and laid it out on the table. He left it there without touching it, without even glancing down at it.

"Great," he said. "And while you're here I don't mind if you borrow some of my books. Do you have any furniture?"

I shook my head. "Nothing but a bag full of clothes."

He smiled, stamped out his cigarette, threw back the rest of his Gin Rickey. "Come on," he said.

As far as I could tell the apartment contained three bedrooms; the middle one served as storage. There were boxes stacked to the ceiling, old, outdated tables and chairs, yellowing newspapers, clothes folded into piles. In the far corner was an old dust-covered desk.

"You can have that desk if you want it. I have no use for it. Been meaning to get rid of some of this shit for a while now. It's real wood, not that pressboard garbage. Heavier than hell but I'll help you carry it down now if you want it."

"Hell yes, I want it. I'll take anything you want to get rid of."

Small scratches were scattered across the desk's surface along with a few nicks here and there, but otherwise it was in good shape. It'd look nice in the apartment. Gene cleared a pathway and then crouched on one side of the desk while I took the other.

"I'm telling you, it's a heavy son of a bitch."

"I have faith in you, Gene."

"I'm glad somebody does. On three. One. Two. Three." We both lifted. He wasn't kidding, it was heavier than hell. Before we were out of the room, Gene's face had turned red; by the time we made it out of his apartment, and before the stairs, it was nearly purple. He went down first, which meant most of the weight was on him, but it was easy weight while I was nearly bent at a ninety-degree angle and straining mightily. By the time we made it down, my hands hurt so badly I was sure they were cut and bleeding.

"Alright, down, down, down!" he said. I lowered my end slowly onto the tips of my shoes to keep from making a sound and smashing my fingers, Gene dropped his when it was within a foot of the floor. "It's yours now. I'm never moving this damn thing again."

We scooted it against the far wall between the two windows and directly below the gaping hole. The desk fit well there, and seeing it made me even more eager to move in. I wished like hell I didn't have to wait six days, and for a moment I considered asking if we could forgo the six-day wait. But I didn't, for fear of pressing my luck. We walked back up. Gene made a second drink. I hadn't eaten yet, and on an empty stomach, I had a slight buzz from the first. We sat and made small talk until I finished. Gene made himself a third. I wondered how many he'd had already, and was even more curious as to how he kept so fit if this was how he passed the days.

But I liked him, and felt a certain lightheartedness by being in his company. There was something entirely agreeable about Gene, the way he didn't seem to pull punches or pretend to be someone he wasn't. *Authentic* was the word. He seemed like a man brought up on honesty, or maybe it had been ingrained in him from the military and he had kept with it post-retirement, a man who told the truth even when the truth was something you didn't want to hear. He radiated indifference to outside opinion: *This is who I am, take it or leave it; it makes no difference to me.* I'd always wished for immunity to those same external concerns, and thus having power over others who use judgment against you.

But there was more to Gene than that, something I couldn't quite put my finger on, at least not then, when meeting him for the first time. It'd be a while yet before I learned that Gene, too, in the quiet way in which he went about his life, was a man with something to hide.

six

BY MONDAY MORNING I was broke. After six days of work I had a good feel for when everyone else arrived. My normal start time was eight, and Cathy, my boss, didn't arrive until a quarter to nine. By arriving at seven thirty, not only did I have the luxury of no supervision for an hour and fifteen minutes, but I'd also receive a half hour of overtime every day by leaving at the normal time of four thirty, thus beefing up my paycheck a bit. But that wouldn't help my current financial plight, or the more pressing matter of what I'd eat for lunch.

I spent the first hour searching craigslist for any short-notice work—helping somebody move, passing out fliers, painting the walls of an apartment, anything, really—but the few inquiries I made went unanswered. I had eaten one of Jeff's bagels for breakfast, something I was sure he'd notice and bitch about, but I didn't care. By ten I was already hungry. By eleven I was starving.

At eleven thirty I walked downstairs to the lunchroom. It was situated between the bathroom and the mailroom, which meant that the bathroom could only be accessed by walking through the lunchroom. I'd have to be quick. I opened the fridge. It was packed full of brown bags and microwavable lunches. I dug through the nearest bag—macaroni salad, chips, sliced carrots, pudding. I pushed it back in and went to the next. I pulled out a ham and cheese sandwich, shoved it into my pocket, rushed back upstairs.

One of the few benefits of my job was my cubicle. It was, as far as I could tell, the best in the building, my desk situated in such a way that nobody walking by could see me or my computer screen, unlike most of the other cubes, which were out in the open. I quickly got into the habit of doing a half hour of work and then surfing the Web and checking email for the next half hour to counterbalance the effort. I ate the sandwich while checking my personal email. My hunger was assuaged, if only for the moment. I went back downstairs and did the same thing an hour later, pilfering a strawberry yogurt that I ate with my fingers in the bathroom stall. When I went down again, at two o'clock, the fridge was empty. The last two hours of the workday were spent in hunger. Just before I left for the day, a company-wide email arrived warning that any employee caught with food that wasn't theirs would be terminated immediately.

❦ 2 ❧

It took forty minutes to get to and from work. When I left at four thirty I always beat Jeff back by an hour, sometimes two or three; the new place would cut ten minutes off my commute. When I got back I went into the kitchen and took four slices of bread and placed them into two plastic sandwich bags. I buried both beneath my shirts in the top dresser drawer. Tuesday's lunch. I was so hungry that the simple thought of food caused me to salivate. I knew I wouldn't last the week by only stealing a bite here and there.

I returned to the kitchen and rummaged through the cabinets looking for something I could eat without giving myself away, a growl coming from my gut. From my days of cutting weight during wrestling, I'd always been very susceptible to hunger, and my hands were quick to shake, which they were doing now. I ate three Oreos, a granola bar, a handful of Cheerios, and a cold spoonful of leftover turkey and stuffing from Jeff's Thanksgiving back home. I took great care to cover my tracks, that everything was as I had found it. The last thing I needed was for Jeff to know I was eating his food. I felt hungry all the time and was getting sick of it and still four days away from getting paid. I'm not sure what else I had expected by paying Gene almost everything I had while leaving myself with eleven dollars for six days. Not the rashest decision I'd ever made, but pretty damn close. If I could just hold on until Friday, then everything would be all right. How in the hell could I hold on until Friday when I had nothing?

❦ 3 ❦

The next morning, Tuesday, I woke to Jeff's heavy footsteps in the hallway. I rolled over, looked at the clock. It was seven ten. I'd been so preoccupied with hunger that I'd forgotten to set the alarm. In twenty minutes I'd be late for the schedule I had set for myself. I still had to shower, dress, catch the train, a process that, at its minimum, took an hour and fifteen minutes. I decided to take my time.

I jumped in the shower while Jeff made breakfast and coffee. Fifteen minutes later, we passed silently in the hall. He walked through his bedroom into his own bathroom, shutting the bathroom door behind him while keeping the bedroom door open.

I slipped on underwear, socks, the same pair of khaki slacks I'd worn the day before. His shower started. I pulled on a white T-shirt and looped a belt through the pants, then walked out of the bedroom and down the hallway. My stomach groaned, and though I had the four slices of bread for the day's provisions, I knew they wouldn't be enough. I was desperate, so wracked with anxiety that I had hardly slept at all during the night. My eyeballs ached; my hands were jittery. I needed help, no other way around it.

I stuck my head in Jeff's bedroom and listened. The sound of water falling inconsistently, a bar of soap clattering against the tub. On the bedside table across the room sat his wallet, watch, loose change, cell phone attached to its cord. I stared back at the bathroom door. Then I took a deep breath and rushed across the room and lifted his wallet.

My heart pounded as I raced through the bills—twenties mostly— totaling $157, enough so that he might not notice if some went missing.

I lifted out two twenties and placed the wallet back on the table just as I had found it, lined perfectly with his watch, beside the tower of change stacked from largest coins to smallest, all heads-up. I hurried out of the bedroom, finished dressing, and sped out of the apartment with a sense of relief, knowing I now had enough to survive the week. I bought a coffee and two breakfast sandwiches on my walk to the train and ate every bit of both of them.

⬦ 4 ⬦

On Friday morning Cathy entered my cubicle and casually dropped off my paycheck. As though there was nothing to it, and for her I suppose there wasn't. But for me the sight of it caused my heart rate to double. I tore away the envelope and brought the check to my nose and inhaled it deeply. Freedom in the form of $411. I stared at it, continually picking it up to feel it between my fingers to be certain it was real. Then I rushed out and opened a checking account at the nearby bank even though it wasn't lunchtime yet. I called Gene the second I returned to let him know I was coming straight over after work.

I shared my cubicle with a fifty-two-year-old thrice-divorcée named Linda. Our desks were situated on opposite sides so that our backs faced one another. Aside from Cathy, Linda was the only person I talked to at work, out of necessity at first, but then because I enjoyed her pert phone conversations and her scorn for the company that, after a few more weeks, I was sure my own would equal. She'd been there four years, lived alone in a house a mile away, and drank no less than eight cups of coffee a day, one an hour. Apparently she had scaled herself back from the twelve or so she used to consume. When I hung up the phone she was eyeing me.

"You okay?" she asked, amused. "You look like you're about to wet your pants."

"I just might, too," I said. "That's how brutal the past few weeks have been."

She was slender and possessed a look that hinted of past beauty.

Dark hair fell to the middle of her back and was, on most days, in a state of disarray as though she'd rolled right out of bed and straight into her clothes. Through our conversations I'd learned that she'd been single for five years after the dissolution of her last marriage to a man ten years her senior who could no longer hold an erection, which was apparently the final nail in the proverbial coffin. Her daughter, her only child from her first husband, was a junior in a college downstate. I continually joked with Linda to let me know the next time she came home on break.

"So you're moving in tonight?"

"Yes, and thank Christ, too. I don't think I can survive another minute in my current situation."

The corner of her mouth lifted into a wry grin. "A passive-aggressive roommate who sleeps in a separate room? Sounds like the last three years of my second marriage."

I laughed. "It's pretty sad that I actually look forward to coming to this place to get away from it all."

"That *is* pretty sad," she agreed.

The day inched by and when it finally ended I literally ran to the train, took it to Belmont, and sprinted several blocks to Gene's. I was guaranteed the place but I couldn't relax until the keys were physically in my hand.

"Stratton, my boy, how are you?"

"Going to be awesome in about a half hour when I'm officially moved in."

I counted out the $250 as we climbed the stairs. I handed it to Gene and he promptly folded the money in half and slipped the bills into his front shirt pocket. That left me with only $161 for the next two weeks, which put me right back in the tight spot I'd been living in, but not even that bothered me when Gene tossed me the keys and allowed me to unlock the door myself. The apartment had been cleaned from floor to ceiling, the walls painted white, the hole at the back plastered over. Even the desk had been dusted and there was now an office chair on wheels to go with it.

"Kick-ass," I said. "You're the man, Gene."

"Nah, just an asshole who has his moments. And besides, I told you I'd whip it into shape before you moved in."

I jogged back to the train, feeling the keys in my pocket and a stupid grin upon my face. Before I had left for work that morning I had preemptively packed my bag. I'd be in and out in thirty seconds. Then I'd be done with Jeff and his passive-aggressive bullshit, his knowing looks, the air of superiority with which he continually viewed me. Maybe I'd give him a final "fuck you" for good measure, draw a big dick on a sheet of paper and leave it on his desk for him to find. Then I could go back to being just another nameless face in a big city with a past that, as far as anyone knew, was no different or remarkable than anyone else's.

When I made it back, I walked in and hung his keys on the hook beside the door. *Good riddance*, I thought. Down the hall and into the bedroom where atop the bed my bag would be waiting. Only it wasn't there. I kept staring at the top mattress as if I'd merely overlooked the bag, and that if I looked more closely it would suddenly appear. And then I heard the floor creak from out in the living room.

Jeff stood firmly in front of the sofa with his arms crossed. His eyes stared through me beneath two tightly furrowed brows. He wore tennis shoes, mesh shorts, and a T-shirt as though he'd been to the gym. His hands were clenched into fists, ready for whatever may or may not happen. Luckily I had two fists of my own, and without telling them to, both tightened into balls.

"Give me back the forty dollars you stole and replace my bottle of whiskey and I'll give you your bag," he said.

"I didn't drink a bottle of whiskey."

"Bullshit," he said, already breathing heavily.

I smiled. "Where's my bag, Jeff?"

"Where's my money and whiskey?" he replied.

"You're kidding me, right?"

"Yes, Stratton, it's all one big joke."

I nodded. "You've sat here all day, haven't you? Thinking this through. But really, Jeff, do you think this is going to turn out well for you?"

"Right, Stratton. You're nothing but a worthless petty thief and I want what you took from me. Hell, you're not even denying that you stole the money."

I shook my head. "You really are pathetic."

"Yeah, I'm pathetic. And you really are a worthless thief. I mean, do you see yourself right now? Like, really? What the hell, man? I helped you out and let you stay here for free and all you did was freeload off me, and when that wasn't enough you stole my money. You're a charity case, you know that? You're—"

"Yeah, you helped me out, and since the day I arrived, you've been nothing but an asshole so you can take your charity and ram it straight up your ass," I said, feeling the anger rise up from wherever it is that it lurks. My balance wavered and I could feel my hands shake. My bottom lip quivered. I couldn't tell if it was noticeable. My throat felt raw. But I wasn't scared. Of all the things Jeff had that I didn't, there were a few things I possessed that he never would. Gravel in my guts. An implacable mean streak a mile wide from a lifetime of scraping by and a desire to do harm to those who never had to. Pent-up anger and frustration. A father who shirked diplomacy and instead taught me how to fight, and how to fight well.

Jeff shook his head. "You've done well, Stratton. Look how far you've come, buddy. You really should be proud of yourself."

"Fuck you," I said, fifteen feet away. Both standing firm staring at each other. It was what I had always done in wrestling, staring down an opponent. Always full of nerves and adrenaline but I refused to look away first. It was another thing my father had taught me. He used to always point it out on those long-ago nights when we'd watch every Mike Tyson fight, years before I started wrestling. To look away first showed weakness, timidity, fear. And now, standing in front of Jeff, who was five inches taller than I was and about forty pounds heavier, it was no differ-ent. I kept my eyes on his. The anger inside of me was quickly boiling to rage, rage that would soon overflow and come spilling over the brim. Channel it, Stratton. Don't let it control you. Then Jeff shook his head and glanced at the floor, giving round one to me.

From the corner of my eye I could see the entrance to his bedroom. The door was closed, which led me to believe that my bag was in there. I doubted he'd go through the trouble of hiding it outside the apartment.

"You think you can go through with this? You think you're man enough to fight me?" I asked. "All the money in the world won't help you out of this, Jeff, you know that, right? No amount of money will make you any less than the little pussy bitch that you are."

I took a step forward.

He shook his head. "Boy, your mom would be proud, wouldn't she?"

And that was it. Something broke inside me. Three quick steps and I was there. I swung. Every bit of strength, every bit of hope and fear and anger and rage, every bit of social injustice, was in that fist hurled his way. It landed flush on his left cheek with a deadening thud. The skin broke. He fell backward onto the glass coffee table. It snapped cleanly in two right down the center, and the sight of it only fueled the fiery red surging through me. I thought about pouncing on top of him. Instead I sprinted toward his bedroom and shouldered through the door. It opened with ease. I slammed it shut, locked it behind me. Jeff yelled something I couldn't hear from the living room. The bathroom door was closed. I kicked straight through it. It busted away from the hinges and crashed forward; the knob broke away and ricocheted straight back and off the wall behind me.

I had guessed correctly. My bag was on the floor in the empty space between the toilet and shower. I grabbed it and rushed out. Jeff kicked the bedroom door open. As he stumbled in I dropped my bag and swung again. I caught him just above the left eye this time. Another cut opened. He fell. Blood ran down both sides of his face. I pounced on top of him, a flurry of punches to his face and the back of his head. Both of us yelling and screaming obscenities. Neither of us hearing them through our own rage, a rage that had been building within me for a very long time. He threw an errant punch and I clasped his head and arm in a front headlock, clamping down hard with perfect technique, another homage to my days on the mat.

"Don't you ever talk about my mom, you piece of shit! I'll kill you!" I screamed. "I swear to god I'll fucking kill you!" I squeezed as tightly as I could. He couldn't talk or breathe, couldn't so much as make a peep. I buried my chin in the middle of his back for better leverage, cutting off the blood flow to his brain. He tried grabbing me, tried grabbing anything that might help. I pushed my knee into the back of his head and this put an end to it. The knuckle of my right thumb was flush against his Adam's apple. I could feel its resistance. Another pound of pressure would probably snap the cartilage in two. What would happen then?

"What about all that Mr. State Champion talk now, huh motherfucker? How about your pissing contest? That's all you are, Jeff. Big talk with Daddy's money. A lot of good it's doing you now, huh?"

I could feel the fight leave him, could feel him quickly drifting off. All I had to do was push my knee down a tad bit harder. That'd do the trick. Instead I squeezed a final time and let go. I grabbed my bag, stepped over him while he struggled to catch his breath. His face was scarlet; blood dripped from his chin. My own nose was bleeding. I wasn't sure if I'd been hit or if I had hit myself in the excitement of it all.

"You're lucky I didn't kill you," I said.

I opened the apartment door and took the stairs two and three at a time. I threw my bag on the ground and turned to see if he had followed. He hadn't, and after thirty seconds I picked up my bag and slung it over my shoulder. Just before I turned I saw him faintly in the front window looking down. The sun's glare covered his face, but the splattered red down the front of his shirt was unmistakable. I lifted my hand and flipped him off. Then I walked away, making a right turn at the first opportunity and zigzagging up and down the streets headed north. I smiled the entire time, my hands violently shaking with the adrenaline coursing through my veins. It was the most alive I'd felt in months.

❦ 5 ❧

I emptied the bag out on the floor. My legal pads were there. So was my bottle of Xanax, my few books, my other pair of shoes, all my clothes. Nothing was missing. Thank god I had packed this morning.

Then a knock fell at the door. My heart sank. My first thought was that Jeff had called the police, but could they have followed me that quickly? How could they even know where I lived? I held my breath and thought about ignoring it, attesting to my innocence by remaining as still as a person faced with a raised cobra, too terrified to move a muscle for fear of being bitten.

"You in there?" the voice asked, and in hearing it I exhaled in a long, slow hiss. I flung the door open and Gene sauntered in, his eyes widening at the sight of my shirt.

"Jesus, what the hell happened to you?"

Blood was splattered down the front of it, and upon noticing, I started to laugh. I bent over to catch my breath, still chuckling. "What?" he asked.

I told him what had happened, sticking mostly to the facts while omitting the more incriminating parts. I wasn't sure why I told him, maybe nothing more than an attempt to impress him with what I believed was a story of valor, even while knowing never to assume the way a person might react to fights. It was a point of pride for me that I could kick my way out of corners when I had to, that I had both landed and taken my fair share of punches, but of course not everybody was as impressed as I was by my own abilities. When I finished the story, I stood there self-consciously while Gene silently stared at me. This time I was the one who looked away first.

"You think he called the cops?"

I shook my head. "I doubt it."

"Did you take the money?"

"Of course not. The man's delusional."

Gene's face softened and I immediately felt better. "Well, good for you for sticking up for yourself. If you don't, then nobody else will." He shrugged. "Shit happens."

"That it does, Gene." I paused and looked around the room. "Hell, now what am I going to do? I have an apartment without a thing in it and it's Friday night and I'm covered in blood," I said, my voice echoing off the walls without the buffer of furniture to absorb it. "I don't suppose you have anything else you want to get rid of?"

He laughed. "You're a mess, kiddo. But let me check. I'm sure I do. Would be good for me to get rid of some of that shit up there."

Gene ran upstairs and returned a few minutes later with his arms full of dishes, silverware, a pot and pan, an old patchwork quilt. He dropped the dishes in the kitchen sink and threw me the quilt.

"Like I said, you're one hell of a guy, Gene."

"Yeah, and I'm starting to believe it, too. You're on your own for the rest, though."

"You've done far more than I could have hoped for. I really appreciate it."

"No problem. Anyway, come up and grab a book before it gets too late. Going to need something to occupy your mind, especially after the day you've had. And it certainly looks like you could use a drink."

"Isn't that the truth?" I said. "It's been one messed-up day."

Gene went back upstairs. I unloaded my notepads, pens, and pencils from my shoulder bag into the desk. The shaking in my hands slowed and I pulled away a piece of skin hanging from a cut on the middle knuckle of my right hand. I licked away the blood, then paced the studio. A train roared by like an earthquake but not even that dampened my spirits.

My own apartment, my own private corner of the world. I was finally in. I had made it.

seven

SUNDAY MORNING. HEAVY GRAY clouds in the leaden sky, bitter cold, empty sidewalks and parked cars with ice-coated windows, stripped trees pushed by the biting wind. Every new day in Chicago, another day of heavy gray clouds. I've yet to find anything quite as lonely as an empty city street on a cold Sunday morning.

I pocketed my hands but it did little to warm them. A new jacket, one equipped to tackle winter, was another in a long list of luxuries I couldn't afford, after a bed, pillows, linens, food, a television, computer, toiletries, a dresser, earplugs, books, hangers on which to hang my clothes instead of folding them into piles on the floor.

I walked to the grocery store a quarter mile away, grabbed a basket, committed myself only to the basics. Anything I could do without for two weeks would be omitted. After paying Gene and after the weekend, I had a hundred and seventeen dollars. Making it on that alone would take a level of creativity I wasn't sure I possessed.

I bought a loaf of bread, small jars of peanut butter and jelly, several packages of ramen noodles, a half gallon of milk, a box of imitation raisin bran, six bananas, a bar of soap, deodorant, a bottle of shampoo. I left with twenty-seven dollars less. At a store across the street I bought a shower curtain, towel, washrag—another twenty-two bucks. When I got home I ate two bowls of cereal and took a hot shower that lasted thirty minutes. Then I sat in front of the window and spent the remainder of the day watching the trains roar by, staring intently as if they carried with them all the hope I'd lost along the way.

❧ 2 ☙

Despite what I'm sure amounted to two separate scars—one over his eye, one on his cheek—in the end, I'm afraid, it was Jeff who had gotten the best of me. His words had cut me deeply, and nothing I did or thought kept the despair at bay. *Boy, your mom would be proud, wouldn't she?* That very question had always haunted me because, let's face it, if we're to be judged by what we leave behind, then my mother's life meant little. I was her legacy, and what have I ever done to be proud of? I would have gladly traded two facial scars for the agony that slowly descended; the first few days were hard, but like a snowball gaining size and strength the further down the hill it rolls, the pain only worsened as the days passed by.

There was nothing in the apartment aside from the desk and chair and piled clothes along the left wall. A monument to bleakness. Even with the passing trains, the place was too quiet. I couldn't stand being there. I went for long walks, or sat and read at the library. Both were feeble attempts to stave off the inevitable: loneliness in all its many disguises. I missed my mom more than normal. In staying with Jeff I had allowed the past to follow me, a past I wished desperately to forget even with the memories of my mother I still cling tightly to. And the past, for those foolish enough to subscribe to it, holds a grudge harder than anything known to man.

❧ 3 ☙

That first week, I went up to Gene's every day. Every day my knocks went unanswered. So did my calls. He was simply gone.

The trains didn't let up. Only two of the CTA lines ran at night, the Blue and the Red, and it was just my luck that the Red Line was right outside my window. The only consolation was that the later into the night the fewer the trains, sometimes forty minutes between. They drove me crazy, despite serving as a diversion away from the banal routine my life had become. Up at six, to work at seven thirty, leave at four thirty, home for dinner, read for a few hours, then sit around for several more staring at the walls. Day in and day out, that was it. I've always wondered why I could never embrace the forty-hour workweek way of life, or at least accept it. But I couldn't, no matter how hard I tried. A good part of the reason, I'm sure, for my perpetual indigence.

❧ 4 ❧

Once we moved, it was my grandmother who raised me. I was a young boy in a small town and had yet to start school; I was restless and had few, if any, friends. She was forced into retirement because of her stroke. Because she worked at the same company for ten years—the entire time she lived in Ohio—most of her friends were from there. But few of them, if any, ever visited.

While her mental capacities remained strong, her physical health deteriorated quickly. Her second stroke came a year after the first and severely inhibited the movement on the left side of her body. She could still get around, but it had become a struggle.

Between them both, my parents had never read an entire book. My grandmother was different; she'd read hundreds. Not a night passed that she didn't read to me, mostly stories tailored to my age, illustrated books, the classics like *Where the Wild Things Are*, *Harold and the Purple Crayon*, Dr. Seuss. My absolute favorite was Shel Silverstein's *The Giving Tree*, a book about the friendship of a little boy and a tree. The tree provides the boy with everything he needs throughout the course of his life, even at a great cost to herself—a shade to sit in, apples to eat, branches to build a house with, and finally, the tree allows the boy to cut her down to build a canoe, leaving her as nothing more than a stump. And when the boy returns years later as an old man, the tree tells him she has nothing left to give, and the old man says all he wants is a quiet place to sit and rest while he waits for death. I bawled every time, could never understand the sacrifice, why the tree would continually give herself to the boy when the boy used her for his own selfish means.

"She loved the boy," my grandmother said. "So much that she was willing to give herself almost entirely to please him."

I sat Indian style at her feet, looking up through tearful eyes. "But why would the boy do that to the tree, Grandma?"

She sighed. "Sometimes people do things that are harmful to others without meaning to. And sometimes people are so blinded by love or loneliness that they don't realize how much of themselves they're losing in the process, like the tree."

I didn't find that a satisfactory answer. I was too young to see the correlation she was making with my mother's marriage to my father, or perhaps even her own relationship with them.

"And besides," she went on, "it has a happy ending, right? After all, they do end up together."

"But that tree must have been so lonely her whole life."

"She probably was," she said with sadness.

The story has always stuck with me. Is loneliness the worst thing in the world? When I was most alone, I thought I enjoyed the solitude. But when I look back at those times now, it's hard to see past the intense feelings of isolation and sadness. Is it possible they existed then without my realizing it, or has the passing of time added sentiments of sorrow during an otherwise happy time? Are our memories sometimes altered without our knowing it? Or do they instead tell the truth about a time we lied so adamantly to ourselves that we then believed it?

− 5 −

The nights cold. Sleeping on piled clothes on the hardwood floor and dressed in sweatpants and three sweatshirts with a single quilt draped over me. I always woke shivering. Sometimes I could fall back to sleep, sometimes I couldn't. Always stiff and aching. Always hungry and scared. Scared of what, I wasn't sure. But scared all the same.

A year and a half later my grandmother had her third and final stroke. She sat on the living room couch reading to me while I sat at her feet. We were alone, and when I first saw the crooked look on her face, I laughed, thinking it was a bit of histrionics for added effect to the story she read. But I knew something was wrong when the book fell from her lap and she tried to speak but only mumbled. I took her by the hand, tried shaking her out of her stupor. She looked down at me with blank eyes. I dialed 911 as I had been taught. I told them something was the matter with my grandma, then in my fear I hung up the phone.

The White Elephant Saloon, the nearby bar my parents frequented most days, was number two on the speed dial, and my mother had showed me several times how to dial it in case something happened.

Loud music blared in the background and in my shaky voice, I asked, "Is my mom there?"

"Your mom?" the voice asked, pausing to look around the bar. "Do you mean Darla?"

I said yes, bawling, terrified. When my mother answered she was laughing at whatever had been said to get her to the phone.

"Hello?"

"Something . . . has happened . . . to Grandma," I muttered through sobs.

"What? What has happened?" she asked. Her laughter drained away into hysteria.

I was shaking my head, unable to do anything but cry.

"I'm on my way, baby."

She burst through the door with my father not two minutes later. My grandmother had since closed her eyes and was slumped forward. I was holding her hand, again cross-legged at her feet. My mother swept into the room and took her in her arms.

"Not now," she repeated through tears of her own. "God, not now, not yet."

My father called 911 though a siren already wailed in the distance. I walked across the living room and sat on the opposite couch, watching my mother rock my grandmother in her arms, telling her to hold on and that help was on the way. My father lifted me into his arms and carried me into their bedroom.

"Shh," he said. I wrapped tightly around him. "You did good, buddy. Everything's going to be okay."

When the ambulance arrived my mother climbed into the back with my grandmother, and my father and I were to follow behind in our own car. One of the officers flashed the light in my father's eyes, asked if he was okay to drive. My father said probably not and the officer left it at that, told him to be careful, and off we went.

❧ 7 ❧

Delirium. Seeing things move in the night. Lying on the floor watching the shadows dance up the wall. Thinking my thoughts and wondering how I was going to survive now that I was broke. And hungry. And cold. Payday still a week away. That would be a fast far greater than any I'd ever done during wrestling. Dapples of light filtered through the tree beyond the tracks and came in the untreated windows, spots of light that brought life to the shadows, glowing eyes and gnashing teeth. Wind and cold. The trains passing. The shrieks of metal on metal piercing the night. The trains forever passing.

❧ 8 ❧

This third stroke didn't kill her, not instantly anyhow, though it plunged her into a lasting decline that would take her six months later. And although the damage to her brain was permanent, she sometimes had moments of clarity not unlike an Alzheimer's patient.

Before I started school, my grandmother had spent so much time reading to me that I had actually learned to read myself. In the last months of her life, while she was at her worst, the roles were reversed and it was I who read to her. Most of the time she simply listened with her eyes closed, though at other times when I finished a story I'd find her looking at me and smiling, a smile that vanished only when she fell asleep.

A week before she died I read to her *The Giving Tree*. She beamed with pride while I read. When I finished she took me by the hand.

"Promise me you'll take care of your mother," she said. "Never trust your father too much. I know he's great to you sometimes, but in the end we are who we are. Don't ever forget that. In the end, we are who we are."

"Okay, Grandma. I promise," I said with the ease of a six-year-old willing to agree to anything to please a person he looks up to.

"And keep reading," she said. "You're a very smart boy, and books are like buried treasure waiting to be found. Don't ever stop digging."

"I won't, Grandma."

She died quietly, in her sleep. My mother was the one who found her. I can still remember the way she sobbed when they carried my grandmother out on a gurney, her bodied covered by a white sheet.

A week later my father took me to the park in town. It was the middle of summer, and the scent of freshly mowed grass was carried on the lazy wind. Together we rode down the rocket-shaped slide, and after, he pushed me on one of the many swings. I urged him to push me higher and higher, and he did. I went so high that when I reached the top of the arc, the swing's chain would lose tension before I torpedoed back down. But I wanted to go higher, and he kept pushing harder. I couldn't stop laughing, butterflies in my stomach, the wind in my hair. And then I went backward so fast that I lost my grip on the chain and went flying through the air, seeing only the empty swing forefront to the blue summer sky. Terror swept through me. My arms instinctively reached out for something to grab. They found nothing but the wind. The certainty of injury flashed through my head. And it was then, anticipating the forthcoming pain, that my father caught me in the comfort of his arms.

"I got ya, buddy," he said, and we both laughed about it all the way home.

⊱ 9 ⊰

I woke shivering on Sunday night, nine days in the apartment, the floor a slab of ice, both windows rattling as though someone was trying to get in. I got up and turned on both burners, then stood over them trying to get warm. After a while I tired of standing and turned them off and went back to my pile of clothes. I couldn't sleep. I sat against the corner of the room and pulled my knees to my chest. A passing train, light and shadows on the walls and the floor around me, swirling shadows that looked like animals hunting in the night. Shaking that I couldn't stop, my hands, legs, lips. A cold that emanated from my very core, a cold exacerbated by the silence in the room aside from the rattling glass. Angry jagged shadows, lunging shadows. So cold. I have nothing I am nothing so scared and alone. I miss my mom I wish she was here I can't stop my hands from shaking my heart from pounding I just want to be anywhere other than where I am I want to be with somebody please somebody keep me safe I have nobody I want to die and to hell with these tears pulled so tightly into myself that everything aches but I say let it ache at least I know I'm still alive that way and goddamn it don't give up so easily you've gotten through worse fuck getting through anything you've gotten through worse you know these moods pass with time but goddamn it I hurt and I don't think I'll ever be better I might as well get it over with and open the window and jump to the tracks and lay my neck across the rail and do the world a favor just do the whole damn world a favor at least I can't hurt or disappoint anyone any longer at least I can stop letting myself down what have I ever done to be proud of other than on that cold March day all those years ago oh yes keep living in the past keep pitying yourself keep feeling sorry for yourself it's always worked so well for you that's just what I'll do I wish I could just go to sleep and never wake up why can't it be that easy. I don't want to die but goddamn it sometimes I do.

❧ 10 ❧

I don't know if I trusted him after that, after he caught me on the swing. I think that maybe part of me did. He was there for us, had helped my mother through her time of mourning, helped her cope with the pain of losing the only parent she had left. For a time it seemed as though we were a real family. I suppose there's good to be found in even the worst situations.

But in the end she was right. We are who we are. There's no escaping it. And I think part of me knew it, too.

❧ 11 ❧

Never have I been so close to utter ruin as I was on that cold winter weekend. But I made it through, somehow, and in the morning every inch of my body ached. Monday before payday, only four days to go. I was run-down, my eyes swollen and sore.

I took the hottest shower I could stand, then I walked to the train and stepped into the front car when it arrived. The heater was broken and I was the only person in it. I bent over in my seat and started crying. I didn't try to stop myself, just let it come. The train running express from Belmont to Howard wouldn't stop again for twenty minutes. I cried the whole way there, then walked the half mile sideways through the biting wind.

I sat at my desk and finally warmed after fifteen minutes of shivering. I placed my head in my arms and sat that way until Linda arrived sometime later. She unloaded items from her bag into her desk, then sat and started typing.

"So any conquests of coeds this weekend?" she asked.

I lifted my head and looked at her. I was in pitiful shape and I knew it. I hadn't intended it to be that way, not initially, but I knew Linda was my only hope and there was no point in hiding it.

"Stratton, are you okay?"

I shook my head.

"What's the matter?"

I shook my head.

"Stratton, what's the matter?"

It took a moment to compose myself. "I haven't eaten since Friday and I can't stop my hands from shaking." I held them up for her to see. "I think I'm losing my mind."

"Stratton, hell, why didn't you say something?" She grabbed her purse from beneath her desk, started rummaging through it, and removed a bill. "Here, take this," she said. She handed me a fifty. I looked at it in my hand, then up at her. I took a deep breath.

"You sure?"

"Yes, of course."

I closed my eyes. "Linda, thank you so much. I'll pay you back on Friday. I promise."

"Take your time, no rush. Go get yourself something to eat."

I left the building without clocking out and walked to a diner two blocks away. I ordered two breakfasts and I sat there trying not to shake until they arrived, and when they did, I ate every bit of both of them.

⟡ 12 ⟡

I hung on until I received my first full paycheck on Friday. It wasn't anything to be proud of—$655—but it was enough. I paid Linda back immediately. As if the check wasn't sufficient, waiting in the mail at home was a credit card with my name in raised letters and a thousand-dollar credit line—a student card I had lied through my teeth to get. I immediately called and had it activated and then rushed out and bought a reasonably priced full-sized pillow-top mattress, a box spring, two pillows, a duvet, flannel sheets, an alarm clock, and a nightstand to go beside the bed. In total it cost over nine hundred dollars but I didn't care because I'd gotten no more than three hours of sleep on any one night. I could have cried when the bed was delivered the very next morning.

eight

ANOTHER WEEK PASSED. I went to work and I came home, still stuck in the same routine despite now having a bed and a few other luxuries for the apartment, all of which helped pull me out of the fugue state I'd been wallowing in. I was finding my footing in Chicago, and even the effect of Jeff's words had faded. However, there was still no sign of Gene. It was almost as though I had imagined him.

I bought a fine cigar for fifteen bucks to celebrate another week in the books at work. I lit it when I stepped off the train. Dominican, full-flavored, rich. I took in the smoke and, with the weekend just beginning, any stress I'd been feeling was purged with that first puff and carried away by the wind. I bought a bottle of Grand Marnier on my walk home. I checked the mail and sorted through it while climbing the stairs, cigar clutched between my teeth.

"You have one of those for me, right?" I heard from the top of the stairs. I looked up. Gene wore a sideways grin with a pair of white slacks, white shirt, and a blue jacket.

"You look like a sailor," I said. "Only thing missing is the white cap."

"You wish I was a sailor, you queer."

I laughed, happy as hell to see him after his three-week disappearing act. I reached into my bag for the bottle of Grand Marnier and held it up.

"No cigar, but I do have this."

"Come on up, my friend."

I dropped off my bag and grabbed the rent check before heading up.

Inside, Gene carried two ice-filled glasses into the living room. I threw the check on the coffee table.

"I'm caught up in rent, so bite me," I said in the friendly banter of men.

He picked it up, folded it, slid it into his jacket pocket without looking at it.

"You did well, kiddo."

"It wasn't easy. Thought I was going to lose my mind there for a few days."

I pulled the cork and filled both glasses. We clinked them together and drank. Gene studied his glass while I closed my eyes and savored the orange and toffee liqueur caressing my palate.

"That's what kills the ghost that haunts us all," I sighed.

"Not bad. Been a while since I've had this."

"My favorite."

He nodded. "I'm going drinking tonight. You interested?"

"You really think I'd say no?"

He laughed. We sat through a long silence while we smoked and drank.

"Where in the hell have you been, anyway?" I asked after a time.

He took a drink and kept his eyes closed. "Sometimes a man has to get lost."

"Fair enough," I said, leaving it at that, though finding it peculiar all the same. Gene had literally vanished, and while he'd been gone a good part of my own sanity had done the same. Regardless of our difference in years, perhaps he and I weren't all that dissimilar.

❦ 2 ❧

We had finished half the bottle before leaving. It was after eight. I had a good buzz and assumed the same for Gene by the amused glint in his upturned eyes. The street was lined with Christmas decorations and an inch of freshly fallen snow covered the sidewalk. We passed a building that blared "Jingle Bells" from an open window. Christmas was a week and a half away.

"You heading home for the holidays?" Gene asked.

"Nope," I said. "You?"

"I'll be here, probably cook a nice dinner. You're more than welcome to join."

I nodded. "Yeah, definitely."

He lit a new cigarette with the dying embers of the one he had just finished. He kept it pursed between his lips, squinting through the smoke.

"You sure do smoke a lot for a military man."

"Show me a man without vice and I'll show you one without virtue," he said, then nudged me and grinned.

The wind howled and I walked sideways for a time to minimize its effect, shuffling my feet to keep from tripping.

"What the hell are you doing?" Gene asked.

"What do you mean? It's freezing out."

He shook his head and chuckled.

It was a small, obscure place, and had there not been a neon sign in the window, I would have never guessed it was a bar. Above the door, in white letters painted by an uncertain hand, a sign read THE LAMPLIGHTER.

It was dark and overly warm inside, giving it a cozy feel. Christmas lights were strung along its walls and ceiling. Above the liquor shelves stockings were taped to the mirror with the names of the employees glued in silver glitter. "Cecilia" played from the jukebox. A couple had just left and we snagged their seats at the L-shaped bar. The place was full, a mix of people ranging in age from twenty-one to sixty-one, though Gene was far from being the only baby boomer. The two bartenders danced to the music while they mixed and poured.

"Mean Gene! Where have you been?" the man behind the bar asked. He was fortyish with a cleanly shaven head that reflected the light around him.

"Goddamn, that's the third time I've been asked that today. You guys need to quit hanging from my nuts," Gene said with a smile, then shook the man's hand. "Sam, this is my new tenant, Stratton. Sam here is an asshole."

Sam shook my hand. "Pleasure to meet you." He dropped a few ice cubes into a glass, filled it with Maker's Mark, handed it to Gene. He looked at me. "Whatcha havin'?"

"Grand Marnier, neat," I said. Sam poured it and Gene and I toasted. "Good bar."

"Yeah, it's not bad. Been coming here for years. Sam owns it. He closes it at eight on Christmas Eve and all the people inside drink for free till ten," he said, and gave me a wink to go with it. "I'll be here."

"Count me in."

I was in a good mood, feeling truly happy for the first time since arriving in Chicago. It was Friday night and I was in a bar with a friend who came in the form of a sixty-one-year-old Vietnam vet. I had received my first full paycheck the week before and all my bills were paid. I comfortably had enough to last until I'd be paid again the following Friday. Relief washed over me. Or maybe it was contentment. Whatever one chooses to call it, I took it in, let it run through me. I inhaled deeply, fingers tingling, feeling light and airy.

"You're aware that that's when you know you've lost, right?"

"What?" I asked.

"When you stare into the mirror like that, that's when you know you've lost. Especially with that god-awful grin you're wearing."

I turned to him, placed my hand on his shoulder, and gave it a good squeeze. "Gene, my man, I conceded defeat years ago."

"Ha!" he said, lifting his drink and toasting the air. "Ditto to that."

We talked and drank at a moderate pace, enough to keep a buzz without becoming a puddle. Gene had a tab and every time I tried paying he'd say something to the effect of "Don't be an asshole," at which point I'd reply that I didn't realize I was being an asshole and then promptly put my wallet away. Eventually he walked to the jukebox and punched in ten dollars' worth of songs, then sat and bobbed his head while they played. Older country stuff—Johnny Cash, Waylon Jennings, Willie

Nelson—even an Elvis song or two. He knew several others in the bar and talked to each when they passed.

After about two hours he went to the bathroom. When he returned he draped his arm across my shoulders and grinned. "Here's the thing, kiddo. There's a pretty girl looking awfully forlorn at the end of the bar. And nobody should be forlorn on Christmas. You're going to go down and talk to her."

I saw who he was talking about. She was somewhat attractive, with dark blonde hair, sitting slumped and cross-legged. He was right. She appeared dispirited, encumbered with some heavy thought while staring blankly into the mirror.

"You know, Gene, this is probably the first time I've ever been in a bar without worrying about pussy. I didn't even notice her."

"Well, now that you notice her, you can go say hello."

I snorted. "Yeah, right."

"Yep, going to go talk to her."

"I don't want to talk to her."

"Sure you do."

"No I don't."

"Why not?" he asked.

"Because I'm shy."

"All the more reason to, my boy. The one thing you're afraid to do is a clear indicator of the one thing you *need* to do."

"Ah Christ, here come the aphorisms."

He smiled. "You miss a hundred percent of the shots you don't take."

"Yep, I knew it. Who's that one from?"

"Beats the hell out of me, but that's of little concern. You should be focusing on the lovely lass at the end of the bar you're going to say hello to."

She turned briefly and I was able see her entire face, which seemed downcast, and a watery look touched her eyes as though she was fighting the urge to cry with only moderate success. It made me sad to see her that way, the way it sometimes does when you notice people in cafés sitting alone emitting faint sighs with drooped shoulders, the people who radiate defeat, who, on one level or another, know they've lost the fight to the extent that it's apparent to others.

"No way," I said.

"Don't be a pussy."

"I'm not."

"I'll knock a hundred bucks off next month's rent."

"Goddamn it, Gene, you would say something like that, wouldn't you?"

He was beaming, clearly amused. "You bet. But that offer's only good for the next three minutes," he said and lifted his watch. "And that three minutes starts . . . now."

I knew I'd do it, and in response I grew nervous as hell. I couldn't pass up a hundred bucks, not in my state. It was an opportunity to get ahead, and I knew that if I didn't say hello, then the contentment I felt would fade away. I was ecstatic to be in a good mood, and though the pendulum would eventually swing the other way, as it always does, I wasn't ready for the shift just yet.

"Hey Sam, grab me a quick drink, will you? I'm going to need one for this," Gene said.

"You're a dick," I said.

Sam poured whiskey straight into Gene's glass.

"Two minutes, kiddo. A hundred dollars. Boy, think of what you can do with that. You can buy that sweet girl dinner. A real nice dinner, actually."

"Alright, alright, quit talking to me, damn it. I need to get my mind straight."

I thought about what I could say, what we might talk about. There are few worse things than having nothing to say post-hello, both just staring at one another while the silence twists you in two. What would I do? For a minute I hated women, hated that I was so awful with them and yet desired them so badly. She looked like the shy type, and conversing with the quiet ones are like solving a Rubik's Cube when sleep-deprived and half drunk. Maybe I could just tell her the truth, point to Gene, tell her that he had paid me to come down, that she shouldn't worry because I wouldn't take up too much of her time. I'd even buy her a drink for her troubles and she'd then be free to all the other, better men in the bar.

But I was still nervous, and in my mind I tried convincing myself why I shouldn't be, why my saying hello was a great privilege and that I'd be doing her a favor. But regardless of the role I created for myself, I knew I was without the tools of artifice to assume it. And the more I thought about it, the more nervous I became until I was nearly in a panic.

"One minute," Gene said.

"Blow me."

I looked back down and studied her while jitters wrenched my body into knots.

"Thirty seconds. A hundred bucks is a hundred bucks is a hundred bucks."

I closed my eyes while the girl sat alone, unaware of the agony she was responsible for twenty feet away. I finished my drink in a single gulp and had planned to stand but my ass was screwed into the stool. My heart was pounding. Why did this make me so nervous? Just another person, alone, sitting in a bar. What harm can come by saying hello? I'm twenty-seven years old; what the hell is the matter with me that the prospect of speaking to another person incites a terror so great that I'd rather streak down the city streets all the way back home? Do I fear she'll see my intentions, know that every time she looks away I'll probably stare at her crotch and drool? Do I fear looking foolish, or being rejected? Of course I do. All of the above. We all do. But still.

Throughout most of my life I'd always believed that by some odd miracle in the mysterious ways of women, every girl I happened to be in love with instinctively knew of my longing, of my deep desire to be with her and of the countless hours I had spent creating idealistic possibilities of our life together, and that in my eyes any other life that deviated from this would be nothing short of oppression. They knew of these thoughts and yearnings, and by not approaching me these girls were in fact attesting to their disinterest in anything connubial or even sexual; they were, in essence, rejecting me. I sometimes took this as an affront, even when, in the years following college, I would sometimes cross paths with these same girls and would learn that a few I'd pined for had in fact liked me back. I never accepted this news in any reassuring or validating way. It just made me angry, and despite my better judgment, my face would turn into a scowl, and in a whine I scarcely recognized as my own, I'd ask, "Why the hell didn't you ever say anything?" To which the only reply has ever been, "Well, why didn't you?"

"Fifteen seconds."

Don't think about it, Stratton, just do it. You can't think of these things, you'll only make yourself anxious. Just do it. Just act.

"Ten seconds."

I stood, took a deep breath, and began walking.

"Atta boy," Gene said behind me.

Each step was a mile. I felt I was walking on razor blades, walking the trail of tears, every step another chance to turn around and say to hell with the hundred bucks. But I kept forging ahead. Another deep breath right before I reached her, just another girl. Alone. In a bar.

She sat against the wall and the stool to her right was taken. I wasn't sure how best to intervene; she'd have to completely turn around in order to talk. I stood behind her and stared at the back of her head, and when I glanced up, I saw that she was watching me in the mirror. I waved at her reflection.

"Hi," I said behind her. "I'm Stratton."

She turned in her stool and smiled casually without showing teeth. "I'm sorry?"

"I'm Stratton."

"Carolyn," she replied.

We shook hands, at that dreaded moment post-introduction when something had to be said and I had no clue of what that something might be. She had a full drink in front of her; offering to buy another seemed excessive. She stared at me, waiting. I shrugged once and let loose a nervous laugh I'd been holding on to since I walked down.

"If you want the truth, I really have no idea what to say right now. Just, um, just wanted to say hello, I guess. I hadn't thought this far ahead."

She chuckled, causing her smile to widen, and in turn revealing teeth that seemed to go in every direction, which explained why she hadn't shown them the first time. She had appeared attractive from afar, and from up close her beauty still held, but the good looks she possessed were greatly diminished by showing those pearly whites of hers, which weren't pearly at all, but closer in tone to the neglected drapes of a smoker's home. Discovering this negative quality allowed me to relax a little; I felt it somehow dropped her to my level, and I could see she was happy I'd come over by the way her face lit up. And in its sudden radiance I discovered an altogether different feature I'd overlooked in the bar's dimly lit interior: what Carolyn lacked in a smile she made up for in her eyes, which were a vivid green, flecked with the cool aqua color of Caribbean water, and framed by perfectly shaped brows. But there was more to them than that. They were big and bright, like a toddler's, though downcast in a way that made her seem vulnerable, maybe even sad. I couldn't stop staring into them.

"So," I said, stalling in the way people sometimes do when beating around the bush. "You live nearby?"

She nodded. "Kind of. I live in Logan Square."

"Have you ever been here before?"

She shook her head. "Nope. Just jumped on the train and wandered around until I ended up here."

"You're kidding me?"

"Nope," she said again. Her voice was soft and timid-like, and she approached the conversation like a student talking to an overbearing teacher.

"That's impressive."

She shrugged and looked away. I assumed that she wasn't used to being hit on in bars. I lifted my drink.

"Well, I'm happy you did. End up here, I mean. There's much to be said for spontaneity, though I'm not entirely sure what any of those things are," I said. "So where is Logan Square?"

"Are you not from here?"

I shook my head. "Just moved here a month and a half ago."

"Oh really, from where?"

"New York City."

Her eyes widened. It was a common response when telling someone I was from New York, a kind of instant respect.

"I've always wanted to go."

"It's a great city."

"Yeah? What made you leave?"

I thought about it a moment. "You know, I'm not entirely sure anymore. Bad luck, maybe?"

"Do you not like it here?"

"I don't really know yet. It's cold, that's for sure." I wrapped my arms around my torso and shuddered for effect. "The wind rips right through you."

"Yeah, the winters suck," she agreed. "But you'll love summer."

We fell silent again. I looked down at Gene and he gave me a thumbs-up. I hoped Carolyn hadn't seen it. Behind him, through the window, snow was falling in perfect harmony with the soft tones of Bing Crosby's "White Christmas" playing on the jukebox, and I suddenly found myself feeling overly sentimental. I turned back to Carolyn and her brilliant eyes bore into mine. They were truly striking, and seemed to shimmer under the subtle glow of a nearby string of Christmas lights. I felt an instant warmth toward her, a desire to forgo the conversation and just wrap my arms around her, pull her into me, and bury my face within her hair. Why was that never allowed? If it's true that the mass of men lead lives of quiet desperation, then why do we still approach one another with timidity and false pretenses? Why do we have to play the game?

"So where did you say Logan Square is?" I asked, hating that I lacked anything more interesting to say.

"Oh, it's west of here, off the Blue Line," she said. I had yet to take the Blue Line. I had no idea where it ran. "It's not very nice. Kind of run-down. But it's cheap."

Sam, the owner, stopped in front of Carolyn. "Gene would like to buy the two of you a drink," he said, and Carolyn looked at me for validation.

"The older man at the other end of the bar," I said. "He's my landlord, or rather my friend, I guess. What do you want?"

She ordered a vodka and cranberry; I stuck with Grand Marnier. Sam delivered both a minute later. Carolyn lifted her drink and sipped at the straw with her eyes closed, giving me the opportunity to view her more closely. She had a single piercing in each ear, and chapped lips so that tiny bits of skin hung raggedly, waiting to be picked away. She didn't look a day over twenty. There was a small hole the size of a dime in the pit of her sweater; had the sweater not been black, and her undershirt white, I doubt I would have noticed. I looked away then, hoping to stay oblivious to any other imperfections I might find. Furthermore, I wanted to protect myself from asking questions to which the answers might bother me, because, truth be told, I really did like her.

"So what do you do here?" I asked.

"I work at Starbucks."

"No kidding. Where? I'm at one coffeehouse or another nearly every day."

"In Bucktown."

I shook my head. "No idea where that is, either."

"West of here, off the Blue Line. Next to Wicker Park. Do you know that area?"

"I've heard of it."

"So what do you do?" she asked.

"Well, I'm supposedly an editor, though the title is a bit of a stretch. I'm actually trying to be a writer, working on a novel right now, which is why I'm always in cafés."

She perked up. "Oh yeah? That's really neat."

I looked down at Gene. The stool beside mine had just opened.

"Would you like to join us at the other end of the bar? We'd love the company," I asked, holding my breath against possible rejection.

"Sure," she said with a shrug, and at the moment I felt like pumping my fist in the air in celebration. I worked hard to suppress a smile as Carolyn gathered herself and stood. She was three or four inches shorter than me, and now that I could see all of her, she appeared a little unkempt, had a somewhat dirty quality to her, but in a naive way as though a subject as mundane as wardrobe selection was something she never thought to consider. I found her even more attractive by virtue of this innocence, or rather, what I perceived to be innocence.

We sat beside Gene and he shook Carolyn's hand. He bought another round though we each held full drinks. Seeing this, Sam gave us two wooden tokens we could exchange when ready. Then Gene stood and said it was time for him to leave.

"This one has gotten me drunk tonight," he said, gripping my shoulder. "But it was a pleasure meeting you. Perhaps I'll see you again." He shook her hand a second time, clapped me on the back, then turned and pushed through the door and was gone.

"He didn't leave because of me, did he?"

"Nah, he's just old and out of practice."

"He seems really nice."

"Yeah, he's great. I've been here a month and a half and my greatest friend is a sixty-one-year-old man who I pay rent to each month. Kind of funny."

I can't recall now what we talked about, but I do know that we quickly grew comfortable with one another and there were no further breaks in the conversation. The longer we sat the closer we became, making subtle gestures at first—a hand to the bicep, looks that lingered—until I eventually put my hand on her thigh and kept it there. Shortly after that she dropped her head on my shoulder and I placed my cheek against the top of it. Something slow was playing, and in the warm and dimly lit bar, I was feeling romantically maudlin. After one more drink I might have even gazed into Carolyn's green eyes and told her that I loved her.

"I'm getting sleepy," she said.

When we left it was tacitly implied where we would go, having arrived there by some mutual understanding there was no need to voice. We held hands at first, and then I put my arm around her and pulled her to me, breathing in the freshness of her hair as we walked in tandem along the city streets as I guided us home, home to the Promised Land, to all things good and loving. Home to the very things that make this life worth living.

nine

A PASSING TRAIN. RATTLING windows, vibrating floor. I opened my eyes. Carolyn's soft breaths beside me. The room flooded with light, a little after nine. She was facing me with her mouth slightly open. I wiped away a small bit of drool from her cheek. She didn't stir. I dropped beneath the covers and nuzzled against her warm body, her lips puckering with each soft breath, the blanket rising and falling. A sense of affection paired with a desperate urge to keep her in this studio, in this bed big enough for the both of us, this girl I'd only just met.

Though we had undressed and lay naked against one another, under a self-imposed abstinence based on the absurd pretense that I was not a lecher, we hadn't actually slept together. I had wanted to, of course, but in an odd moment of consideration, my desire to show I was a good and decent man had won a rare victory over my burning loins, which was the main reason, I'm sure, that I woke with a raging hard-on.

I kept my arms around her. My stomach rumbled and I had an idea: The path to a man's heart was through his stomach; did the same hold true for a woman? It couldn't hurt. I might have been a subpar cook regarding lunch and dinner, but when it came to breakfast I was a pro. It was the meal I most often skipped when I had wrestled, and in retaliation for those lean days, when I could finally eat at will I taught myself to make a mean breakfast, and make it well.

I crawled from bed and dressed. Carolyn's panties rested atop my shoe and I glanced at her to be certain she was asleep. I grabbed them and held them up to the light. They were red plaid, string bikini. There was a tear in the band, the cloth thin and slightly discolored at the crotch. I felt gleefully dirty with them in my hands. Then I stuffed them into my pocket and rushed out the door.

I wasn't hung over, was curiously sharp when I should have been groggy, as though my mental clarity depended on something as simple as who I happened to sleep beside the night before. I thought of going back to leave a note in case Carolyn woke, but I didn't and ran down the dusty stairs and out into the freezing Chicago morning through the flakes of snow that fell from the low sky and melted in the waiting slush; the cold air came sharply into my lungs and numbed the edge of my nose. I made it to the grocery store in five minutes, up one aisle, down the next, the entire time feeling the indentation of Carolyn's panties through my denim pocket while wondering why in the hell I had taken them in the first place. Well, because I was a pervert. That's the answer I came up with, and true to form, I continued relishing their presence.

I left the store and hurried back, quietly opening the door to keep from waking Carolyn. But she was already awake, sitting up with her back against the wall and pulled tightly into herself like a bouquet of flowers. The blanket was pulled to below her pits, revealing the white in her throat and the delicate line of her barely visible collarbones. Her clothes lay untouched on the floor. I grinned at her as though we shared a secret unknown to the rest of the world.

"Hi," she said playfully.

"How are you feeling?"

"I'm okay. A little bit of a headache."

"Are you hungry? I picked up a few things for breakfast. And I bought coffee, too."

"Yes, I'm starving. But I really have to pee," she said, as though the two were somehow connected.

I pointed to the bathroom, and in a display of diffidence Carolyn retreated further into the duvet, pulling it to her nose while watching me through the tops of her eyes. She looked kittenish and I could tell that she was smiling, and with the bottom half of her face covered, she appeared far more beautiful than she really was. Her eyes were truly stunning, and I was happy she was awake just so I could have the pleasure of seeing them. But what I had failed to realize the night before was just what made them so striking. It was the way she looked at me, her intense gaze creating the sensation of what photographers call depth of field; I felt I was standing sharp at the forefront while everything around me blurred away or was blacked out entirely. It was as though, in her eyes, everything else existed only as an afterthought. This I liked very much.

I gathered her clothes and lay them on the bed for her. They smelled of the bar. She sorted through and lifted her jeans and her shirt.

"Do you see my underwear?"

"Were you wearing underwear?"

She rolled her eyes.

I feigned confusion, crinkled my brow, and looked at the floor. "I don't see them," I said, and then I got down on my knees and peered beneath the bed. "Aha," I added, creating an excuse to crawl completely beneath it (which I could barely do) to get them out of my pocket without her noticing. "Here they are."

I handed them up and she looked at them forlornly.

"Do you want something of mine instead?"

She nodded, and in her shyness she seemed about ten years younger than she really was. I removed a pair of sweatpants and a T-shirt from my clothes pile and turned my back to give her the privacy to dress. She walked to the bathroom. I could hear the tinkle as she used the toilet and I turned on the kitchen faucet to drown it out. I started frying bacon. Carolyn walked out and sat on the edge of the bed watching me. I handed her the cup of coffee.

"Thank you," she said.

The sweatpants were too large and the cuffs hung over her feet and dragged along the hardwood floor, which I found endearing. She kept silent, and her coyness started to make me a little uncomfortable. I focused on breakfast, giving the appearance of concentration where little was needed as though I was silent because our meal depended on it and not because I wasn't sure of what to say. The trains went by, the world outside gray and white while the snow continued to fall. When I finished cooking I handed Carolyn a plate and took my own and sat at the desk while she stayed on the bed.

"I'm getting a table soon," I said, suddenly self-conscious about the apartment's lack of furnishings.

She nodded. I kept glancing at her and when our eyes met we smiled politely at one another and looked away.

"Do you have to work today?" I asked.

"No. Not till tomorrow morning."

"Have anything planned?"

She said no, and without the effect of alcohol, her voice was even softer than it had been the night before. I've always felt more at ease with shy women, more confident, but that was only after becoming comfortable enough to be unfazed by the long silences. Then, however, there was only misery in them.

"Want to do something?"

"Like what?"

I shrugged. "I don't know. Maybe see a movie or something."

She thought about it a moment. "Yeah, sure. I really need to go home and shower and change, though."

I took her plate when she finished and she lay back down. Her sweatshirt had lifted, revealing two inches of her belly. I felt the urge to press my lips to it and give her a raspberry to get her laughing, but when I jumped on the bed, I quickly lost the courage to and instead dropped beside her and placed my arm in the gap beneath her neck.

"How do you want to work this?" I asked.

"I don't know."

A train thundered by.

"Right on cue," I said. "Damn trains are horrible. I'm finally starting to get used to them. Did they keep you up?"

"Not at all. I can sleep through anything."

"I wish I could."

Carolyn yawned deeply and turned and burrowed into me with her face in my neck. My chin rested on the top of her head. A few minutes later her lips began to pucker and I knew she was out cold. I wasn't tired and instead lay there with my eyes wide open. My arm began to fall asleep but I didn't want to disturb her by removing it. Eventually she twitched, rolled away from me. I turned on my side and propped my head on my hand, watching Carolyn sleep, happy that I could reach over and touch her.

After a while I rose and sat at the desk. I looked out the window and studied the blank rear of the building across the tracks. Beyond it, to the east, I could see a faint sliver of the watery blue smudge of Lake Michigan. The snow kept falling and I sat for a time wondering if it was also falling further east, in Ohio. With my hands behind my head, staring pensively out the window, I heard Carolyn stir behind me. I turned around. She was wide awake, and by the thoughtful look on her face, I felt certain she'd been watching me for a while.

"Are you okay?" she asked.

"Yes, of course. Why do you ask?"

"You looked very sad staring out the window just now. Are you a sad person, Stratton Brown?"

"No, not really."

"What were you just thinking?"

"I don't remember," I lied. "Mostly just watching the snow fall. What about you?"

"Me, what?"

"Are you a sad person?"

"What do you think?"

"I think you just spent a delightful night, and about to spend one hell of a day, with a ruggedly handsome man you can't help but adore. What could you possibly be sad about?"

She grinned. "You're awfully full of yourself."

"Nah, just a little happy you're here. So what's the plan? Shall I get showered and we can go to your place? You can even shower here if you want." I jumped on the bed beside her and mirrored her same pose, on my side with my head propped by my hand.

"Um, well . . . ," she said and trailed off. "I'm in kind of an odd living situation at the moment."

"What does that mean? Do you live at home with your parents?"

She shook her head. "My parents are in Iowa. I'm living with my ex-boyfriend."

"Oh jeez, how is that working out?"

"It's horrible."

"How long have you been broken up?"

"A week."

I nodded. "I guess that explains being alone in the bar last night."

"Yeah. I don't know what I'm going to do yet."

"Do you have friends you can stay with?"

She sighed. "Not really. The only friends I've made are from work, and I only started there a month and a half ago."

"How long have you been in Chicago?"

"A year."

"From Iowa?"

She nodded. "We moved here after we graduated. He would get really jealous when I made friends, so I never really did until a month ago."

"I know the type," I said. "So that makes you what, nineteen? Twenty?"

She nodded. "Nineteen."

"How did you drink last night?"

"Fake ID."

"Are you considering moving back to Iowa? *That* might turn me into a sad person."

"I sure hope not. That was why we moved in the first place. My parents hated Jimmy. They wouldn't let me see him and said it would never work out. So we moved here. And they were right and they'll make sure I know it if I go back."

"Wait, his name is Jimmy? What is he, a mobster?" She laughed.

"Did your parents not like him because his name was Jimmy? Is it even possible to take someone named Jimmy seriously?"

"Shut up, jerk," she said playfully.

"Me? What did I do? I'm not the one named Jimmy here."

"You're mean."

"I'm as sweet as pie."

"Are not."

"Am too," I said, batting my eyes and attempting to make a cute face.

"You look like a squirrel when you make that face."

I stuck out my bottom lip. "Now who's the mean one?"

"Me? How am *I* mean?"

"You called me a squirrel."

"Squirrels are cute, silly. Like the cutest thing in the world."

"Are you saying I'm the cutest thing in the world?"

"You're nuts."

"Squirrels love nuts."

She laughed. I lay there on my back looking into her bright eyes that appeared even greener in the light of day. I reveled in our lighthearted banter, had forgotten I was supposed to be shy around her, that we had only just met. Both of us were at ease now.

"So, you tell me the plan, then," I said.

She looked out the window, out into the gray and the cold and the accumulating snow. "It's freezing out, isn't it?"

"Yep."

"Can I wear this home?"

"Are you sure you want to? I mean, will it get you into trouble?"

"No. He's working today."

"Then wear it home. But if you don't come back I'm going to hunt you down."

"I'll come back, silly."

I gathered her dirty clothes in a plastic bag. She pulled on her jacket. It was too big on her small frame and fell to her knees. With the sweatpants too long, and the jacket too large, she looked like an orphan wearing hand-me-downs waiting for the train. It made me smile.

"I'll see you in three hours," I said.

She nodded. I put my number into her phone and then called it so I had her number as well. Then I kissed her, and she walked out the door.

❦ 2 ❧

Carolyn arrived a little before three, dressed in jeans, a black turtleneck sweater, a red scarf wrapped around the bottom half of her face so that her eyes shone brightly. She had lost most of the unkempt qualities I'd noticed the night before. In her right hand she held the same plastic bag she had taken with her, my sweat pants and hooded sweatshirt on top, but beneath those she had tried hiding a fresh set of clothes I assumed she intended to wear tomorrow. The sight of them made me buoyant. I unraveled the scarf and pressed my lips to her cold face. She was wearing makeup, her cheeks gently rouged, hair pulled back into a ponytail.

"You look very pretty," I said.

She smiled. "You shouldn't seem so surprised."

"I'm not surprised. Just paying you a compliment."

"Well thanks," she said and bobbed a curtsy.

We took the train downtown, holding hands until we reached the theater on Illinois. The snow had ceased falling, though several inches now blanketed the ground. Carolyn wanted to see *Charlotte's Web*. I didn't mind. I loved the book. It was one my grandmother had read to me.

I paid for two tickets, two sodas, and a large popcorn. There were several other couples inside the theater and I was happy to be among them. It had been a very long time. Before the movie started and after the lights went down, Carolyn leaned over and kissed me on the cheek and nuzzled against me, wrapping herself around my arm with her head on my shoulder. It became obvious how the rest of the day would go and I sat there with a grin as the opening previews played.

We both cried at the end. I knew I would. The damn spider had put me in another sentimental mood, and when we walked outside, the snow was falling heavily again and the flakes landed upon Carolyn's face and melted. I yearned desperately to drink the water from her cheek, and I told her so. I pulled her to me, kissed the top of her head through the hood pulled over it, and it was then that I knew I was in trouble. Loneliness. I had learned to live with it for so long that I had forgotten how nice it was to have someone. I had lived with it and now I was a fool to remember this other way.

We stopped at a wine shop on the way back, walking hand in hand up and down its three meager aisles. I grabbed a bottle I knew well that I used to sell while working for the wine importer.

"What is that?" Carolyn asked.

"About as close to heaven as I can ever hope to get."

She punched me in the arm. "No, really."

"La Pousse d'Or. A French Burgundy."

"What kind of wine is it?"

"Pinot Noir."

She looked at where I'd gotten it.

"It's a sixty-dollar bottle!" she said.

"It's worth double that."

"You're not going to get it, are you?"

"I will if you promise to stay the night."

"I'll promise to stay the night only if you don't get it."

"How about this: I buy the bottle, make a nice dinner to complement it, and you stay the night anyway?"

"Stratton, that's too much money," she pleaded.

And she was right, of course, but in the end I bought the bottle and justified it by reminding myself of the hundred dollars I had knocked off my rent by talking to her. In my way of thinking I owed it to her.

We stopped at a grocery store and Carolyn insisted on buying the items for dinner. I was happy to let her. When we made it back to the apartment I uncorked the bottle and poured the wine into plastic cups while cursing myself for not having wine glasses. I sniffed at the body of the wine, inhaling it deeply, and then I tapped Carolyn's cup with mine and we each drank. The flavor was full-bodied and bold, just as I remembered, carrying hints of fig on its backside.

"Like falling in love," I said.

She rolled her eyes. "It tastes like wine."

"You bet it does. *Real* wine."

I made dinner and we sat cross-legged on the hardwood floor with our wine and plates. By the time we finished eating, the bottle was empty and we were both slaphappy, the night before us stretched out with illimitable possibilities. We kept smiling coyly at one another, both knowing what was to come yet relishing the patience of it all. Eventually we began making out on the floor. I lifted Carolyn into bed and it was then that we made love for the first time, slowly, gently, the small studio folding around us. Shy with one another in our tenderness. There was never an interruption with the always awkward question of protection. She had simply taken hold of me and kindly showed me the way. I didn't last long and I didn't pull out, and once finished, we fell asleep wrapped in each other's arms. I woke near midnight to her soft kisses on the nape of my neck and we made love again. Afterward I lay on my back for the longest time with my eyes closed, and in the dark room a faint smile somehow found its way to my lips.

ten

‹ 1 ›

MUCH OF MY CHILDHOOD was set in the smoky, dimly lit interior of the White Elephant Saloon, a low-slung place usually half filled with tired men content to be in the company of others. There was a jukebox in the back, a pool table up front, a dust-covered television in the corner that nobody ever watched except when the Browns played on Sundays. Behind the bar a long mirror was wallpapered with dollar bills that had been signed by the patrons, sometimes just their names and dates, but the more creative drew lewd pictures of women's tits or wrote witty jokes. The bus dropped me there every day after school, and until my father arrived at five I busied myself with schoolwork or coloring books or pestered the men until they bribed me with quarters to play pinball.

Some of the men at the White Elephant were drunks and alcoholics, some stopped in for a beer or two after work, and others didn't drink at all and simply went for the company. Of these three my favorite group was the first: the drunks. They were a raucous bunch more willing to put up with the repetitive questions of a kid, loose with their money and their tongues, and there are few greater joys for a child than listening to the curse-laden rants of an adult. And in the areas that went beyond the limits of my father's own paternal knowledge, the men, as a collective group, filled the holes.

For instance, I remember Ray Scanlon, a mostly deaf man of about seventy who once drunkenly told me what he perceived to be the three keys to a happy life, namely, a comfortable pair of shoes, a tight pussy, and a warm place to shit—it struck me as being rather profound at the time (and to this day I'm still hard-pressed to argue with it). I also remember a tall, scrawny man with buggy-whip arms whom everyone called Denver by virtue of his being from there. He was quiet and mostly brooding, and in direct retaliation for the effete way he looked he once gave an uncharacteristic sermon on winning, passionately looking me in the eye as though banishing past regrets by saying, "If you want to win, Stratton, then always be the aggressor. Always. Get on offense and stay there and don't you dare let up. Ever." And then he looked into his beer and not another word was spoken.

And then there was Timmy East, the self-proclaimed "King." Of what, it never occurred to anybody to ask. He was a compact, energetic man with the gone-craggy face of a successful boxer at the end of a long career. But the King was far from retirement, and though he was one of the more genial people I've ever known (and who I still miss today), he always seemed cocked, poised to strike whenever the situation called for it, though I don't remember this ever happening. He had an uncanny ability to solve crossword puzzles and never missed an opportunity to spout vulgarities that often segued into long-winded monologues about past conquests. And there were a lot of them. Years later, when my own sexual encounters began, it was the King's lectures I relied on to give me a leg up on the competition, though all I probably did was scar a few poor unsuspecting girls far from ready for such moves as the "standing wheelbarrow" or the "cross-fingered crippler."

But aside from the "fuck a lot of women" and "stay in school" and "never give up" lessons that were oft repeated, I also became privy to things I'd have rather remained ignorant about, such as jealousy and its destructive tendencies. Of all the things I didn't learn from my father, that was something I certainly did.

Though my mother was fifteen when my parents met, before my father she had already acquired two lovers. He was enraged that he was not her first—tormented, really—by thoughts of her with the two men who came before. Ostensibly he feared she'd stay promiscuous or, in his words, would forever remain "a fuckin' whore," but really I think he couldn't stand the thought of somebody else having what he did, that on some level my mother might still think about them, even make comparisons. He reverted to it during every fight they had, throwing it in her face when she had gained the upper hand, never mind the dozens he had slept with before her.

My first memory of this came when I was six, seven at the oldest. I was sitting at the bar drinking juice and waiting impatiently to go home. My father walked in after five. It was winter and he wore a full beard and a flannel shirt tucked into faded jeans. The month before, he had started working as a machinist in a factory ten miles away. The rigid tenseness in his hands, the way he flexed his jaw with a raised brow, and the creases deeply cut across the length of his forehead all told me we wouldn't be leaving anytime soon. I slouched as he took the stool beside me. My mother walked down. He ordered a boilermaker without saying hello and she eyed him suspiciously.

"Just get me the goddamn drink, Darla," he said in the slight Southern drawl he was never able to lose entirely. My mother spoke with one, too.

She shook her head, poured a shot of Jack Daniels and a mugful of Bud Light, and set both in front of him. She walked away to finish the conversation he had interrupted. There were ten people, give or take, mostly those of the "stopping in for a quick one" variety. My father took the shot, didn't touch the beer. He leered sideways at my mother as she talked to Danny, a bear of a man who I had always loved for the simple reason that he treated me as an adult. He was around my father's age, midthirties, and had kind eyes. He worked construction and had the eternally chapped hands and muddy boots that came with the job. My father turned away and stared down at the empty shot glass.

"Darla," he said, not in a yell, but loudly enough so that everybody heard.

My mother sighed, walked down. "What?"

"I want another." He flicked the glass forward and my mother had to catch it to keep it from flying over the bar's edge. She didn't object, merely poured him another, and he took it as he had the first. He slammed the glass down, thus garnering everybody's attention.

"Another."

"Jesus Christ, Mark, what are ya tryin' to do?"

"I'm tryin' to drink a shot."

She rolled her eyes, sighed, wiped her hands down the front of her shirt. "Sure, I'll get ya another. But it's the last one."

He kept his fingers around the glass while she filled it. He took it the second she pulled the whiskey bottle away.

"I guess I don't need to ask you how your day was," she said.

He looked at her so fiercely that I felt uncomfortable sitting beside him. She shook her head, walked away. I stayed beside him until I could no longer handle the silence, could no longer stand looking at his hand white-knuckled around his beer mug. I hopped from the stool, pushed it in, began walking toward Danny and my mother.

"Where ya goin'?" he asked when I had taken my second step.

"Nowhere," I said. I turned around and climbed back up. I was scared to look at him and instead eyed the dollar bills on the mirror, searching for the ones carrying my own name. I had found two when he spoke.

"How was school?"

"Good."

"Learn much?"

I shrugged. "I think so. How was work?"

He snorted. "Work's really fuckin' up my world." He lit a cigarette, took a deep drag, breathed the smoke out his nostrils. "Just make sure you study real hard so you don't have to deal with this bullshit." I wasn't sure what bullshit he was talking about, and sensing that, he took it upon himself to tell me. "Goddamn hands so filthy they won't never come clean, breaking your back for shit above minimum wage," he said, leering down at my mother. "A wife who don't work in no bar and wouldn't fuck the first man that said hi."

I looked over at him. He wasn't a large man, standing five feet nine, slender though muscularly defined. He had blond hair just long enough in the back to be worn in a ponytail, the top and sides clipped short. He finished his cigarette, lit another, threw his Zippo onto the bar and watched it clatter away, the sides and corners of it worn to the brass.

"Momma wouldn't do that," I said.

He snorted a second time. "Wait a few years before talkin' 'bout shit you don't know nothin' about." He looked down to where she was laughing at something Danny had said. He shook his head, said, "Fuckin' whore."

Hearing those words brought tears to my eyes, though I remained silent.

"Why you cryin'?"

"I'm not."

He sighed, slight remorse crossing his face. "Ah hell, don't listen to me none."

I stayed silent and stared ahead, tears fueling my anger. My mother saw me and came charging down.

"What's the matter, baby?" she asked me. I looked at her, tears still coming. "Goddamn it, Mark, what'd you say?"

"Nothin' that wasn't true."

She shook her head. "Come on, Bubby," she said. She reached over the bar and I stood and climbed toward her.

"Sit back down!" he yelled, pounding his fist onto the bar. "I'll be goddamned if you two are gangin' up on me again."

He placed his hand on my shoulder and forced me down.

"Nobody's gangin' up on you. You had a shitty day and now you think you can be an asshole to everyone around you."

"Oh fuck you," he said.

She swung at him. My father threw up his hands and ducked so that her fist grazed the top of his head. She turned before he could retaliate, and while she rushed away to come around the bar to get me, he picked up his drink and threw the entire contents at her while keeping the glass in his hand. Beer covered most of her back.

"Quit fighting! Quit fighting! Quit fighting!" I yelled while banging my own glass onto the bar in rhythm with the words.

"Shit, Mark," Danny said, standing. I jumped from the stool and ran away.

"Leave. Now!" my mother yelled.

"Yeah, I'll leave. But I'm takin' Stratton with me."

"The hell you are."

I stood behind her, my arms tight around her waist, and she stood behind Danny, who outweighed my father by a good hundred pounds, taller by five inches. Though I'd been scared, I felt perfectly safe behind my mother.

"You should probably just call it a day, Mark," Danny said.

"Come on, Stratton, let's go home."

I buried my face into my mother's shirt so I wouldn't have to look at him.

"He's stayin'," she said.

My father clenched his hands into fists and nodded. "Okay. I'll deal with you both at home. And you," he said, pointing at Danny. "You'll get yours another day."

"I doubt it," Danny said.

My father turned, grabbed his jacket from the stool, and left.

"What's up his ass?" Danny asked when the door shut behind him.

"Who the hell knows."

"Are you alright?"

She laughed. "Same shit, different day."

Danny handed me a crisp dollar. "Play us some tunes, buddy."

I stood at the jukebox, punched in four songs, then sat beside Danny while he drank his third beer and talked to my mother.

"Will everything be okay at home?"

"Yeah, it'll be fine."

We stayed until my mother's shift ended at seven and then drove home. She slowed when driving by the house as though she intended to pass it by, but when my father's car wasn't there, she turned the wheel hard at the last second and pulled into the gravel drive. There was no sign that he'd even been there, and when we lay down to sleep at ten, he still hadn't come home. I was too scared to sleep in my own room—really I was just scared to leave my mother alone—and I instead curled in bed beside her. We both heard his truck pull in some hours later. I held my breath. I could feel my mother do the same. He stumbled into the room and flipped on the light, saw us both in bed pretending to sleep, then turned the light back off and slept on the couch. When I woke for school the next morning, my father had already left for work.

I was restless all day, couldn't concentrate in class, ate little of the lunch my mother had packed. The bus ride was hell, my stomach in knots by the time I finally arrived at the bar. I rushed off and saw my mother standing in the front doorway waiting as she did every day. Relief flooded through me and I hurried across the street and through the snow to get to her.

"Hi, Momma," I said, hugging her tightly. She hugged me back.

"Hi, Bubby. How was school?"

"It was good," I lied.

We walked inside and I took my normal stool while my mother went back around the bar. There wasn't a single thing amiss that day, no acknowledgment of the events of the day prior. Danny came in at four thirty, posted up in his normal stool, and drank his three beers as he always did. My father arrived at a quarter after five carrying a dozen red roses. The others fell silent and stared without trying to be obvious. He ruffled my hair and gave me a quarter.

"Go rack 'em up, buddy."

I went to the table and did as I was told, watching closely as my mother approached. He leaned over the bar and kissed her, handed her the flowers, said something that I assumed was an apology. She put the roses in a pitcher and poured my father a beer, and just like that, all was forgiven. He walked up to Danny. The two men shook hands and talked for a minute or two, and then he came down to me where I'd been waiting at the table with the balls already racked. We shot two games. He let me win both and then we drove home. My mother arrived an hour later, cooked a nice dinner, and afterward the three of us piled into my parents' bed and watched a movie together. I don't recall what the movie was, but what I do know is that I had learned something that day even though I was still too young to understand it. My father's outbursts were common, but so too were the grief and sadness that followed in their wake. Even if it took him days to reconcile in his mind what had happened, he always apologized, always made certain we knew just how badly he felt, and assured us that he'd try to do better while somehow making it up to us. And he'd be fine for a while, but of course his violent swings always returned. And my mother and I knew they always would.

eleven

I WOKE AHEAD OF the alarm on Monday, rolled over, wrapped myself around Carolyn. She moaned, burrowed against me.

"You don't have to get up yet, do you?" she asked.

The clock read 5:14. "Not for another hour."

"Good," she cooed. "I wish you didn't have to go today."

"Me too. But I have to make money to pay for that expensive bottle of wine you made me buy on Saturday."

"Hey!" she said and elbowed me in the ribs. She had come straight from work the day before, and aside from her seven-hour shift, all of our time had been spent together since meeting Friday night.

She rolled over and faced me.

"I'll miss you."

"I'll miss you, too," I said.

"Will you still be up when I get back?"

"I'll stay up," I said.

She had to work at four and wouldn't get off until eleven. The commute back would take another half hour. What she didn't know was that I planned on surprising her at her work after my own workday ended.

We stayed awake and made love before I crawled from bed. I showered, and when I walked out of the bathroom, Carolyn had just finished making breakfast. She looked adorable wearing light blue pajama pants covered with little white clouds, a maroon tank top, her hair in a ponytail.

I took the plate with a towel around my waist. We sat on the edge of the bed. "I desperately need to buy a table."

She nodded. We finished at the same time and she took my plate away while I dressed. Then she lay beneath the covers and watched me until I was ready to leave. I climbed on top of her.

"You going back to sleep?" I asked.

"Yes."

I shook my head at her. "You're evil, making it so hard for me to leave."

"I'm not evil. I'm an angel."

"An evil, evil woman. A termagant, really."

"What's a termagant?"

"A violent, spiteful woman."

"Hey! I'm no termagant. I'm an aaangel," she said in a cute voice.

"That you are." I kissed her. "Have a great day. I'll give you a call when I can."

She nodded. "Don't miss me too badly."

"Impossible," I said, then walked out the door.

I made it to work by seven thirty. Linda walked in an hour later.

"It's Monday morning; what in the hell are you so happy about?" were the first words from her mouth.

I was smiling at her, and her tone made it widen.

"How in the hell do you do that?"

"Wisdom and age," she said. "And people so rarely smile here that it's hard not to notice when they do."

"Good point."

She sat and faced me in her swivel chair.

"So are you going to tell me, or do I have to beat it out of you?"

"Just had a good weekend is all."

"I can see that. What's her name?"

"You're an amazing woman, Linda. You know that?"

"Of course I do."

"Her name is Carolyn."

"Pretty?"

"In her own way, yes. Very pretty."

"Well, good for you. If we all could be so lucky."

"Eh, don't worry. I'm sure I'll screw it up in time."

"That's the attitude."

I laughed. "The eternal optimist. How was your weekend?"

"A bust. Had a terrible date on Friday with a man who seemed to have irritable bowels and a small bladder. Excused himself to use the restroom six times during dinner, I shit you not. Excuse the pun. Six times."

I laughed. "How do you feel about a retired sixty-one-year-old military man named Gene who smokes and drinks too much?"

"I would say he sounds like my second husband. Can he hold an erection?"

"Surprisingly enough, Linda, I don't really know. But I'll see if I can find out for you."

"You do that." She turned back around and began shuffling through the papers on her desk. She sighed, then said to herself, "Just another damn day in paradise," a comment that kept me laughing most of the day.

❦ 2 ❦

I made a quick dinner that consisted of an apple and a peanut-butter-and-jelly sandwich, then walked out the door. It took an hour to find the Starbucks, and when I got there, I was somewhat giddy to walk in and see Carolyn, the girl who had held a firm grasp on my mind all day.

There were two baristas, a man and a woman. The woman was not Carolyn. There was no line. Half the tables were occupied. I walked to the counter.

"Is Carolyn Reyug working?"

"Yes, she is," the woman replied and looked to the back. "Let me go grab her."

"Thank you."

I waited at the counter, the anticipation making me a little nervous.

Then Carolyn appeared. Her face lit up and I smiled at her. She came around the counter, holding her head at an obvious angle. I didn't know why until she was a few feet away. On her cheek, just below her left eye, a bruise had started to form.

"Hey you," she said and hugged me.

"How are you?"

"I'm good."

She pulled away and I was able to see just how bad the bruise really was. An inch long and wide, a deep purple starting at the lower eyelid and turning a yellowish hue as it rolled down her cheek. There was little doubt in my mind as to how it had gotten there. I simply stared, feeling myself tense up. She made an apologetic face.

"I'm sorry," she said.

I pulled her back into my arms, my right hand cupping the back of her head. "Don't be sorry." I closed my eyes and counted backward from ten trying to dispel the rage. My first impulse was to kill the son of a bitch. "Are you able to sit a few minutes?"

"Yeah, I can take a short break. Did you want a drink first?"

I sat in the corner as far away from the others as I could get. Carolyn made a latte and brought it over and sat across from me. I smiled and tried to show her I wasn't angry, though beneath the smile, I wanted to rip Jimmy's throat out.

"So what happened?"

She talked in circles. I had to calm her down to get to the heart of the story. She went home to get her things in order to come straight to my place after work. She didn't think he'd be there, but he was. He'd been drinking. He asked her where she had been. She told him it was none of his business. He threw a beer bottle at her but it missed and shattered against the wall. He ran over, grabbed her by the arms and shook her, kept repeating "Where have you been?" When she wouldn't answer he slugged her in the eye and she fled the apartment and came straight to work without getting any of the items she had gone for.

She wiped away a tear that had begun to roll down her cheek.

"I'll kill him," I said.

"Stratton, please, no."

I took a deep breath. "So this was what, two and a half hours ago?"

She nodded. I leaned forward, closed my eyes, pinched the bridge of my nose. I had feared it would come to this from the second I learned of her living situation, feared having no choice but to do the thing it was far too early to do. I looked at her, seeing the sadness in her eyes, the confusion and uncertainty.

"I'm really sorry," she said.

"Carolyn, don't be sorry. It's not your fault," I said.

She nodded, looked down at the table. I reached over, lifted her hand, and kissed the back of it.

"How much stuff do you have there?"

She shrugged. "Clothes, a television, the bed is mine. Everything else is things he brought or bought once we got here. I have a cat."

"A cat," I said and smiled. I took a deep breath. "Do you think two people can manage it without renting a car or truck?"

"I think so. Why?"

"When is he supposed to work next?"

She thought about it a moment. "Tomorrow morning until, like, three."

"Well, this is what we'll do," I said, reluctant to say the words. But I knew I had to. I couldn't stand the hurt in her eyes. But that wasn't all. After the few days we had spent together I couldn't bear the idea of losing her. If I allowed her to leave now and move back to Iowa, then I'd be haunted by the what-ifs and what-could-have-beens. Sometimes that's what life comes down to, minimizing future regret. "I'll take the day off. We'll go over together and gather your things and bring them to my place."

She looked uncertainly at me, as though she was about to say no. I spoke before she had the opportunity to.

"It doesn't have to be permanent," I said. "We'll see how it goes. But it's obvious we have to get you out of there."

"Stratton, are you sure?" she asked, and her words had the calculated tone of an argument rehearsed for hours. Certainly she had pondered the option herself. And sure, maybe she was just as reluctant as I, but what choice did we have? Sometimes the world makes decisions for us. Sometimes people enter our lives neatly, without notice, in the same unexpected way we sometimes lose the very people who seemed as though they'd be with us forever.

"Of course I'm sure," I said.

"Don't feel like you have to do this."

"I don't, Carolyn. But I've enjoyed being with you over the last few days. I'm thinking it might not be so bad having you around a little more," I said.

She nodded, looking at me with kind, unburdened eyes.

"Are you able to part with the bed?" I asked.

"Yes."

"Good. Now, a more important question: How big is your boyfriend?"

"My *ex*-boyfriend," she corrected me. "And he's not as big as you are."

"I was really hoping you'd say that."

❦ 3 ❦

I stayed for the duration of Carolyn's shift. If Jimmy was drunk at four, then he was surely embalmed by seven. My father always was. I feared that Jimmy would show up. There was nothing I could do to change what had already happened, but I'd be damned if I'd allow any further harm to come.

The temperature had dropped considerably by the time we left. We huddled against one another waiting for the bus I thought would never come. It finally did and we took it down to the train, then the train up to Belmont, and we walked the rest of the way home.

"Home sweet home," I said when we walked through the door. "For us both, I suppose."

Carolyn smiled. I had hoped she would. If we were to live together, then why dance around the facts and call it anything other than what it was?

She went to the window and stared out. Above her on the wall, the hole that had been plastered over was beginning to show, small cracks on the surface, the entire circle turning tawny through the off-white paint. I felt embarrassed by it. Then Carolyn turned around, and I was happy she was here. The apartment felt far cozier than it ever had before. She had grown comfortable to me, and in that comfort there was beauty.

twelve

I'VE ALWAYS BEEN HABITUALLY irascible, or as my father often put it, "full of piss and vinegar," but fighting, at least the technical half of it, didn't come naturally. I had learned how to fight from him. He himself had picked it up while boxing for the navy in the three and a half years prior to being dishonorably discharged, the punishment received for stabbing a man who'd hustled him in a game of pool outside of a bar in Ansted, West Virginia. I didn't learn of this last fact until it was brought up in a courtroom many years later, but considering what I then knew, I wasn't at all surprised . . .

I am nine, in the fourth grade. It is the age when children have become aware of the world outside their doors, have begun to understand it, or at least believe they do. My mother is a visible part of our small community, somebody different, talked about at dinner tables. She's far younger and much more beautiful than my classmate's mothers, and for that I am ridiculed. It never occurs to them that it's their fathers on the receiving end of the beers my mother serves, their fathers' lustful looks that fuel discussion. That it's my mother's being off limits that incites the very jealousy that often turns to bitterness. I fight often. I lose more than I win. I'm small for my age, but I'm quick. Little do I know I'm toughening myself for the trials that lie ahead.

I enter the bar. It's Thursday and my father's already here. He's been out of work for two months and we're solely supported by my mother's tips. The fact that he's out of work should negate my being dropped off at the bar, but it doesn't. With him not working, and in turn drinking more without the misery of early-morning rousings, he's much nicer and far less volatile, so my mother lets it slide.

I walk past him and head around the bar and hug my mother. My bottom lip is cut, beginning to swell.

"What happened to you?" she asks.

"I got into a fight."

"With who?"

"Donny Smith."

"Why?"

I shrug. There's no point in transferring the hurt that I felt onto her. Even at my young age I know that much. The truth is that he called her a whore and said that she'd let everyone in town slip it to her if it weren't for my father always hanging around. It's obvious these beliefs were recycled from something his own father had said, a father who comes in most days and drinks past the time he's due at the dinner table.

"Jesus, Stratton," she says with a sigh. "Go sit and I'll get you an icepack."

I slide onto the stool beside my father. The crooked grin on his face, the slack wrinkles across his forehead, tell me he's been here awhile.

"Hey buddy!" he says, wearing an expression of puzzled stupidity as if I'd just materialized from out of thin air. His eyes swim above two rosy cheeks. Sitting in front of him is a half-drunk beer and an empty shot glass. "What's up, man?"

"Nothing."

My mother brings over a washcloth with a rubber band wrapped around several ice cubes and presses it against my lip and tells me to hold it there.

"Stratton got into a fight today," she says.

"A fight?" my father asks.

I nod.

"So what's the other guy look like?"

I shrug. Donny Smith is bigger and stronger than I am. I'm not even sure I hit him once during the twenty-second brawl.

My father lifts my right hand, inspects my knuckles.

"Damn, son, you even throw a punch?"

"I tried to."

"Darla, let me buy this man a drink," he says, picking up two dollar bills and slapping them back down onto the bar. My mother smiles and pulls a root beer from the cooler, pours it into a frosty mug, and sets it in front of me.

"Cheers," my father says.

We touch our glasses and drink. My mother doesn't take the money. She rarely does. He gives me one of the dollars to feed the jukebox and the other he changes for quarters to shoot pool. He racks the balls, allows me to break. I hit the cue as hard as I can but only a few of the balls break away. He plays left-handed, which is the handicap we've established when playing together. My father is the best shooter in the bar. He rarely loses. I've seen him win games without the other person even taking a shot.

"So why'd ya fight today?" he asks.

"Donny Smith called Mom a whore."

"He did, eh?"

I nod.

"You know why?"

"Because he's a dick?"

He laughs. "Because his father's a drunk and a loser. He's in here every day starin' at yer mom's ass. It's pathetic. Hell, he'd come in with his dick hanging out if he thought he'd get away with it," he says, watching me earnestly. He then unzips himself, shoves his hand down his pants, and pokes his thumb out of his fly to demonstrate how it might look for a man to have his dick hanging out, albeit a grossly undersized one. Then, to further illustrate the point, he thrusts his hips back and forth and grunts with gusto.

"What the hell are ya doin'?" my mother inquires from the bar.

He grins sheepishly and waves her off with a flick of the wrist. She rolls her eyes.

"The point is," he says to me, zipping himself back up and bending over the table, "if you ever want to sleep at night, then don't marry a young, beautiful woman. I married both." I can't help but blink. Apparently he doesn't consider this remark a non sequitur, but I do. And as I stand there confused at the relevance, he promptly sinks every one of his balls on the table.

"You remember how to throw a punch like I showed ya?"

I nod.

"Show me," he says, holding out his hand for a target. I punch it awkwardly. My fist only grazes his palm.

"Damn, son," he says, and cuffs me in the back of the head. "You're everywhere. You can't flail your elbow like that. Your whole body is slack."

He steps back, bounces on the balls of his feet, and punches the air. The movement of his body is a work of art, everything turning with machine-like precision.

"A punch is ninety percent mechanics and ten percent force and strength, and even power comes from technique. You gotta stay balanced. Look, look at the way I'm standin'. Feet planted, shoulders parallel. Do it."

I try mirroring him. He comes over, repositions my feet, then my body.

"Like that," he says, tucking my chin.

"Whatcha doing over there?" my mother yells, still behind the bar.

"Nothin'," he yells back, again waving her off.

"Yer supposed to tell him to stay out of fights, not show him *how* to fight."

"Mind yer own business, woman." He turns back to me. "Okay, before throwin' a punch, you want to be loose, but firm. Then, in the very moment you throw from your shoulder, all the weight in the back comes forward, centered on your front leg. Your torso pivots, and though yer weight's movin' forward, you always, *always*, keep yer back foot planted. And then you imagine everything inside of you is in the fist yer throwin'."

He does it slow for me to observe. I try doing the same.

"Keep yer elbow tight. You can't let it flail out like that. You'll dislo-
cate yer shoulder, have less accuracy, and little force."

I do it again, focusing intently on doing it right.

"Perfect."

Then he teaches me to jab. "Unless yer a boxer and practice throwin'
a jab, very few people ever take the time to learn how. It's just awkward for
'em. But if you practice and learn it yourself, then you'll have the upper
hand. After a while, after practicing how to do it, you'll be able to throw
a hard punch from any angle regardless of how yer body's positioned.
Then you'll be a damn dangerous man, just like your pop," he says and
cuffs me in the back of the head a second time, and pretty hard, too. "Aim
for the nose. You hit a man square in the nose, and he'll be momentarily
blinded and worthless. Right here," he says, pointing at the bridge of his
own nose. "Now hit my hand again."

I do it, this time hitting it dead-on. He pulls his hand away and
shakes it. "Atta boy, you'll be punching like Mike Tyson in no time," he
says. "You just have to practice like a motherfucker. Boxing's one of those
things you have to drill over and over and over again to get good at. Ah
hell," he says for no apparent reason, and then walks to the bar. I don't
hear what he says to my mother, but she reluctantly gives him a few bills
and he struts back. "Come on, we're getting out of here," he says.

"Drive carefully, damn it," my mother yells from behind us.

We drive to Medina, the nearest city with a sports equipment store.
My father buys a heavy bag and two pairs of boxing gloves. The cashier
looks at my busted lip and smiles. He knows exactly what's happening:
a father teaching his son to fight. I doubt it's the first time he's seen it.
When we arrive home, my father, who has never been what one would
call a handyman, sets about hanging the bag in the center of my bedroom,
which is small to begin with; I'll have to shuffle around the bag to get in
and out. He screws a thick eyebolt into the center of the ceiling without
bothering to check for a stud. He stands back for a moment admiring his
work, and I too look upon the bag with pride.

"Whatcha think?" he asks.

"I love it."

He walks to the bag, grabs the top of it with both hands, and puts a little weight on it. The bag puts up no resistance whatsoever and comes tumbling straight down, ripping a softball-size hole in the ceiling and scattering chunks of plaster all around the room. My father falls over the bag and crashes shoulder first into my dresser, knocking everything on top of it to the floor.

"This fucking house," he says, as though the house is merely continuing on with some long-standing grudge my grandmother had started. He stands and massages his shoulder while peering up into the hole. He shakes his head. Beside the hole, and now visible, is the thick, heavy stud required for the suspension of heavy weight. "Missed the damn beam by an inch," he says, confused at why the damn beam wasn't in the center of the ceiling in the first place.

He goes through the same ordeal again, this time screwing the eyebolt into the stud's center. When he's done he hangs the bag, gives it a good jerk, and then jabs it a few times. Satisfied, he shows me how to hit it, correcting my technique until I get it right.

"Good. Now do that no less than a thousand times each day and you'll be good to go in no time. Then nobody'll fuck with you."

❦ 2 ❦

I punch the bag every day, not a thousand times, but a hundred, fifty times with each hand when I wake, fifty more before I go to bed. My father watches some nights, corrects me when I get sloppy, hits it himself while I hold it from behind. After a few weeks he no longer has to correct me. I'm becoming sure of myself, and this newfound confidence finds me in far fewer fights, as though it was my apparent insecurity that had opened the door to discord in the first place.

After I learn the heavy bag, my father begins boxing with me. We go at it in the middle of our living room, my mother usually cheering me on from the couch, making sure my father doesn't get too rough. The irony is that I want him to be rough, have begun to look forward to the bloody noses I sometimes get. He boxes on his knees, throws careless punches he expects me to duck, but at times gets caught up in the excitement of fighting again and throws punches far too hard, uppercuts that floor me, left hooks I never see coming that send me reeling into the wall.

"Goddamn it, Mark," my mother says, and during those first few weeks I go to her so that she can soothe me.

"What? I'm toughenin' him up."

"Yer being an asshole is what yer doin'."

"Don't baby him, Darla."

She voices a make-believe bell for our three-round fights, usually sounding it when it looks as though I could use a break. I go to her corner and she whispers encouragement into my ear, and then she rings the bell again once I've caught my breath.

After two months of this, and for whatever reason, my father announces that tonight's loser will be the first one who bleeds.

"Not a chance in hell," my mother says.

"First one who bleeds loses," he repeats, ignoring her. "Ring it."

I punch my gloves together as I've seen Mike Tyson do to let her know I accept his stipulation. She sighs, sounds "ding ding" in her high-pitched voice, and then adds, "Don't be an asshole," just for good measure.

I bob and weave in a way that makes my father laugh. I've learned that mobility and quickness are my greatest advantages since he can only shuffle while on his knees. He toys with me, wraps me up and lightly punches me in the ribs. I break away, charge and duck right into an uppercut he's thrown too hard. He threw it playfully, theatrically meaning to miss, but it's a solid shot to the forehead that knocks me backward into the TV.

"Goddamn it, Mark," my mother says. My father laughs.

"What? I didn't mean it."

"I don't give a shit if you meant it."

I get up, tears in my eyes. I'm angry. My father has assumed I'd quit and is in the process of taking off his gloves. It's then that I wind up with everything I have. What am I, forty-five, fifty pounds at the most? However much I weigh, every ounce of it is in the fist hurling his way, a fist that hits him flush, squarely in the nose. It does exactly what he had said it'd do, temporarily blinding him, forcing tears to his eyes. Blood gathers in his left nostril and a thin red line trickles down to his upper lip.

"Shit," he says, touching the back of his glove to his nose. He pulls it away. A small drop of blood stands out on the red leather. "I think I just lost."

My mother and I are both laughing.

"You little bastard," he says. "You've got one helluva punch when yer angry."

"That's my little champ," my mother says proudly.

"Now we just have to get you wrestling. Then you'll really be a bad man, just like yer pop."

The next day, my father watches me walk into the bar after school, eyes me with a prideful grin as I take the seat beside him. He nods approvingly.

"That's my boy," he says.

My mother rolls her eyes. Apparently I've developed a hop in my step, am beginning to walk into places with a proprietary air as though I'm the one who grants the patrons entrance each day. It's a trait I've always noticed in my father. A trait I've always loved.

3

It's the first warm day of the year, and outside, the snow and ice have been melting since dawn. From the window outside the principal's office I watch pools of water gather. My hands are shaking, partly from the fight not yet twenty minutes old, partly from the anticipation of which parent will pick me up. I'm sure one will be livid, the other approving. Aside from the trouble I'm already in I fear this will pit them against one another, that I'll have to sleep through yells from the room beside my own, perhaps broken dishes and overturned furniture. It wouldn't be the first time.

The clock on the wall reads three. The fight happened during that rush between the day's last class and the boarding of the buses. It started during recess, when Donny Smith called me poor because there was a large hole in the front of my sweater. He then went on to say that it made sense I had a shirt with a hole because my mother was a whore and that was all that whores deserved. Everybody in the schoolyard had heard it, and laughed, and then hyped it up for the rest of the day. Jeff was there. He was Donny's best friend, and with that, the majority of kids took Donny's side while the rest—a small, embarrassing bunch happy to be included at all—took mine. By the end of the day there was no doubt there'd be a fight. I was nervous as hell and feared being hurt or, even worse, being embarrassed. But I've learned over the years that a fear of failure is as good a motivation for success as anything else this world might offer.

At two forty the last class let out. Everybody began yelling and forming a tight circle in the hallway outside the room, pushing Donny and me toward the center. I could see him, and being forced into the situation filled me with a black hatred, the words about my mother replaying in my mind. I remembered the last time we had fought. The swollen, busted lip that burned for days each time I brushed my teeth or drank something acidic. The way I was laughed at. As we neared one another the hatred turned to rage and I became blind to everything else, my fists tightly clenched at my side. *Stay loose but firm*, my father's voice echoed. I was ready, breathing heavily, my eyes wide and focused on Donny. He laughed the second he saw the expression on my face.

We got to the center and he came at me. His arms were up and away from his body as though he intended to bear-hug me. I stood firm, my feet parallel to my shoulders despite several hands shoving me from behind. Then I let it go, transferring everything that I am and everything that I can ever hope to be into that fist. I never closed my eyes. I watched it all the way in. As soon as it was thrown I knew it'd connect. I felt the cartilage give way, heard the pop. The feel of the crunch beneath my knuckles sickened me. I closed my eyes to it. The whole group groaned in harmony, and when I reopened my eyes I saw that there was blood everywhere and I instantly knew I was in deep shit. Donny dropped straight down. Then I felt the principal's hand grab me hard from behind and drag me away. I held firmly to the story, told it just as it had happened. And now I sit waiting.

❦ 4 ❦

I breathe a sigh of relief when my father's rickety old pickup truck comes around the bend and enters the school lot. He walks in cocksure and confident, wearing jeans and a black long-sleeve tee, the sleeves of which are pulled halfway up his forearms. He winks at me and together we walk into the principal's office.

"It should be obvious that fighting cannot go unpunished," the principal says from behind his desk. He's an older man, bald with gray hair at the sides and back of his head. "Especially since your son apparently broke another kid's nose."

"He did, eh?" my father says. He looks at me. "And what'd the other kid do to deserve it?"

"It was Donny Smith," I answer. "He called Mom a whore and said we were poor and that I deserved to wear clothes with holes in them."

My father nods. "And what punishment did Donny Smith get?"

"I'm not sure you heard me," the principal says. He removes his glasses, throws them onto the desk. "His nose was broken, and pretty badly at that. I saw it with my own eyes."

"I heard you the first time, and it sounds as though he deserved it. This ain't the first fight they've had, nor is it the first time Donny's said these things about my family."

"There's a protocol for such taunting. Your son should have brought it to my attention."

"Yeah, and what would you have done? They're kids; kids fight."

The principal closes his eyes. "Well, it's apparent where your child gets his aggression," he says in a derogatory tone, challenging my father.

"Stratton, go wait in the truck," he says without taking his eyes off the principal.

I do what he says. When he comes out a few minutes later my suspension has been reduced from three days to two. We pull out of the school parking lot.

"What happened in there?" I ask with something resembling amazement.

"Just chitchat between grown men."

"I'm not sorry for breaking his nose."

"I'd be pissed if you were."

"I did just as you taught me."

He looks over and smiles. "Ya did good, buddy," he says and cuffs me in the back of the head. "Though you better not tell yer mom that."

"Is she going to kill me?"

"She may kill us both, but she'll get over it."

I shrug, nervous the whole ride back over how she's going to respond, but when we walk into the bar, she simply smiles and hugs me and tells me that she loves me. I hug her back, and accept that women are one of the many mysteries of this world I have no hope of ever understanding.

❧ 5 ☙

It's six o'clock when he finally walks in, livid, dragging his son by the arm. Donny's nose is encased in cotton beneath a metal splint held in place with several strips of white surgical tape. My father has been waiting for this, turning his head each time the door has opened since we arrived. He drinks what's left of his whiskey and turns in his stool. He smiles in a way that can only be taken as a taunt.

"Mike Smith, I thought we might see you today."

"See what the hell your son did?" he asks, stopping five feet from us.

"Well, no, but I certainly see it now. Did a pretty good number on him, eh? And by the sound of it yer boy deserved it."

Everyone in the bar falls silent. They've heard the story proudly recounted by my father. Several of them have stuck around out of pure curiosity as to what might happen. Donny stares at his feet, never once lifting his head to look at me. I don't feel a shred of regret.

"You know how much this is going to cost us?"

"No, and if you want the truth, I don't really give a shit, Mike."

I'm certain my father's been waiting a while for this opportunity. He's never liked Mike and is tired of the opinions voiced behind our backs that somehow still reach us. I'm certain he has a cache of acrimonious quips he knows will only tempt the larger man, who's taller by three inches, some forty pounds heavier. My father shows no fear.

"Go wait by the pool table," Mike says, his eyes never leaving my father's. Donny lumbers away, his head still drooped.

"You think you're tough shit, don't you?" Mike asks.

My father grins. "You bet yer ass I do."

"Fuck you, Mark Brown. Fuck you and yer whole goddamn family."

My father smirks but stays silent. He's wound like a rattlesnake, just waiting. For what, I'm not exactly sure. Maybe that right combination of words that'll push him over the edge.

"Yeah, go ahead and smirk, you cocksucker," Mike says. He shakes his head and turns to leave, but before he's able to take a single step, my father hurls his beer bottle at him and it hits Mike squarely in the back. He springs from his stool and, as Mike lifts his arms in defense, my father hits him in the jaw with a left jab that's followed by an overhand right. It lands flush on the chin and knocks Mike to the floor. The crowd swarms to break it up. Mike stands and rubs his jaw with his right hand.

"You motherfucker," he yells and charges into the group. Just as his son had done earlier in the day, he doesn't throw a punch and instead tries grabbing my father by the shirt but there are too many people between them, my mother included. She tries calming Mike down and puts her hands on his chest to push him away from the crowd and toward the front door.

"Get yer damn hands off me, you whore," he says to her.

Her mouth drops open. Mine does, too. Without hesitation, she reaches back and slugs him in the face with her right hand, around the fingers of which she's wearing several rings. One of them splits the skin below his left eye. She then grabs a fistful of his hair while the crowd rushes to now separate them. She won't let go, and they're pushed apart so forcefully that when they finally do separate, a large patch of hair is clutched in my mother's hand. Mike staggers backward, one hand to his head while he grabs his son by the arm with the other. Together they stumble awkwardly from the bar.

I turn around and my father is already sitting on his stool watching my mom. When their eyes meet he winks at her, and she smiles, a private moment passing between them. He's as calm as though he's just walked in waiting to be served, completely devoid of the effects I've come to expect from fights. Shaking hands. Heavy breathing. A numb face. My parents, no strangers to bar fights and brawls. I want to hug them both as tightly as I can, filled with so much pride that I don't know what to do with it all.

thirteen

I WOKE AT SIX forty-five, had become accustomed to my work schedule and would wake early regardless of the time I went to bed. I made coffee and showered. I waited until eight thirty to call the office, a time I knew Cathy wouldn't be there yet so that I could leave a message without scrutiny. Then I lay beside Carolyn and traced her eyebrows with my thumb.

"I love that you don't have to work today," she said in a sleepy voice.

"Me too."

"What time is it?"

"A quarter till nine," I said. "What time does Jimmy go to work?"

"Seven."

"Well, then, we should probably get moving."

"Does that mean I have to get out of bed?"

"Afraid so, darlin'."

"Nooooo," she said and buried her head beneath the duvet. I burrowed beneath it as well until I could see her eyes staring back at mine beneath our darkened tent. Her cheek had completely blackened in the night.

"Just think, we'll go and do what we have to do and it'll all be done and over with in two hours." She nodded. "Are you sad?" I asked.

"No, of course not. I'm happy."

"Good. I am, too."

She showered, dressed, made offhand comments about how bad her eye looked and how there wasn't enough makeup in the world to cover it. I reassured her that it wasn't nearly as bad as she thought, which was a lie. I started getting nervous. Jimmy was supposed to be at work, but it was hard to imagine that holding true. It was too convenient. Would Carolyn's prolonged absence only stoke the flame of anger? Well, I'd match his with my own if that's what it came to.

We left at ten thirty. By the time we arrived, the hundred or so things that could go wrong were racing through my head. I wished I had grabbed a knife, though I figured it was probably better that I hadn't. I wanted it done and over with, one of those punishments to endure for a little reward after. There's always a price to pay. Always.

The building was in a greater state of disrepair than Gene's, and an air of dilapidation hung over the entire neighborhood. Flattened beer cans lined the curb while sheets of newspaper and plastic bags were wrapped around parking meters and telephone poles; an abandoned warehouse with busted windows stood across the street. A dog barked from somewhere unseen.

"How do you feel?" I asked.

"I'm okay. Kind of nervous. Are you?"

"Nah," I lied.

Carolyn took a deep breath as we marched up the stairs. We entered the living room of the third-floor apartment. It was small and dimly lit; dirty sheets hung over the windows. Silence. I relaxed a little. *Hustler* magazines covered the top of the coffee table along with dirty dishes, empty beer bottles, an ashtray full of cigarette butts.

"What can I do?" I asked.

"Get the TV. I'll gather my clothes in the bedroom."

I unplugged the television, lifted it off the table, set it beside the door. It was caked with dust, as were most of the other surfaces. The walls were bare. There was broken glass against one of them and what remained of the thrown bottle was on the floor below it. Then a sudden burst of yelling came from the bedroom.

"Where the fuck are you going?" a man's voice roared.

He held her tightly by the shoulders when I entered.

"I'd let her go if I were you," I said.

"Yeah? And who the hell are you?"

I was instantly sickened by the look of him. He was scrawny, his face covered in acne scars and the beginnings of a pencil mustache that looked more like dirt than hair. He wore a white tee that fell nearly to his knees, a gold chain around his neck, a tattoo of a snake wrapped around his right forearm. Large ears and closely cropped hair dyed blond. Was this really who Carolyn had spent the last two years of her life with, this piece of trash? And why did it piss me off so badly? For a split second I felt I deserved better than somebody who'd be with him. But then seeing his hands on Carolyn made me quickly shrug that thought away. He had hit her the night before, and I feared he'd hit her again. We had come to get her things and that is exactly what we'd do.

He stared at me. The anger he emitted was an obvious attempt to cover fear, and recognizing it allowed me to settle into a role I knew well, that of the favorite, which is what I was for nearly every match in the last two years of my wrestling career. The one expected to win.

"It doesn't matter who I am," I said. "But I'm telling you now, if you don't take your hands off her, then you're going to find that answer out very quickly, and I don't think you are going to like it very much." It came out far better than I had hoped, as though straight from the scenes of a Clint Eastwood Western. My heart was racing. Deep, slow breaths.

"Yeah, man? You think I'm scared of you?"

"I don't really give a shit, Jimmy. We're here to gather Carolyn's things and we're not leaving until we do."

He let her go by shoving her against the wall. She stayed there, her back to the corner, too scared to move.

"Get the fuck out of my apartment!" he yelled.

The cat emerged from beneath the bed and trotted over to Carolyn. She picked him up and clutched him to her chest. He was a large, black cat that seemed indifferent to the tension in the room, while Carolyn was on the verge of tears. I don't think she believed Jimmy would be home, that it'd come to this. Jimmy glared at her furiously.

"You're a fucking whore," he said. "I hope you rot in hell."

Familiar words. I knew what they meant in the context of my own life, not exactly verbatim, but close enough, and there wasn't a chance in hell they'd take away the things they did the last time they were uttered. Diplomacy had failed. I stepped forward and swung. A clean punch, square on his jaw with a resounding thud. Carolyn shrieked and dropped the cat. She covered her face with her hands. Jimmy absorbed the punch and tried to counter. He was quick, but I was quicker. I hit him between the eyes and was sure it'd blacken both of them. He fell onto the bed behind him but quickly stood. I gripped him around the throat and pushed him backward until he hit the wall so hard that the drywall cracked inward. I kept my hand on him waiting for him to counter. He didn't, and instead stayed put while breathing heavily and scowling at me.

"Get your things, Carolyn," I said. She didn't move, her hands still over her face. "Carolyn!" She snapped back to attention. "Gather your things."

She began rushing around the room. I kept my hand pressed to Jimmy's sternum. The punch had caused his nose to bleed. Blood trickled from both nostrils and dripped onto his white shirt. Some landed on my hand.

"Couldn't leave well enough alone, could you?"

"Fuck you," he said.

"She's going to be living with me from now on, you understand? So keep the fuck away from her. You screwed it up, plain and simple."

"You think I'll miss that whore?"

"Yes, I do."

"I'll be banging somebody else by this weekend."

"Good. And Carolyn will be with me. Everybody wins."

"Fuck you."

"Very original, Jimmy."

Carolyn retrieved a garbage bag from the kitchen. She began rifling through drawers, tearing clothes from hangers. She was crying. I hoped she was crying at the unexpected violence and not because she was sad to be leaving. I didn't want to think that she might, on some level, still love Jimmy, that she might somehow miss him. It was hard to imagine anyone missing him, or being with him, for that matter.

"Hey," I said. She looked at me. "Slow down. Everything's fine."

At that, Jimmy decided he'd seen enough. He swung while my head was turned. I instinctively ducked when I felt his body jerk, and his fist grazed the top of my head. Carolyn shrieked. He swung again, this time missing completely. The force of the punch spun him around, and I wrapped my right arm around his throat, then tightened my grip by placing my hand in the crook of my left arm. A rear naked chokehold. I had full control. He couldn't breathe. I dragged him out of the bedroom and into the bathroom. I must have outweighed him by thirty pounds. I let go and thrust him forward by shoving my foot on his ass. He sprawled forward full length, crashing into the side of the tub. I slammed the bathroom door shut. It was the kind that opened outward. I swiped a chair from the kitchen table and placed it beneath the doorknob. It wouldn't hold him for long.

I went back into the bedroom. Carolyn was trembling. I put my arms around her.

"I don't like this," she said, shaking her head. "I don't like this at all."

"I know you don't, but it's almost over. You have to be sure you get everything so we don't have to do it again. You get it all and then it's over."

She nodded.

"But be quick."

I carried the filled garbage bag into the living room and set it beside the television. When I walked back in, a second bag sat on the bed, half filled.

"I think I have everything in here," she said.

"Is there anything I can help with?" I asked, carrying the second bag out and placing it beside the first. The bathroom knob jiggled one way, then the other.

"No."

"Where are the cat's things?"

She sighed. "His litter box is in the bathroom."

"Of course it is."

She walked out of the bedroom carrying an oscillating fan.

"Leave the fan here," I said.

"What, why?"

"Because I don't want it."

"But it'll help drown out the trains."

"I don't care," I said, not bothering to explain.

She left it there and began rifling through the kitchen drawers. The bathroom door was beginning to be forced now. It was cheap, flimsy wood. If Jimmy shouldered into it, it would break. Carolyn was to my left, the bathroom to my right. He would have to get through me to get to her.

"I think you can leave anything we don't need."

She didn't respond, instead growing increasingly agitated by the noise at the bathroom door.

"What does Jimmy shave with?"

"Why, why does that matter?" she asked.

"Because I want to make sure that when he comes through that door there's not going to be a straight razor in his hand."

"Just a regular razor," she said with her hands on the edge of the kitchen counter.

"Do you have it all?"

She nodded. "I think so."

"Good. Now we need to rush down the stairs with the bag and the television. We'll come up and get the rest and then it's over. Okay?"

She nodded.

"Let's go then."

I took the television and raced down first. Carolyn was slower, but that was what I had wanted. I sprinted back up and passed her on the second-floor landing as she continued down. I grabbed the other bag and met her outside. Then we walked back up together.

"Do you have your keys?" I asked.

"Yes."

"Give them to me."

"Why?"

"So we can leave them."

I took them from her and dropped them on the kitchen counter.

"Get the cat," I said.

I walked out to the hallway and grabbed the fire extinguisher I had noticed when we first came up the stairs. Carolyn already held the cat in her arms when I reentered.

"Go on down," I said.

She was frightened. "Please don't do anything bad."

"I won't."

She left just as Jimmy kicked the bathroom door. It broke away from the jamb, but the chair still held. I pulled the safety pin from the extinguisher and hoped like hell that it worked. I kicked the chair away and the door swung open. I aimed the rubber hose at Jimmy's face and squeezed the handle. Powder shot out of it and knocked him backward so that he tripped over the toilet and crashed into the tub. I kept it aimed right at him. Neither of us could breathe, all the oxygen sucked from the room while the powder filled my mouth and burned my eyes. I could only imagine what it was doing to his. I released the trigger and threw the extinguisher on top of him, grabbed the cat box, and walked out.

Carolyn stood on the curb beside her belongings. She gazed up at the apartment with a sad look on her face. Then she looked at me.

"Why are you covered in white?"

I was coughing a little. "The fire extinguisher."

"Is Jimmy okay?"

"Yes, he's fine. Do cabs come by here?"

"Sometimes."

I peered up. Jimmy was in the window staring down at us. "Does he have a gun?"

"Why would he have a gun?"

"Because he's a thugged-out white kid from Iowa who wants to be tough. Why does anybody have a gun?"

"No, he doesn't."

"How in the hell could you be with him?" I asked a little more callously than I had intended.

"Please don't be mean."

I shook my head. "He's a piece of shit," I said. Carolyn didn't respond, which irritated me further. The whole situation made no sense, and I wanted to understand her validation in being with him.

We hailed a cab and loaded her things into the trunk. Carolyn scooted in first. I peered up again to see Jimmy still in the window with the downtrodden look of a dog left at home. Nobody suffers worse than a lover left behind, and I felt certain the next few days would be hell for him. I'd been there before. Well, to hell with him and his agony. I hoped he'd feel it in his bones. I flipped him off, hopped in the cab, and closed the door. The car sped off. I patted the cat's head. He purred in Carolyn's lap, unfazed by it all.

"What's his name, anyway?"

"Thomas," she said.

I patted the cat's head while I spent most of the ride back trying to talk myself out of the jealousy coursing through me. I was now to share a bed with a girl who had shared the same with a worthless lowlife. I tried convincing myself that her past didn't matter. Hell, I had put my penis in places I sure as hell wasn't proud of, but still, I couldn't get the image of Jimmy out of my head, nor the *Hustler* magazines scattered across the coffee table. Why would Carolyn allow such a thing?

"Jesus Christ," I said.

"What?"

"Nothing."

I took a deep breath. It was supposed to be a happy day, and I needed to allow it to be. I reached over and took hold of Carolyn's hand when we arrived, though there was nothing tender or loving about the act. It was done simply because I knew it was the right thing to do.

"Home," I said, trying to add levity to my voice.

We got out of the car and emptied Carolyn's things onto the front yard. We passed Gene coming down the stairs as we were going up, the television in my arms, Thomas in Carolyn's. I hadn't seen him since Friday night.

"Hey Gene," I said. He stayed on the stairs looking confused. "Let me drop this off and I'll be right back."

I unlocked the door and Carolyn tossed Thomas on the bed. I put the TV in the opposite corner. "I'll grab the rest of the stuff," I told her.

Gene was still in the stairwell. "That's the girl from Friday night, isn't it?"

"Yes. See what the hell you've done, ya bastard?"

"What the fuck?" he asked with a grin.

"I have no idea."

He followed me down and grabbed the second bag while I lifted the first.

"She's living here now?"

"Yeah."

"Holy shit, kiddo. You move even faster than I do."

"Yeah," I sighed. "Just kind of happened that way." I told him the bare essentials of the story. We stood outside, both freezing from the hard wind.

"Well," he said, drawing the words out slowly. "You did an admirable thing. And I wouldn't worry about it. I'm sure everything will be fine."

"I sure as hell hope so."

"Oh, to be young and reckless again," he said whimsically.

He followed me up the stairs.

"Hi there," he said to Carolyn. "It's good to see you again."

"You too."

"So you're with us now, huh?" She nodded. "Great, great. Well, I'm heading out now. I'll have extra keys made and drop them off when I return."

"Thank you," she said.

Gene shut the door behind him. Thomas investigated the apartment and sprinted beneath the bed when the first train passed. A half hour later, after a few had gone by, he approached their roar with indifference.

"He's a fearless cat," I said.

"I watched him be born. He's from my mom's cat back home."

I was still feeling a little rotten about Jimmy, but receiving Gene's affirmation helped pull me from my funk. I kicked off my shoes and jumped on the bed. "So what do you say we officially christen the new arrangement?"

Carolyn crawled in beside me with a devilish grin. She ran her hands up my back and my reservations melted away. Maybe it wouldn't be so bad after all.

fourteen

THE FIRST LETTER ARRIVED a few days later, on Christmas Eve. A Saturday. The familiar Ohio State Penitentiary return address in the upper left-hand corner, the same red stamp on the back over the seal. My name and previous address written in pencil in the same thick block letters I'd grown accustomed to, all uppercase. Carolyn had gotten the mail and placed the envelope on top of the pile. I grabbed it from the counter. The post office had rerouted the letter from New York, which meant the sender would be notified of the change of address, which meant my father would soon know where I lived. Out of habit, I had set a forwarding address the day I moved into the apartment. It was a stupid mistake I now regretted.

"Are you okay?" Carolyn asked from the bed. I was scowling down at the envelope, biting my bottom lip.

"See this?" I asked, a little more hostility in my voice than I had intended. Carolyn had only been with me for a week then and we were still shy around one another; my tone was one she had yet to hear.

"Yes?" she asked, confused.

"Throw them away when they arrive. Don't open them, don't set them on the counter so I can find them first, just throw them away."

"Why?"

"Because."

"I don't get it. Who are they from?"

"A prisoner serving time in Lucasville, Ohio."

"But who's the prisoner?"

"It doesn't matter."

"I don't get it. Why don't you read them?"

"Because he's a piece of shit and I hope he rots in hell. So please, just throw them away whenever you see them, okay?"

She narrowed her eyes. "I don't understand."

"I know, and I'm sorry, but I don't want to talk about it." I threw the letter in the trash. I didn't open it, didn't allow it to see the light of day by first tearing it up. I threw it away, tied the garbage bag though it was only half filled, and carried it to the downstairs can. I walked back up, bypassed my apartment, and continued up the second flight of stairs and knocked on Gene's door. He was in a navy blue bathrobe, unshaven, holding a tumbler full of what looked like Scotch in his right hand.

"How goes it?" he said.

I walked in and plopped on the living room sofa, then slid down until only my head rested against the back of the couch. I loved the smell of that room, redolent of paper and glue, like the inside of a bookstore. Books everywhere; we were literally surrounded by them. I knew my grandmother would be in her own personal heaven here, and I vowed to have a room just like it someday.

"I think I messed up."

"What do you mean?" He knocked back the rest of his drink and set the glass down. He sat in the chair and crossed his legs.

"Carolyn is downstairs sitting on the bed with the cat."

"Okay. Go on."

"That's it."

"Well, wasn't that the whole damn point in having her move in?"

"Well, Gene, I hadn't thought that far ahead."

"You do realize you're crazier than a rat in a brick shithouse, right?"

"Yes."

"Well, good. Knowing's half the battle. Now how in the hell did it come to this after just a few days?"

I sighed. "It happened so quickly I'm not even really sure," I said, and then filled in the rest of the details I had omitted the day Carolyn moved in. I told him about Jimmy hitting her, of being faced with the choice of letting her go back to Iowa or insisting that she move in with me, all of the events leading up to me sitting on the couch and him looking at me with his legs crossed while wearing a blue robe. When I finished he leaned back and smiled.

"What?" I asked.

"That's some story. Christ Almighty. Better you than me, kiddo."

"Yeah," I said. "I didn't think this through. She's already asking me stuff I'm years away from being ready to tell."

"Like what?"

"Just stuff."

Gene lifted his hands, showed me his palms in a questioning gesture, then dropped them on his thighs. "What the hell can you do? Give it a shot. You might be surprised. There's no way of knowing whether or not a thing will work until you've tried it. But for Christ's sake, put yourself in her shoes for a minute and quit thinking about yourself. Do you know how anxious she probably is, how vulnerable she must feel down there? She has almost no choice at this point but to try and please you. What would she do if you had a change of heart? She'd either crawl back to Iowa or to her ex, and it sounds as though neither is a very attractive option."

I nodded. He was right; I hadn't thought about it from her point of view. She had to be just as scared as I was, if not more. "I just wish we could have taken it a little slower."

"Stratton, my boy, I married my wife after knowing her for seven days. If you don't think I was scared shitless, then you'd be dead wrong. But when it's right, it's right. Don't worry yourself over how quickly everything happened. Sometimes it's better that way."

I studied Gene's earnest face staring back at mine. I had no idea he'd been married before. "We really don't know that much about each other, do we?"

"I'm not the one you need to reveal yourself to. That's the benefit of friendships over relationships."

I smiled and nodded to the library. "Which of those books did that come from?"

"It comes from all of them. Now get your ass downstairs and make that girl happy."

I guffawed. "I can't even make myself happy."

"Few of us can, kiddo."

Downstairs, Carolyn was sitting on the edge of the bed with her hands on her knees.

"It's good to see you," I said. "How was your day?"

She shook her head. "You're crazy."

"Crazy about you, maybe."

She rolled her eyes. I sat beside her.

"I'm sorry for getting angry just now. I was mostly upset with myself for setting a forwarding address with the post office, which now means those letters will arrive every week or two, without fail."

"Will you at least tell me who they're from?"

"My father. He's been writing me letters for twelve years now, and I don't like talking about him. But still, it was wrong of me to take it out on you."

"Why is he in prison?"

I shook my head. "I'm sorry, Carolyn, but I don't want to talk about it. I really don't. Can we please just let it go for now?"

We sat staring at each other. I was thinking of Gene's words, about Carolyn and how vulnerable she must feel. I smiled, and as I did I tried gathering every good thing about myself and placing it in that smile, hoping Carolyn might find some comfort in it.

"How are you?" I asked.

"I'm good."

"I mean, with everything, with this, with us? It all happened so quickly."

She nodded. "I'm good. I mean, it's a little scary, but it's nice, too. We have a lot of fun."

"Of course we have fun. I'm awesome."

She laughed. "And modest."

I lay on my back and stared at the specks of dust dancing in the lamplight. Carolyn reclined beside me. I put my arm around her and she placed her head on my chest. It was dark out, and cold, but the apartment was warm and cozy and I again felt that sense of contentment I had found the night in the bar when we first met.

Carolyn let loose an impatient sigh.

"What?" I asked.

"I don't like that you're already keeping things from me. We've only been together for a week, Stratton."

"I'm not keeping anything from you," I replied, which of course was a lie, and Carolyn knew it, too.

A silence passed between us.

"I'm not asking you to tell me everything now, because I get that it's a tough subject and that we haven't been together very long, but will you tell me eventually?"

I thought about it a moment. "I'll do my best, okay?"

She lay still for a time, and then ever so subtly shook her head. "Fine," she said, and in that one word, there resided the unmistakable hint of impatience.

fifteen

❦ 1 ❧

UP EARLY, A LITTLE after six, the studio masked in darkness, without definition. I crawled out of bed and sat at the desk. The sun still hidden but to the east a purplish glow growing in the cloud-swollen sky. I pushed the chair in front of the window and propped my feet on the ledge. Thomas jumped in my lap. We watched the silent dark, and in time the coming dawn chased the darkness to the west, the dawn of a new day. The trains passed. Most of the cars were empty.

I placed Thomas beside Carolyn. She didn't stir, which didn't surprise me since I had quickly learned the girl could sleep through anything, even her alarm, which she did most mornings. I dressed and kissed her on the cheek and placed a few slices of bread in a plastic baggie and walked out the door. The weather was brisk but not too bad, midthirties by my guess, which was a welcome break from the usual single digits. An overcast sky above a landscape that looked faded. I kept my hands pocketed, wandering the silent streets. Everything was closed, deepening the already desolate feel the holidays seem to worsen for the lonely of the world. Christmas, that time when you yearn for the very things you don't mind doing without at other times of the year. An occasional car passed, but for the most part, the city remained indoors. What were they doing? Did families still wake together on Christmas morning, eat breakfast, open gifts, snap pictures with arms draped over shoulders?

I sat at a bench near Wrigley, removed the bread, and broke the slices into small pieces I then threw to the pigeons. There were three at first but the group swelled to over thirty by the time the bread was gone, and once it was, the birds quickly vanished and then there was only me.

I sat and thought of my mother and of all the Christmases we had shared. They now seemed so far in the past that they were instead a part of somebody else's life, a life that had been recanted to me in a bar late one night at a table littered with bottles. I missed her terribly, and hated that her image was no longer sharp in my mind, no matter how hard and how long I thought of her. What remains of my mother are those things I still remember, and what I remember, sadly, is growing smaller each day.

I took the long way home, trying to rid myself of the gloomy fatigue that had found me after the letter had arrived the day before, a mood that had stayed with me through the night. It was after nine when I arrived. Carolyn still slept, though she had rolled over to her other side. In her arms lay Thomas with his four furry paws pointed toward the ceiling. It was an adorable scene. Carolyn twitched. The comforter was askew and her entire left leg showed to her crotch.

I sat on the bed beside her and stroked her cheek with the back of my hand. She opened her eyes and looked at me.

"Hey you," she said.

"Merry Christmas."

"Mmmmm. Is it Christmas already?"

"It doesn't have to be."

"I love Christmas."

"Then merry Christmas," I said and placed upon her chest the gift I had gotten the day before. It was a square box, slightly bigger than a deck of cards, wrapped in a sheet of newspaper.

"Aww, you bought me a gift?"

"Of course I did."

She sat up, began tearing away the paper. Beneath the wrapping was a wooden box, and within it lay a gold ankle bracelet embellished with a dangling heart charm. She held it up in her hand and twisted it in the light.

"I love it," she said.

"I was hoping you would." I took it from her. "Which ankle?" She held up her right and I clasped the bracelet around it. It fit perfectly.

"Thank you so much," she said and kissed me. She climbed out of bed and stood in the center of the room with her legs shoulder-width apart. The ankle bracelet was the only thing she was wearing.

"I'm sorry," I said, "am I supposed to be looking at the bracelet right now?"

"You can look at whatever you want."

I did. Her blonde hair was disheveled in a sultry way, sliding down the sides of her face and falling past her shoulders. She had a tremendous body, slender and firm, her breasts a buoyant B cup, a thin line of pubic hair she kept trimmed in a vertical strip. And those eyes. No matter how long I looked at every other part of her, my gaze always returned to her eyes.

"Come here, you," I said, lifting my hand out and beckoning her.

"Come where, over there? And what makes you think you can have me that easily?"

"Because I rule."

"You're at least going to have to let me give you your gift first."

"You're gift enough, darling."

"Oh shush, you already know you're getting laid."

"Enough said."

She lifted from beneath her pile of clothes what I could already tell was a book wrapped in green and red paper. When she handed it over I grabbed her arm and pulled her to me. She fell forward and I began kissing her neck.

"No," she laughed, playfully pushing me away.

"Okay, okay." I took the gift and tore away the paper. It was Hemingway's *A Moveable Feast.*

"How the hell did you know?"

"Know what?"

"This book. How did you know to buy me Hemingway? How did you know this was one of the only ones of his I've yet to read?"

"Oh yay!" she said, sitting on her heels with her hands together. "I was hoping so badly you hadn't."

"I hadn't, but how did you know?"

"I went through your books, and six of them are by Hemingway, but none was this one."

"Carolyn, Jesus, thank you so much."

"You're welcome. I'm so happy you like it."

I did like it, she was right. And after that we made love, such a beautiful love that during it I forgot all my past loves and lovers and slights of the world, such a sweet love that I wished I could've lived in it forever.

⊰ 2 ⊱

Carolyn labored over a chocolate cake. She couldn't leave the damn thing alone, getting up and opening the oven door every few minutes to be assured of its progress. I didn't say anything, just smiled over the binding of Hemingway at her nervousness to make a good impression on Gene. It was cute in its own way.

When the cake was done, at noon, we went upstairs. Gene's apartment smelled of honey-baked ham and candied yams. At Carolyn's insistence she was to help him with the rest of the dinner. He had two drinks already made. He handed one to me and I clinked his glass and took a long swig. It was a mojito.

"You know why I love you, Gene?"

"Because I have a big peter?"

Carolyn laughed so hard at Gene's unexpected rejoinder that she nearly dropped the cake.

"Yes, Gene, of course, it's because of your big peter. That's why I love you."

He stood grinning.

"You know how many people drink mojitos in the middle of winter?" I went on.

"At least one."

"Precisely. You're one hell of a guy."

He ushered us into the dining room, took Carolyn's cake, and set it upon the table.

"Carolyn, this looks lovely."

"Thank you," she said, proud of herself.

"I didn't know what you wanted to drink, unlike this one," he said and motioned to me with his glass, "who would drink turpentine if I were to put it on the rocks, so I waited. I can make most anything."

"Yeah you can," I said with emphasis.

"Stratton, please, the adults are talking here," he said.

"You have wine?" Carolyn asked.

"Of course. Red or white?"

"White, please."

"White wine in the winter? It's almost criminal," I said.

"Stratton, please," Gene said.

Carolyn grinned while Gene pulled the cork on a bottle of Riesling he had grabbed from the fridge, correctly assuming that Carolyn was unfamiliar with wine, and would thus probably prefer something sweet. He poured a glassful, handed it to her, and made a toast.

"Merry Christmas, you two. I'm happy to have you both." He didn't look at either of us, and instead stared at some abstract point between our glasses, then took a deep breath and exhaled.

"Happy to be here," I said.

"I mean it."

"So do I."

We drank. Gene handed Carolyn a dark apron. She lifted it over her head and I tied it in the back for her.

"How late did you stay last night?" I asked Gene.

"Until Sam kicked us out, close to midnight."

"Not bad," I said. Carolyn and I had gone ice-skating at Millennium Park, which is where I bought the ankle bracelet, and on the way back we met Gene at the Lamplighter for free drinks but we were both tired and only stayed for one.

I watched them cook for a while, and when I realized I'd do little more than stand there with my dick in my hand, I ran downstairs to grab the book. Thomas sat regally on the bed watching me. I patted him on the head and he began to purr. I swiped the book from the desk, and just before I walked out, Carolyn's phone rang atop the nightstand. I looked at the caller ID. It read JIMMY. I held the phone until it stopped ringing. A knot formed in my chest, and even though I knew I'd be breaking some unspeakable bond of trust, I had to know if there were other calls. I opened the phone. From the past week alone, there were four calls from Jimmy, all of them missed. I would have been satisfied with that, but my eyes were drawn to something else, the call *to* Jimmy, three days ago, while I was at work. They had talked for seventeen minutes.

I sat on the bed with the phone in my lap. My face was flushed. I lifted the phone and checked her text messages. There were none, not even the ones I had sent over the past week and a half, which could only mean she made it a habit of deleting all messages, and not just the frivolous ones. Was there significance behind it? It didn't really matter, because all I could picture was Jimmy with his pencil mustache and baggy clothes and pockmarked face oil-rigging the girl with whom I now shared my home.

The phone beeped; one new voicemail. I didn't know Carolyn's password but if I did there's no doubting I would have checked it. Thomas rolled to his side and swatted at my arm. I was in no mood to play with him.

I dropped the phone and paced while trying to talk myself out of a jealous rage. I sat on the edge of the bed. I took a deep breath, filling my lungs and holding in the air as long as I could, then exhaled in a long, slow whoosh. Was I always going to have to put up with these calls, always wondering what goes through her mind when they arrive?

"Screw it," I said. I picked the phone up and called him right back. He answered on the first ring.

"Hey you," he said in a soft, tender voice.

"Merry Christmas, Jimmy. Why are you calling my girlfriend?"

He was silent a moment. "Where's Carolyn?"

"Sitting right next to me."

"Give her the phone."

"Nothing doin', Jimmy. That ship has sailed," I said, and prayed that I was right. Was I? Carolyn did, after all, have a seventeen-minute phone conversation with him three days prior.

"You think?"

"You're goddamn right I do."

"Yeah? You sure? I was nailing her while she was dating somebody else and I'm still banging her now that she's with you, Stratton."

He knew my name. She had obviously told him. Did it matter? It made me angrier than hell, and I gritted my teeth and bitterly said, "With me? Please, she's not with me."

"That's funny since you called her your girlfriend not twenty seconds ago."

I snapped the phone shut, dropped it on the bed, and then punched a pillow over and over and over yelling "motherfucker" each time I hit it. I had just been outwitted, no other way of putting it. Was Carolyn prone to cheat, as he had said? And more importantly, had she seen him? I knew I wouldn't be able to swallow the curiosity. I had to know, even if it meant giving away the fact that I had checked her phone.

I plugged it back into the charger, sat at the desk, waited for the trains. I watched them and took refuge in the bedlam that erupted as each car passed. I took deep breaths to calm myself. I could feel my face twisted into a scowl. I sat that way for twenty minutes before the door opened behind me. I turned and Carolyn smiled, the front of her apron covered with powder.

"What are you doing down here, silly?" she asked.

"Nothing," I said in a voice without emotion, which she picked up on.

"What's the matter?"

"Nothing."

She walked to me and sat on my lap.

"Are you sure? You seem tense."

"I'm sure."

"Dinner is almost done. Twenty more minutes. I've had two glasses of wine already," she said and looked me in the eye with her forehead pressed to mine. "And Gene made me take a shot of brandy with him."

"I missed shots?" I said, trying to sound sweet.

"You did."

"Was it good?"

"Mmm-hmm. It was really sweet."

I nodded. I had a hard time looking at her. It was hard to look at anything. I tried taking all my frustrations and anger from the past half hour and pushing them into the pit of my stomach. To hell with my emotions, my ego and pride. Ego. Nothing more than a fickle friend who's in the bathroom whistling loudly with his dick hanging out when you're slugged in the face and need him most.

"Hey," she said and nudged me. "What's the matter?"

I wanted to be quiet, to let it go and kiss Carolyn and hug her and get her laughing and just live in the here and now and not worry about what may or may not reside in each of our respective pasts. But I couldn't. I looked her in the eye, tried to bring lightness to my voice, and asked: "Jimmy called your phone when I came down here. I didn't answer it, but I got pissed off and called him right back."

"Okay," she said.

"He said you guys were still sleeping together."

She guffawed. "Give me a break. I haven't seen him since we got my things."

"Really?"

"Yes, of course. He's called me a bunch of times. I called him back once because he left a message asking what to do with some of the things we left behind."

"What did you leave?"

"Some clothes, dishes, a necklace, a pair of earrings, my bed."

"Did you get them from him?"

"Stratton, I would have told you if I'd seen him. I haven't."

We were both silent as a train rolled by.

"I'm sorry. I had no right to ask, or to check your phone. I'm never really myself on holidays. Kind of missing my mom today," I said.

She kissed me on the forehead. "Of course. You never talk about her. If you want to talk about it, then you know I'm here for you."

"Thank you," I said. "I'll keep that in mind. Now let's go enjoy dinner."

&3&

Carolyn set the table while Gene and I carried everything in. When we were ready Gene rushed out of the apartment, down the stairs, and came back a minute later carrying a dusty bottle of wine.

"Stratton, my boy, you're going to love this."

"What is it?"

"A 1994 Domaine J. L. Chave Hermitage. Been waiting to open this for a long time."

"You're kidding me? That's like a hundred-fifty-dollar bottle, right?"

"Almost double that, actually, but who's keeping track?"

He peeled away the foil, worked the cork out of the bottle, poured three glasses.

"You guys and your wine," Carolyn said, rolling her eyes. "It's crazy how much you spend on it."

"You're in for a treat, darling," I said.

Gene handed us each a glass. I stuck my nose in it, inhaled deeply, pulled it away and gave the glass a swirl, stuck my nose back in.

"Get your nose in there, babe, like this," I said to Carolyn. She did. "Now breathe it in. You smell that?"

"It smells like wine."

"You bet it does. Wine with hints of black currant and smoke and a little pepper," I said. Gene held his glass up and we all clinked and drank. I sighed. A long finish, slightly sweet.

Gene nodded, looked at his glass. "That's what kills the ghost that haunts us all."

"You stealing my lines now, you bastard?" I said.

"It was a good line."

"Of course it is. Took me a hell of a long time to come up with it."

There was enough food to feed four families. We sat and ate and drank and talked for nearly two hours. Carolyn and I cleaned while Gene split the leftovers in half and placed our portions in large freezer bags to take with us. I'd be eating well for days. Carolyn was beginning to slur. She continually giggled though nobody had said anything funny. We went into the living room. Carolyn sat in the recliner and closed her eyes with the glass of wine on her tummy and her hand around its stem. I removed it and set it on the coffee table. Five minutes later she was out cold.

"She's a sweetheart," Gene said. "Other than your anxiety on Friday, how's it going?"

"It's been good so far."

"She has a big heart. I'm sure you know that's a rare find these days."

"I know."

Gene reached beneath the coffee table and removed a wooden box, from which he took two cigars and handed one to me.

"Christ, Gene, you're full of surprises today."

"Don't get used to it. I feel charitable around Christmas," he said. I thought he was pretty damn charitable all the time but I didn't say so, and instead lit the cigar and the two of us sat there smoking and drinking and relishing the fact that neither of us was alone on Christmas.

"How's the book coming?"

"It's not really. But I'm going to start again on the first of the year and write like hell until it's done. A thousand words a day, every day."

"Sounds like a plan. You think you can keep the pace?"

"I'm going to keep that pace even if it kills me. I think I can finish the first draft by March. I'll write at work if I have to, which reminds me that I have to go back tomorrow. God, I hate work, and I've only been at it a month."

"It doesn't get any easier, kiddo. Keep on writing is my suggestion."

"How long have you been retired?"

"Twelve years now. Retired just before my fiftieth birthday."

"Man, it had to be nice to retire that young. Not a day of work for twelve years. I can't even imagine."

"Stratton, my boy, thirty years in the military is like having a job for sixty."

"Did you hate it?"

"Nah, not all of it. Like anything, it had its pros and cons. It allowed me to see the world."

"Where was your favorite place?"

"Have you ever been to Paris?"

"Only through the eyes of Hemingway."

"That's probably my favorite. If you ever get the chance, then go. There's such beauty there that it'll make you weep to be a part of it."

"The city of love, no?"

"It is where I met my wife," he said in confirmation.

"She lived there?"

He shook his head. "She was from Germany, vacationing there with her family. I met her in a café where Rue Bonaparte meets the river. I had been in the city for a month after my last tour of duty," he said and briefly paused. "I did three tours in Vietnam and had no desire to come back to the States after seeing what I did. I was twenty-five. I had gone to that café every morning, just sitting outside drinking coffee and trying my damnedest to forget everything I had just been through. And then one day, alone in the corner, sat the most beautiful blonde I'd ever seen, wearing a long white dress that fell to her ankles." He looked at me and smiled. "Hell, I had just survived the war and knew I was never going back. I had all the courage in the world back then. I walked right up to her and introduced myself. She could hardly speak a word of English, but I sat beside her and we made it work. We mostly just gestured and smiled and winked at one another until we left the café and bought two translation dictionaries, communicating by pointing out words to one another. We both knew right away, no doubt about it. Her family returned to Germany two days later and she stayed with me. Five days after that we got married." He let out a pleasurable sigh. "That was by far the best time of my life. We'd wake up, eat breakfast in bed, and make love all morning, drink some of the best wine in the world, walk along the streets until we were both exhausted and then we'd crash in each other's arms, and in the morning we'd do it all over again. We stayed in Paris for two and a half months, until I had spent every damn dime I had. And if I would have had more money, then we'd have stayed even longer."

I smiled, trying to imagine Gene as a much younger, more brazen man living a dream in Europe, a man falling headlong into the kind of love only the truly lucky ever find.

"What did you do after that?" I asked.

"Reenlisted in the Marines and came back to the States. I got sent to California that time and we stayed there for three years."

We sat through a silence. Then I asked the question and almost immediately wished I hadn't.

"Do you want to tell me what happened?"

He drank what was left of his wine, set the glass upon the table, and just like that all the happiness and smiles of things remembered drained out of him and were replaced with a pervasive sadness cut deeply into the wrinkles across his face and neck.

"You know why I offered this place up to you so quickly, even when you hardly had a penny to your name?"

"No."

"Because I could tell the things you'd been through just by the way you carried yourself, that they were probably pretty damn equal to the things I myself have endured. If you live with pain long enough you learn to recognize it in others."

I stayed quiet, unsure whether he'd give me anything else. But I knew he was right about recognizing pain in others. I had noticed it myself.

"My wife and son were killed in an automobile accident twenty years ago this month. And poof, just like that, everything in my life that I loved was gone," he said. "My son was only ten."

I shook my head. "I'm sorry, Gene."

"Thank you," he said.

I picked at a ball of lint on my sweater, looked at the way the light reflected off the rim of the glass in my hand, and watched Gene flex his jaw while he stared out the window. Then he turned to me and I took a deep breath. I could have told him then, and I wanted to, but I didn't. I'm still not sure why.

"Stratton, my boy, you don't want to go through life the way I have. This shit life is all we have. There's nothing else. Just this one life to do whatever we deem necessary. Nothing, if that's what you choose, like I have. Or everything. We can end it or we can go on, through the sun and the shit, and sometimes it's hard to tell the two apart. We'll be lied to, sacrificed, forsaken, crossed, let down, and betrayed, but if we're lucky, we can be loved, too," he said. He looked at Carolyn, then at me. "And if we're truly lucky, we might learn to love ourselves. That's what life is about, taking the good with the bad and somehow going on. As I'm sure you know by now, there's a certain pride in being shit on and still forging ahead. This life is the best fight we have. The only good fight for some. So don't be like me and give up on it."

"You really think you've given up?"

"In my own way, I have. In your own way, I'm pretty sure you have, too. But don't."

I nodded, wanting to keep talking. But just then Gene lifted himself from the couch and walked into the kitchen.

❧ 4 ☙

I shook Carolyn awake. She opened her eyes and looked around the room, smiling at Gene when finding him on the couch across from her.

"Hi," she said to me. "How long have I been sleeping?"

"About two hours. Come on, let's go downstairs."

"Will you carry me?" she asked, reaching her arms up and around my neck. I grinned and was oddly thrilled for the opportunity. I hefted her up.

"Thank you for dinner, Gene. It was great," she said.

"I'm happy you enjoyed it."

I went down the stairs slowly. Between the two of us, Gene and I had finished two bottles of wine on top of what we had had with dinner. I was pretty drunk, but I was careful with Carolyn and made it back without tripping. I placed her in the bed. She was in that lucid trance between wakefulness and sleep, that place where one is aware of dreaming and can either decide to fall headlong into it or wake and let it dissipate. I undressed her, pulled the duvet out from under her, and covered her with it.

"Mmm. Thank you," she moaned, her eyes closed. She pulled the duvet to her chin, balled up one corner, and wrapped her arms around it.

"You're welcome."

"Are you coming to sleep?"

"I will soon. I'm going to read for a bit."

"Okay."

She sighed, shifted, and then almost in a whisper, said, "I really like Gene. I think he's lonely up there."

I bent over and kissed her forehead "We're all lonely, my dear."

I read for an hour and a half and finished *A Moveable Feast*. When I lay beside Carolyn, I found I couldn't sleep. I kept thinking about Gene and what he had told me of his past. Part of me wished I had told him about the dark side of my own. I suppose I should have been content with having made it through another painful holiday, but I still wish I had opened up to him.

My mind was racing and I gave up on sleep and went back up to Gene's. It was only nine o'clock.

"You have any more of the white paint you used on my walls?" I asked, wanting some thoughtless activity to occupy my mind.

"Yeah, it's in the basement. Why?"

"I want to paint over that plastered hole. It's turning a creamy color and small cracks are showing on the surface."

"Yeah, I was afraid of that. Probably from the vibrations of the trains."

The basement was small, a fifteen-by-ten foot rectangle. Stacked boxes with black marker across the sides, landscaping tools, cans of paint and cleaning supplies, an old rusted bike with flattened tires, twenty or so bottles of wine in a wooden rack. It smelled of mold and was dimly lit so that I had to squint to read the paint labels. I grabbed the one that looked the most like a match to what was on my walls and went back upstairs.

I pulled the desk away from the wall, forced the can open with a butter knife, poured the paint into a pan. I added a thick coat to the plastered hole, stepped away, and could see the cracks still showing. I let it dry for a half hour and then added a second coat. When I finished, it didn't look any better than it had before. I stared at the hole for a long time. The paint was drying unevenly and the spot looked dreadful, maybe even worse. I vowed to buy something that'd cover it. Then I cleaned the brushes in the kitchen sink, took the paint back down to the basement, and returned Gene's keys.

sixteen

THE ALARM RANG AT five thirty on Monday morning, the day after New Year's, which I had off because of the holiday. I hit the snooze button. Carolyn lay undisturbed. I whispered into her ear that it was time to get up. She grunted, snuggled into me, fell back asleep. In reality she didn't have to be up for another hour, but in the few weeks of living together I'd quickly discovered it takes nearly that long for her to finally crawl from bed. I had learned to adjust the alarm accordingly.

I jumped in the shower. Halfway through it the alarm began again. It was still ringing when I finished. I dried myself and shut it off. Carolyn hadn't moved an inch. I dressed, watched the first train roar by while adding to my bag the things I'd need for the day.

I ripped the duvet off Carolyn. She grunted, opened her eyes.

"Hey!"

"It's time to get up."

"Why?"

"Because you have to go to work."

"But it's so cold! Give me back the blanket."

"You have to get up, darling. I'm leaving and you can't oversleep."

"Where are you going?"

"To write."

"Why so early?"

"So I can spend all day writing a best seller that's going to make us rich."

"Mmmm, I like that idea. Now give me back the blanket."

I folded the duvet in half and set it against the far wall, away from the bed. Then I went into the bathroom and started the shower, making sure the water was hot to the touch, which is how Carolyn liked it.

"You're so mean."

"Am not. You have to get up so I can get out of here. The shower is running for you."

"I'm up."

"No you're not," I said and reached out my hand. "Come on, time to get up, my lovely."

"I hate it."

"I hate it, too."

She grabbed my hand and I pulled her out of bed. She blew the loose strands of hair from her face and slouched as she walked to the bathroom, looking crestfallen and glum.

"Hey," I said. She turned and faced me, and I added, "Have a great day."

She walked back and wrapped her arms around me. "You too. Have a great day writing."

"Thanks." I kissed her on the cheek. "I'm sure I'll be here when you get back."

She jumped in the shower. Before I walked out the door I grabbed a sticky note and on it I wrote, *I miss you already.* I left it on the kitchen counter for her to find.

I breathed in the cold air and kept my hands pocketed while I walked. A thousand words, four pages, every day until the book was finished. I wouldn't pretend that everything I was writing was good or the best I could do, but I'd write it all the same. You can't edit what isn't there. Discipline. I'd tattoo it down my arm if that's what it took. Remember what your old wrestling coach used to say: "Talent without discipline is worthless."

I walked in at ten after six just as the café opened. I was the only person there, aside from the two baristas, neither of whom looked any more awake than Carolyn had twenty minutes ago.

I bought a coffee and sat away from the door. I turned my phone off and removed the legal pad, sharpened for the first time all four pencils that'd be my ally in war for as long as they'd last, or for as long as I would. I took a long drink of coffee. Getting started is the hardest part. Write one sentence and go from there. You know the story. You know where it's going, so go ahead and get on with it.

I tried to take every good and bad thing in my life and let go of it all, put all of it on the shelf so I could pick it up later. There was no place for any of it in my story. Let us stop worrying about ourselves. It's Barrack Gray, my protagonist, who we worry about now. It is he who will be hit by the world and try with everything to hit back.

I had a paragraph after twenty minutes. The coffeehouse was still empty. There was something pleasurable about working while most of the world still slept. I had always worked best in the morning, though I didn't anticipate being able to do it much because of my job.

It took another forty minutes to finish the first page. I counted the words in each line and wrote the numbers in the margin and tallied them up and had 357. Two more pages and I'd be done. Then I'd smile for the rest of the day.

I walked outside. The weather was mild but the wind barreled through the streets and the trees shook in the pale light of the coming day. I bounced on the balls of my feet. I could make it another two hours. I went back inside after ten minutes.

It took a long time to get started again, but when I did the words came easily and I kept at it until I had three and a half pages, 1,127 total words. A success by my definition. It was a quarter till ten. It had taken three and a half hours. I hoped it wouldn't take that long every day.

"Take it easy, Stratton. Rushing these things only hinders quality. Remember, patience is a virtue."

Fuck patience, I thought. *I don't have the time for it.*

I jumped off the train on Friday after the shortened week and stopped at a thrift store. Cheaply priced artwork hung in the windows. I perused the paintings, most of which smelled of dust and looked to be from the seventies, but there were a few I liked, one being a panoramic photograph of a placid lake with the front of a rowboat showing in the foreground. It was dusk in autumn, and the surrounding pines at the lake's shore reflected in the calm waters, everything dark, golden, and brown. Everything silent. It was titled *Quiet Places*. A caption along the bottom read, "The quieter you become, the more you can hear." I wasn't sure if it was large enough to cover the hole but I liked it despite its terrible cliché. I bought it for ten dollars and carried it home. Carolyn was sitting on the edge of the bed with her phone to her ear. She bit her lip and looked at me apologetically. I held the picture up. She nodded, smiled approval. I climbed on the desk. The picture was only a foot in height, but three feet wide. It wouldn't quite cover the hole, leaving a slight discoloration at the top and bottom, but not enough to bother me. Plaster skittered down the wall each time the hammer struck the nail. Carolyn stuck her index finger in her free ear to hear the voice on the other end of the line while I worked.

"Fine," she said sternly into the phone. "I'll be there in a half hour." She paused and sighed. "No, it's fine. I'll see you in a half hour."

I finished hanging the picture and sat on the desk with my feet in the chair.

"Where are you going?"

"I have to get my things from Jimmy."

"You're kidding me?"

"No, he's moving back to Iowa next week and it's now or never."

"I'm going with you."

"No, Stratton. I need to go over there alone and talk to him so he'll quit calling me."

"I'll kill the piece of shit."

"Which is precisely why I don't want you to go. I'll be fine. I'll only be there a few minutes."

"I don't trust him," I said. "What if something happens? What if he hits you again?"

"Hey," she said and walked over and took my right hand and massaged open my fingers, then stared at me until I met her eyes, which I was reluctant to do. "It'll be fine. I'll only be gone an hour."

I sighed and shook my head.

"I really like the picture. It's peaceful," she said, then stood and began readying herself. I said nothing and watched her dress, silently scrutinizing her choices, turning suspicious as she pulled on my favorite pair of her jeans, which were faded and tight and made her ass look spectacular. She threw on a nice sweater, then pulled the rubber band from her hair and brushed it in the mirror.

"Why are you getting dolled up?" I asked, and even I could hear the accusatory tone in my voice.

"I'm not," she said, slipping her feet into her shoes, tying them, throwing on her jacket. "Are you going to go write?"

"I doubt it."

"Well, I'll see you in an hour or two then."

I looked at the clock. It read 5:20. "So you'll be home by seven?"

"I should be."

"What do you mean, *you should be*? Either you will or you won't."

"Stratton, I'll be back before you know it." She came over and kissed me on the lips. I didn't kiss her back. "You should go write."

"How are you getting there?"

"The train."

I could feel myself sneering, my face tight and warm. "Are you going to sleep together?" I asked, which was stupidly impulsive but I couldn't help it. I had to ask even though her answer was obvious. My foolish pride ached for reassurance.

"Ugh," she said impatiently. "No, Stratton. I'm getting my things and talking very briefly. I'll be back in two hours."

"Firstly, just a minute ago, you said it would take one hour. Now you're saying two. Secondly, you were supposed to have gotten them when we were there weeks ago."

"Yeah, I know, but it was a little hard to think clearly at the time, okay?"

"It takes a half hour to get there, a half hour to get back. What the hell are you guys going to talk about for a full hour?"

"I don't know, okay? I'm not the one wanting to talk."

"But you're the one going."

She shook her head. "I have to go so I can get this over with. I don't want to do it, either."

"So don't, then."

"Stratton, please stop. I won't be gone long."

I didn't move from the desk when she left, just sat there staring at the door. Nothing about her going felt right. Something was off. I should ignore it. Ignoring it would make me a stronger man, a more trusting one. But then again, what comes to those who coast through life ignoring things, those who let the world come to them without reaching out to it first? Nothing great comes to those who simply wait. Ignoring this isn't going to make me a stronger man, not when something could be done. Being proactive was the way to go. Just like Denver once told me in the bar: "Always be the aggressor. Always. Get on offense and stay there and don't you dare let up. Ever."

I threw on my shoes and jacket and rushed out into the cold and the dark. I hailed a cab and had him drop me off two blocks away from Jimmy's apartment.

I felt tight as I walked to the building and stood on the opposite side of the street. The lights were on, but the windows were still covered with the dirty sheets. I receded into the shadows of the alleyway. I tugged my hat down as far as it would go and pulled the hood of my sweatshirt over the hat. After ten minutes I began to shiver. I walked out to the street and positioned myself between two cars to ease the wind, and then I finally saw Carolyn coming down the street. I crouched on my haunches. She removed her phone and dialed but I was too far away to hear what she said. Jimmy opened the bottom door thirty seconds later. He hugged her and kissed her on the cheek. I burned inside. His words echoed in my ears. *I was nailing her while she was dating somebody else and I'm still banging her now that she's with you.*

Only then did I realize that coming was a horrible idea. The only way it'd turn out well was if Carolyn walked out now, didn't linger inside any longer than it took to grab her things. But I knew she wouldn't. My whole body felt rigid and I tingled in the way of suspecting betrayal from the one you love. My fists were clenched so tightly that my fingernails left crescent-shaped indentations in the palms of my hands.

I couldn't see a thing looking up through the windows. Even if there was movement on the opposite side of the sheets, I didn't think I'd notice. I remained between the cars. I didn't know what to do. People passed and eyed me suspiciously but nobody said a word. I walked to the end of the block, walked back. Five minutes passed.

I crossed the street and tried the bottom door. It was locked. I was desperate, didn't really care any longer about being caught. I could always say it was fear for her safety that had led me there.

I gathered small pebbles into the palm of my hand and stood behind a parked SUV. I hurled the first stone at Jimmy's window. It hit the side of the building. I threw another and it clinked off the window of what I remembered to be the living room. I ducked behind the SUV and watched. Nothing. I threw another and it again hit the window. Nothing. What in the hell were they doing where they wouldn't even look out the window after a stone had hit it?

I was becoming frenzied. I paced. Another five minutes. "Goddamn it," I said. I called Carolyn's phone. It rang twice and went to voicemail, which meant she had hit the ignore button when seeing it was me. I searched the ground for something larger. I was seconds away from pounding on the door and yelling her name. I lifted a piece of concrete that had broken away from the curb and I threw it far harder than I had meant to. It crashed straight through the window. The whole bottom pane shattered, half of the glass falling into the apartment, the other half breaking into smaller pieces on the sidewalk. I lunged behind the SUV. Jimmy and Carolyn both appeared in the window, both alarmed and, thankfully, both dressed. They couldn't see me. Jimmy rushed away. Carolyn stayed and I couldn't sprint away for fear of being seen. She'd recognize my jacket, maybe even the way I moved.

Jimmy charged out of the building door. There wasn't really much I could do, so I stood from behind the SUV and walked to the center of the street. Jimmy stared at me and took a few steps my way. He stopped ten feet short.

"Are you fucking serious right now?"

"You bet I am."

"You just broke my window."

"Sure did, Jimmy."

The sounds had drawn others outside. I felt cornered. I was sure somebody would call the police. Carolyn raced out into the street and walked to me.

"Stratton, what the hell?" she said so that only I could hear.

"I was scared for you."

"Why?"

"Because I don't trust him and you wouldn't let me come. I just tried calling you, and you sent it to voicemail."

"We were only talking up there. Jesus, Stratton."

"I didn't trust him."

She closed her eyes, shook her head, took a deep breath.

"You guys are fucked up," Jimmy said behind her. He turned and walked inside. A siren rang in the distance. I didn't know if it was because of me and I didn't want to stick around to find out.

"We should probably go," I said. "Did you get your things?"

"Goddamn it, Stratton. Why couldn't you just trust me?"

"It wasn't you I didn't trust."

Jimmy appeared in the window and cleared away some of the glass that remained. He disappeared and came back ten seconds later with a box in his arms. He held it out the window and dropped it. Some, if not all, of the dishes broke on impact.

"You guys are both fucked up," he said again, this time from above. "You two deserve each other."

I went to the sidewalk, picked up the box, and began walking.

"You coming?" I asked.

Carolyn shook her head again, looked down at her feet, and followed. We rounded the first corner and hailed a cab.

"I'm sorry," I said. She didn't respond. I grabbed her hand. "I didn't trust him."

"No, Stratton, you didn't trust *me*."

"Bullshit," I said. "He's a lowlife. I've seen what lowlifes can do. My father was one."

Not a word was said the rest of the ride home. Carolyn climbed into bed and kept her back to me. I separated her jewelry from the box and then picked away the shards of porcelain from her clothes. Only one of her dishes remained intact, a white coffee mug reading JOE'S DINER on the side. I folded her clothes, placed them in a pile beside her others, and took the box out to the garbage cans.

Back upstairs Carolyn had removed her clothes and was beneath the duvet. The cat lay in her arms. It was eight. Her right ankle hung over the edge of the bed and the golden ankle bracelet with the heart charm I had bought her for Christmas sparkled beneath the light from the lamp on the nightstand. She had yet to take it off, and seeing it now made me realize that I had been wrong, plain and simple. Worse than that, I knew I had failed her.

"I'm sorry, Carolyn," I said. "I screwed up."

She shrugged, keeping her back to me. "It's fine," she said.

"No, it's not. You're right, I should have trusted you. But I couldn't bear the thought of him hurting you again."

"I know, Stratton."

I climbed into bed with her. She kept her back to me but after a while she turned so that our faces were inches apart. She reached up and rubbed her thumb over my left eyebrow, and then my right.

"What are these scars from?" she asked.

"Fighting."

"The scars over both your eyes are from fighting?"

"Yes."

"From the same fight?"

"No."

"Do you fight a lot?"

"More than I care to admit."

"Have you ever lost any?"

I nodded. "Again, more than I care to admit."

"Why do you fight?"

"Because I'm an angry person."

"You don't seem that angry to me."

"Really?" I asked, not believing her since she'd witnessed both altercations I'd had with her ex.

"Well, maybe sometimes. But mostly you seem cuddly and lovable."

"Give it time," I said. I held up both my hands in front of her face.

"What am I looking at?"

"The scars on my knuckles. I can't let you think that I only get hit."

She took my right hand, turned it over, and studied it.

"There's literally a scar on every single knuckle except your thumb."

"Damn right there is," I said proudly.

"You're crazy," she said. She dropped my hand and placed her head on my chest and draped her right leg over my waist.

"I really am sorry about tonight."

"It's okay," she said. "I understand. We're still new to each other. I just hope you'll learn to trust me."

"I will," I said. "Promise."

seventeen

ANOTHER LETTER ARRIVED IN the middle of January. It was addressed to my Chicago apartment, not rerouted from New York, which meant my father now had my new address. It was a surefire way to put me in a shitty mood.

Most days, Carolyn checked the mail before I made it home, and she would place whatever there was on the kitchen counter, but that day, the letter was the only thing in the box. Had she found it and left it there as if she hadn't? Perhaps. I ripped it in half, walked outside, tossed it into one of the garbage cans, went upstairs. The apartment was empty. Carolyn's shift was supposed to have ended at two, and she should have been home. I called her phone. It didn't ring and went straight to voicemail. I left a message, then called again. Again, straight to voicemail, which I assumed meant her phone was turned off.

I walked around the apartment, surveying the mess she had made that morning—clothes strewn across the floor, covers bunched at the bottom of the bed, the uncapped tube of toothpaste in the bathroom sink. It had taken a few weeks for the two of us to stop being self-conscious around each other, and now that we could be ourselves, the things I had originally viewed as somewhat cute and endearing had quickly become annoying. The bar of soap she always left at the bottom of the shower so that it became soft and mushy; unrinsed dishes left in the sink so that the food hardened and was tough to wash away; the way she never plugged in her phone until the battery died; the way a roll of toilet paper lasted only a day or two whereas I could make a single roll last for months. That isn't an exaggeration. I understand that she's expected to use much more than I do, but if I require a single sheet or two to wipe my own ass, then why did she need half the roll when she peed? Much later, once our level of comfort had grown even more, to the point that we each peed with the door open, I'd watch her with nothing short of amazement. When she finished tinkling she'd take a delicate, albeit misleading grasp of the exposed sheet, and with the force of starting a lawnmower, she'd yank it hard in a backhanded swipe that sent the roll a-spinning. After a good two or three pulls, she'd then ball it all up into a tissue-y mass and wipe twice before dispensing of the entire wad, ninety percent of which (and I'd be willing to wager my life on this) was still dry.

I cleaned Carolyn's mess and checked my phone. No missed calls or texts. I called her again. It still didn't ring and I left another message, then walked upstairs to Gene's. He was clean-shaven, wearing khaki slacks and a starched, white button-down beneath a dark blazer.

"Where are you going?" I asked.

"I have a date in an hour, kiddo."

"You're kidding me?"

"What the hell do you think, I dress like this just to sit alone and read?"

"How did you get a date?"

"How does anyone get a date?"

"Fair enough. Where did you meet her?"

"At Sam's on New Year's Eve. Even kissed her at midnight. Hell, I might even get lucky," he said and nudged me.

I scratched my head. "I feel as though I'm missing something."

"I hate to break it to you, kiddo, but you're missing a lot of things."

"Touché. So why are you dressed now if it's not for another hour?"

"Wanted to make sure I looked good. What do you think?"

I eyed him from head to toe. "I'd sleep with you."

"I bet you would, you bastard."

We walked into the living room. Gene went to one of the shelves and plucked down a book and handed it to me. It was called *A Fan's Notes*, by an author named Frederick Exley. I'd never read it or even heard of it before.

"Been meaning to give this to you. One of my very favorites," Gene said. "It's a book any aspiring writer can appreciate, as it's more or less about an alcoholic madman trying to be a writer himself. Might give you a little shove in the right direction. The man was an amazing writer, and terribly deranged."

"Thank you," I said. "Are you saying I'm deranged?"

"What would give you that idea?" Gene said with a grin.

"Just making sure."

I flipped the book over and read the synopsis on the back. *Sure, why not*, I thought. Since I had gotten serious about writing again, I did in fact yearn for some validation that my own attempt wasn't being done, and besides, in vain, that I wasn't merely staring up the ass of a dead dog with fleas. And besides, I had always found inspiration from books about writers. I tucked it under my arm to take it with me.

"Have you seen Carolyn today?"

"Afraid not. Why?"

I shook my head. "She got off work at two and isn't answering her phone. I don't know where she is. She usually lets me know when she's going to be late," I said, slightly irritated, partly from Carolyn, partly from my father's letter having arrived at my new address, leaving in its wake a bad taste in my mouth. I looked at Gene. He was fidgeting, working his hands together, gripping one and then the other, and it was then that I discovered the chink in Gene's armor. This man, despite surviving three tours of duty in Vietnam and the death of his wife and child, and who appeared calm and confident every time I'd ever been around him, was uneasy in the company of women. Or at the very least, at the prospect of going on a date with one.

"You nervous?" I asked.

"A little bit."

"Really? I thought it'd get easier with age."

"Hell no, it gets harder. I'm sixty-one. I haven't been on a date in three years."

"Well, you look rather dapper. That's half the battle."

"Thank you."

"Ask lots of questions, and listen to her answers. The key to a good date is to let her do most of the talking, and then to react to what she says so that it encourages her to talk more. If she thinks you're interested, she'll relax, grow confident, and be more willing to share."

"You sure?"

"I might be a mess when it comes to women, but I promise you, I know how to date. It's all the other stuff that gets me."

"Spoken like a true optimist."

I laughed. "That's me alright," I said. "At any rate, say as little about yourself as possible. And it's a good practice not to stare at her crotch and drool. Rarely goes over well. I've had problems with that myself."

"I'll keep that in mind."

"Don't point at your own crotch and say 'touch me here.' She might be down with it, but it's too risky on a first date."

"Anything else?"

"Don't tell this joke: What is the definition of an eternity? The time between your orgasm and when the girl finally leaves."

"Ahh. So you don't think misogynistic, sexist jokes are the way to her heart?"

"Probably not. But maybe tell her you think boxing is a barbaric sport that should be abolished."

"You're shitting me?"

"Of course I am. You say that, and she'll think you're a pussy," I said, then I heard a noise in the hall. I rushed to Gene's door and stuck my head out into the hallway, but it was only my neighbor carrying out the trash.

"Damn it," I said. I removed my phone. No missed calls.

"What's the matter?"

"Nothing."

"You worried about Carolyn being out without your knowing where she is?"

"No."

"Bullshit," he said, calling my bluff. "You're a weird kid, Stratton Brown."

"That's certainly true," I said and looked at him. He was still working his hands together. He took a deep breath, lifting his shoulders, and then dropped them.

"Christ, Gene, you're making me nervous just watching you. Make yourself a drink or something."

"I was trying not to drink."

"Well, do. You'll feel better. Just one though. Showing up drunk is another of those things best avoided."

I wished Gene luck and went back down with the book still under my arm. I dropped it on the bed and took out my phone and tried calling Carolyn again. Nothing. I plugged in my phone. Then I sat at the desk and removed the pages I'd printed at work earlier that day. I already had 132 of them.

I read the last paragraph, then tried adding to it but couldn't focus. I reverted back to my old practices in the weeks I'd lived alone before Carolyn moved in, trying to see how many words I could get down between one train ending and the next one beginning. The trains came, the words didn't. I glanced at the door every time I heard a noise, repeatedly checked my phone to make sure I hadn't accidentally silenced it. I was tense and agitated. My father had written; Carolyn was missing. I felt best served to cut the anxiety off at the knees before it snowballed to something else, which I knew it would. I took a Xanax and then paced the apartment waiting for it to take the edge off.

Unlike others, I've never taken Xanax recreationally, or as a warm-up to a night on the town, or for any other reason that went beyond its intended purpose, which was to put the kibosh on mounting anxiety before it became destructive. Xanax, quite predictably, always put me to sleep if I just took one, or knocked me out completely for a minimum of eight hours if I took two. I merely wanted to take a nap, but that didn't stop the question from coming before the pill started working: Where in hell was Carolyn? This right here, this worry, this is why I hate relationships.

I'm still the same person plagued with insecurity and jealousy and the past. I started worrying that we had moved too fast. With the benefit of hindsight, her moving in was the wrong decision. Then I shook my head. Screw hindsight; there is no benefit to it. It's deceptive. Hindsight isn't twenty-twenty because we can never know what would have happened had we chosen otherwise. There's no point of comparison. Every decision we make is the death of a thousand other possibilities, and with that to contend with, who the hell knows what is or isn't the right choice? You can never know anything for sure unless you try.

I undressed and fell into bed and finally started to drift away when the door opened.

"Hey you," Carolyn said. She flipped on the lights.

"Hey," I said, my speech sounding slurred. I lifted my head, squinted up at her. She wore the same black pants she wore every day to work and her green apron was in her hand.

"What's the matter?" she asked.

I shook my head. "Nothing. Where were you? I kept trying to call."

"Did you? I'm sorry. My battery died while I was at work. I had to cover someone's shift for a while. It sucked. Are you okay?"

I shrugged. "I took a Xanax. I'm going to be out cold soon."

"Nooooo," she said and sat beside me. "It's Friday. I want to go do something."

"What do you want to do?"

"I don't know, something. Maybe get a drink somewhere. Or have dinner."

I groaned. "I don't really think going out is the proper move for me right now."

"Stratton," she said in a whine, shaking my arm as though to wake me. "Why did you take Xanax?"

"I don't know. I couldn't get ahold of you, and then I started worrying where you might be, or if something bad had happened. I kept calling your phone because all I really wanted to do was talk to you but it kept going straight to voicemail. And on top of everything else,

I got another letter from my father, just sitting there patiently waiting in the mailbox for me."

She sighed. "Why do you always worry yourself like that?"

"I'm neurotic."

She kicked off her shoes and undressed. I dropped my head back on the pillow.

"You should have called. I was worried."

"I would have but my phone died."

"From the Starbucks phone then."

"Stratton, I don't have your number memorized."

"Well, memorize it then," I said, trying to reclaim a bit of the anger I had had before, but the pill was working, and any anger I found was nothing more than a mouse's squeak from the room next door.

Carolyn stepped into the shower and I closed my eyes. She shook me awake sometime later. She was fully dressed, wearing makeup and looking pretty.

"Where am I?" I asked. It felt as though the bed was spinning.

"In bed, silly," she said.

She grabbed my pants and pulled them up my legs. I lifted my ass so she could work them over my hips. Then she grabbed a shirt at random and pulled it over my head and arms.

"Why are you dressing me?"

"Because you're going to take me out for a drink."

"I am?"

"Yep."

"What time is it?"

"Eight."

I groaned and begrudgingly climbed out of bed. We walked down Clark Street. Or rather, she walked and I stumbled, dizzy, fighting the effects of the pill. It seemed to have hit me harder than one normally would have, and all I really wanted to do was sleep. I paid no attention to where we were and instead focused on putting one foot in front of the other and staying upright. Carolyn kept looking in the windows of the bars, sighing, then walking on. Five minutes later, she stopped.

"Oh look," she said with a grin.

I looked. Without my realizing it she had navigated us to the Lamplighter.

"The place where it all began," I said, opening the door for her. "After you, my queen."

The bar was half full and we sat in the very same seats we had before. Sam, the bartender, recognized us and said hello. He poured us both a drink without us having to tell him what we wanted, a Grand Marnier, neat, for me, a vodka and cranberry for Carolyn.

"Cheers, darling," I said. Carolyn touched her glass to mine and we drank. Then I shook my head.

"What?" Carolyn asked.

"I'm really high on Xanax."

"I thought you were tired."

"I was. Now I'm high."

"I wish you wouldn't worry about me," she said. Her face was blank, but I could tell something was bothering her by the way she stared straight ahead at the mirror behind the bar.

"That's how you know you've lost, you know?" I said, echoing what Gene had said to me the night we had come here.

"What do you mean?"

"When you stare in the mirror like that, that's when you know you've lost."

"That doesn't even make sense, Stratton."

I shrugged. It had made perfect sense when Gene had said it, but without him, I was at a loss for how to explain it. I took a long drink of the Grand Marnier, well aware that no good would come from pouring liquor on top of the pill. I could feel myself teetering on the barstool.

"Carolyn, sweetheart, you have about three minutes before I become a worthless puddle. I suggest you tell me what's going on in that head of yours before that happens. What's the matter?"

"Nothing."

I sighed, dropped my head on the bar, then lifted it back up and could feel the dizziness sink in even further.

"We've been living together for almost a month now. I promise, I know when something is troubling you."

"I just want you to trust me, Stratton. I had to stay a few extra hours at work, and you took a Xanax because you thought I was off doing something else."

I shrugged. "I couldn't get ahold of you."

"I told you, my phone was dead."

I sighed. "Fine. You're right, I shouldn't have worried myself. But it wasn't just because of you. How about we make a deal: You memorize my phone number and call me when you're going to be late, and I'll do my best not to worry about where you are anymore and promise not to take any more Xanax."

"I'll memorize your number, but how about you just trust me?"

"I'm working on it, okay? I'll get there. Trust isn't an easy thing, you know."

I lifted her hand and kissed the back of it. She turned and faced me.

"You really do promise, no more Xanax?"

"No more, at least in regards to your whereabouts," I said, and I was genuine in agreeing to it, but I knew myself, and I wasn't very confident it was a promise I'd keep.

"Good," she said. "It's a deal." We sealed it by toasting one another.

All the Christmas decorations had been taken down from inside the bar, and it wasn't nearly as warm and cozy as it had been on the night Carolyn and I had met. The music pouring from the jukebox was a little blurry. I missed the ambiance created by the strings of Christmas lights; the bar seemed brighter now even though the lighting itself appeared hazy. I continued to sway on the stool.

"Wow, I'm smoked," I said to Carolyn as she ordered another round of drinks.

❧ 2 ❧

We went to several other bars after the Lamplighter, and some hours later, when we finally made it home, Gene was outside throwing trash into one of the garbage cans. I was absolutely shit-canned. My arm was draped over Carolyn's shoulders and she was supporting most of my weight.

"Gene!" I yelled. "You cocksucker! How the hell did the date go?"

He smiled. "Christ, kid, you're wrecked. What happened to you?"

"Been doin' a little boozin'," I said, feeling myself sway.

"I would never have guessed."

"So, come on, man! How'd it go?"

He laughed and shook his head. "Halfway through dinner, she tells me she's married. I stood up from the table and left, right then and there."

"No shit?"

"No shit."

"Jesus, did you at least let her blow you first?"

"Ugh," Carolyn groaned. "Come on, Casanova. Let's get you upstairs."

❧ 3 ❧

I woke at ten the next morning. I felt surprisingly good. I lifted my head and squinted at Carolyn sitting Indian style at the foot of the bed watching the muted television. The screen was fuzzy, more static than picture.

"I think I dreamt of Gene," I said.

She turned. "Yeah? What did you dream?"

"He told me he had a date but the girl was married so he got up in the middle of dinner and left."

"That wasn't a dream. He told us that when we got home last night."

"No shit?"

"No shit."

I dropped my head on the pillow. "Huh. I was even drunker than I thought."

"I believe *smoked* was the word you kept using last night."

I laughed. "I must have been then. I only use that word when I am."

"You always use that word."

"That's because I'm always smoked."

"You're dumb," she said, and turned back to the television.

❦ 4 ❧

There was something else about that day.

When I finally woke up for good, I went to a café to write for a few hours, and when I returned, Carolyn was feeling restless from being pent up in the apartment. It was midafternoon and we went for a long walk with no destination in mind. It was snowing. Despite being from Iowa, Carolyn had the least tolerance for cold weather of any person I'd ever known, and I was certain she wouldn't last long without the refuge of a cozy place in which to warm up.

"Maybe we should stop for coffee?" she said fifteen minutes later, and I smiled at my accurate prediction. We'd been walking south. Her face was red and she had a runny nose. She wrapped her arms around herself as though this might help.

"You cold?" I asked.

"A little."

We entered a café on Diversey, and Carolyn sat on the couch in front of the fireplace while I went to the counter. It was very warm inside. I ordered a regular coffee for myself and a cappuccino, extra froth, for her. By the time I carried them over, she had taken off her jacket and was holding her hands up to the fire. I sat beside her.

"I wish we had a fireplace, don't you?" she said.

"It'd certainly be nice."

Neither of us said much and I stared at the fire feeling the heat coming off the flames. The frothing machine was going at full blast, but over it you could still hear the soft music. I had had a good day of work and with the fire and the instantaneous caffeine buzz, I was feeling very affectionate. I turned to Carolyn. Her eyes were closed, and in the fire's lambent light, her tilted face looked profoundly content. She held the cappuccino in her lap, but when she had taken her last sip, she had stuck her nose in too deeply and on the tip of it hung a spot of froth she was unaware of. She felt me watching her and slowly turned toward me, looking cute and innocent. Her cheeks were still red. I was already smiling, and the second her eyes bore into mine, a shiver ran up my spine. Butterflies flittered about in the pit of my stomach. I reached over and wiped the froth away with my thumb. I kept my hand against her cheek, and she pressed her face against it, watching me through the tops of her eyes. I could see the fire dancing within them.

"I love you," I said.

A tender grin played across her lips. "I love you, too," she replied.

It was the first time either of us had said it. And I couldn't stop smiling.

eighteen

I was the smallest kid in the seventh-grade class, weighing a whopping seventy-four pounds and still waiting impatiently for puberty. In the fall they called all the boys into the cafeteria to tell us about winter sports. The wrestling and basketball seasons both began in a month. Though my friends were divided, there was never any doubt which of the two I'd choose.

After school, I found my mother at the dining room table. Her legs were crossed and she held a cigarette in the fingers of her right hand.

"How was school?" she asked.

I sat beside her. "It was good. They went over winter sports with us today."

"Yeah? And what do you think?"

Just then my father walked through the door. His face was rigid, brows crinkled together. He dropped into the nearest chair and began working his dirt-covered boots off, pushing down on the heel of one with the toe of the other. He sighed, said, "Work is really fuckin' up my world." It was his line.

"Most of my friends are playing basketball—"

"You're not playing basketball," he interrupted.

We both looked at him.

"I know," I agreed, but he felt inclined to give his reasons why, anyway.

"Basketball is for pussies and you're too short. You're tough enough to wrestle."

My mother shrugged. "He's right."

He got his boots off and tossed them on the mat beside the door. His days in a factory were behind him and he now worked construction. It was as good a setup as he could hope for, seven months of work through summer and fall followed by five months of unemployment during winter.

"Of course I'm right. You're an ass kicker, just like your old man. Discussion closed," he said, stood, retired to the bathroom to shower.

I smiled at her. "I was going to wrestle, anyway."

"I know, Bubby," she said with a wink.

❧ 2 ☙

Jason Daniels, my best friend, was slightly bigger than me. He had sandy blond hair and pale skin and wore glasses so thick that when he took them off, his eyes appeared small and beady, drawing laughs from whoever was around to witness it. At the age of twelve, he knew more about sports than any other person I knew. When we had a question, he almost always fired back with the right answer. We called him, creatively enough, "The Answer" because of it. We had played baseball together for years and, as he was no taller than me, there was little doubt he would wrestle as well, just as his older brother had before him.

They weighed us all in on the first day of practice, writing our names and weights on a chart that hung on the wall beside the scale. They kept track of our weight before and after every practice. The lightest weight class was eighty pounds, which meant I'd be outweighed by six pounds every match I wrestled. Six pounds is nothing to a heavyweight, but it's a lot to a lightweight.

We were all nervous that first day; few knew what to expect. You could tell the ones who did know because they were already wearing wrestling shoes—usually because they had an older brother, such as Jason, who had wrestled before—while most of us wore tennis shoes. Those completely in the dark wore to practice what they'd worn to school.

Our coach was a slightly overweight fifty-year-old who taught shop at the high school. Every day, he wore the same pair of black nylon shorts that were nearly pulled to his chest, so tight that we could see his balls on each side of the permanent camel toe no less than an inch deep. He carried himself as though the world conspired against him and his only defense was profanity, which he used constantly. He had graying hair at his temples, was always squinting though he wore no glasses, and had a ruddy complexion that gave the appearance of high blood pressure. None of us would become close with him, but in his own way he was endearing to us all.

He gave a brief tutorial in the locker room. In total there were twenty-nine of us for fifteen weight classes. He expected that by the end of the week, he'd be left with only twenty, twenty-two at the most. Wrestle-offs would be the Tuesday before our first match, which was a month away on a Thursday. There was one other person in my weight class, and I knew there was no way he could beat me even though I knew next to nothing about wrestling. Heart and determination had to count for something.

As the coach passed out equipment, I leaned over and whispered in Jason's ear.

"How much did you weigh?"

"Eighty-five," he said.

"I'm still going to screw you up."

"Maybe after I screw yer momma," he snapped back. I laughed. The coach glared at me.

"What the hell is so funny?"

"Jason said he's going to screw my mother."

"And you thought that was pretty goddamn humorous, huh?"

I nodded, drunk with spastic energy to get on the mat and do whatever it was we'd be doing. "Yeah, because he doesn't realize my mom doesn't go for blonds."

"Your dad is blond," Jason argued.

The coach nodded. "Okay," he said. "We'll see if you're both still laughing after running twenty laps after practice."

Over the years, I'd lost none of my fiery nature, not a single ounce of piss and vinegar. After I had learned to fight and thus acquired the confidence such knowledge brings, I think I'd grown even more restless. The problem was that I no longer had an outlet for my natural aggression after the fight with Donny Smith. Sure, there was still the occasional scuffle, but they were hardly fights, always broken up immediately after starting, and I believe that was half the reason for my eagerness that day; I was certain I'd found the outlet the heavy bag still hanging from my bedroom ceiling no longer provided.

That first day was mostly boring, full of instruction, that is, the basics of a match, how points are scored, what's legal and what isn't, neutral, top, and bottom positions, and so forth. At the very end of practice, however, we learned a single leg takedown. It was a start, and already, after learning just one move, I was in love.

Before that day, which is to say, before wrestling, my greatest worldly concern revolved around a constant assault on my own penis while lustily gazing at the pictures in *Hustler* magazines I'd bartered from older brothers of close friends. But on that day, I'd found something those spread-eagle, sly-smiling girls couldn't compete with, at least not for the next couple of years. The inherent competitiveness, the discipline I knew it'd take to be successful, the strength of mind and body, the necessity of endurance and balance, raw purity, the fact that it was an individual sport and ultimately all the glory or all the blame would rest on my shoulders and my shoulders alone, ignited such passion that I craved desperately to know everything at once, up front, but yet I knew it'd take a long time at a slow pace. That was the justification I had made up in my mind back then, but really I think it was much simpler than that: Wrestling was the first thing I was certain I could be good at. And I was ready. I even smiled during the extra twenty laps after practice, which turned into thirty when our coach thought we were sandbagging it, smiled even when I thought Jason might vomit.

❦ 3 ❧

Wrestling is repetition, drilling the same move over and over until it becomes a reflex, until it becomes instinct. That is how you learn and how you become good. You do it and you have faith that you're getting better. It's hard to gauge success in the practice room. All you can do is hope your effort pays off. If it doesn't, then there's no one to blame but yourself. If it does, then there's a whole heap of people to thank. In this way, wrestling is like writing.

Jason and I were drill partners from that very first day and would be for the rest of our careers. We learned the sport together and would always walk out onto the mat one right after the other for six straight years. In that time I'm certain I hit no fewer than 6,437 low singles on him in the practice room, probably wrestled a minimum of three thousand matches. I won most of them, but he wasn't without his victories, too.

❦ 4 ❧

A week before our first match, the coach ran whistle drills for the top and bottom positions. Jason was down; I was up. Drilling stand-ups as a team. The room would fall silent, and after the top person assumed the position, the coach would blow the whistle and the bottom person was to explode to his feet and try to escape. All twenty-four wrestlers who remained on the team, or twelve pairs, burst up at the same time. The key was for the bottom person to anticipate the whistle, to rush up in the fraction of a second between the ref's lips puckering and his cheeks expanding but before any sound escaped. The top person, for this drill, wasn't allowed to watch the whistle and had to react to the bottom person's movement. If he escaped, the top person had to run one lap after practice. If he didn't, the lap went to the bottom man.

"Goddamn it, Lincoln, my grandmother could hold you down and she has an artificial hip!" the coach snapped at one of our teammates. "Stand up so that a fuckin' tank couldn't hold you down, all of you, you hear me?"

Everyone got down again.

"Okay, top man on," the coach said.

I got on, placed my left hand on Jason's elbow, my right arm around his waist with my hand on his navel. The room completely silent, all anticipating the whistle, ready to fight for twenty seconds. Before it blew, however, I removed my hand from Jason's gut and rammed my thumb straight up the crack of his ass. He yelped and lurched forward as though diving for a ball. He landed on his side and looked back at me with a hurtful expression.

"Daniels, what in the fuck are you doing!?" the coach screamed.

"Nothing, sir."

"That had to be the ugliest goddamn stand-up I've ever seen! You didn't even stand. It was like you were diving straight ahead for pussy. Do you see pussy anywhere in this gym, Daniels?"

"No, sir."

"Christ, that was hideous! Just for that, everyone here gets five extra laps."

The room groaned. I tried with everything to suppress my laughter. Thankfully my face was already red from the workout.

"Well then, get back down. Shit, don't let me see that again. I'm liable to forfeit the whole goddamn match next week."

"Yes, sir."

He got back down, and I assumed the top position while still trying not to laugh.

"You're a dick," Jason whispered to me.

❦ 5 ❧

The day before our match, we received our warm-ups and singlets. I took both home, put on the solid black singlet, and stood in front of the bathroom mirror admiring myself.

"Come out of there and let me see," my mother yelled.

"You sure you don't want to wait till tomorrow?"

"Yes, I'm sure."

I walked from the bathroom. My mother gasped. I flexed my right arm, then got into my stance, made a mean face, and growled. She smiled, eyes full of pride.

"My money's on you," she said.

"Damn straight it is," I replied and pointed at her. She burst into laughter.

That night she made a big dinner of spaghetti and pork chops, mixed vegetables, applesauce, garden salad with Italian dressing, and a tall glass of milk. My father arrived home as I was setting the table. He removed his boots and sat.

"Wow, this looks wonderful. What's the occasion?"

"Today's nutrition provides tomorrow's strength," I said, reciting the exact phrase our coach had used earlier in the day.

He nodded. "Of course, of course. Well, enjoy eating meals before matches while you can. As you get older, especially in high school, you'll probably have to cut a little weight."

We dug in and started eating.

"So you ready for tomorrow?" he asked.

I nodded. "You bet."

"Nervous yet?"

"Nope."

"You will be."

He was right. When I woke the next morning, a slight nervousness had settled in my gut and grew as the day wore on. Most of the other students were coming—friends, acquaintances, girls who I had crushes on and who I had, at one point or another, masturbated to. I grew more and more jittery, and an hour before the match, standing in line for weigh-ins, I was scared shitless. Jason stood behind me with a blank stare that I knew meant the same. They weighed in both teams together, by weight class. I was the first person to step on the scale. I'd also be the first match wrestled. I weighed 74.5. My opponent weighed exactly 80. He was the team's eighth-grade captain. That didn't help my nerves, though I wasn't impressed by the look of him. He was an inch taller than I was and somewhat lanky with shaggy, dark hair and a pimply back. I noticed immediately that he had armpit hair, which made me more nervous than anything else as I had none of my own. Then our team dressed together and sat in the locker room beneath the gymnasium while the other team warmed up first. Most of us were silent. Then our heavyweight lifted his leg and ripped a fart that echoed off the locker room walls and made us all laugh, assuaging a bit of the collective anxiety we were all feeling.

Our middle school gym was small—half the size of a normal one— but when our team ran into it, the crowd had packed the bleachers and made the gym appear even smaller. Everyone was there—even people who had no children of their own—standing and yelling when we ran around the outer circle of the wrestling mat and warmed up. I spotted my parents immediately, front and center, and beside them sat four or five of the men I recognized from the bar. I hadn't seen most of them in a long time. The King was there, as he would be for most of my matches during all six years, and beside him sat Ray Scanlon, who years before had told me the three keys to a happy life. My mother flashed "I love you" in sign language. My father gave me a thumbs-up.

When we finished warming up, the other team came back and they lined us up on opposite sides of the mat and announced each name. My opponent's name was called first, and he walked out and waited for me in the center of the mat, which is where I met him when they called my own name next. I shook his hand and walked off. The crowd clapped but I could hear my mother yelling loudest. I could only imagine how loud she'd be during the match.

Jason walked off after shaking his opponent's hand and slapped me five while I stripped down to my singlet.

"Whip his ass," he said.

I nodded, waiting for all the names to be called. My stomach was full of lead; my hands were shaking. Breathing heavily, sweating. I stared at the ground, then looked at my parents. My father watched the other wrestlers being announced but my mother was watching me. I could tell she was just as nervous as I.

The referee and captains from each team met in the middle of the mat. I had no idea what they were doing out there. The ref flipped a double-sided disk, red on one side, green on the other, and some decision was made. Then our captain walked off and my opponent stayed. My name was announced again and I stepped onto the mat and walked to the center where he stood waiting. The room was spinning. I wasn't at all sure I was breathing. Nonetheless, I shook my opponent's hand. And the ref blew the whistle.

I was heavy on my feet, a product of nerves and inexperience. I wasn't low enough. First line of defense: head. Second line of defense: hands. My head was too high, hands too heavy. My opponent shot in, grabbed hold of both legs, and scored two points by taking me down. We rolled out of bounds. I rushed back to the center and got down. *Anticipate the whistle, just like practice.* I raised my head, saw my father lift both his thumbs in an upward motion. Then I looked at the ref as my opponent climbed on. I exploded up in that split second before the whistle blew. I was quick and scored a point for an escape. I felt lighter now. Everything faded away, and I forgot about the nerves and the crowd, though I could still hear my mother and the collective sighs and gasps as each of us took errant shots. We ended the period in a tie-up. He was leading, two to one.

For the second period, my opponent had the choice of top, bottom, neutral, or defer. He chose down. I tried like hell to keep him there, to turn him to his back, but I eventually got too high and he escaped, scoring another point. There was little time left, and in my desperation to score before the period ended, I took a bad shot. He caught me in a front head-lock and windmilled me around, scoring another takedown right before the period ended. I looked at the scoreboard. I was losing, five to one.

It was my choice for the third period. I wasn't really tired. I looked at my opponent. He was bent at a ninety-degree angle with his hands on his knees, struggling to breathe. His face was red, sweat-covered. I felt certain he didn't have the strength or endurance to hold me down.

I got into the down position and lifted my head. I saw my parents, saw the others from the bar who had come to cheer me on, saw the entire crowd. Then I looked at the ref. *Anticipate the whistle*, I thought to myself. My opponent must have done the same because he picked my ankle and thrust me forward as soon as I tried to stand. I was flat on the mat. He worked my arm into an arm bar but I pulled it free and struggled back to my base. I tried standing again but he forced me back down.

One more minute. That's what my mother yelled. I tried another stand-up without success. Then I realized he wasn't trying to turn me; instead he kept his arm tightly wrapped around my waist pretending to try. He only wanted to run out the clock, and in sitting on the lead, he had gotten careless, allowing his elbow to drop.

I clamped it tightly with my right arm and turned into him as hard as I could. A barrel roll. It was a chump move, strictly for suckers, and yet I could feel the momentum shift. I couldn't believe he had become that careless. He went all the way over and landed flat on his back. I followed through and trapped him there. The ref yelled, "Two points, reversal." Then I heard him counting back points. The whole gym erupted. My opponent tried bridging off his back but I squeezed him as tightly as I could, lifting his head and going for the pin. I couldn't remember the score, didn't know if I'd win once back points were added. But I knew damn well I wasn't letting him up. Then the buzzer sounded. I rolled off and stared up at the ref. He held up three fingers to the scorekeeper. I looked at the scoreboard as the points were added. The final score was six to five, me. I pumped my fist as I stood and looked over at my mom. She was jumping up and down and yelling, her arms raised in celebration. Relief flooded through me. I had won. My very first match, and I had won it in dramatic fashion.

I shook my opponent's hand. The ref raised my arm. I walked off the mat as Jason's name was announced. I slapped his hand. He looked terrified.

"Now it's your turn to whip some ass," I said.

I was shaking from the adrenaline, sweating, completely out of breath.

But I had never felt so good in my entire life. I looked at my parents, and both were looking at me. My mom winked, Dad gave another thumbs-up and nodded approvingly. I dressed and scanned the crowd, seeing my classmates I had yearned desperately to impress. I couldn't wait for school the next day. I looked across the mat to the person I had beaten. He was slouched in his seat, catching his breath. Then I looked at the mat. I yelled for Jason but my yells were in vain. He was pinned before the first minute expired.

nineteen

AT THE END OF February the workload had worn me to a nub. In addition to my job, I worked on the book every night when I got home. It took everything I had to keep going. I wasn't tired of the story, or even the writing itself. Quite the contrary. I was tired of working eight passionless hours and then coming home to write for another three, four, sometimes five, tired of waking at five fifteen after going to sleep past midnight. Same shit, day in, day out. All I wanted to do was come home and fall straight into Carolyn's arms, and of course that was the whole point of finishing the book, to make that very idea a reality. I felt the possibility of this life, and in the way I had idealized being with women I adored when I was younger, I knew that any other life that strayed from this would feel like prison.

When I wrote, my mind wandered. I thought of everything to keep from starting. And eventually I'd picture Carolyn sitting in our shitty little apartment, happy to be there, to be with me. During the times I wasn't overly insecure or in the throes of a bout of jealousy—bouts that were becoming more and more common—I felt an intense desire to give her the life I thought she deserved, the life we talked about during the late nights when neither of us felt like sleeping. I wanted to give her the things she never had. She deserved that brand of happiness. That's how I'd start, telling myself that I'd finish this book and sell it and we'd finally live this idealistic dream we both created. To hell with the odds stacked against us.

I worked late every night the first week of March. The company's biggest book of the year was coming out, and overtime was required from all employees to finish it. On Friday I didn't get off the train until after seven. It was freezing out but the snow had melted the week before and the ground was dry. Gene stood outside gathering broken limbs and detritus that had blown into the small plot he called a yard. There were gaping holes in the apartment where entire sections of the vinyl siding had been ripped away.

"Hey kiddo, how goes it?" he asked.

I shook my head. "Work is really fuckin' up my world," I said, and then stopped dead in my tracks. My breath caught in my throat. My father's words, what he had always said to justify being an asshole.

Gene looked at me as I stood frozen in silence. "What?" he asked.

"Nothing."

I dropped my bag and helped him pick up the trash, but I did so absently because the only thing I could think of was my father's words I had so casually repeated. Work didn't affect me the way it did him. Just because I had repeated one stupid thing he always said didn't mean I was becoming him. Not even close. I wasn't my father. I was nothing like him.

"What the hell are you doing?" Gene asked.

"What do you mean?"

"You're poking at the same spot on the ground with that stick."

I shrugged and, with the end of the stick, lifted a used condom that lay stiff in the grass and held it up for him to see.

"This yours?" I asked.

"What do you think?"

"It's sure as hell not mine. These things went out of style in the eighties."

Gene laughed. "Well it looks like we have ourselves some kind of mystery then."

I dropped it into the garbage can. We worked quietly for a time. Gene raked while I picked up what little was left and tried taking my mind away to some benevolent place, but of course my father's words were the only thing I could think about.

"You okay?" Gene asked again.

"Yeah, I'm fine. What happened to the siding?"

"Tore it down. Going to have a crew come in here and fix up this old wreck of a building."

"What are you having done?"

Gene studied the building with his hands cupped over the rake's rounded handle. "Give it a facelift, and fix all the broken parts. New roof and siding, maybe have all the windows replaced. Make the place look respectable, or at least try to keep the piece of shit from falling down on us."

"Nice," I said, loving the idea of windows that'd reduce the noise of the trains.

"So how's the book coming?"

"Ugh. I'm burned out, Gene. I don't think I can keep going at this pace. I need a break in the worst way, especially with my current schedule. I worked fifty-one hours this week."

"Sure, you can keep going."

"It's making me stressed and irritable as shit. I don't know how Carolyn puts up with me." I sighed. "I'm getting pretty close, though. Just don't think I can go much further without taking a break."

"Eh, you can always go further than you think you can. You just need to discover what gives you that extra push."

❧ 3 ❧

I was bothered all night by my father's words, and I moped around the apartment until Carolyn came home. I was wide awake when she walked through the door, though I pretended to be asleep. When she fell asleep herself, I was still awake, and I stayed that way for hours before finally passing out.

I woke early the next morning and walked to my usual café. The writing was a bust. I got the words down, but they were garbage, hardly cogent, nothing more than the rambling thoughts of a troubled neurotic, most of which I'd later delete.

I was writing the last third of the book, maybe the last quarter. When I flipped through all the pages, I couldn't believe how many there were—over two hundred of them. I was certain the book would be under three hundred. A year of my life, this was its equivalent on paper, the pages filled with a story that came from the heart, one loosely based on my little hometown of Spencer and the people I still remembered from there, and maybe the book would be worse because of it. But the story had occupied my mind for a while, and I had to tell it for no other reason than to be done with it.

I gave up at noon and walked home. Carolyn was showered, dressed in a red sweater and dark jeans, standing at the window looking out. She turned and could see that the day's work had been hard. She walked across the room and hugged me.

"I love you," she said.

"Love you, too." I dropped my bag on the floor beside the desk. "You going somewhere?"

"I feel like going downtown. I dunno, walk down Michigan and shop a little. Do you want to come?"

I dropped face-first into the bed. "Oh darlin'. I'm tired and cranky and the weather outside can gargle my nutsack. Going downtown is the last thing I want to do."

"Pleeeeeeeeease."

"Babe, I'm in Krumsville right now," I said, and remembering Krumsville nearly made me smile. I hadn't thought of it in years. It was part of the interior language of a relationship I'd had after college with an ill-tempered, irrational blonde named Marcie. She was from Pennsylvania, and on an idle weekend, we rented a car and drove two and a half hours from New York to her little hometown of Frackville, passing along the way a highway sign reading KRUMSVILLE. The name struck me as dispiriting and forlorn, and all I could picture was a large, furry creature wearing an equally large frown, and from that point on, Krumsville became a cutesy part of our secret dialogue, meaning I'm not feeling well today, that I'm a little down but don't worry I'll be better soon, but please be gentle in the meantime. Uttering the word always made us feel better, if only marginally. But of course our relationship couldn't be sustained by sweetly optimistic adjectives alone, and in the end we parted ways, as I have with many others. People enter our life and then they leave it, and once we reach a certain age it becomes a question of sustainability. Are we gaining as many people as we're losing? Because we're always losing people.

"Come on," she said, almost in a whine. "I'll buy you lunch."

We took the train down to Michigan Avenue. We held hands and weaved through the hordes of tourists, most of whom stood smack-dab in the middle of the sidewalk gazing up at the various buildings, forcing us to walk around them to get by. The sun shone brightly in the cloudless sky, giving the appearance of summer, but the cold and wind said otherwise, though neither had dissuaded the tourists from coming in droves.

"Any place in particular?" I asked.

"Nope. Just want to walk."

We started by entering a bookstore for coffee and stayed long enough to find Hemingway so I could thumb through a few books and read Carolyn some of my favorite passages. She went along with it, helping lift a portion of the morning's bad feelings, but when we walked outside, the pervasive crowds brought it all right back.

We stopped in clothing stores, a store that sold cologne and perfume, a chocolatier, a lingerie store. Carolyn sifted through pairs of panties and bras until I had to leave. Throughout my life I've always had trouble maintaining any degree of civility in the presence of women's panties. Even when they're flat and lifeless on a store table, the sight of them incites an increased heart rate so that I can feel my pulse in my peter. And when there are other women around, especially those of the attractive variety, delicately holding a particular pair in their slender fingers to feel the quality of the fabric . . . Forget about it. It's just too much.

She dragged me in one store, then another, then another. I felt hot, my patience wavering. We ended up in a jewelry store and Carolyn tried on a pair of diamond studs. They looked beautiful on her. I checked the price. Six hundred dollars. She took them off and handed them back and we left.

"One day we'll be able to afford earrings like that," I said.

"I don't care if we're ever able to afford them," she replied, leaning over and kissing me on the cheek. I didn't believe her for a minute.

We entered a store advertising summer sales and Carolyn tried on two dresses.

"I think I like this one better," she said, holding up a somewhat trashy floral print with a liberal back, so short that whoever sat across from her would see her crotch every time she crossed her legs. The fabric was thin and I was sure it'd be rendered transparent by the glare of a bright light behind it. Carolyn seemed oblivious to this and it reminded of the time when, a month or so after she had moved in, she undressed and plucked from her pile of clothes a black lace halter she thought looked provocative, but to me made her look cheap and tawdry for the sole reason that it was something I imagined Jimmy would've loved. As far as I knew, he had bought it for her himself. How many times had Carolyn modeled it for him in the exact way she did for me? No man wants to see a woman he loves in something so intimate as lingerie he's certain she's worn for another. It doesn't matter how sexy it looks on her. Actually, the sexier she looks the greater the jealousy, and I burned with it that day and asked her to take it off, after which she turned sullen and we didn't even make love.

"Yeah? How come?" I asked.

"It's pretty."

"Okay," I said.

"Do you not like it?"

I shrugged. "It's not that. I just think you look prettier in the blue."

She put on the blue dress again and twirled for me. It really did look great on her, and I'm not just saying that because it was longer and covered more, but rather it made her look graceful; it was a dress I couldn't imagine her wearing before we started dating. I knew she had nothing like it at home. She bought it. I carried the bag outside. My feet hurt from walking and my back was stiff from sitting all morning at the café. Carolyn could sense my agitation and dragged me into a restaurant on Ohio.

"How are you guys doing today?" the server asked in a fake falsetto and a surfeit of enthusiasm.

"Good," Carolyn said.

"Great! Well, my name's Jimmy and I'll be taking care of you guys today. Can I start you out with something to drink?"

Carolyn bit her lip and looked at me with a face full of concern. Though we had gotten into plenty of arguments over her ex in the months we'd been together, and while certain reminders of her past still bothered me most days, I would have been fine then if I only had the server's name to contend with. But then there was Carolyn's fearful veneer to go with it, staring at me as though she expected me to be riled, and maybe even hoped for it. I sighed and asked for a Grand Marnier neat while Carolyn ordered a soda. I was already tense from walking the length of Michigan Avenue, but by assuming that something as simple as meeting a man named Jimmy would incite within me the petulance of an irritable child, Carolyn caused my tension to grow.

"Jimmy," I said with disgust.

"Stratton, please don't."

"Carolyn, I don't give a shit that the server's name is Jimmy," I said, which might have been true at first, but hearing the name roll off my tongue made me realize I was wrong. I suddenly did care.

I glared across the table, and seeing Carolyn sit cross-legged in a dainty way as though emulating how she believed a *lady* was supposed to sit suddenly brought to mind crisp images of her ex-boyfriend, a tattoo-covered, thugged-out douche bag with a pencil 'stache, banging my girlfriend in every square foot of their filthy little apartment. We had never once talked about her past sex life—and by this I mean the actual details of it (not that I didn't want to know, because some part of me—the masochistic side, perhaps—truly did want to know)—or her relationships before me, but in my mind the images I saw were as real as the cold and the wind outside. So vivid that I could almost hear the way Carolyn must have moaned beneath him. I couldn't shake the damn things away, and they kept coming, the two of them going at it in bed, in the shower, on the floor. Why did her past even matter? What about my own? Surely hers couldn't be as bad as mine. But it didn't matter, and that was the worst part. I could have slept with a thousand women instead of just twenty-one and I'm certain these same thoughts would still drive me insane.

"Are you okay?" Carolyn asked.

"Yes."

She reached across the table and placed her hand atop mine. "Hey," she said, and shook my hand until I looked at her. "What's the matter?"

I stayed silent, making one final attempt to push the images away. But they refused to leave, clinging to me as tightly as a cat clings to the upper branches of a tall tree when you try pulling it free.

"What was it? I mean, really, what the hell was it that attracted you to him?"

She closed her eyes and shook her head.

"Why, Stratton? Why does it even matter? I had a relationship before you, big deal. God only knows how many you had before me."

"What was it?" I asked again, this time with such calm intensity that I hardly recognized the sound of my own voice.

She stared down at the table. "What do you want me to tell you? I'm not going to sit here and apologize for dating somebody before I even knew you. He was a nice boy from my hometown and I fell in love with him and then I fell out of love. He wasn't always the way he is now."

Hearing Carolyn admit that she loved him did nothing to assuage my anger; it only made it worse. "Are you still talking to him?"

"No, Stratton, I'm not. I've told you that a hundred times already. How many times are you going to ask me?"

Our waiter returned. He placed our drinks on the table and, sensing the tension, quickly left. Carolyn stared at me. I lifted my drink and took it down in one big gulp.

"I don't care about him anymore. I don't. All I care about is you. But I don't understand why you keep pushing me away with this shit."

Her eyes turned watery and she dabbed at them with her napkin. I remained silent. I was being cruel, of course, and I knew it, for I wanted the very tears she had just dried. I needed them, and for no greater reason than to feel the reassurance that words alone couldn't provide. I've witnessed in others the ability to seek approval without seeming needy or insecure, but I've never mastered it myself. My problem is that I sulk and turn mopey, so instead I learned to become mean. It took me a long time to figure this out about myself, and I certainly didn't understand it then, in the restaurant. But that's life; it only even makes sense when looked at backward.

She lifted her hands and slapped them down on her thighs. "It helped make me who I am, Stratton. It made me appreciate so much more what I have with you now. That's all I can say."

I shook my head, and even though anger still lurked on my side of the table, the images had stopped. I was still upset, but salvaging lunch seemed like a faint possibility then. I even unrolled my linen napkin and draped it across my thighs. Then Jimmy returned and asked if we were ready to order. I motioned to Carolyn.

"I'm not ready yet," she said, leading Jimmy to walk away. And then she bore into me, her eyes filled with such ferocity that they lifted me up and hurled me well beyond my original point of irritability. My anger not only returned, but in reaction to Carolyn's defiance, it had grown stronger, bringing back all the images that had riled me so badly in the first place.

"I don't want to keep defending myself over my ex. I never ask about your past. I don't even mention the letters from your father. Everyone has a past. Everyone wishes they could change certain aspects of it. Everyone makes mistakes. I'm sick of being beaten up over mine. It's like you're trying to punish me for it."

"Oh give me a break. You act like I bring it up every goddamn day."

"You do!" she said in the whiny, high-pitched voice she always used when angry.

"Well, Carolyn, if that's how you feel, then fuck you," I said, and without another word, I stood and threw my napkin onto the table. She didn't try stopping me, which is of course what I had wanted, and instead sat silently in her chair, giving me no choice but to swipe my jacket and leave.

I only vaguely knew how to get back to the train. I walked up Ohio, turned down Wabash. My phone rang. It was Carolyn. I hit the ignore button and turned it off. Five minutes later, I turned it back on and checked my voicemail. She hadn't left a message. I turned it off again, found the train, went down the stairs and waited in anger.

All the seats were taken when the train arrived. I turned my phone back on but I was underground and wouldn't emerge for ten or fifteen minutes, which frustrated me further. I remembered a fight my parents once had when my mother still worked at the bar. My father was home and she had called. I wasn't sure what was happening on her end of the line but my father was screaming into his, then he told her to go fuck herself and slammed down the phone. She called right back and he ripped the phone from the wall to silence its maddening ring. Five minutes later, after he had calmed a bit, he tried fixing it but he couldn't, because it was broken. Then he started cursing the busted phone as though he had nothing to do with it himself.

I kept a tight grip on the metal pole the entire way back. The train resurfaced and I checked my messages. Nothing. When I returned, Gene was in the yard again, rake in hand, looking up at the building.

"What are you doing?" I asked.

"Trying to figure out what I'm going to have done," he said. "What's up with you?"

I told him about the fight and how I'd left Carolyn sitting at the restaurant table.

Gene shook his head. "Who gives a shit about her past? We all have one."

"I don't care," I said.

He guffawed. "Okay, well, here's what we'll do then. You go down there and break up with Carolyn, and when you get back, we'll walk down to the middle school and scope out all the twelve-year-olds. We'll find you a nice young one with no past at all."

I looked at him, then dropped my head and stared at the ground.

"Piss off," I said.

Gene snorted. "Let me give you a little advice, Stratton. Something I'm sure you already know but for some reason have yet to accept. The woman you want, the perfect one you seem to be looking for, she doesn't exist. She doesn't exist and she never has. So I suggest you stop looking and love what's standing right in front of you, which is a girl who happens to love you, and you're damn lucky to have her, too," Gene said, and then he bent his head and went right back to raking. "Or don't," he added. "But you'll regret it when she's gone."

I walked upstairs and took a Xanax and then paced the apartment waiting for Carolyn to come home. I knew she would. That's the beauty of living with someone, knowing they always had to return. I just didn't know how long it would take her, but I received that answer twenty minutes later, and by then, the pill had kicked in and all the fight had left me. I wanted to still be angry, but I knew my earlier argument was an untenable one and there was no anger to be found.

Carolyn's eyes were red and I felt bad for what I had done, but I wasn't in the mood to tell her so, or to apologize. If need be, then I'd just shut down and retreat into myself, certain that she'd concede if I held out long enough. But I wasn't sure I had the endurance for even that. Mostly I just wanted to ignore it, pretend that nothing had happened and take a mulligan on the whole day.

"What the hell, Stratton?"

I looked at her, then shrugged.

"You left me sitting alone at a restaurant table. Do you know how stupid I felt?"

I climbed into bed. Carolyn took off her shoes and threw them across the room. I pulled the duvet to my chin.

"I'm sorry," I said truthfully but without much conviction.

"Oh great, you're sorry," she mocked me.

"I am."

"Why do you insist on being such an asshole?"

"I told you I didn't want to go in the first place."

I rolled away from her and pulled the pillow over my head. She turned on the television and said nothing further. When I woke up, the sun had set and Carolyn was in bed beside me. The television was off. I was drowsy and had forgotten about the fight and rolled over and curled around her. Then I remembered, but by then it was too late. I don't know if she had also forgotten or whether she took my cuddling as a peace offering, but she responded by grabbing my hand and pulling my arm more tightly around her. We didn't speak of that particular fight again.

€ 4 ϡ

The next day, on Sunday, Carolyn opened at Starbucks. Together we crawled from bed at four in the morning. Wounded pride still hung in the air between us, but we both seemed intent to ignore it. I kissed her good-bye when she left and then I waited for the café to open. I felt tired and cranky, and even though it was no longer an issue, I was still a little hung over from the fight.

Snow was falling when I left the apartment. The wind howled and the temperature hovered in the low teens even though we were well into March. I had my doubts that winter was ever going to end.

I entered the café. Gene's words echoed: "You can always go further than you think. You just need to discover what gives you that extra push." I hadn't the slightest idea from where that extra push might come.

I dropped the pencil on the legal pad and people-watched. There were two pretty girls sitting a table over. They were dressed in sweatpants and looked as though they had just crawled from bed, talking loudly enough so that I didn't have to strain to listen.

"I don't know, he's just not very good-looking and he's terrible in bed."

"So why even try, then?"

"Because he makes a hundred and fifty grand a year."

"He told you that?"

"Yes."

"So what's the problem, then? Hell, if you don't date him, then I will!"

They laughed. I shook my head. Never mind the conversation; the girl facing me wore small triple-hoop earrings. The two outer hoops were gold; the inner was silver. My mother owned a similar pair, and I remembered them perfectly because I had bought them for her. It was the summer before high school. There was an open tournament in which I wanted to wrestle at a venue an hour away from home, but I knew she already had plans and I didn't bother asking because it was on her birthday. I placed the flyer on my bedroom dresser and went out for a run. When I returned, my mother was on the couch with the flyer in her lap.

"You didn't mention this," she said.

I shrugged. It was mid-July and I had already wrestled in six tournaments that summer. I had won four of them, took second at one, took fourth at another. "It's your birthday," I said.

"So what?"

"You have plans."

"So? I could cancel 'em. I'd rather watch you wrestle."

"You've seen me wrestle like forty matches this year. Your birthday only comes once."

"And every one of those matches was greater than all my birthdays combined."

"You're crazy, Mom."

"Okay, how about this. You promise to win it for me, and we'll go."

"Puh-lease," I said. "I'll win that shit for you."

She tossed her hands in the air. "Well, it looks like we're going then."

On the day of the tournament, we had to wake at seven to arrive in time for weigh-ins. It was just the two of us, which had never happened before. I was usually able to talk one of my friends into wrestling with me, or one of my mom's friends would tag along for the ride, or on rare occasions, my father came. But it was never just us. She would be the only one in my corner for each match, which meant she'd have to coach me. Her coaching came in the form of yells of yes or no, or simply just shrieks of encouragement. Sometimes that was all I needed.

I won my first match by three points, my second by a score of ten to six, and my third went into overtime before I took the kid down with an ankle pick to win five to three. That put me in the finals against a kid who had won all his matches via pin.

"You'll beat him," she said. I appreciated her optimism, but I had my doubts.

"I'll do my best."

"I know you will, Bubby."

As soon as the match began it was apparent that he was far better than me. I was taken down twenty seconds in and quickly altered my strategy from trying to win to instead keeping it close until the end, at which point I'd try for a throw. My mother kept yelling. I was losing nine to four heading into the third period. I earned a point by escaping but got desperate, took a bad shot, and got taken down again. I escaped again with thirty seconds left, but every move I tried was countered and the match ended. The final score was eleven to six.

I walked off the mat breathing heavily. My mother hugged me. I went to the locker room, changed, walked out, and we climbed into her car. Before we pulled out of the parking lot, she stopped and looked over.

"You did great," she said.

"I'm sorry I didn't win it for you."

"Hey," she said. I looked at her. "You did great."

"Thanks, Mom."

I reached into my bag and removed a jewelry box that contained the triple-hoop earrings I had bought the day before with money I'd earned mowing lawns, which I did every summer. They weren't expensive—only seven dollars—but I thought they'd look nice on her.

She opened the box and lifted them out. "They're beautiful," she said in a breathless sort of way that embarrassed me. That's how she always was, overly sentimental and impressed by simple gestures. She put them on and asked me how they looked. I told her they looked great.

"Thank you, Bubby," she said. "But I still think that tournament was a better gift."

I rolled my eyes. "No way."

"Yer going to be my little state champion someday. You might not believe it, but you are. You've busted yer butt to accomplish every goal you've set for yourself thus far. How many of your friends wrestle in every tournament?"

"None."

"How many wrestle year-round?"

"Zero."

"Exactly. Yer workin' harder than everyone else and yer gettin' so good. It makes me proud to watch you work as hard as you do."

"Thanks, Mom."

"You don't have to thank me; it's true. And when you win it all, I'm gonna be the proudest mom in the whole world."

Remembering that moment, I found the extra push Gene had talked about. I sat reliving the memory for twenty minutes and, at one point, laughed out loud when recalling how out of place my mother had looked sitting alone in the coach's chair, cheering me on. Then I picked up the pencil and started writing.

twenty

FOUR AND A HALF months in Chicago, three months with Carolyn. For a time, she asked many questions, about my mother, my father, my childhood, where I grew up, what I dreamt about when I was a kid. How much of my past, I wondered, could I keep hidden? There was no doubt my coyness frustrated her, but what worried me most was the chance of that frustration turning to despair, which would inevitably segue to hopelessness. How long would she stay? We were living on dreams in those days; was that enough? But I tried to keep hidden, a fool's hope if there ever was one. Not only the past, but me, the present, my emotions, my thoughts, the negative aspects that encompass the person I had allowed myself to become. Did she see through it all even then? Probably, and in time, the inquiries stopped. I figured she was sick of asking questions she knew I'd evade. Quite a bit later, I learned just how wrong I was. The past was with us both then, all the time.

From the northern walkway that runs between Lake Shore Drive and Lake Michigan, the Chicago skyline, in its own way, looks every bit as majestic as New York's. The buildings rise, they fall. The land itself gently curves like a crescent moon and the buildings curve with it, making the skyline look much bigger than it really is, pristine and proud. Indiana smokestacks far in the distance. Harsh weather to the east. Nothing but a great expanse of land to the west.

I trudged along, the neighborhoods to the right, sand, water, ice, cold, wind to the left. I headed inward. Lakeview with its pubs and galleries, its independent shops and bookstores. The city's youth, the passionate, the down-to-earth, the self-sustaining eking out a living on their own. Coffeehouses, tree-lined streets, brownstones. Then to Lincoln Park, with its money, high rents, darkly lit bars, and cafés playing soft music. Wider streets housing trust fund kids. An extension of collegiate Greek life, former sorority sisters and frat brothers. People well into their twenties still living on daddy's dime, still living without consequence, living without having to survive. Then into Gold Coast with its extreme wealth, the snobbish, the haughty, the old money, fur coats, big hotels, condos, suits, expensive cars, and tall buildings. Martini bars, nightclubs, world-class dining. The city's conservatives, where the few celebrities live. Beyond here the Magnificent Mile begins, Michigan Avenue with its stores and crowded streets filled with tourists. The locals stay away unless they absolutely must go, and when they do, it's like entering tourist hell not unlike an inhabitant of New York City visiting Time Square. Times Square is not New York. Michigan Avenue is not Chicago.

I walked by the Hancock Tower, turned up Chicago Avenue, took the Red Line back home. I had walked for two and a half hours. I arrived home, sat at the desk with the pencil in my hand, took a deep breath, and started writing.

❦ 3 ❧

Chicago, that somber city once known for dirty meatpacking plants and even dirtier politics, for Al Capone and the lowly Cubs, for being the birthplace of Hemingway before he got the hell out, and I can't blame him for it, either. How can I make one understand the misery that that lone winter brought me? It never let up and seemed as though it would never end. The cold and the wind. It's far worse than what I'd been told, worse than what was possible in the realm of my own imagination, so cold that it can make you cry, though the irony is that you're far too chilled to cry. The low, gray sky and the wind has an impressive knack for taking the most optimistic of moods and wiping its ass with it, tossing it on the ground, stepping on it without regard. Day in and day out. Layers, that's how you get through it. Thick socks, thermal underwear, heavy sweaters, wool caps. Don't concern yourself with wearing too much. You can't. Keep the heat as high as it'll go, or as high as you can afford. Plastic over the windows helps, and so do space heaters. Don't depend on the trains. When you're most cold is when they're sure to be late, and when they do finally arrive, their heaters are certain to be broken. Find someone. Find someone to curl around and to curl around you. There's no greater source of heat in the world than passion and love and affection. Find it and coddle it and it'll keep you warmer than you could have ever imagined. And don't you dare let it go. Or let it go, but know that the cold you once felt is nothing to the cold you'll now feel.

❦ 4 ❧

My mother. Most of the time I can no longer remember what she looked like, her face, her hair, her eyes, all memories that are failing me. I can only picture her in context. When I try really hard I can still see her at the campsite, legs crossed in profile while staring out into the far trees on the opposite side of the road all those years ago. I can still see her soaking-wet hair and her arms propped on the side of the boat on that lazy summer day at the lake. And I'll never forget her face in the crowd, always yelling for me, always watching. Always there.

❦ 5 ❧

My father. Sometimes I struggle to forget the good times, the times he taught me to box, the encouragement during the years I wrestled, the days he'd have the whole bar laughing, had me laughing so hard that I could hardly breathe. He lived on opposite sides of the spectrum with no in between. Extremely encouraging, extremely happy on one side, miserable and hating the world and everything in it on the other. A good man almost half of the time, though the rest of the time he was so far gone there was never any doubt where he would end up. And I hope he stays there forever.

❦ 6 ❧

After I had gotten serious about writing the book again, I began punching in at work every day at 6:30 A.M., two hours before my actual shift started. I didn't know who unlocked the door. I never saw anyone and of course I never asked. All the employee time cards sat within a metal shelf beside the time clock near the entrance door. We were required to keep ours there, removing them only to punch in and out. Each day, I carried mine to my desk and hid it in my drawer, removed the dummy card, and slid it in with the others so there wasn't a gaping hole where my card was supposed to be. Then I left and walked to the coffeehouse down the street. I'd sit and write for an hour and a half, sometimes two if it was going well. I could usually get down five hundred words that way, or half my daily quota. Then I'd walk back, punch in with the dummy card to keep up appearances, and start the day's work. I again exchanged cards when I clocked out for lunch. I had been doing it for two and a half months, and no one seemed to notice. In this way, I was being paid to write. I desperately hoped that it wouldn't be the only way.

❦ 7 ❧

The worst part about writing back then was when I had finished for the day; the second I stopped working is when I'd start thinking, which opened the gates of insecurity, second-guessing, and a general malaise over the quality of my work. The night is a dreadful time for anxious people, and on the harder nights when I left the café and walked home, I could feel myself coming unglued. When Carolyn was there, I'd usually get better through the simple power of her reassurances; when she wasn't, I always got worse. I'd wash a Xanax down with a beer or two and many nights I was able to fall asleep, though there were others on which I'd lie awake for hours listening to the trains. Then, in the morning, the anxiety was always gone, as though it had been delivered by the darkness itself, and thus carried away with it.

❦ 8 ❧

On the good days, nothing, and I mean nothing, stood between me and my greatest ambitions. Between me and greatness itself and the posterity that comes with it. The days when the words seemed to pour from my brain, roll down my arm, and leak onto the page from the tip of the pencil. During these highs, I knew that someday Carolyn and I would laugh about the enduring poverty of our early days just as I'd come to laugh about the poverty of my own childhood. Nothing, that is, except my inclination to doubt myself and my own fickle abilities. I thought I was a talented writer almost half of the time. The rest of the time I felt I had no business trying to be one in the first place. I wasn't sure on which side to park my beliefs.

❦ 9 ❧

For the first few months of writing, I thought little about what might happen when I finished the book. As I neared the end, however, the anxiety washed away and I could no longer keep myself from getting excited, from building up possibilities I hoped would soon be real, the most prevalent being that I'd no longer have to wake at five to go to a passionless job. It was destructive thinking, of course, as are most desires that are left to roam freely, but that didn't stop the thoughts from coming. Carolyn got on board, too, and many nights we'd talk about what we'd do if the book actually sold. To keep her expectations low, I made sure she was aware that the average advance for a first-time novelist was small, sometimes only a few grand. But she insisted mine would be better, that it'd go for more. I agreed with her, though at first I didn't explicitly say so. In my mind, I wanted to underpromise and overdeliver so that if we did hit it big, it'd feel as though we'd won the lottery. But then we'd talk about it more and I couldn't help myself, and the next thing I knew I'd start throwing out extravagant ideas that went well beyond her own modest thinking so that no matter what the book sold for, it'd still fall far short of our bloated expectations. At no point during those nights did we allow reality its due consideration.

We'd talk about giving New York a try, her first tour, my second. We'd talk about buying a country home with a wraparound porch and a white picket fence in some sleepy New England town. We'd talk about moving to Iowa to be near her parents, but I never had the heart to tell her that rabid warhorses from hell couldn't drag me to Iowa. But we knew we'd leave Chicago. I didn't think I could survive another winter, regardless of how gorgeous she insisted the summers were. We talked about traveling far and wide, about having cars in the driveway, a fat bank account, carpeted floors, guest rooms, dinner parties. We talked about dancing barefoot in the cool grass on warm summer nights. And we talked about love, sweet and pure, such an innocent love that it's all there is and all that matters. A love that makes you believe there's nothing else.

❧ 10 ❧

On the better nights when Carolyn worked, I'd sometimes walk to the lake and sit with my legs dangling over the break wall while watching the waves and the windswept ice to the east. I'd think about winters in Ohio, about my little hometown of Spencer. I wondered how much had changed since I'd left, if my parents' home was still there, if somebody now lived in it. Did the town shrink, or did the farmers sell their land so that new houses could be built? Was the White Elephant Saloon still

open? How many of my friends still lived there? Were there still signs at
the town borders that read:

Home of Stratton Brown

2002 Ohio Wrestling State Champion

and National All-American

It's funny now to think of myself as an All-American, and I wonder
if I'm still remembered as such, if anyone remembers me at all. Would I
recognize any of them if I were to venture back? I knew I never would,
but I still wondered, anyway.

❦ 11 ❦

The days pass. They're in no great hurry to pass but they pass all the
same. I write. I think of Carolyn. I sit in my quiet apartment and watch
the world in a rush beyond these walls, while within them, little changes.
I sit and I wait for the trains and the vibrations. Sometimes Thomas sits
with me; sometimes he does not. We've become a family. Like the one
I was born into, it's not a perfect family. But it's a family all the same.

twenty-one

I SAT STARING AT the computer screen in front of me, eyes fixed on the blinking cursor. I printed the new pages and added them to the pile. It was ten and I had yet to spend a single minute on actual work, and instead created an outline of the few events yet to happen. It didn't take long, and when I finished I just sat there taking it all in. It was an odd sensation, the feeling I assume a marathon runner experiences when hitting the last mile. If I included the months of thinking about the novel before I started writing it, which I did while still in New York, then it had been with me for slightly over a year.

"What the hell are you doing?" Linda asked behind me, a reasonable question, given that I was staring at the computer screen with an awkward grin.

"Just taking it all in, my dear. I think I'm going to finish my book this week. And it's about damn time, too."

"That's great. How far are you now?"

"Two hundred and fifty-one pages."

"Hot damn, Stratton, that's excellent! You going to celebrate?"

"You know, I haven't really thought about it. Maybe, though. Interested?"

"Absolutely," she said, and I was flattered by the genuine excitement in her voice.

I finished ten days later, on a Friday.

I had clocked in earlier than normal and was seated at the café by six fifteen. I had intended to write for two hours, but when I realized how close I was to finishing, I refused to stop for the sake of my job and I was still there four hours later. And then I finally came to the last paragraph. I paused before writing it, certain about what I needed to capture, namely, American loneliness, uncertainty and fear, insecurity, the inclination to always look ahead or behind but never in the now. The end of any story can either make or break it, and I felt I had to embody these things to make mine a success, to make it worth reading.

Barrack Gray leaves his little hometown as he had always yearned to do, but it's not the way in which he had intended. He simply begins walking with a bedraggled old beagle named Charley. Walking, but toward what? He doesn't really know, but he hopes it's something worth walking toward, that it's worth leaving behind everything he knows, for there is comfort to be found in the familiar. He holds to this hope, the very hope that resides in bulk in this country, the hope that keeps the human spirit alive. Regardless of how dire any situation might be, there is always hope to lift it.

I took a deep breath. Then I wrote that last paragraph as I had written all the others—simply, truthfully—and I prayed it did justice to the fifteen hundred paragraphs that had come before it.

When the last word was written I dropped the pencil and cried. I didn't care that I was in a café, feeling both exhilarated and crushed. Everything I had been working for, this was it. Done. Finito. No más. Writing a great book is no guarantee of anything, but it's the bare minimum to have a chance, and I really felt like mine was good. After ten minutes, one of the baristas asked if I was okay. I looked up at her with my tear-streaked face and told her that the world was a fierce place and a tough place but goddamnit it's still worth fighting for all the same.

I left the coffeehouse, and as I walked by work, I called Cathy and told her I wouldn't be coming in today. I bought a dozen tulips after I jumped off the train. March 23, winter still forging on with confidence, the temperature in the midthirties, the ground wet with standing puddles from the melting snow. Carolyn lay asleep when I made it home. I shook her awake and placed the flowers on her chest. She opened her eyes.

"Did you buy me flowers?"

"I did."

"Why, silly?"

"Because I finished the novel this morning. It's done."

"Really?"

I nodded. She sat up and wrapped her arms around me.

"That's so great. I'm supposed to be buying you flowers, though."

"Nah," I said and kissed her on the lips. "I was thinking of going out for a nice dinner tonight. You, me, and Gene, maybe Linda from work."

"That would be great. I would love to meet her."

"Good. I'm going to walk up and ask Gene."

She leaned into me and kissed me on the lips again. "Congratulations, darling. I'm so proud of you."

"Thank you," I said, flying inside.

Gene was already showered and dressed, drinking coffee and reading the paper.

"Kiddo! What are you doing home?"

"Just finished the first draft," I said. "No way I could sit through work."

"You did? Very nice. Congrats."

"Thank you, Gene."

"How do you feel?"

"Pretty damn good."

"Good, good," he said.

"Anyway, I wanted to see if you'd be interested in coming along for a celebratory dinner tonight."

"Well, I did have a couple date offers I was entertaining."

"Really?"

"Hell no, of course I'm in for dinner. Where are we going?"
I laughed. "Not sure yet. But let's plan on eight."

෴ 3 ෴

Carolyn, Gene, and I took a cab up north to an Italian restaurant in
Ravenswood. Linda was meeting us there, though I didn't tell Gene.
We arrived a few minutes before eight. The restaurant was small,
dimly lit, smelling of olive oil, freshly baked bread, and wood smoke.
Soft Italian music played through hidden speakers, and on the walls
hung old Italian advertisements for products that hadn't been made
since the fifties.

"Reservations for four under Stratton Brown," I told the hostess. She
guided us to a table in the back. Gene sat across from Carolyn and me.
He smiled, looking dapper in tan slacks and a vertical striped white shirt
beneath a black blazer.

"You look damn good, Gene," I said.

"I was thinking that very same thing," Carolyn added.

"Yeah? Well thanks, guys. This old man can still put a few things
together from time to time." He grabbed at his lapels and gave each a
firm tug. "So who's the fourth?"

"Oh, just a friend from work," I said, intentionally downplaying it.
"Her name is Linda. She's great. I think you'll like her."

He nodded, asked nothing further, and looked at the wine menu. He
handed it to me. "Any preference?"

I didn't recognize any of the bottles. "Nope," I said. "Your choice."

He ordered a Barbara d'Alba. Before it arrived, Linda walked in. I
had never seen her in anything other than dated pantsuits and almost
didn't recognize her in a dark blue dress that fell to her ankles. Her hair
was down and she was wearing makeup, both of which were also firsts.
I had to admit, she looked radiant. I gave her a hug and then made
introductions.

"It's great to finally meet you," she said to Carolyn. "I was getting awfully tired of this one talking about you all the time without knowing who you were."

"You too," Carolyn said. I could see that Linda did a double take when Carolyn smiled. I had forgotten how her teeth had affected me when I first saw them, how they must still affect others. "Apparently you're the only thing that keeps him from going crazy in that place."

"Ha! None of us can stay sane there forever. I've merely slowed the inevitable."

Gene was silent, looking up at her.

"And you're the man who lives above him, right?"

He nodded, said yes.

"I've heard a lot about you, too."

"Well, you should hear my side of the story before making judgments," he said, intending for it to be funny though it sounded more like a threat. Poor Gene. I was now seeing firsthand how bad he really was with women. He became fidgety, unsure of what to do with his hands. He became anal about his silverware, positioning each piece parallel and equidistant apart. The server brought the wine. She uncorked the bottle and poured a small amount into Gene's glass. He went through the motions, giving it a swirl, holding it up to the light, a quick sniff, and then finally taking a sip.

"That'll do," he said.

She filled our glasses. Gene lifted his and spoke with far less gusto than he normally would have had Linda not been sitting beside him.

"You've done well, kiddo. But the first draft is the easy part, and now you have the task of making it good. I have no doubt you're up to it. Make us all proud," he said.

"I'll do my best, Gene."

The wine was very good, sweet and ripe with hints of plum and black cherry, full-bodied. It was what I had learned to expect from Italian reds. We placed our orders and had finished the bottle before our meals arrived. Gene looked back at the wine menu.

"I think we can do better than that first," he said.

He ordered two more, a French Bordeaux and a South African Shiraz, and I figured he did so to placate his nerves more than anything else. I didn't know how much the wine was, and I began to worry.

"I have no idea how much each bottle is," I whispered in Carolyn's ear. "I don't think I have enough to cover our share of the bill. Did you bring money?"

"I have like thirty dollars on me."

I shrugged. "Eh, I guess we'll figure it out."

When the wine arrived Gene poured the Bordeaux first.

"This is really good," Carolyn said.

"Not a bad choice, Gene. You were right, we could do better than the first."

"This ain't my first rodeo, kiddo," he said, fumbling with his linen napkin. He placed it in his lap, then lifted it for no apparent reason and set it down on the table.

"Do you know a lot about wine?" Linda asked him.

"Not as much as I should with as often as I drink it," he said.

Linda laughed. "Ain't that the truth?"

"Gene spent a lot of time drinking wine in Paris back in the day. I'm sure that didn't hurt," I said, trying to get him talking by directing the conversation to something he was comfortable with; watching him realign his silverware for the umpteenth time was making even me nervous. I wasn't sure how a man who seemed to be in such firm control of his life could unravel so completely around women, and that comes from a man who's always been notoriously bad with them.

"Well, I learned about *good* wine there, anyway," he said. "My father actually owned a vineyard in Oregon when I was growing up, right in the middle of Tillamook County, in the western part of the state, about twenty minutes or so from both the ocean and Portland. It was a small vineyard and I don't think it ever made much money, but he gave it a go. Made Pinot Noir, Gewürztraminer, and Riesling. I used to love the Riesling, probably because of the sugar in it. Couldn't stand the other two, though. But I was just a kid. I have no idea if any of it was worth a damn."

"Really? I never knew that," I said.

"That's because you never asked, you self-centered son of a bitch," Gene said with a sideways grin causing us all to laugh.

"So you're not from Chicago?"

"Afraid not, kiddo."

"What happened to the vineyard?" Linda asked.

"My father died when I was nineteen. I was in the service then. My mother never had much interest in it, so she sold it and retired to Florida." He took a drink. "How about you? Are you from Chicago?" he asked. I wanted to lean across the table and pat him approvingly on the shoulder for refocusing the conversation on Linda, just as I had coached him.

"Born and raised," she said. "Left for four years for college in Minnesota, but have been back ever since."

"Been here for ten years myself. It's a good city. Whereabouts do you live?"

"In Evanston."

Just then our food arrived. We continued drinking and talking. Gene finally relaxed midway through the third bottle, and he and Linda became engaged in conversation.

"I think they're getting along just fine," I whispered into Carolyn's ear.

"I think I'm getting drunk," she whispered into mine.

"Sweet, does that mean I'm getting lucky tonight?"

"I wish you could get lucky right now."

"I'm sure there are bathrooms here," I said.

She nudged me in the ribs. "Not *that* lucky."

Gene ordered a fourth bottle, and Linda excused herself to use the restroom.

"You're a cocksucker for not telling me," Gene said as soon as she left.

"What do you mean? I thought we were just having a friendly dinner."

"Bullshit. I know you."

I winked at him. "You're doing well."

"You think?"

"Absolutely."

The wine arrived before Linda returned.

"How much are these, anyway?" I asked. "Between the two of us, we have a hundred and twenty bucks."

"You make me smile, kiddo, you really do. But don't worry, dinner's on me tonight."

"You don't have to do that," Carolyn said.

"You guys are my friends. It's a celebration. What kind of world are we living in if a man can't pay for a celebratory dinner when something good happens?"

"First off, you'd pretty much be living in *my* world," I said. "And secondly, you should have told us you'd be paying before we ordered. I'd have gotten the prime rib."

Gene laughed. "There wasn't even prime rib on the menu."

Linda returned. Gene filled her glass.

"You guys up for shooting some pool after this?" I asked.

"Definitely," Linda said before Gene could respond, and I knew that sealed it.

❦ 4 ❧

We took a cab back to Lakeview and went to a bar Gene knew. It was run-down and dirty, which I liked, and mostly empty, though all four pool tables were occupied.

"First round is on me," I said. "Whatcha guys want?"

"No way," Linda said, shoving two twenties into my hand. She ordered a martini and Carolyn ordered the same, a Scotch on the rocks for Gene. I got a Corona for myself. I carried them back. Gene stood with a chalked stick already in his powdered hand.

"You look ready to go," I said.

He winked. "These guys are about to leave."

Carolyn sat slumped against the wall with her eyes closed.

"You okay, babe?"

She fluttered her eyes open. "I'm really drunk."

"I don't think this martini is going to help much. There's nothing but booze in it. You want me to get you a water?"

"No, I'm fine."

"You sure?"

"I could use a hug."

I laughed and wrapped my arms around her and she buried her face into my chest. I pulled away and she again closed her eyes. I didn't think she would last much longer. Carolyn is not what you'd call a drinker. It took me about three weeks to understand this about her when, every time we went out or had a few drinks with Gene—and though she had a full stomach and was bone sober when the night began—she was a wreck and had to be carried home when it ended. Her problem was that she understood nothing of the fine points of drinking, namely, the social aspect of it. Nor did she have any grasp of her own meager tolerance. She didn't savor alcohol and was possessed by an odd compulsion to keep pace with whoever the fastest drinker happened to be, regardless of how big that person was or whether or not they'd been drinking before she was even born. Quite frankly, she refused to be the only one not ordering when another round was being poured.

I went to the bar and got her a glass of water. When I returned, half the martini was gone. I nudged the water into her hand.

"Thank you," she said.

"If you still want to drink the martini, promise me you'll take two drinks of water for every one drink of that."

"Okay."

"You promise?"

"Promise."

The balls rattled from the bowels of the table and Gene racked them as they fell.

"Doubles?" he asked.

"Umm . . . Maybe we should play singles right now," I said and nodded to Carolyn.

"She okay?"

"Yeah, she's fine. I don't think she ate very much today. All the wine just hit her at once."

Fear that had little to do with Carolyn registered in Gene's eyes.

"Don't worry, we're not going anywhere," I said, though I knew that wouldn't be the case. "You want to play first?" I asked Linda.

"Nah, I'll take on the winner."

I grabbed a stick from the wall, chalked it, and put a line of powder between my thumb and forefinger of my left hand. I lined the cue, broke the triangle, and sent balls in all directions. A solid and a stripe fell in.

"I ever tell you I was raised in a bar?" I asked Gene.

"I think you've mentioned it a time or two."

I made three balls in a row before I missed an easy bank on the two.

"I usually play better with a few drinks in me," I said. "But I have to admit, I think I've entered into the law of diminishing returns."

Gene made four but scratched on the fifth. The remaining balls were in good order, and for some reason I was playing well beyond my abilities. I made every shot and left the eight for an easy straight-in, thus relegating Gene to the role of spectator. I bent over the table and lined the cue. I took the shot and the eight dropped in the corner pocket with ease.

I racked the cue and walked to Carolyn. Her chin rested against her chest and the martini glass was empty. The water remained untouched. I shook her awake and she opened her eyes.

"You okay?"

"I don't feel very good. Can we go home?"

I looked at Gene and Linda. They seemed to be getting along just fine.

"Sure. Give me two minutes."

I walked over. "I'm going to have to get her home," I said. "I think she's ten minutes from passing out. You guys should stay and play."

Gene looked at Linda. "Want to stay?"

"Well hell yes. You can't cheat me out of my turn just like that."

I shook Gene's hand and hugged Linda. "Thanks so much for coming out."

"Of course. Thanks for the invite. Now get that poor girl home," Linda said.

Carolyn stumbled up and I placed her right arm around my shoulder, supporting her weight as best I could with my arm around her waist. We were only four blocks from home, but it felt more like twenty. On the last block, I picked her up and cradled her in my arms like a child. She wrapped her arms around my neck.

"Thanks for taking care of me," she said. "I'm sorry I got so drunk."

"It's okay," I said. "We had a good time."

"We did," she cooed, her lips against my stubbly cheek. "I love you."

"Love you, too."

I got her upstairs and gently lowered her onto the bed. I undressed her and covered her with the duvet. I placed the trashcan beside the bed and prayed she'd use it if it came to that. The cat lay at her feet. I undressed and snuggled up beside her. I was drunk myself, and feeling pretty damn good about everything.

❊ 5 ❊

I woke sometime later to Carolyn retching into the toilet. I filled a glass with water and carried it to the bathroom with two Aleve. Her cheek was against the toilet seat and she looked up at me despairingly without moving her head.

"You okay?" I asked.

"No."

"Anything I can do?"

"Just love me, okay?"

"I do love you. Here, drink some of this water and take the Aleve."

"Oh god, I hurt."

"I know, darling, but try to take these and drink as much of this as you can. You're dehydrated. It'll make you feel better."

I flushed the toilet and sat beside her on the floor. She released a deep, helpless sigh. I gently rubbed her back.

"I don't understand. I didn't even drink that much."

I was inclined to disagree, but instead said, "Yeah, it sometimes sneaks up on you like that."

I helped her up. She took the pills, drank the entire glass of water, and crawled into bed.

"Will you get me more?"

I filled another glass and this time she finished half.

"Will you hold me?"

"Of course," I said.

❧ 6 ❧

The next time I woke, it was eleven and I heard footsteps above me. Carolyn was still asleep. I climbed out of bed and went upstairs. Gene answered the door but only opened it six inches. He was already showered and dressed.

"How'd it go?" I asked.

I tried walking in but his foot was stopped against the bottom of the door. I was confused at first, but then I heard the shower click off and the reality of the situation slowly dawned on me. I flashed him the biggest shit-eatin' grin that ever graced my face.

"You son of a bitch," I said. "She stayed here last night, didn't she?"

He tried suppressing a smile but the corner of his mouth defied him and subtly curled upward. He then brought his index finger to his lips as if to tell me to keep quiet.

"You're the man, Gene," I whispered.

I went back downstairs and couldn't stop smiling. Carolyn was still asleep but I wanted desperately to wake her up and tell her the news. I lay beside her.

"You awake?" I asked. Nothing. I gently shook her. "Hey, you awake?"

"Mmmmm," she groaned.

"You're not going to believe this. I just walked upstairs and Linda's still there."

I waited for a response. She remained silent.

"Hey, did you hear me?" I said, nudging her.

She opened her eyes. "Of course she's still there. Didn't you see the way they kept looking at each other?"

I thought about it a minute. "You know, I think I give you far less credit than you deserve sometimes."

"Yes, you do," she said.

She fell back to sleep. I went to the desk and removed all the pages I had written, all 268 of them. The whole damn book. I wanted to see it and bury my nose in the middle and breathe in the smell of ink and toner and paper. I thumbed through them all and stopped randomly to read a sentence or two, smiling proudly. I moved the chair and propped my feet up on the windowsill with the book in my lap and sat staring out.

"What are you doing?" Carolyn asked behind me twenty minutes later.

"Just thinking."

She swung her feet over the side of the bed and sat up. I turned in the chair.

"How are you feeling?" I asked.

"Much better now, thank you. What are you thinking about?"

I shrugged. "Just proud, you know."

"You should be. You just finished a whole book."

I nodded. "Not just that. About everything."

"What do you mean?"

"I don't know, this whole move. You should have seen me when I arrived. I was a mess, completely broke and miserable and didn't know what in the hell I was going to do. I was literally terrified of ending up on the streets. But then I found a job after only a few days of looking, got this apartment, and for the most part have stayed on the straight and narrow like I promised myself I would. And if that wasn't enough, on a cold winter night in December I happened to meet a delightful young lass I fell head over heels in love with. And, well, then I wrote this book. I don't know. I guess I didn't think I really had it in me, but I stayed focused and got shit done. It's been a long time since I was that way. And now I have you, and Gene," I said, feeling myself becoming emotional.

"Oh darling," Carolyn said. She removed the book and sat in my lap and hugged me. "You've done great."

I squeezed her back.

"Thanks," I said. "I know I struggle with a lot of stupid shit, but things seem like they're getting better, and maybe a little easier, too."

"That's great, Stratton."

"And I feel so close to something great again, something I can be proud of."

"You should be proud already. You've done so much."

"Thank you," I said.

"It's true."

"I mean it. I know I'm not the easiest person to deal with sometimes, and I know I can get kind of mean and a little jealous, but you've been great and it really means a lot to me."

"Just a little jealous?"

"I know," I admitted. "I'm trying to get better."

She kissed my forehead. "I know, Stratton. I love you."

"Sometimes I love you so much it hurts."

"Just sometimes?"

"At all times. So much that I feel like I might die if I loved you any more."

She pressed her forehead to mine. "I love you, too."

twenty-two

FOR ONCE, ON THE following Monday, I arrived at work at the normal time; the book was done, and in order to come back to it with a fresh eye, I planned on taking a full month off, which meant there'd be no early mornings for a while. I grabbed my time card to clock in but it was my dummy card and something dropped inside me. I knew immediately what had happened. I had clocked in on Friday, gone to the coffeehouse and meant to return, but instead had called off and gone home.

I went to my desk and grabbed the real card. Sure enough, clocked in at 6:08 A.M., didn't clock out.

"Shit," I said.

"You talking to yourself?" Linda asked, entering her cube.

"I didn't clock out on Friday."

"What do you mean, you didn't clock out? You weren't even here."

"Well, Linda, that's the truth in theory. But in actuality, I'm afraid it's not."

"I don't get it."

I explained to her what I'd been doing.

"You sly son of a bitch, you. That's one of the greatest things I've ever heard."

"Thank you, thank you. Now what the hell do I do?"

She shook her head, then shrugged. "Not much you can do, really. If I were you, I'd tear up your card and say it was missing when you arrived

this morning. Cathy will give you the thirty-two hours you worked last
week, sans overtime."

"But that means I'm going to lose like a hundred bucks."

"For as long as you've been doing your little trick, I think you're still
coming out ahead."

"Ugh." I ripped up both cards, buried them in the bottom of my
trash bin, and clocked in with a new card.

"So how was the rest of your night with Gene?" I asked.

"It was good," she said, keeping her back to me.

"That's great. Gene's an awesome guy. I might have hanged myself
by now if it weren't for him."

"Yeah, we had a nice time."

She turned in her chair and realized I was grinning at her like a
swindler.

"You know, don't you?"

"Not because he told me," I said, and then explained what had happened Saturday morning, when Gene wouldn't let me in, and how I'd
heard the shower turn off.

"Damn," she said.

"Ahh, Linda, after all we've been through. I'm hurt you would try
to hide such a thing. And here I thought you and I were the real deal."

"Yeah, yeah. I would have told you. Just might have given it a day
or two."

"I don't know if I believe you, but I think it's awesome all the same."

She nodded but remained silent. I wanted to know more.

"So are you going to see him again?"

"Tomorrow night for dinner."

"Hot damn! My man, Gene, and my darling, Linda," I said. "Well,
was he at least able to hold an erection? I know you had voiced concern
for that at one point."

She rolled her eyes like a teenager. "Yes, he did quite well. Now quit
asking me stupid questions."

During my month off I still spent two hours every day at work research-
ing agents and writing query letters describing who I was and the book I
had written. If the letter intrigued any agents they'd ask to see a portion
of the novel or maybe even the whole thing. If they liked what they read
and thought it sellable, they'd offer representation. Such is the process.
After two weeks I had ten letters. It was my goal to send out fifteen before
I started editing the book. After each reply, whether it was a request or
a decline, I'd send another. That way, I'd always have fifteen letters in
circulation.

At the end of April, I printed the fifteen letters. I signed them all
and sealed them in individually stamped envelopes addressed to agents
in New York City. I carried the letters home, smiling proudly at what I
was certain was the dawn of a new era. Carolyn was at the desk when I
sauntered in. I removed the letters from my bag and handed them to her.

"All the queries," I said. "Bless them for good luck."

She took them in her hands. "This is them?"

"You bet."

She thumbed through and tenderly kissed each and every one, and
when she was done she looked at me with those big green eyes of hers and
they were full of such confidence that I knew I couldn't fail, not this, not
now. It was a look that alone made the time and energy it took to write
the novel worth it, reminding me again just how beautiful her eyes really
were. Never once in the months that we'd been together had they ceased
to amaze me, and I knew they never would in much the same way that
regardless of how many times a person flies into and out of New York,
the city's skyline, as viewed from above, never fails to inspire.

"All ready," she said and handed them back.

I took them from her and walked out into the April air and glided to
the big blue mailbox at the end of the street. "Godspeed," I said aloud,
and then let them all fall from my hand into the box.

twenty-three

❦ 1 ❧

LIKE MOST MEN IN rural America, my father owned a gun. Jason's dad owned several, and on lazy summer days when there was little else to do (I was still an underdog where the opposite sex was concerned, and a good year and a half away from getting laid for the first time, whereas I think Jason was even further away than that), the two of us would shoot cans and trees in the woods behind his house. One day in the summer after my freshman year, instead of using one of his as I'd always done before, I took my dad's gun, which I'd long since discovered in one of the drawers beneath my parents' bed. I grabbed the gun and box of ammo and wrapped them in a towel. Without considering the laws I might've been breaking, I placed the towel in my backpack, pulled the straps over my shoulders, and headed out the door.

Jason lived in an isolated farmhouse eight miles away. His dad was a part-time farmer who raised sheep and grew several acres of hay we all helped bale at the end of summer. His name was John and he was an affable man with white hair and a beard, and I liked him a lot. He was a sports fanatic—which is how Jason had come to know so much about them—going as far as to collect and sell trading cards and memorabilia at events around Ohio and surrounding states. He had a vast gun collection despite never having the heart to be a hunter.

When I rode up on my bike, he was standing outside holding a glass of ice water and looking at the yard that one of his sons—there were three—had just finished mowing. I waved at him as I went into the house.

I found Jason sitting on the edge of the coffee table watching *SportsCenter*. He wore green shorts and a plain white T-shirt.

"What up, yo?"

"Shit," he said. "What's in the bag?"

"My old man's gun."

He smiled. "He's going to whip your ass."

"Nah. He might try."

Jason laughed. "Right. What is it?"

"Beats the hell out of me."

I pulled it from the bag and handed it to him. The gun was two-toned, silver and black. That was the extent of my knowledge.

"Is it loaded?"

"Probably."

"You're an asshole."

"Why?"

"Because," he said, popping the clip and inspecting it. "Yep, that's definitely a full clip. You just rode ten miles on your bike with a loaded gun. The safety wasn't even on."

"Eh, it was only eight miles," I said. "What kind is it?"

"Don't know." Just then his father walked in. "Dad, what is this?"

He took the gun and turned it over in his hand.

"Not bad," he said, one eye looking down the barrel as though aiming at something. "A Ruger forty-five caliber, Centerfire." He pulled a bullet from the clip. "The clip holds eight rounds. These bullets are hollow-point."

"What does that mean?"

"It means they'll expand once hitting their target, thus damaging more tissue the deeper they penetrate, which is to say, they'll do some serious damage."

"Cool," I said. "You want to come with us?"

"Nah, you boys have fun. Be careful out there."

Jason snagged a black revolver from the gun cabinet while I grabbed a plastic bag full of pop cans from the kitchen. We walked out across the field and into the woods. Jason carried the guns in a duffel bag. His father insisted that we always carry them in a bag, unloaded with the safety on, until we got to where we were going, which was a circular pond forty yards wide that sat in the middle of the woods a ten-minute walk from the house. But when we entered the woods and knew we couldn't be seen, we always removed the guns, loaded them, and tucked them into the waistband of our shorts like bandits of the Old West.

"You work out at all this week?" I asked.

"I haven't done shit since we last ran."

"Lazy bastard, that was a month ago."

"Eat it," he said and grabbed his crotch. "How about you?"

"Been running," I said. "Lifted a few times with the football team."

I had been the starting 103-pounder my freshman year of high school. Jason wrestled 103 as well, but I had beaten him at every one of our wrestle-offs. He had gotten much better since the seventh grade, when he'd won only a single match all year. This past year, wrestling JV, he had had a fifteen and seven record and had won his first tournament ever. Wrestling varsity, I had enjoyed a good year as well, finishing the season at twenty-four and nine. I had placed third at the sectional tournament and qualified for districts. If I had placed in the top four there, I would have made it to state. Since then, I had worked even harder, going to open mats twice a week at neighboring schools and wrestling in every open tournament I could find. I started lifting weights for the first time and ran four or five miles every two or three days. I could feel myself getting stronger; my endurance, which had always been good, was improving, too.

We made it to the pond. Off to the left stood a wooden pavilion, beneath which were scattered chairs and picnic tables and two artificial deer with bull's-eyes on their sides meant for arrows. On the opposite side of the pond, to the right, was the wooden table on which we stacked our cans. It was a flimsy thing that had seen its share of errant bullets, and because of this, the table was splintered and largely held together with layers of duct tape. I walked to it, dumped the cans on the ground, and lined up five for Jason. I walked back and stood behind him. He was forty feet away. He unloaded the gun as though in a Western, snapping the hammer back as quickly as he could with his left hand while pulling the trigger with his right. He hit only two cans in the six shots fired. He then set them up for me.

"I don't have to cock this after every shot, do I?"

"I don't think so," he said. "I think it does it itself."

I pulled back the slide and a bullet clicked into the chamber. I held it up with both hands, looked down the rear sight, and lined the front sight on the middle can. I took a deep breath, held it, and slowly squeezed the trigger. I hadn't anticipated how hard the kick would be, or how deafening the sound. The gun snapped back in my hands so hard it nearly hit me in the chin. I couldn't hear anything other than the shot's echo.

"Damn," I said.

Jason had his face screwed up with his hands pressed tightly over his ears.

"Shit, that was loud," he said. "I think I'm going to go deaf now."

The can had shot straight in the air, which meant I had aimed too low. I set the gun on the ground and we walked to the table. The bullet, which had missed the can entirely, had split the front board in two, and half of the board beside it. There was nothing clean about the impact. The hollow-points were meant for destruction, as Jason's dad had said, and the bullets held up their end of the bargain.

"Man, I pity the fool that breaks into your house in the middle of the night."

"No kidding."

We walked back and I picked up the gun. Jason shot a few more cans with his, and when it was my turn, I took aim at a large oak fifty yards away and unloaded the seven remaining bullets into the side of it. He had been right, there was no need to cock the gun after each shot. We walked to the tree. Each bullet had taken a grapefruit-size chunk out of its side, four or five inches deep.

"My dad will be pissed if he sees that."

I put my arm around him as we headed back.

"You scared, sweetheart?" I asked.

"Eat a dick," he replied.

twenty-four

⊹ 1 ⊹

I HADN'T RECEIVED A letter from my father in over a month. Since it was rare for two weeks to pass without one, I assumed Carolyn was throwing them away as I had asked. I took note of this only because I had become completely obsessed with the mail. I had mailed the queries during the second week of April, and by the end of the month I had yet to receive a single reply. I tried forgetting about them but it was useless; they were all I could think about.

The mail was delivered at three o'clock every day. On the days Carolyn didn't work, I'd call no later than 3:05.

"Hey you," she answered on Friday, exactly three weeks from the day I had dropped them in the mail.

"Surely there has to be at least one letter today?" I said.

She opened the apartment door and I listened to her shoes thump down the steps. She opened the mailbox and then gasped.

"What?" I bellowed, jumping out of my seat.

"We definitely have replies!"

"You're shitting me?"

"My god," she said. "There are eight of them here."

"All with my handwriting on them?"

"Yes. This is exciting as hell. Do you want me to open them?"

I sighed, dejected. "You can open them if you want. It doesn't really matter."

"What do you mean? Why?"

"If they bothered to send the envelope back, then it's a rejection. If they were interested they would have emailed or called."

"Well, then why do you bother including return envelopes?"

"Closure, my dear."

"This process sucks."

"That it does. Anyway, I'll be home in two hours. Love you bunches."

"Love you, too."

I hung up. I had an hour and a half left of work. To hell with work. I removed the novel's next section and began moving over it with a red pen. I wasn't as disappointed by the rejections as I thought I'd be. So I had received eight letters on one day after not hearing a word for three weeks. So much for the steady stream of keeping fifteen in circulation. But that's life. It gives you nothing and then all of a sudden it's crammed up your ass just to let you know you haven't been forgotten.

❧ 2 ❧

I entered the apartment a few days later and found Carolyn standing at the sink washing dishes, which she never did, and I was immediately suspicious in the way some women are when their significant other surprises them with flowers, believing they must be making amends for some wrong they've committed. It was Monday, the start of another infinitely long week. I went to the sink and kissed the nape of her neck.

"Mmm, thank you," she said.

"How was your day?"

"It was okay. Yours?"

"Hell, as always."

She finished the dishes and dried her hands.

"So I talked to my mom today. I was thinking of going home for a few days."

"All right," I said, beginning to understand why she had washed the dishes.

"Are you okay with that?"

"What do you mean? Are you asking me if you can go home?"

She shrugged. "I don't know, just wanted to make sure it was okay."

"Why would you think you would have to ask me?"

"I don't know."

"When was the last time you went home?"

"Thanksgiving. It's my parents' anniversary on Friday. I kind of miss them."

"Well hell," I said.

"What?"

"Nothing," I said. "I'll just miss you. When are you leaving?"

"Not sure. I wanted to talk to you first and still have to figure out work. I'll have to get my shifts covered since it's such short notice, but I shouldn't have a problem."

                                  ℰ 3 ℈

She left three days later, on a Thursday. She worked the early shift and her bus was scheduled to leave at four. I left MDI at two so we could ride down to the station together. It'd be our first time apart. I was a little bummed, and wasn't sure what I'd do during the six days she'd be gone.

I arrived home at two forty. She was packed and showered, looking vibrant and beautiful in faded jeans and a black tee. She had sprayed perfume on her wrists and neck.

"Why are you all dolled up?"

"I don't know. Want to look nice for my parents. It's been a long time."

"Are you going out with friends tonight?"

"No."

"Are you sure?"

"Yes, Stratton," she said with hints of frustration. "I'll probably go to dinner with Mom and Dad."

"Alright," I said. "All ready?"

We took the train down to Union Station. It was a nice day, the sun shining, spring finally waking from its long, insufferable sleep.

"What are you going to do while I'm gone?" Carolyn asked.

"Cry myself to sleep at night."

"Shut up," she said, nudging me in the ribs.

"I don't know. Have a ménage à trois."

"Don't be mean."

"Are you going to be good to me while you're gone?"

"Yes, of course."

"Promise?"

"Yes, Stratton. Quit worrying."

"I'm not," I said unconvincingly.

"What are you really going to do?" she asked again after a brief silence.

"I don't know. Try to get some editing done, hopefully write more queries," I said. On Tuesday another four rejections arrived, the next day, two more. Zero for fourteen with only one to go.

"Well, I'll miss you," she said.

"I'll miss you, too."

"Do you realize that tonight will be the first night we've spent apart?"

"Yeah, I was thinking that today," I said.

"It makes me sad. Are you still going to love me when I get back?"

"I don't know. All these women keep knocking on our door, leaving love letters and worn panties."

She laughed and shoved me. "Don't be a jerk."

"I'll still love you," I said. "And I'll keep the bed warm and toasty and waiting."

We found the bus and I stowed her bag in the storage area beneath it. Then I scoped out the other passengers, looking for any swinging dicks that might hit on Carolyn. There were a few halfway decent-looking guys, and judging by the number of people milling around, the bus would probably be full; she'd have to share a seat with somebody.

"I'll be back before you know it," she said, and leaned in and hugged me.

"Hope you have a great time," I said. "I miss you already."

"I miss you, too."

Then I kissed her and hugged her tightly, lifting her off the ground, which was done mostly for show while hoping that anyone who had noticed her was watching. Then she pulled away and climbed the stairs and I watched her scoot down the aisle of the bus that'd take her home, back to Iowa and her past. She found a seat beside a matronly woman in her forties. I relaxed a little, feeling much better about the next six hours or so.

I stayed until the bus pulled away, and then I waved at Carolyn waving back until I couldn't see her anymore, the bus disappearing around the turn.

❦ 4 ❦

Saturday, late afternoon. Carolyn had been gone for two days and would be gone another four. I called her at noon, no answer, and again at two, the same. I forced myself not to add meaning to it, supposing she was out and about with her parents and away from her phone. But I've never been good at controlling my thoughts and it was no different then.

The day before, I had bought two books on writing successful query letters. I read the first that night and the other the next morning, then I wrote five letters. From the books, I gleaned there were ten major rules to follow. In the previous letters, I had broken eight of them, so of course I hadn't received any requests.

To mix things up, I kept the windows open as I worked at the desk, the wind pushing in, filling the apartment with the cool, crisp air of spring. I had to wear a sweater to keep warm, but the sky was blue and the sun was out and it was great hearing the birds sing again. Then Gene's familiar knock interrupted me. I opened the door and found him brimming at the threshold.

"You have to come up and check this out," he said.

I followed him up and found, atop his dining room table, a wooden crate with its lid pried off. Inside the crate lay three bottles wrapped in tissue paper. Out of the box stood the fourth, divested of its wrapping to reveal a green bottle with a simple white label written in French. Gene picked it up and carefully held the neck with one hand while the other cupped the bottom as though it was a delicate newborn.

"You know what this is?"

"Not a clue," I said. "I can't read French."

"Real absinthe, made with grande wormwood, unlike the American shit they're now selling as 'absinthe.'"

I perked up. "You're shitting me? How in the hell did you get real absinthe?"

"Had it shipped from France."

"Is that legal?"

"Hell no, it's not legal. But they made it here, so who cares."

I smiled in the manner of a man about to be privy to one of life's great mysteries, a mystery that, until then, had completely confounded him.

"Well are we going to drink it, or what?" I asked.

"That's the spirit," he said. "I was hoping I wouldn't go it alone."

He grabbed two glasses that were bulged at the bottom, a flat, slotted spoon, several sugar cubes, and a bottle of Perrier. He laid the spoon across the mouth of the glass and placed a sugar cube in its middle. Then he slowly poured absinthe over the cube until it completely dissolved and the bulge of the glass was filled. The absinthe was light green. He filled the rest of the glass with Perrier, about three times the amount of absinthe. The liquid turned to a milky white. He handed me the glass and then made his own, pouring in more absinthe and less water.

"I've always wanted to try this," I said.

"I thought you might appreciate it. Well, here goes nothing."

We clinked glasses. It was extremely cool and refreshing, slightly bitter, tasting of black licorice. With that first drink came the slight dizziness you sometimes get with the first gulp of anything alcoholic.

"Whatcha think?" Gene asked.

"Not bad," I said. "Not too bad at all. Can't say it's necessarily what I expected, but I like it."

"Wait till you've had a few glasses."

"I will."

"Just don't start hugging me."

"I make no promises, my friend."

We finished one glass and started in on another. The more we drank the more we talked and the more certain I was that I knew exactly what I was talking about, regardless of the topic. That night, at Gene's dining room table, we solved all the world's problems in regard to politics, the military, universal health care, social security, art and literature, relationships and women. After a while I became numb but I was completely attuned to the conversation and only vaguely noticed anything else. I was in a place of rare honesty, feeling that I could say precisely what I thought and felt and have it received without judgment.

"So how are things with Linda?" I asked sometime around the fourth glass.

"Not bad. Been a month and a half now."

"Hey, you've made it longer than I usually do."

"Yeah, but you're an asshole and a misogynist."

"Nah, I don't hate women. I just hate that they hold so much power over me."

"Fair enough. And how are things with you and that angel of yours?"

I shrugged. "Mostly good."

"And the other times?"

"Like you said, I'm an asshole."

He nodded. "You can't try to control her, kiddo."

"You think I do?" I asked. I knew damn well that I did, but I didn't know that Gene knew.

"I've seen it. It might work for a while, but eventually she'll have had enough. You'll lose her if you keep it up."

Any other time I might have gotten pissed, felt cornered, and stormed out of the apartment. But I didn't then. I was drunk, or maybe high—I couldn't decide which of the two I felt more like—and in my present frame of mind, I craved advice from somebody I trusted. Things weren't bad between Carolyn and me, but they weren't great, either, and just because we had gotten a little off track didn't mean we couldn't get right back on. We had our good moments, and much of the time things were right, but that night, "much of the time" wasn't good enough.

"Yeah, I know," I agreed, pouring another drink. "You know, every one of my past relationships has always failed because of the same bullshit: jealousy, insecurity, fear of the past, my need to control. I always think I'm better, that I can control my actions the next time around. And I do for a while, but they always catch back up."

"That's because you're focusing on the wrong thing," Gene said. He nodded toward the coffee table. "Give me a smoke."

I grabbed the cinder box and removed two cigars and handed him one along with the cutter. He snapped the end off his cigar, and I did the same to mine. We lit up. Then he stood from the chair and walked to the bookcase, removed a book, flipped through it, landed on a page, and handed it to me.

"Read that," he said.

It was a poem by Charles Bukowski. I read it and handed the book back.

"I have no reason to doubt Bukowski," he said, "but I'll be sixty-two soon and I've yet to realize that loneliness isn't the worst thing in this world. And if I decide someday that he's right, you can bet your ass it'll be too late, and there's nothing worse than too late."

I nodded, remembering an ex-girlfriend who, just after she broke up with me but before walking out the door, assured me that I was going to die alone. Those were her words. But I was young then and the world had yet to beat me to my knees and I shrugged away her unsolicited aside, never once suspecting that she might be right, that one day I'd wake up as a fifty-year-old man, lonely, poor, and drifting into depression, suddenly aware that the world had passed me by and doomed to remember the days when I had felt another way, not happy, exactly, but still years away from the bitterness and gloom that, by then, would be coursing through me.

I took a long drink. "I can't necessarily say that I consider loneliness the worst thing in the world. Hell, I even think I'm happier sometimes when I'm alone."

"You know why?"

"Why?"

"Because you're a haunted motherfucker always in contention with himself. Ask yourself what you're so afraid of."

"I know what I'm afraid of."

"Yeah? And what's that?"

I waved away the question with the back of my hand.

"Try me," he said.

"Ah hell, I don't know. Being cheated on. Being crushed and having my heart ripped out of my chest and stomped on the ground. Being with somebody for long enough so that she regrets being with me. Being pitied, or thought of as weak. Being viewed as a failure, or viewing myself as one. Most of all, being left or abandoned."

"And what's the product of all those fears?"

I saw his point. I didn't need him to tell me that it made me guarded or that I never allowed anyone all the way in for fear of them learning the truth, that I'm almost always paranoid and afraid, which in turn makes me controlling even while knowing that the surest way to be wrong in any relationship, as with life, is to think you control it, and that it's because of these fears that I've been mostly miserable in every relationship I've ever been in. It was no great epiphany. I already knew these things. I also knew that just because I had had my heart broken in the past didn't mean it'd happen in the future, which was the conclusion I felt certain he'd try leading me to.

Gene sat, waiting for me to answer. And then he slowly nodded once. "Yeah, I know you get it," he said, and it was as though he had read my mind. "She's a good girl, Stratton. You're missing out on a lot by keeping her at an arm's length. Like I told you before, just after she had moved in: I'm not the one you need to reveal yourself to. That's the benefit of friendships over relationships."

I looked at him, the cigar in his left hand, the absinthe in his right.

He knew far more than he should have. I hadn't considered it before, but it made perfect sense.

"She comes up here, doesn't she?"

"Of course she does. Most days when she doesn't work. Sometimes we have breakfast together, sometimes tea. She loves you, you know."

I looked away. Even her talking to Gene upset me. What had she told him that I wished he didn't know? But then I realized there was little Carolyn could disclose to Gene that would bother me; I had revealed a good deal of myself to him already. There was but one secret I kept, and I had kept it from them both.

"And if you get jealous at that, I'm going to slap the shit out of you."

I smiled. "I did just get jealous. I don't know why."

"Yes you do."

"Yeah, I do," I said. The thought of Carolyn enjoying herself and having a laugh with somebody else made me resentful, even if it was only Gene. It was stupid but true.

"Things bother me too, you know. Every time I'm with Linda I feel so goddamn guilty that it eats me alive. My wife has been gone for over twenty years now and I still can't spend time with another woman without feeling like I'm betraying her."

"That bad?"

"That bad."

I nodded, and in Gene's admission I realized the topic of his wife was one he had already discussed with Carolyn. They had probably shared everything, things about themselves that even I didn't know, and I was oddly okay with that. Maybe it was partly due to the absinthe that was making everything tingle, or maybe because I had grown so close to Gene that I trusted him, knew he accepted me despite my many flaws. But whatever the reason, I was fine with it, and that was something new.

"I'm starting to see shit," I said.

He laughed. "That happens sometimes. Switch to water for a while. Some people lose their minds if they drink too much of this, or too quickly." He held the cigar between his teeth. "Do you know the moral of the story?"

"Maybe, but why don't you tell me just to make sure."

"Don't be controlled by the past. All you have to do is let it go, as simple as that. Life's way too short to go through being somebody you don't want to be."

I smiled. "Easy for you to say."

"Yeah, real easy. Like I've said before, knowing's half the battle. But take a chance, kiddo. Things might not turn out so badly. Fear will hold you prisoner for as long as you allow it to, but there's hope for us all in the end, in some form or another. Even you. And you'll never be happy if you don't give it a shot anyway, so you might as well go for it."

"I believe that, too," I said, staring blankly at nothing at all. Then I downed the rest of my absinthe, set the glass on the table, and went about the routine of refilling it.

twenty-five

ON MONDAY MORNING, I arrived at work at the normal time. I stood at the clock looking for my time card. It was missing from its normal spot, and while I initially feared that I had misplaced it, I distinctly remembered clocking out on Friday. Nevertheless, I clocked in with a new card and walked to my desk.

"Hey there," I said to Linda. "Was your time card missing today?"

"No. Why?"

"Because mine was. I wonder if somebody really did take it this time? Eh, shit happens. How was dinner with Gene last night?"

"Dinner was just fine. I heard you two had a raucous time on Saturday?"

I nodded. "I think we did. If only I could remember it all."

"Been there myself a time or two," Linda said.

I opened my desk drawer to grab my notepad to start making calls.

"Oh shit," I said.

Linda turned. "What now?"

"My dummy card is missing, too."

"No way?"

"Yes way. I keep it in my drawer and it's not there."

"You're sure it was there Friday?"

"Positive."

"You think they figured it out?"

"How could they? I was careful as hell except for when I had clocked in and called in sick," I said. "What do you think I should do?"

"What can you do?"

Just then Cathy entered my cubicle.

"Stratton, you mind coming into my office for a minute?"

"Sure," I said.

She turned. I stood and flashed Linda a frightened face. She frowned in response. Then I followed Cathy. The second I entered her office, I knew I was up shit creek without a paddle. There were two others waiting for us: Stan, the executive editor, who was Cathy's boss, and another person I knew to be the head of human resources.

"Have a seat," Stan said.

I sat across from them feeling like a parolee in front of the board.

"Care to explain these?" Stan asked, reaching across the desk with my two time cards. I took them.

"No."

"No, what?"

"No, I don't care to explain them."

"Well, I'm a little confused as to why you have two cards instead of just one."

I could feel my legs shaking. My heart was racing and I'm not entirely sure why I felt so uneasy. There was nothing I could do but sit there and eat the shit sandwich they were serving. I had to let them fire me because if I got up and left, it would be considered quitting, and if I quit, I'd be ineligible to collect unemployment. I'd been through this process before, but that didn't make it any easier.

"Well, I'm a little confused as to why you went through my desk without my permission," I replied, intentionally using his own phrasing to piss him off.

"MDI's desk, you mean."

"No, my desk."

"The desk you're privileged to use that is owned by MDI."

"Now we're just splitting hairs, sir. And I wouldn't call it a privilege."

"No, you wouldn't, would you?" Stan said.

"No, I wouldn't. That's why I just said that."

Stan smiled. "There's also this," he said, and handed me a sheet of paper. "It's a list of everything you've printed here. Correct me if I'm wrong, but I don't believe there are any MDI documents titled *As Far as the Eye Can See?*"

"No, I wouldn't think there would be," I said. *As Far as the Eye Can See* was the title of my novel, and I had printed it using MDI's printer more times than I could count on the sheet Stan had given me. Each instance was listed, and the title repeated itself about a hundred times, maybe more. I wasn't surprised, seeing as I only ever printed small sections at a time, and sometimes just a page or two.

"You do know it's against company policy to print anything that isn't for company use?"

"Sure do," I said, smiling at Stan, who I had always thought was an asshole.

"It's funny, is it?"

"A little bit, yes," I said, continuing to smile.

The HR man chimed in before Stan, who was on the brink of erupting, could reply.

"Well, Mr. Brown, we appreciate your six months of service to this company," he said, looking very uncomfortable. "But we're afraid we're going to have to let you go."

I counted the months in my head. I had started in November and it was now the beginning of May. He was right, I had only been there for six months.

"Sounds good," I said. "Is there anything I need to do before leaving?"

"No. We'll be sending your final check in the mail. You can expect it in two weeks."

"And the overtime I'm owed?"

"And the overtime."

"Wonderful," I said. I stood, winked at Stan, then walked back to my cube.

"Well, Linda, my darling, it's been real."

"Oh no, that's it?"

"Afraid so," I said, grabbing my bag and filling it with stationery.

"Hell, Stratton. I'm really sorry."

"Don't be. This is the best thing that could have happened. I'll be able to collect unemployment and live the good life for six months. It'll be a nice vacation."

The head of HR stood outside my cubicle while I finished.

"Have everything?" he asked.

"Yep." I bent over and hugged Linda. "I'll see you again soon."

"Have a great day. Get some writing done."

"Will do," I said, then turned and walked out of the building for the very last time, and thank Christ for it, too.

⬦ 2 ⬦

I felt relieved I no longer had to report to an office every day, but I was also a little disheartened. I felt somewhat like a failure for losing this job. Don't get me wrong, I was thrilled I no longer had to wake before the sun had risen, or sit in a sterile cube for eight straight hours a day, or walk into a building that, by pure virtue of its existence, killed off a little bit of myself each time I entered, but I still felt as though I'd let myself down.

I called Carolyn when I got home.

"Hey darling," she said.

"This vacation business of yours isn't working out too well for me."

"What do you mean?"

"Without you, I think my life tends to fall apart."

"What do you mean?" she asked again.

"I'm home right now."

"Okay?"

"I got fired about an hour ago."

"What?" she asked. "Why?"

"Because I'm a fuck-up."

"Stratton, you're not a fuck-up. Are you okay?"

"Yeah, I'm fine. Just feeling like shit. At least I'll be able to collect unemployment and devote myself entirely to selling the book and loving on you."

"Will you be able to *get* unemployment?"

"Yeah, I shouldn't have a problem."

"Well, good. I think I'd better hurry back then."

"Nah, take your time. I've gotten a lot done. I'll just be here, waiting on you with bated breath, counting down the seconds."

"Me too. Two more days!"

I was silent a moment. "Do you still love me?" I asked.

"Of course I do. You still love me?"

"More than ever."

I hung up, and wondered if that was the truth. Then I spent the rest of the day writing more queries.

❧ 3 ☙

That night I finally got around to *A Fan's Notes*, the book Gene had given me several months before. I'm not sure why I had waited so long, and when I picked it up I had only meant to start it, read a chapter or two, and then go to bed. But before I reached the end of the very first page I realized the book was akin to magic, amazing to the point of discouragement, so brutally honest and beautifully written that I knew I could live ten lifetimes and still not write anywhere near as well as Exley. It was unlike anything I had ever read before. I drank in every word, eyes burning with exhaustion by the time I reached the halfway point at three in the morning, but I couldn't stop there, not until I finished, all 385 pages of it. And when I finally turned that last page, I was so enthralled and inspired that I wanted to rush out immediately and have the word *Exley* tattooed somewhere on my body. But the sun was only then beginning to crawl over the horizon, so instead I curled into a ball and had a good hard cry that I reveled in. It had been a long while since my last, and when I finished, I then lay waiting for sleep, hoping for once that it might come easily. But it never does. Still today my mind forever races, wracked with either anxiety or worry or nothing at all, and I don't remember there ever being a time when I could relax or immediately fall asleep without the benefit of a sedative. And even when I do sleep I'm tight and restless and wake often. It's not a good thing, but so it goes.

❦ 4 ❧

My paperwork went through two weeks later. I was to receive $211 each week for the next six months. If I carefully watched my spending, it'd be just enough to get me by and would thus allow me to devote my time to selling the book, and that was all I really wanted.

twenty-six

AT THE BEGINNING OF June we were finally able to keep the windows open. There was hardly a spring. One day it was forty degrees; the next day it reached eighty. The sound of birdsong and the smell of clipped grass filled the warm air. After the insufferable, long winter, I thought that summer would never arrive, but here it was at last. Even the leaves on the trees seemed to have sprouted overnight. But it was a blessing and a curse; without the buffer of the windows, sleeping through the trains was like sleeping through a hurricane. We elected to battle the noise rather than the heat. Neither of us made it through a night without waking at least once. Carolyn suggested we buy fans. I objected. I didn't want fans and didn't feel like going into why; nor did she ask. In our time together, she had learned to simply take my eccentricities at face value.

On the first few really hot days, the wind blew in and filled the room with smells of creosote and oil and worn steel that had baked in the sun. The smell made it just as hard to sleep as did the trains, penetrating our dreams, becoming a part of them just as the smell of manure had during the August months when I was a kid. It was a dreadful smell, but it was hot and we had little choice but to tolerate it. Without my working we didn't really have the money for an air conditioner.

On a particularly hot night when the open windows only marginally helped, I lay on my back staring through the darkness. It was the middle of June. My birthday was the ninth of July. I could never get used to birthdays, hadn't enjoyed them in a good twelve years. Not while I knew what was right around the corner. My mother's birthday was the twenty-fifth, my father's the thirtieth. And then there was August, which always made things worse.

"Do you want to talk about it, or are you going to keep us both up all night?" Carolyn asked beside me.

"Hey," I said. "I didn't know you were awake."

She propped herself up on her elbow and touched the side of my face. "So what's the matter?"

"I don't know, just thinking about my birthday in a few weeks."

"Okay." She ran her fingers through my chest hair, up my neck, then traced my brows with her thumb.

"You ever think back to all your birthdays to try remembering what you did on each?" I asked.

"Sometimes. Is that what you were doing?"

I nodded. "I was thinking of my favorite birthday, which was when I turned seven. My mother organized this big party at the little park in our town, invited all my friends from school, made a big cake, bought a piñata, the whole nine yards. It was only a few months after my grandmother had died, and I think half the reason she made it so big was to keep herself occupied. Everyone came, even kids I barely knew. There were all these swings and slides and stuff, and I remember my mom bought me a baseball glove while my dad got me a silver Easton bat and a ball to go with it. And then my dad and I played catch, or tried to anyhow, but of course I wasn't very good yet. And from out of nowhere, these huge, dark clouds moved in, but neither of us cared and we just kept throwing the ball while the adults scurried to clean. Then it started to pour, and with the rain came loud claps of thunder and lightning. Everyone else huddled beneath the pavilion, but my dad and I just kept throwing the ball. I could barely even catch the damn thing, couldn't throw it more than twenty feet, but we kept at it until my mom finally made us come in."

"Sounds like a fun birthday," Carolyn said. "Why were you thinking about that one?"

"I'm not really sure."

Carolyn rolled toward me. In the distance I could hear a train. The wind came in and padded over the bed.

"Mmmm. That breeze feels good," she said.

"Yeah, it does."

She started kissing my neck, ran her hand from the side of my face down to my chest.

"Well, this year we'll make sure you have a great birthday," she said, "even better than that one."

I meant to respond but the train started passing, shaking everything inside. More plaster rattled from the hole above the desk and tumbled down the bowels of the wall. I closed my eyes, listening to the train and the wind and the plaster.

❦ 2 ❧

The first request came at the end of the month. I walked to the library to check my email, something I was doing several times a day then. I had seven new messages, but my eyes nearly popped out of my head when I read the subject line: "Your Query—As Far as the Eye Can See." I began to shake with excitement. In total, I had received twenty-nine rejections and was losing heart fast. Hell, I had begun to panic. And now here it was! I opened the email.

Dear Mr. Brown,

Thank you for your query regarding As Far As the Eye Can See. I would like to consider your project for representation. Please either email me with a Word attachment or send about 50 double-spaced pages. Please also send a synopsis, if you have not done so already, and a list of prior publications. You may address these materials to my attention.

Mark the envelope or email "Requested Material" and remember to enclose proper postage for the return of your materials. My

response time is approximately a month (I hope!). I'll be in touch as
soon as possible and do look forward to reading your work.

Yours,
Simon James

I printed the email and sprinted out of the library. I yelled "*Yes!*" from
the top of my lungs. I dialed Carolyn's cell. She didn't answer. Then I
dialed her work number, and she answered on the third ring.

"Thank you for calling Starbucks. How can I help you?"

"Guess what," I said.

"Stratton?"

"Yes, of course. Guess what."

"What?"

I read her the email. I stumbled over several sentences, reading it too fast.

"You're kidding me?"

"Nope, and it's from one of the bigger agencies, too."

"Oh my god!" she said.

"I know! It's about damn time."

I rushed back inside. I had already written a synopsis and was
torn between an efficient email reply and taking the more professional
approach and having the pages mailed. I based my decision on the fact
that I hated reading anything on the computer, so I rushed to a print
shop, printed the pages, and sent them two-day express.

I stopped at a little pub I had been to a time or two. There were two
others inside, both dejected and miserable looking and unworthy of my
company. I sat at the bar nonetheless and ordered a shot and a beer. I
was a man caught up in the certainty of his own genius, and as such, I
tried projecting this image so the others there could pay heed, maybe find
comfort in holding the company of a man on the rise. They paid me no
notice, and I had the urge to feign a conversation on my phone so that
I could espouse the good tidings loudly enough so that everyone could
hear. Perhaps they'd find inspiration in it. But then I came to my senses

and slammed the shot and beer and strutted back home. I knocked at Gene's but he wasn't there. I went downstairs but felt cooped up in the apartment. I walked to the lake. I skipped rocks across the water, watched the runners and bicyclists while breathing in the summer air and feeling the warm sun on my face, which had begun to ache from all the smiling. Carolyn wouldn't be home for another two hours, and it took forty-five minutes to reach North Avenue Beach. Half-naked bodies were strewn everywhere, and I sat in the sand and stared at all the pretty girls in bikinis. I sat for about an hour and then I left and took the Red Line home.

❧ 3 ❧

I couldn't sleep that night. I lay for a while and then got up and walked to the bathroom mirror. I took pleasure in the confident eyes staring back and fantasized about fame, imagining what I'd say when introduced at book signings, how I'd act far cooler than I really was, or maybe by then I would actually fit the role I'd spent most of my life creating. I decided in my mind what passages I'd read, what I'd write when personalizing my autograph. I stood answering questions, showing my witty side with ease, making everyone laugh. The crowd would be enthralled. Even the booksellers would act awkwardly around me, unsure of what to say. Then they'd thank me for coming and ask in an almost pleading way if I'd please consider returning.

I crawled back into bed.

"What are you doing?" Carolyn asked.

"Thinking I might never step foot in another office again. Can you imagine?"

"No, I can't. That'd be amazing."

"I mean, even if it doesn't go for that much, I've always been able to live on little. Twenty-five grand would last me a year and a half, enough time to write and sell another. And even if it does go for a smaller amount, it could still get a huge following and pay a ton of royalties over time."

Carolyn was silent, and I almost felt betrayed that her enthusiasm didn't match my own.

"We could go on vacation somewhere," I said. "I don't know, maybe Hawaii, or Paris, which Gene insists is beautiful."

"That'd be wonderful," Carolyn said. "I've never even been in a plane before."

"You're kidding me?"

"Nope."

"Wow," I said, and in my mind I began recalling book advances for first-time writers I had researched over the years. Where would mine rank? When I first started, I would have given the book away if that meant seeing it on a shelf somewhere. But not anymore.

The thoughts of book signings and adoring fans and dollar signs swam in my head until I fell asleep, and in my dreams the fantasies continued. I kept waking up. When morning came I was still smiling. I had a whole day to get through before the package would even arrive.

❧ 4 ☙

My fantasies were short-lived. The package arrived at 1:47 P.M. They must have reviewed the materials immediately, because at 3:01, I received the following email.

> *Dear Author,*
>
>   *Thank you for your query.*
>   *I am afraid your project does not seem like one I can success-*
> *fully represent at this time. My client list is quite full, and I am only*
> *able to offer representation to projects about which I am wildly*
> *passionate.*
>   *Thank you for thinking of me, and best of luck in your search*
> *for representation.*
>
> *Yours,*
> *Simon James*

Dear Author? Did they think so little of my work that they couldn't be bothered to type in my name? I was in utter disbelief, and couldn't believe the gall of these people.

Without thinking I hit the reply button, intending to write a long, impassioned email about all the things wrong with the process, about how writers who poured themselves into their work deserved far better than a form letter after their hopes had been bolstered by the personalized request, but in the end I decided a terse reply was more appropriate and typed, "Go fuck yourself" and hit SEND, knowing that I wasn't doing myself any favors.

I left the library and walked home. Carolyn was in the shower. I took off my clothes and slid in beside her. The shower was so small that for both of us to fit, our bodies had to be pressed tightly together. And that's what I wanted just then, to feel her body up against mine.

"They said no."

"Already?"

"Already."

"I'm really sorry," she said. "But don't worry, it's their loss."

I struggled to remain optimistic, and my confidence was gone, but I didn't want Carolyn to know that.

"No worries, my dear. There are plenty more," I said, which was true, but I wasn't convinced any would respond differently.

I pressed against her and bit her neck, running my hand down her stomach until striking gold. She arched her back and moaned. I tried to enter her but couldn't get hard.

"It's okay," she said after a minute of this.

I sighed, closed my eyes.

"Hey," she said, cupping my chin. I looked at her through the water that poured heavily over our heads. "You'll get more requests."

"What if I don't?"

"Then so what. You'll write another."

I stepped out of the shower, walked across the room, and went to the window without toweling off. I stared at the tracks. The rejections had opened the doorway of doubt. I started to doubt everything, my writing, my relationship, my current living situation, the fact that I had been without a job for a month and a half and was already anxious about rent. I stressed every time I bought a cup of coffee. I had entered into a predictable trance of complete and utter insecurity that reached into every aspect of my life. The notion that people wrote stories and were paid for them seemed ludicrous. It was as though the whole concept of writing and books was nothing more than an elaborate ploy at my expense.

Carolyn walked out of the bathroom wrapped in a towel. I left the window and sat on the bed.

"Do you think I'm screwing up?"

"What do you mean?"

"I don't know, do you think it's stupid for me to keep writing?"

"Of course not, Stratton. You're following a dream. It's not supposed to be easy."

I sighed. "It just seems like one of those things reserved for other people, not me. It's like the whole world is playing a trick on me and everyone knows it but me. And they're all having a great hearty laugh watching me try."

She hugged me from behind, pressing her wet head against my shoulder.

"Why do you say that?"

"I don't know, it just seems kind of silly. All of it. It's hard imagining actually being a writer. Like, it's too good to be true, and half of me believes I'm only doing it to keep from being a responsible adult in the first place."

"But you love writing, and books."

"I don't know what I love anymore."

"Stratton, you're just doubting yourself. It's normal."

I nodded and stood. "When the hell don't I?"

She groaned and fell back into the bed with her feet still touching the floor.

"You sure do make yourself hard to love sometimes," she said.

"Yeah, you should try living in this brain. It's no pretty place. All Stratton, all the time. Yippee! It's like watching a movie in which the main character comes out of the screen every few minutes to sucker punch you right in the gooch."

She laughed. So did I. I didn't intend for it to be funny, but it was. Even I saw the comedy in it. When all else fails, use humor. Maybe I should write that down, put it over my desk, read it the next time I'm stuck. Humor, that'll be the thing to bring me out of the lull and push the story forward.

Yes, I thought. *Isn't it pretty to think so?*

twenty-seven

On Saturday, July ninth, a deep malaise pulled me from sleep. I had expected it to. Morning, a new day, the sun still hidden, dark and silent in its gloom. Happy birthday to you too, world.

It was 4:37 when I crawled from bed. Too early to do anything other than walk, everything closed, resting in the gray calm of early morning. I pulled on shorts, a T-shirt, tennis shoes. I grabbed a few slices of bread and pushed through the door and walked down the stairs and out into the darkened streets, where nothing stood sentinel save the buildings and trees and the streetlamps casting pale shadows across the faded terrain. I walked east and in ten minutes I crossed Lake Shore Drive, no cars other than what I could see in the distance. I entered a park of green grass and trees. To the south, a harbor full of boats; to the north, tennis courts and a golf course. God forbid the rich be without theirs.

I sat at the break wall with my feet over the edge while the waves below lapped endlessly. There were no birds to feed. The sun starting to rise, not quite on the horizon, but close, a pallid glow slowly breaking on the eastern edge of the vast expanse as far as the eye could see. I watched it grow, the colors fade and change and brighten, a new day beginning. I was certain the sun was already up in Ohio.

I broke the bread into small pieces and tossed it in the grass for anything interested in eating it. Walked home. Carolyn still asleep. I undressed, curled beside her. I knew I wouldn't sleep, but didn't know what else to do. I did know, however, that I didn't want to be alone. I nuzzled against her warm body, slid my arm in the gap beneath her neck. Let the day begin and let the earth brighten. Let it all pass without me. Let this bed and this girl be my haven from the world beyond my walls. And may I stay safe within them.

❦ 2 ❧

I woke to my cell phone ringing. I rolled over, swiped it off the nightstand, looked at the caller ID. It was Carolyn. I glanced behind me. The bed was empty.

"Hey you," she said.

"Hey." I cleared my throat. "Where are you?"

"Upstairs."

"What are you doing?"

"Gene needed help hanging a painting. I'm not really strong enough to hold it for him, though. Wanna come up? It'll only take a second."

I wiped my eyes and looked at the clock. 10:47. I was surprised I had fallen back to sleep. "Yeah, sure. Be up in like two minutes."

I still felt horrible, not physically, but the other, far worse kind, a pain in my chest, as far down as the pit of my stomach.

I knocked at Gene's door, then pushed through, yawning, down the hallway and into the living room. I stopped. My mouth dropped open and I stared in disbelief. In the center of the room Gene, Carolyn, and Linda stood smiling. Gene was in the middle holding a birthday cake covered in candles; Carolyn was to his right holding two wrapped gifts; Linda, wearing a black sundress with her hair pulled back, stood at his left holding a bouquet of helium balloons.

"Surprise!" they all yelled.

I just stood, unmoving, staring in disbelief. I thought I might tear up.

"Oh darling," Carolyn said. She placed the gifts on the table and hugged me, cupping the back of my head with her right hand. "It's your birthday."

I gazed up at Gene.

"Happy birthday, kiddo. Now blow out these damn candles because I'm sick of holding this thing."

I took a deep breath and made a wish, blowing out the candles with a single whoosh. Gene placed the cake on the table. Linda hugged me and slapped the balloons in my hand.

"Happy birthday," she said.

"Thanks, Linda. It's great to see you again."

"Nothing like fat and sugar at eleven a.m.," Gene said, cutting four slices.

"I can't believe this. I've never had a surprise party. You guys are great," I said. "Thank you so much."

"You bet, kiddo."

Carolyn was beaming. She stood on her toes and kissed me on the cheek. We sat at the table and ate. The cake was good, homemade chocolate, thick, rich, loaded with icing. Gene made himself a drink. I looked at him, then at the clock on the wall.

"Bite me," he said, in a seemingly crotchety mood, which I suppose is why he had made himself a drink in the first place.

There were two gifts, both meticulously wrapped, and Carolyn handed me the first.

"That's from Gene," she said.

It was a small package, an inch thick, probably six inches long, and somewhat heavy. I ripped away the paper. It was a green leather case with the name "Parker" etched into the side, an emblem of an arrow shooting through an open circle. I knew what it was and that it was pretty damn expensive.

"Well, open the damn thing," he said.

I lifted the top. Inside was an acrylic black and gold fountain pen, elegant, stylish, far too nice for me to ever use. There were two refills and a manual. Gene had bought me a pen that came with a manual, which I found absurd. I removed the pen and ran my thumb down the length of it and felt several etchings. I twirled it to see "Stratton Brown" engraved in its side.

"Jesus Christ, Gene," I said.

"If you can't write a book with that, then you can't write a book at all," he said.

"Thank you so much." I shook my head disbelievingly. It must have cost at least a couple hundred. Far too much for him to spend on me.

"You're welcome."

Carolyn handed me Linda's gift next. It was again thin, but long and wide. I smiled knowingly at Linda.

"You bought me fancy paper to go along with this didn't you?"

"I don't know. Did I?"

I tore away the wrapping. It was a soft black leather portfolio, smooth and polished looking. Inside was a legal pad of fine paper, a pen sleeve, compartments for loose papers and notecards. I took the pen in my hand, uncapped it, signed my name on the top sheet, the ink sliding thick and heavy and soaking into the page in a dignified way.

"Thank you so much," I said to Linda. "I love them both. How in the hell is an asshole like me supposed to get used to nice things like these?"

"You'll find a way," Gene said.

I capped the pen, slid it into the sleeve of the portfolio. It fit perfectly. I took a deep breath and looked at everything, the cake, the balloons, the gifts, then at Gene, Linda, and Carolyn. "You guys are too good to me. I mean, really, thank you so much. I can't tell you how much all this means."

"It's your birthday, kiddo. Enjoy it."

"Thanks, Gene."

"So, dinner tonight?" he asked.

I looked at Carolyn. I didn't necessarily want to do anything other than spend a quiet evening at home, but how could I say no? Plus, it'd be good for me to get out of the apartment, which I hadn't been doing very much of.

I shrugged. "Sure, why not? Where do you want to go?"

"We'll figure it out. Let's say seven."

I carried the gifts and balloons downstairs, Carolyn carried the cake. I sat at the desk and started doodling in the notebook. The pen felt comfortable and the ink went on thick, which is what I preferred when I wrote by hand.

"Hey there, birthday boy," Carolyn said behind me. I turned around. She stood in the doorway with tousled hair wearing white lace panties with a small black bow over her pubis, matching stockings attached with garter straps to a bustier, the ankle bracelet I had bought her for Christmas around her right ankle. In all our time together I had never once seen her take the bracelet off, and in its own way, it had become a symbol not unlike an engagement ring. I was always happy to see her wearing it, and I hoped she always would.

She walked across the apartment—long, sexy runway-model type steps—and sat in my lap facing me. She grabbed my head and buried my face between her breasts. I breathed her in, the smell of perfume and fresh skin. I began kissing her, moving my hands up her spine. She moaned and arched her back, mouth open, looking down at me seductively. Then she stood and led me to the bed. She dropped my hand when we reached it, and I could still feel the warmth of her fingers between mine and I nearly wished there was someplace else for her to guide me. Instead she pushed me backward, and then, while still standing, she slowly ran her hands up both legs. She reached my hips, took a firm grasp on my shorts, and pulled them off. I removed my shirt myself. She started at the top of my right foot, kissing, licking, moving slowly and tenderly up with her wet tongue. By the time she reached my knee I was rock hard. She took me in her mouth, slow and sensual without using her hands. I moaned. It had been a few days since we had last made love. She looked up at me, using her hand now, then she removed her lips and used only her tongue.

I sat up and grabbed her head, kissed her hard, and threw her on the bed. I was in a frenzy and tried pulling her panties off but couldn't until first unclipping the garter straps. She helped, then pushed her panties down herself. I ran my hands up her smooth inner thighs. She was glistening even though I had yet to touch her, but I did then, moving impatiently. I buried my face for a quick thirty seconds just to taste her and then I jumped up and entered her and the apartment swam with moans and sighs. I was ready to burst before I was even in, and it took no time at all to finish, a minute at the most. I pulled out of her and came on her stomach. I was still raring to go. I wiped the cum away with my wadded-up shorts and went back down on her until she came, then I entered her again and did it right this time, taking my time, moving slower, more sensuously. We reached at the same time, then collapsed into one another, breathing heavily, satisfied, smiling and kissing until it was time to go again.

❧ 4 ☙

"You sure we have to get up?" I asked, naked, exhausted, only half awake. It was six o'clock. All told, we had made love six times. It was a new record for me. I hoped it was for her, too.

"I don't want to."

"Me either," I said. "Ten more minutes."

She leaned over me and reached under the bed to grab her shirt. I laughed, being reminded of the time I crawled beneath the bed to remove her panties from my pocket the morning after we had met.

"What are you laughing at?" she asked as she pulled on her shirt.

I told her the story.

"Please tell me that isn't true."

I smiled. "I'm afraid it is, darlin'."

"You're a pervert."

"You're not figuring that out only now, are you?"

"Well, I guess not."

"Atta girl," I said.

Just then I thought I heard a noise from upstairs.

"Did you hear that?" I asked.

"Hear what?"

I sat up, listening closely.

"Hear what?" she asked again.

"Shhh."

We were both silent. I could hear a train in the distance, thirty seconds off.

"Damn it," I said.

"What?"

The train passed, obstinate and loud. Ten seconds after the last car passed, another train ran in the opposite direction.

I threw up my hands. "Of course, why wouldn't another train pass right now?"

I crawled out of bed and pulled on my underwear.

"I thought I heard yelling upstairs, something breaking."

"You sure?" she asked.

"No."

"From Gene's?"

"Yes, I think so."

I sat on the edge of the bed listening. Then a door slammed shut, followed by the sound of feet racing down one flight of stairs, then another.

"Well, I definitely heard that," Carolyn said.

"Shit. That didn't sound good." I took a breath. "You think I should go up?"

She opened her mouth to respond but Gene's familiar knock came first. I opened the door. He was tense and his eyes were red, still dressed in the same clothes he'd been wearing this morning. He tottered in front of me, shifting his weight from one leg to the other, holding his right hand in his left. It was bleeding. I reached out to steady him but he swatted my hand away.

"Are you okay?" I asked.

"We're going to have to reschedule dinner," he said through heavily slurred words. I had never seen him drunk before, and I could only guess at how much he must have put away to be as bad off as he was.

"Yeah, sure, no problem at all. But are you okay? Do you need to come in?"

He shook his head. "I'm fine. I'm sorry to have to cancel."

"Don't worry about it, Gene. No problem at all."

He turned and went up the stairs. I watched him slowly and cautiously take one step at a time. Then he disappeared and his door closed.

"You have to go up there," Carolyn said.

"I know," I said, though it was the last thing I wanted to do. I went up ten minutes later and knocked at his door. I waited there a full minute before I came back down and called his phone. He didn't answer. I wanted to call Linda but I didn't have her number, so there was nothing else to do but let it settle. Hell, I had been in the same position more times than I could count. Most of the time I wished people would have left me alone, too.

❦ 5 ❧

Late night, Carolyn beside me. I watched her sleeping, her sounds, her twitches, her fluttering eyes beneath her lids. I ran my hand down the side of her face. Softly, so as not to wake her. She had tried so hard to make my birthday a good one, and it was. The gifts, the love, the hour massage when the sun had set, the time and complete attention. It had been a great day, but despite everything, at the back of my thoughts came all the same old nagging shit that comes with every birthday—fear, insignificance, regret, and, bringing up the rear, patient and confident in its power, was the past.

❦ 6 ❧

The wind kicked up hard that night and came swirling in so forcefully that it woke us both. I lay there with my eyes open, and though she remained silent, I knew that Carolyn was doing the same by the way she was breathing; when she was asleep, her lips puckered in a soft cadence. A train rumbled by, and halfway through its passing, a loud bang split the night, and in its wake there followed the unmistakable sound of shattering glass. Carolyn simultaneously jumped and yelped and pressed tightly against me.

"Shit," I said.

"What was that?" she asked, taking a firm grip on my arm draped over her.

"The picture just fell and shattered on the floor."

I climbed out of bed and turned on the light. The hole in the wall the picture had covered was wide open; almost all of the plaster had broken away save a few insignificant pieces that held stubbornly to the hole's perimeter. The interior brick was fully exposed now, rough-hewn and shoddily done for anyone who cared to look.

"Shit," I said again, studying the hole. "What in the hell are we going to cover it with now?"

"It's not so bad," Carolyn said. "Besides, maybe some holes aren't meant to be covered."

I looked at her, turned off the light, and went back to bed.

twenty-eight

❦ 1 ❧

THE STACKED LEGAL PADS on my desk had become synonymous with defeat, with failure. On the days Carolyn worked, I'd lie in bed casting contemptuous glances at them. I would look at them, just sitting there in a neat little stack, and then I'd lie back down and close my eyes and try to sleep.

How many queries had I sent? Sixty? Seventy? I had kept a list but I didn't bother checking it anymore. The number was irrelevant. What *was* relevant, however, was that I was almost out of options. In total I had received seven requests, then received seven rejections soon thereafter, each one generic and without substance. Almost out of options, out of agents to query. Then what? Carolyn ceased asking anymore. Half of me was happy she didn't; the other half wished desperately that she would.

❦ 2 ❧

I sent the last batch out the last week of July, seven letters, written, signed, and stamped. My last hope. There was no observance or ritual this time around, no kisses to envelopes or wide eyes of excitement. I didn't even tell Carolyn. I just printed the damn things, signed them, folded them into the envelopes, and dropped them in the mail. *Good riddance,* I thought.

It took two weeks to receive the seven replies, each and every one accounted
for. Out of the last batch, I had gotten one final request, and a few days
later, I received one last rejection. To celebrate I went out and bought
a bottle of vodka and Jack Daniels and a jug of grapefruit juice. I came
home, and though I knew it'd be in vain, I walked upstairs and knocked
at Gene's door. No answer. He'd been gone for a month, no word at all,
not a sound from upstairs since the night of my birthday. The rent check
sat on my desk gathering dust.

Downstairs I made two drinks, a Greyhound in one glass, whiskey
and water over ice in the other. It was stifling hot. I sat at the desk, opened
the portfolio Linda had given me, and uncapped Gene's pen. I drank and
stared at the yellow page wondering what I could write. But the tank was
empty of ideas, free of ambition. I finished the Greyhound and half the
whiskey when Carolyn returned from work.

"Hey there," she said.

"Hi."

"What are you doing?"

"Drinking."

She looked at me closely to gauge how much I'd already had.

"Don't worry, I'm only on my second. I have ambitions of several
more, though."

She sighed. "Did the mail come?"

"Only this," I said and threw the last rejection on the bed. She picked
it up and relaxed a little when realizing what it was. I wasn't sure why.
"That's the last of 'em."

She removed her shirt and added it to the pile of dirty clothes.

"When are you going to send more?"

"I'm not," I said. "That's it."

"What? Why?"

"There's no point. The book is shit and I know it now and nobody
wants it."

"Stratton, you've had eight requests. Why would you quit now?"

"I sent out over seventy queries. I'm not quitting."

"So send more."

"Carolyn, there are only so many agents in the world. I've gone through most of them," I said. "I mean, Christ, I even sent a letter to an agent in a place called Red Hook, New York. Do you have any idea where in the hell Red Hook is?"

"No, Stratton."

"Well, neither do I."

"But you said there were hundreds."

"Christ, Carolyn. I don't know how to find the rest, okay?"

"Don't get mean."

I placed my head in my hands and looked at her through the gaps between my fingers. "I don't know what the hell else I can do. I'm hurting and I feel like a worthless piece of shit. I wrote a book I thought was good, but it isn't. I can see that now." I held out my hands, palms up, pleadingly. "I don't know what else to do, okay?"

She rolled her eyes, finished undressing, walked into the bathroom, and closed the door. The shower kicked on. I sat there for a minute, then stood with my drink in my hand and walked across the apartment and stood at the kitchen counter. I couldn't believe how callous she was, and I kept replaying in my mind the way she had rolled her eyes when I had opened up to her and made a tacit plea. Where was the support, the encouragement? I was tightly wound and growing angrier by the second. I finished the whiskey and looked at the hole across the room, exposed brick surrounded by small pieces of jagged plaster. Then I took the empty glass and hurled it as hard as I could. It hit dead center, exploding against the brick. *Steee-rike three!* I thought. Most of the broken glass rattled down the bowels of the wall, though several shards found their way to the desk and floor.

"I'm no damn good at anything else!" I yelled at the closed door. I wasn't sure she had heard me, so I kicked it hard to make sure she knew I was pissed.

Then I pulled out the bottle of Jack and took a hearty swig, set it back on the counter, and walked out the door.

❦ 4 ❧

I wasn't sure where to go. I was feeling a bit dizzy from the drinks. I pulled out my wallet. I had twelve dollars. My bank account was empty save the $500 the rent check was made out for. I would be paid again in two days, but I was reluctant to borrow money against Gene's rent. My credit card was maxed. I could afford two drinks, three if I didn't tip.

I turned off my phone. Three minutes later, I turned it back on and stared at the display to see if I had received any messages. I hadn't.

I walked to the Lamplighter. There were three others there, two men in suits and a female bartender I'd never seen before and who looked ten years removed from dancing at an off-the-beaten-path strip club catering to long-haul truckers.

"Hi, what can I get ya?" she asked.

"Just a Corona please."

It was happy hour; the Coronas were only three dollars. I finished one and ordered another. I leaned back and crossed my legs and drank the cold beers, trying like hell to keep from panicking or feeling sorry for myself.

I drank a third beer, which left me with three dollars. I thought of ordering a fourth, but the bartender had been nice and looked as though she'd have more use for the tip than I would the beer, so I left the money on the bar and walked home. The apartment was empty. I called Carolyn and it went straight to voicemail, which meant her phone was off. I left a message, then kicked off my shoes and walked to the desk. On the way there, I stepped on a piece of glass and cut the shit out of the bottom of my foot. I hopped around while hollering like some deranged Indian doing a rain dance, and then sat on the bed and pulled off my sock. The shard was half an inch thick and still lodged in my foot. I pulled it free. *Karma's a bitch*, I thought.

My foot was bleeding pretty badly. I walked to the bathroom, leaving behind a trail of blood. I rummaged through the medicine cabinet even though I knew I wouldn't find any gauze or Band-Aids. Instead I lined the bottom of a sock with toilet paper and pulled the sock over my foot. The blood seeped through but the paper and sock sopped up enough so that it didn't drip. Then I hopped around picking up the glass. Satisfied, I poured another whiskey over ice. I stacked all the pillows at the bottom of the bed and lay down, propping my foot on the pillows to keep it elevated. A little while later Carolyn came home.

"What happened?" she asked.

"I stepped on a piece of glass."

She laughed spitefully. "Serves you right."

"Piss off."

She went to the fridge and made herself a drink.

"Why didn't you answer your phone?" I asked.

"Because I didn't want to talk to you."

"Great. I love you, too, babe."

"Stratton, you shattered a glass against the wall. Then you left without telling me where you were going. Do you know how upset you'd be if I did that?"

"I wouldn't be upset."

"Bullshit," she said, scanning the floor. "Did you clean it all up?"

"I tried to."

"Look at all this blood."

"I cut the hell out of my foot, okay? What do you expect?"

"You to wipe it up, for beginners."

"Well, excuse me if I was more fucking concerned with stopping the bleeding first."

She sighed. "Great, more profanity."

"Fuck you."

"Wonderful way to talk to your girlfriend," she said indignantly. She walked into the bathroom and slammed the door shut. A fit of rage gripped me, and from my back, and for the second time in two hours, I hurled the whole glass of whiskey at the door. Just as it left my hand, but before it shattered against the door, I knew I had messed up. Whiskey and glass went everywhere. The cat leapt from the windowsill and sprinted beneath the bed. The door flung open and Carolyn surveyed the scene.

"What in the hell is the matter with you?" she screamed.

Images of my dad came rushing in, memories of his temper tantrums and sullen moods and the way he'd throw drinks at my mother when she still tended bar. It had been a perfect day thus far, so why not make the comparison? Perhaps we're more alike than I acknowledge. Or, as one of my ex-girlfriend's pops used to say, *You can't change the spots on a leopard.*

"There is glass and whiskey all over everything! Look at all this!"

"I'm sorry," I said, sitting up. "I'll clean it up."

"No shit, you'll clean it up. Goddamn it, Stratton! I'm getting sick of this!"

She shook her head and slammed the bathroom door while leaving me to ponder just what she meant by *this*. Was she sick of just me, or of our overall situation, both of us barely getting by while living in a hole? Well, I was sick of it, too, and now that the book had been universally rejected, I knew my prospects for improving our situation were slim, if not altogether nonexistent, and that depressed the hell out of me.

I could still hear her ranting on the other side of the bathroom door, but her voice was muffled and I wasn't sure what she was saying. I hopped around on one foot and cleaned up the ice and broken glass, while in my mind I wondered how and when the shift in power had taken place, when Carolyn had shed the shy and somewhat submissive skin for this thicker, more assertive one. Was I to expect this from here on out?

I finished with the big pieces and swept up the rest with a broom. I wiped away the whiskey that ran down the wall onto the floor. Thankfully none of it had reached Carolyn's clothes.

I lay back on the bed and propped my foot on the pillows. The sock was soaked with blood and I didn't really care if any was dripping.

"Great, the whole apartment smells like whiskey now," Carolyn said as she walked out of the bathroom.

I closed my eyes. "I'm sorry."

She made a sandwich and a drink of her own, taking her time at both tasks. She seemed to relax a bit in the silence.

"I'm sorry for throwing the glass," I finally said.

"What the hell has gotten into you?"

"I already told you, Carolyn."

She didn't respond. A train passed and a rush of wind blew in the windows. She was right; the whole apartment smelled like whiskey.

"Where were you?" I asked.

She dug through her purse and removed the copy of my book. I looked to the desk. I hadn't noticed it missing.

"Reading this," she said, and I wasn't sure what to feel. Flattery? Anxiety? Anger at her for not asking? Mostly I still felt like an asshole.

"How far did you get?"

"Fifty pages. Are you going to be mad about that, too?"

I thought about it a minute. No, I wasn't mad, more nervous than anything. Nobody had read it but me. And a few agents. But had they really read it, the whole thing? I highly doubted it.

"No," I said. I was quiet a moment. "What did you think?"

"I don't know yet. I want to read the whole thing first."

"You're really going to read it all?"

"Only if you're willing to let me."

I shrugged. "I don't mind if you do."

"Okay, but I'm not answering any questions until I'm finished, so don't ask."

She carried her sandwich to the desk. "Jesus, Stratton." She stopped eating and lifted my ankle, inspecting the bottom of my foot. "You're dripping. You cut yourself really badly."

"I know, it hurts like hell."

She pulled off my sock, studied the gash, then shook her head. "If you weren't so goddamn ignorant sometimes, then things like this wouldn't happen."

"I know."

I closed my eyes while she cleaned the wound with a wet rag. Then she covered it with ointment and bandages she had in her purse, pulled a fresh sock over it, and kissed the bottom of my foot. I felt remorseful, and knew I was far from deserving of her tender attention.

twenty-nine

I'M SWEAT-COVERED, OUT OF breath. Four miles today through the stifling heat beneath the cloudless sky, the rancid smell of manure filling the heavy air. Not bad for wrestling season still three months away. I reach home and neither car is in the drive. I walk around the block to cool down. When I return, my mother's car is there. I hear it ticking and can feel the heat coming off its engine. She's at the dining room table, legs crossed, smoking a cigarette. She smiles, and is somewhat done up, wearing makeup with her shiny hair past her shoulders. But there's something else there too, something a little harder to put my finger on, and it goes beyond the powder on her cheeks or the lilac perfume on her wrists. A sense of happiness perhaps, maybe even tranquility. It's been a long time since I've seen either of these things in her.

"Hey Bubby, out for a run in this heat?"

"You betcha."

"I don't see how you do it."

"Sometimes I don't either, Momma."

"I'm going shopping in a bit, maybe go to the mall. You interested?"

"Umm, I was planning on going to Jason's."

"No problem, just figured I'd ask."

"What are you going for?"

"Just browse around, maybe buy a new outfit. Been a long time," she says.

I find it odd that she'd go to the mall. The only times we ever go are

for school shopping, and while that's still a few weeks away, nothing has
been said about it yet. And besides, things are tight around the house, as
they always are. Disconnection notices arrive monthly, and my parents,
the models of perpetual insolvency that they are, are never less than a
month behind in bills, sometimes two. But I shrug it off.

I take a cold shower, and when I finish, my mother has already left. I
quickly dress in shorts, a tank top, and sandals. Jason and I have planned
on shooting guns today, and I grab the shoebox in which my father keeps
his and take it out to my car. I've had my license for a month and no
longer have to pedal the eight miles to Jason's house. I'm still dehydrated
from the run, and I go back in to grab a Gatorade from the fridge. I drink
the whole thing and throw the bottle away, and as I turn to leave, my
father arrives in his rickety pickup truck. He comes into the house, and I
can tell immediately that there's something wrong, his eyes red-rimmed
as though he's been crying, or maybe they're merely watering from the
heavy smell of urine and manure wafting into town. I can't tell which.
But I can see that he's tense. He pulls his shirt off, sweating profusely,
the faded wolf tattoo with its teeth bared glistening and looking alive on
his right pectoral.

"Have you seen yer mom?" he asks, fixing me with a cold stare.

"No," I say. I'm not sure why I lie. Something in the way he's carrying
himself, the rigid way that he sits. From the opposite side of the room,
I can feel anger rolling off him in torrents. And I know how volatile he
can be when he gets like this. Whatever the cause, he's been this way
for a month or two, always angry and yelling, poised to snap in a flash.

He goes into the kitchen and grabs two beers from the fridge and
sits at the dining room table. He pops the top of the first and drinks the
entire thing without once pulling it away, and then he smashes it down
on the table and throws it across the room but misses the garbage can.

"Is everything okay?" I ask.

He gives me a hard look of malice. "What the fuck do you care?"

"Jesus," I say.

"Fuck you."

"What the hell is your problem?" I ask.

He locks his eyes on mine. I'm sweating again and anger bubbles up inside me. I'm sick of his moods and of the way he's been talking to my mother and me, tired of him pushing us around and his temper tantrums and the way he kicks and breaks things like an angry child.

"Like you give a shit," he says and opens the second beer.

"Why are you being such an asshole?"

He smiles. "Think yer hot shit, do ya? Think yer ready to take on yer old man? You just remember who taught you those moves that have ya feelin' so cocky right now."

I shake my head. "Piss off," I say, and instead of waiting to see how he'll respond, I turn and walk out the door and get into my car, holding my breath while praying that he hasn't followed me. He hasn't. I start my car and pull away. My hands shake for most of the drive. I have the urge to go to the mall instead, to find my mother and warn her against coming home. But there are three malls the same distance away and I have no idea to which she has gone. And I doubt I'd be able to find her if I did.

I arrive at Jason's and carry the box with the gun and ammo up to his house. He walks out wearing black shorts and no shirt. The high is 101, and it feels every bit of that now, no wind, not a cloud in the sky, humid as hell. The good thing about Jason's is that he lives far enough away to evade the smell of simmering manure.

"What up, fool?"

"Shit," I say. "It's hotter than hell."

"Yeah it is."

I look at the Pepsi can in his hand and shake my head. "Empty calories," I say.

"Blow me. When I bust in your face you'll be covered in empty calories."

"Actually, I think there's a lot of protein in jizz."

We both laugh. I follow him into the house, which is hot and stuffy, and several fans do little more than circulate the hot air. Both of us are sweating.

"You mind if I use your phone?"

"No, go ahead."

I pick up the receiver and call my mother's best friend. She answers on the second ring.

"Hi, Dee, it's Stratton."

"Well, hey there," she says cheerfully.

"I was wondering, have you talked to my mom today?"

"Well no, haven't seen her since yesterday morning. Is everything okay?"

"Yeah, everything's fine. But if you see her, could you please tell her to call me at Jason's," I say, and then I give her the number. "And warn her away from going home. My father's in a really bad mood."

She pauses in such a way that suggests she might know the reason behind it. "Did he say why?" she asks.

"No."

"Well, I'll make sure she knows if I talk to her."

I pause. "Do you know why?"

"No idea, I'm afraid," she says, and I know it's a lie but I don't press her. I know I should, but at sixteen, I'm shy, still fighting for my share of worldly confidence.

I make two more calls to two of my mother's other friends, but neither answers. When I put down the phone I sigh.

"Everything okay?" Jason asks.

"I hope so. I got into an argument with my dad before coming here. He's pissed off about something, and I can't get ahold of my mom to find out."

"I wouldn't worry. Your mom would probably whip his ass if he tried anything."

"Maybe," I say. My mother's a spunky woman. The days of being pushed around by my father without fighting back are long since over. The last big fight, six months ago, I watched him smack her, then watched her slug him hard in the nose with a straight right, bringing an end to the fight and blood and tears to my father's face. *Yes,* I think, *I'm sure she'll be fine.*

Jason's holding a twelve-gauge shotgun in one hand, a black duffel bag filled with shells and a handgun in the other. A long piece of straw hangs from his mouth, and he looks like an outlaw ready for the high noon showdown in some dusty town.

We cross the field and enter the woods and reach the pavilion with its targets and cans. The sun is high in the sky, directly overhead. No wind, everything silent, the tall grass unmoving, the small pond with hardly a ripple on its glass-like surface. Jason says something and I stare at his lips without hearing a word. I'm still worried about my mom. I set the box with the gun on the ground and look out over the woods. Everything still. A discordant tranquility. I wipe the sweat from my eyes. Jason sets up a couple of one-gallon jugs full of water on the rickety stand and walks back. I remove the loaded gun and pull the slide. A bullet clicks into place. Jason stands behind me. I aim at the jug on the right and then unload all eight bullets into it. Water gushes out of it as it sails through the air. I release the clip and catch it in my left hand, hold it out to Jason, and tell him to refill it without looking behind me. He crouches down and reaches into the shoebox. "There aren't that many bullets left," he says.

"Just fill it," I reply.

He does as I've asked and hands it back. I slap it in the gun, pull back the slide, and again fire until I'm pulling the trigger and hearing nothing more than hollow metallic clicks. The jug has completely disappeared.

"You alright?" Jason asks.

I shake my head. "Something doesn't feel right." I stare at the woods, but they offer no answers, unmoving, indifferent, the jug lost somewhere in the thickness of them. "Something doesn't feel right at all."

"What do you mean?"

"I don't know," I say. "I'm going to go home, though."

"You want me to come with you?"

"Nah, I'm sure I'm just overthinking it. Probably nothing."

I reach down and grab the box to reload the gun just as I had found it, but then I realize there's but a single bullet left.

"Did I really use them all?"

"All but one."

"Shit. I don't even know where to buy ammo. Eh, whatever, just another thing my dad can be pissed about," I say, sliding the last bullet directly into the chamber.

"Well, good luck."

"Thanks," I say, then slap him five and head back. Jason's shots ring loud through the stifling heat when I make it to my car. I get in, speed out of the driveway, and race home. I make the usual ten- to fifteen-minute drive in five. The driveway is empty. I walk into the house and put the gun back in the drawer, covering it with clothes as I had found it. On the dining room table are five empty beer cans, and crumpled beside the trashcan are another three. An hour has passed since the argument. There's nothing for me to do but wait. I turn on the television, watch it for five minutes, turn it back off. I walk outside and sit on the porch swing and stare at the light traffic, waving and saying hello to those who walk by. The smell of manure becomes too strong and I go inside and punch the bag still hanging from my bedroom ceiling.

Four hours later, after the sun has set, my mother returns home, looking as she did when she left, smiling, happy, bouncing on the balls of her feet. She's carrying two bags, one in each hand.

"How'd it go?" I ask.

"Was very nice. You should have come."

I nod and agree. "Is everything okay with Dad?"

"Yeah, why?"

"He was really pissed off earlier and started an argument with me for no reason. He's been drinking pretty heavily."

She brushes the notion aside with a flick of the wrist. Why wouldn't she? We've both seen it a hundred times before, if not more. "When isn't he angry?"

"Yeah, I know. I just wanted to make sure. He seemed pretty bad this time."

"It'll be fine, I promise. He's probably drinking it off somewhere now."

"Cool," I say, and I think nothing else of it.

My mother showers and changes into a large tee that falls to her knees, then talks on the cordless phone for a half hour with her bedroom door shut. She's beaming when she comes out. We sit on the living room couch together and watch a scary movie that's so bad we laugh through most of it. She drinks a glass of white wine and I drink water. When the movie's over I brush my teeth and change into mesh shorts and do two hundred sit-ups and push-ups. She watches from the couch, and I know she'll probably sleep there, as she does most nights. When I finish I stand and point at her in a funny way and say, "I'm going to make you proud someday, Momma."

She smiles her crooked smile and the soft light shines upon her freshly scrubbed face. "You already have, Bubby," she says.

I carry the two strongest fans into my bedroom. I turn them both on high and aim them at my bed to combat the humidity. It takes forever to fall asleep. Not only is there the heat to contend with, but there's also the manure, which will linger for at least another week, maybe two if the weather stays hot. But eventually I do fall asleep, closing my eyes on a world in which my greatest foes are the heat and the manure, having no idea that when I next reopen them, hours later, it'll be to an altogether different life, one in which I've been robbed of everything I feel sure about and everything I think I know.

When I recall that night, I like to think that my mother's hair was wet, that she sat on the sofa and ate a bowl of orange sherbet, which was her favorite, and that in her mind there were thoughts of happier days on the horizon. I like to think that she watched *Golden Girls*, which was her favorite show, and that our dog, a black and white mutt no bigger than a beagle that my mother absolutely adored, sat with her and kept his head in her lap for her to scratch, and that for once all was right with the world. But I don't know if her hair was wet, or if there was sherbet in the freezer, or even if *Golden Girls* was on that night. I don't know if any of those things are true. What I do know is that on the final night of my mother's life, we watched a terrible horror movie that made us laugh, and that instead of hugging her goodnight and telling her that I loved her, I merely pointed at her and said that I was going to make her proud. And those were the last words I spoke to her, the last time I ever saw her alive.

thirty

AFTER A MOSTLY UNEVENTFUL two weeks following my shattered whiskey glass tirade, Carolyn walked in and dropped the manuscript on the desk. It was after seven in the evening and I was still in bed.

"Did you get out of bed today?" she asked.

"I did not."

I looked at the manuscript. I'd been impatiently measuring her progress by the look of the pages, slight creases and folds for the ones she'd read, straight and crisp for the ones she hadn't. There were no crisp pages left and, as Carolyn poured herself a glass of orange juice and stood drinking at the kitchen counter, I realized that I no longer wanted to know her opinion. I was in a glum mood and didn't feel my ego could take another beating. Besides, I figured that if she liked the book, she would've already said something, perhaps mentioning a scene or a line that had made her laugh, but she hadn't said a peep. In the last week, I had resigned myself to letting it go, accepting it for what it was. I was still learning, still teaching myself to write, and I hoped the book's takeaway was that it had somehow made me better.

"So it was all for a girl?" she asked. "Why he was so messed up, because he lost the girl when he was twenty?"

"I hope you really don't think that," I said.

"That's how it seemed."

"I mean, that's certainly part of it. He lost her and his mother while he was in Vietnam. Leave happy, come back empty and hollow, the world gone to shit, mother dead, fiancée far away and in the arms of another. Thus he found refuge in the warm interiors of the local bars and from the men who entered each day seeking the very same company."

"Do you think that's believable?"

"Yes, of course. Hence why I wrote a two-hundred-and-sixty-eight-page book about it."

"Don't get defensive," she said.

I sighed. "You didn't like it, did you?"

"I haven't decided. There are parts I liked a lot, actually. I loved the dog, Charley. He made me smile. And I liked the two old men he drank with, Harry and Smokie. They made me laugh and reminded me of Gene. I don't know, I think I got annoyed that he blamed everyone around him for his problems."

"He didn't blame anyone but himself."

"You think?"

I closed my eyes and stayed silent for a while.

"Did you at least like the end?"

"I don't know. He gets arrested, misses his bus, and just starts walking because he's out of money?"

"Just starts walking. He had had enough. Did you understand the river and the clock tower in the final paragraph, that the river is symbolic for a baptism, as though he and Charley were being washed of the town and his past, but yet the clock tower reminds him that regardless of where he goes, he'll never be fully absolved?"

"Hmmm," she said. "No, I didn't pick up on that."

I nodded and imagined that there were a ton of these sorts of symbols and nuances she had missed, and I almost felt the need to explain them all to her, about how I perceived the book to work on different levels, but the thought of trying to clarify in five minutes what it had taken me a year to figure out was too daunting, even if I did think it might sway her opinion. So I didn't say anything and tried discounting Carolyn's view by reminding myself that I had never seen the girl read a book before. Hell, maybe mine was her first. What did I expect? It's a masculine book, and while the vast majority of the world's readership is women, it was never written with women in mind. It wasn't written with anyone in mind. Just a story I felt was true to the world I knew.

"I really wish I knew where Gene was," I said. Every day, I went up and knocked at his door; every day, my knocks went unanswered. He'd been gone for a month and a half. Who knew if he was ever coming back?

Carolyn sat at the foot of the bed and I stared at the back of her head. The more I thought about it the sadder I became that she didn't like the book. She had been my ideal reader and I had written almost every page of it with her in mind, writing certain lines with the ulterior motive of making her smile while hoping she might fall further in love with me. She was who I had wanted to most impress, and I think that had she'd known how important it was to me, or known just how badly I needed some semblance of positive reinforcement, or any encouragement at all to keep this dream of mine alive, regardless of the source, then she might've lied and said she loved it. But she didn't, and instead I lay there feeling insignificant.

"Did I ever tell you I was a state champion in wrestling?"

"Yes, several times."

"I also took third in the nation. I was an All-American."

"I know you were."

"I should have won it all."

"Yeah?" she said, sensing that I had a profound need to tell her this, and by obliging me, she reminded me of one of my mother's old tricks: During the times my father was in one of his moods, she'd ask him to open a jar, claiming that its lid was screwed on too tightly for her to manage herself. Once I even witnessed her tightening it further before handing it over to him, and afterward, my father always seemed a little better, and thus I'd learned that the easiest way for a woman to restore a man's virility is by asking him to open a jar.

"Yeah," I said, my eyes still closed. I then spent the next ten minutes telling her all about wrestling in the national tournament and, more specifically, about the semifinal match I should have won but didn't because of a terrible call by the referee, which was the only reason I didn't win it all. As I told this story my voice grew softer and softer until it was barely audible, nothing more than the tinny click of two pennies in your pants pocket. I opened my eyes and studied Carolyn's quiet face as she looked out the window. I sighed, allowing myself to remember the glory days, when I believed my life amounted to something, and I wondered which is worse: to reach the level of success I once did and then spend the rest of your life trying to replicate it, or to never know the taste of glory in the first place? Which is worse: to never do a damn thing worthy of pride or envy, to never even try and thus being spared the knowledge of defeat, or to earn a glory so great that the rest of your life is spent in pursuit of replicating that very same feeling that came all those years ago?

Carolyn was drawn back from the ruminations the darkening windows momentarily encouraged, and the way she looked at me, as though I was a man she still loved but who she had since given up on, caused my heart to break.

"I'm sorry," I said.

"Sorry? For what?"

"I don't know, I'm just sorry. I don't understand why you stay with me."

"Because I love you."

"Even though I'm no goddamn good?"

"Stratton, that's not true."

"I'm a mess and you know it," I said, and all of a sudden, I became terrified I was going to lose her—I was certain of it, really—and even worse than that was the insufferable belief that I couldn't survive without her. She was all I had, and stumbling upon this truth, I grew hopelessly despondent and willing to say anything that might take that awful realization away.

"I'd marry you tomorrow, you know?" I said, and I believe I would have for the sole reason that marriage, in its simplest definition, is a relationship with the one person you can't get rid of except via death or divorce. No matter how enraged I might become, or how many times I stormed away, I'd always have to come back to her, and she to me. I'd have sold my soul for that security.

"I don't think we're quite ready for that, Stratton."

"I know, but I would. You're all I've got."

"That's not true," she said, and for a second, I wanted her to explain to me how it wasn't, for who else was there? But I didn't ask, because I wanted to believe her, if only by extension of her own thinking, however feeble it might be.

"I wish I wasn't the person I am half the time. But I always realize what a fuck-up I am in the end. I always do."

"I know."

"Please don't leave me alone," I whispered, feeling myself tear up.

"I'm not going to," she said with hints of exasperation. This was a conversation she didn't particularly care for, and who could blame her?

"Please don't be impatient with me right now," I said, and then swiped a tear from the corner of my eye and massaged it dry between my fingers. "I'm sorry, okay? You're all I have, and I know you deserve better."

"Stratton, I'm not going anywhere."

"You promise?"

"Yes, I promise. I'd never leave you alone. And besides, it's me we're talking about here. Cute and lovely little me. You shouldn't be mean to *me*. I'm your laaaady, remember?" she said, drawing out the word in the adorable way she sometimes did.

She then reached over and wrapped her fingers around my foot. Her hand felt warm and lovely and the feel of it made me realize I had to end the self-pity and neediness. Nothing good was coming from either, as nothing good ever does.

"I'm sorry," I said, feeling somewhat embarrassed after a minute or two of silence.

"It's okay," she replied.

❧ **2** ☙

The next day, on Thursday, Carolyn worked the early shift. She kissed me on the cheek before leaving and I hugged her good-bye. I wasn't tired but didn't feel like getting up, and so I stayed in bed. I climbed out at ten to urinate, climbed right back in. Thomas lay with me, but after a while, even he had had enough and sat at the window instead. At noon Carolyn called and I was still there. I talked to her for three minutes. She asked if the mail had come and I told her no, then hung up. I didn't feel like reading, certainly didn't feel like writing. It had been four days since I had left the apartment. I just lay in bed, awake, sometimes with my eyes open, sometimes with them closed. I didn't even bother turning on the television. When the mail came I didn't check it. Nor did I care about what I may or may not have gotten through email.

Carolyn came home at three. She looked tired and in an altogether sour mood.

"Have you been in bed all day?" she asked.

"No."

"What did you do?"

"Lie in bed."

"All day?"

"I got up to go to the bathroom a few times."

She rolled her eyes. "Did you get the mail?"

"No. Why?"

"Because I just checked it and there was nothing there."

"I heard the mailman come in. I guess there was nothing today. Why are you still preoccupied with the mail?"

"I'm not. I was just curious. Did you really not do anything today?"

"Not a damn thing."

She undressed and climbed in bed beside me.

"Everything okay?" she asked.

"Nothing is ever okay."

"Oh Christ, Stratton," she said, disgusted. She rolled away and didn't bother saying anything further. I had the urge to kick her out of bed, but I didn't have the ambition to do even that. Instead I stewed in anger for a few minutes, and when that was gone, I simply languished.

"When is the last time you left the apartment?"

"Sunday."

"Why don't you go outside and do something?"

"Fear," I said. Then I rolled over and tried sleeping.

❖ 3 ❖

The next day, I felt slightly better. Carolyn didn't work. I woke at ten, finally got out of bed an hour later and showered, then listlessly shuffled out of the stuffy apartment. The sun was out, midseventies, blue skies and smooth sailing. I checked my email at the library but found nothing important. I ate lunch at a cheap Mexican restaurant and made it home by one. The mailman was sorting the mail. He was early. I waited for him to finish, then unlocked the box and pulled out three envelopes. The first two were junk. The third was a letter from my father, and I gave it nothing more than a cursory glance as I turned to throw it into one of the garbage cans outside. But then I stopped. Something didn't add up. I had literally received hundreds of letters from him, each one the same—the capital block lettering, the return address, the penitentiary stamp over the back seal. But I had noticed something different in the split second my eyes had flitted across the envelope's face with the preconception that comes with the overly familiar, and it was with heavy dread that I finally looked a second time. My heart sank, and the hand holding the envelope began to tremble. I couldn't believe my own eyes. The name across the front, written in faint blue ink . . . it wasn't mine.

It was Carolyn's. And upon that realization, the world, and everything in it, seemed to stop moving.

❧ 4 ❧

I stared down at it. I stared and stared, and yet I couldn't believe just what I was seeing. After I had told her no, made it perfectly clear that this part of my life was off limits, no questions asked. And suddenly it all made sense, the fact that my father hadn't written in months, the reason Carolyn had been obsessing over the mail. I had completely attributed it to the excitement over query letters and the possibility of selling the book. And I now knew why she had stopped asking questions about my past months ago; she instead had asked my father, and I have no doubt that he had told her everything she wanted to know.

I looked at the letter again. I pondered tearing it to pieces and throwing it away. But I knew we were past that point. There was no ignoring it. Not at that point.

I hoofed it down the street and stood on the corner for a few minutes, trying to calm myself, but really the anger was only building. I could have trekked all the way to Indiana and I highly doubt I'd have been any less upset.

I took my time climbing the stairs, and when I reached the top, I took a deep breath, exhaled slowly, and pushed through the door. Carolyn was watching the fuzzy television with Thomas in her lap.

"Hi," she said.

I bent over, placed my hands on the kitchen counter, and closed my eyes.

"What would you do—" I began.

"What's the matter?" she asked, turning off the TV.

"What would you do," I started again, opening my eyes and lifting my head. I glared at her. My fingers hurt from the death grip I had on the counter. "If somebody you loved . . . went and did something behind your back they promised they wouldn't do?"

She deflated, hanging her head until she was staring at the floor. There was no doubt in her mind as to what had happened, and I'm sure she had feared it for some time.

"I'm sorry," she said, looking so sheepish and sad that I almost couldn't continue.

"I'm going to ask you a question, and I want the truth."

"Okay," she squeaked.

"Do you love me?"

"You know that I do."

"Then tell me, Carolyn," I said, my voice controlled even while I struggled mightily not to erupt. I wanted to, badly, wanted to break the counter in half and beat down the walls with it. "Why in the hell you wrote my father when I asked you not to, when I told you no?"

She shook her head and closed her eyes.

"I'm sorry," she said again.

"How many letters?" I asked. She kept slowly shaking her head. A tear rolled down her cheek. "How many goddamn letters have you written him?" I screamed this time.

"I don't know, okay?" she yelled back. She lifted her head, revealing her own tear-streaked face. Everything about her seemed pitiful and scared. Everything about me had turned numb with anger. Then I shook my head and started to cry myself, a hard, angry cry.

"How could you?" I asked.

"Because you don't tell me anything!" she screamed, her voice high and whiny.

"What did you tell him about me, huh? What in the hell did you tell him?"

"Why, Stratton? Why does it matter?"

"Because the son of a bitch doesn't deserve it, that's why! Now what did you write?"

"Everything!" she screamed back.

"Fuck!" I yelled and kicked the cabinet door, hearing the wood crack. A train roared by. Carolyn dried her face with the hem of her shirt. She was still crying. I simmered, waiting for the train to end. She had told him everything, so of course he had reciprocated by telling her the same.

"See this?" I said, holding the letter when she could hear me again. She looked up with her angry face, and the sight of it only made me madder. "This is the last one," I said. I took a step back and turned on the burner and it ignited with a whoosh.

"No!" she screamed.

I dropped the letter into the flames. She swept across the room and tried grabbing it, but I intercepted her before she could and pushed her backward. Her face was red and leaking and her eyes bore into me. She swung and I instinctively ducked her fist, then lifted her up and threw her on the bed. She landed on her stomach and stayed that way, lying flat with her arms over her head, bawling so loudly that I feared Gene might hear. Then I remembered Gene was gone.

"It's the last one," I said.

She just cried. Cried and cried while shuddering with each breath. I watched her, her breathing, her crying, the back of her head and body both delicate and frail, and all of a sudden I hated myself more than I ever had before. I turned away and looked to the stove. The letter had been reduced to ash. Small bits of it broke away and floated in the air. I turned off the burner. Carolyn continued to cry. I thought of leaving, walking to the nearest bar and drinking until I forgot the reasons why.

Instead I turned back to Carolyn. Her hands were over her head, her body inflating with jagged breaths, contracting in sharp wails. I started to cry again, silently, and I knew that if I were any sort of man at all, then I would go to her and take her in my arms and tell her that I was sorry for so many things. I wanted to do this, for at that moment, I suddenly realized the pain to which I still held tightly had ceased being mine alone; it had become her pain as well, and in some odd way, it bound us together every bit as much as love did. But instead I just watched her, two feet away from me yet a hundred miles apart. Then I wiped my face on my sleeve and walked out the door. I could still hear her when I reached the bottom step, and even then, I knew that it wasn't too late and that I could still turn around. I paused there and looked at the top of the stairs, where, on the other side of the wooden door, the only thing that mattered in my life lay crying in the middle of the bed we shared. But I couldn't do it. I tried, and I wanted to, but I just couldn't.

❦ 5 ❧

I didn't know where to go, anywhere to stop feeling like an asshole, like I'd done something wrong. Had I? I couldn't decide. I told her no and she went behind my back and wrote my father anyway. Those were the facts. Sure, maybe I should have answered her questions. But still, there are boundaries in every relationship each person must acknowledge. I had clearly established mine, and yet Carolyn walked right past them without batting an eye.

When I made it to the lake, I sat in the sand and placed my face in my hands and bawled. I couldn't get the sound of Carolyn's sharp wails and jagged breaths out of my head, or how frail she had looked lying facedown on the bed. It made me sadder than hell to think that she might still be that way, alone in our shitty little apartment. And of course, I missed my mother, as I always do that time of year, unhealed scabs yet again torn open. The anniversary of it all was only a week away. I shook my head. I couldn't go on the way I was, and I knew it, but as Gene had said, "Fear will hold you prisoner for as long as you allow it to." And so will the past, I realized. And it was my own damn fault for allowing both to do so.

I looked out over the water while the sunbathers cast furtive glances at the beaten man weeping in the sand. What a sight I must have been. My nose ran and I blew snot rockets on the ground and wiped away what was left with the back of my hand. Somebody handed me a wad of paper towels and said they were sorry. I said thanks and blew my nose. Then I stood and was blindsided by the crushing certainty that Carolyn had left the apartment, and maybe for good. I became frantic to get back and to try in some way to save what little was left between us, if there was anything left at all. It's one of the great fallacies, it seems to me, that love and relationships are all puppy dogs and ice cream cones. They aren't. They're about war, about coming back to the person after the big fight, about the big fight itself. No happily ever after, no Hollywood ending. Every relationship sees its share of struggle because there's no such thing as a relationship without fault. And now *I* had to return, had to do my best to make things right. I was the one who had been unwilling to meet her halfway, and goddamnit she was owed that much.

I sprinted the whole way back and was a sweaty mess by the time I rushed up the stairs and pushed through the door. Carolyn was still there, in nearly the same position I had left her, facedown on the bed with her hands over her head. She didn't appear to be crying, though I wasn't certain; she hadn't moved an inch since I had entered. I stared down at her, wanting badly to wrestle my arms around her and squeeze tightly. But I feared she wouldn't allow it, that she'd push me away in the very manner I deserved, and I couldn't take that sort of rejection then. Instead I sat at the foot of the bed and kept my back to her. I didn't know what to say, and when I tried speaking, my eyes misted over.

"I don't know what to say," I finally said. "I'm sorry I got so angry. I shouldn't have left."

Her weight shifted, but I didn't turn around.

"You're an asshole," she responded. Her tone was that of a sulking child protesting in frustration while knowing it'd bear no result. I turned around. She was sitting up, peering at me through narrow slits, and I searched her rigid face hoping it'd reveal none of the answers to questions I yearned to ask. But it disclosed plenty in the way it held itself aloft in self-righteousness, as though she felt justified in writing my father and had no regrets about doing so. She had looked forward to his letters, and I imagined the way she must have torn open each envelope and raced through his words with the giddy impatience of a schoolgirl, perhaps finding him endearing, maybe even charming.

"I don't want to talk about it," I said.

She pressed her lips into a thin, straight line.

"How about what I want? Has that ever mattered to you, Stratton?"

"In regard to my father? No, it doesn't matter to me," I said, my own eyes narrowing into piercing slits to match her own. Anger lurked around the room now and had chased away whatever sadness had been present.

"Do you even know a single thing he's gone through over the past twelve years?"

"Please tell me that's a joke."

"Does it matter that he's spent every day wishing he were dead because of the guilt, Stratton? Does it matter that he's written you hundreds of letters begging forgiveness?"

"No, it doesn't matter, Carolyn," I replied, mocking her by adding a little extra edge as I said her name.

"Stratton—"

"No, it doesn't matter, okay? I'm not talking about this with you. Some things in this world are unforgivable. I'm done. Some people don't deserve forgiveness for what they do, for the way they treat others. Fuck him."

"I'm sorry you believe that."

"What, you don't?"

"No, if you want the truth, I don't. God believes everyone deserves forgiveness."

"Carolyn, do not even start in on the God shit with me," I replied. "I'm not listening to 'the invisible man in the sky who grants wishes and sees and hears everything' bullshit, okay? I hold more faith in Santa Claus. They're one and the same as far as I'm concerned."

"Have you ever even heard his side of the story?" she asked after a pause.

I started nodding my head, rapidly, like a madman. "Yes, I have, okay? I've heard the whole damn thing, trust me."

"Well, I bet he's never heard yours."

I threw up my arms. "Christ, what the hell do you want from me?"

"I really wish you'd write him back."

I shook my head and muttered, "I just can't win."

"It's not a competition, Stratton. We're on the same team."

I groaned and dropped on the bed. Neither of us moved an inch and after ten minutes I rolled to my side and looked at her. I remembered how she had appeared the night we met, her body slack, everything about her seeming downcast and beaten while radiating such a deep sadness that I had felt it myself on some level. I had wrongly attributed it to virtue and naïveté, which were two of the features I had found attractive about her.

And then I talked to her and everything brightened, and it continued that way for a long time. An emotional convalescence. But it was over now, and as I stared at her I realized she looked almost exactly as she had back then. But she had become hardened too, containing an almost indiscernible tension that bordered on fatigue. Every so often a tenderness would sneak into her face and push the stress away, but it never stayed gone for very long.

I stood and went to the window. It hadn't rained in weeks and dust covered the brittle-looking leaves of the oak tree. As quiet as any other day in the hot sun, but a train was quickly approaching and the silence wouldn't last.

"There's not much hope for us anymore, is there?" I asked just before the train reached us. I had timed it that way, wanting her to think it over before answering.

"I don't know, Stratton," she said when the room fell silent again, and I couldn't help but notice the unhappy finality in her voice.

I turned away and we didn't talk about it any further, not my father or the growing uncertainty of our relationship. I sat at the desk and tried reading. Carolyn turned on the TV to rid the apartment of silence. She watched from her side of the bed and I climbed in and watched from mine. After an hour she asked if I wanted to help with dinner. I took it for what it was, a peace offering, a "let's agree to disagree and move on for the time being" sort of thing. I accepted. We baked two chicken breasts and whipped up mashed potatoes and peas. I drank a few screwdrivers to fight my discomfort. I teetered back and forth between feeling angry and feeling sad, and not a minute passed without my wanting to bring it all back up again. But I knew it'd only open the door to another fight I was far too tired to endure. So I just bit my tongue and pushed it all down into the pit of my stomach, as deep as I could bury it, just as I'd been doing for twelve straight years, though knowing the subject was far from being closed.

thirty-one

I WAS STILL IN bed when Carolyn left the next morning. I stayed there for most of the day. It was again hot and humid, which made the apartment almost unbearable. I considered taking a cold shower. I had the shakes, partly from hunger, partly from the miserable belief that my relationship was coming to an end.

I got up and walked to Carolyn's side of the apartment and sorted through her things. It had been a while since I had last snooped. I sifted through her clothes, her papers, little jewelry boxes that housed knick-knacks, searching first for my father's letters, and then, failing those, anything else that seemed suspicious—phone numbers on slips of paper, pictures of ex-boyfriends, old love letters. I found nothing and wasn't sure if I was relieved or disappointed, and then I wondered where else she might be keeping his letters, because surely she wasn't throwing them away, was she?

I sat in front of the window. It was two thirty and Carolyn would be home any minute. I didn't want her to see me like that—unshowered, stinking, downtrodden—so I undressed and took a cold one. When I stepped out she still wasn't home. I considered going for a walk but just then I heard footsteps and a thud on the floor above me, and in hearing it, I thought my head might explode. I snatched the rent check from the desk and took the stairs three at a time.

I pounded on his door. He answered it wearing a full beard, his hair long and shaggy.

"Jesus, where in the hell have you been?"

"Come on in, kiddo. I've been everywhere."

His apartment was suffocating, all the windows closed, the blinds drawn. A large suitcase sat in the middle of the living room, explaining the thud I had heard. I handed him the rent check. "I guess I'll have to give you another in a few days."

"Thank you, thank you. Going to need this after the trip I just had. Only walked in thirty seconds ago."

He coasted through the apartment turning on the air conditioners he had mounted in various windows. Once they were all on, we sat at the dining room table.

"Where in the hell did you go?" I asked.

"Well, first off, let me apologize for your birthday. The day kind of slipped away from me and I drank too much, and as sometimes happens when I drink too much, everything came flooding back."

"Yeah, of course, don't worry about it, Gene. What happened, anyway?"

"Let's just say I messed up pretty badly, and when it came right down to it, I preferred falling apart overseas. I wasn't in good shape and I don't remember much of what happened. After knocking on your door, I apparently came up here and packed, hailed a cab, and went to O'Hare. I got on the first flight to Paris. The plane was descending into New York before I was fully aware of what in the hell I had done. And by then I was almost a thousand miles from home."

"So you were in Paris this whole time?"

"I was there most of the time, putting old ghosts to bed, or something like that. Then I visited my wife's family in Germany, went to Italy for a few days, and spent the last week in Spain."

"Wow, I couldn't imagine. Had to be amazing."

"I assure you, kiddo, the trip wasn't all fun and pleasure; it was something I should have done years ago. Hell, you can only run from things for so long before they catch back up to you. And now I'm here, where the consequences of my actions sit waiting. And what will I do? I'll face them, and try to learn from my mistakes, because what else can I do? Even at my age. But enough of that, how are things with you?"

"Just dandy," I said. "The book has been universally rejected, I'm still jobless, and my relationship is on its last leg. So, let's just say it's good to see you."

"Damn, kiddo. You can't be left alone, can you?"

I nodded. "Something like that."

"We're a hell of a pair, me and you. Really, you hanging in there?"

"I'm hanging in there. Have you talked to Linda?"

"Nah, that ship has sailed, I'm afraid."

"Shit, Gene. I'm really sorry."

"Such is life, kiddo. We live and we learn, or we try to anyway."

I sat for a minute while he sorted through six weeks' worth of mail.

"So things are okay?" I asked.

"Things are okay."

I watched him, the top of his bowed head as he went about creating a pile of the important mail while the rest went into the trash. He looked very different with a beard, but he was the same old Gene—a fierce clarion who had a knack for spouting truth in ways both succinct and unexpected.

I bent over and wrapped my arms around him. I gave him a firm squeeze and he lifted his arm and patted me on the back.

"It's damn good to have you back," I said.

"Yeah," he replied.

❧ 2 ❧

I walked downstairs and Carolyn still wasn't home. The apartment was stifling, imbued with creosote and oil and grease. I stuck my head out the window, the sun high in the sky, beating down brightly. A bell tolled somewhere, loud, deep, consistent bongs that were near, but not near enough to detect where they were coming from. To the east, far off over the lake, dark, heavy clouds turned the sky into a menacing haze, and within it lightning strikes were followed by the low, veiled growls of thunder that'd reach us before the sun set. I watched the clouds gather and billow westward, moving faster than I originally thought but still a ways off. I tossed a book into my messenger bag and walked out the door. I called Carolyn when I got outside.

"Hello," she answered in what I took to be an impatient sigh. In the background, I could hear talking, music, laughter.

"Are you still at work?"

"No. I stopped at a bar to have a quick drink with Holly. She works with me."

I tried hiding my irritation. "You know when you're coming home?"

"No."

"Fine," I sighed.

"I'll talk to you later," she said.

I hung up without responding. I shook my head and realized it had taken Carolyn about fifteen total words to put me into a foul mood. But she called right back while the phone was still in my hand. I pressed IGNORE and slid the phone in my pocket.

I entered a café three blocks away, got a coffee, and sat by the window. It was only a quarter after three, but the thick, tenebrous clouds had swept in and blotted out the sun, turning day into night. The wind howled, its brisk sibilance heralding the promise of the coming storm's ferocity. Deafening thunder sent people scurrying. The café's tables filled and those left to stand did so while peering out with morbid curiosity. And then the rains came, hard and heavy as though, by some cataclysmic curse, the lake itself had been flipped upside down and dumped on top of us. The world turned to a milky soup only a foot beyond the glass, yet the constant strikes of lightning lit the land and offered occasional glimpses of wind-bent trees and inside-out umbrellas bouncing by. Deep torrents formed and cleansed the streets of the dust and dirt that had settled in the long stretch since the skies last opened. And as the storm grew, becoming darker and fiercer and taking on the mythic proportion of something pulled from a fairy tale, I began to wonder if I'd ever seen one quite so perfect before. And then, without notice, the storm ended, every bit as abruptly as it began. The rain had poured for fifteen straight minutes without once letting up; it didn't lessen and there was no tapering off. The storm was there and then all of a sudden it wasn't, as nothing that burns with that rate of intensity ever burns for very long.

The sun returned, shining high and bright as though there'd been no interruption. The air was rich, smelling of wet pavement; wisps of steam lifted off the cars, and stooped trees looked like bedraggled drunks fighting gravity. The temperature drop was only transient and the day grew warm again and the humidity was even worse. Water stood in deep puddles while nascent streams raced along the curbs carrying away broken branches, clumped-together leaves, and other detritus that dammed the sewer grates and created ponds that reached from one side of the street to the other.

My feet were soaked when I got home. I kicked off my sandals and called Carolyn but she didn't answer. I hadn't expected her to. I made dinner and ate with my feet propped on the windowsill. The trains ran slowly. One inched by and then another came five minutes later and completely stopped. I could see the people sitting impatiently. I toasted them with my sweaty glass of ice water but none acknowledged me back.

I called Carolyn again at seven. She didn't answer. My face and arms were hot with perspiration, and the occasional bead of sweat trickled down my spine. Early in the summer, I had noticed a direct correlation between the heat and the tracks: the higher the humidity, the more power-ful the creosote, which, at its worst, smelled like a burning mound of tar. It was making me nauseated and I was already irritated by the humidity and the perpetual sweat, and when I called Carolyn for the umpteenth time and her voicemail kicked on, I was feeling up to the task of leaving a long-winded, curse-laden rant telling her to go fuck herself and to not bother coming home, but thankfully, for reasons beyond me and for a split second only, the piercing beep snapped me back from the jaws of rage and allowed me to quietly press END.

To celebrate what I took to be a moral victory, I made a whiskey over ice, then a second, then a third, and by ten o'clock, I had polished off five. I kept calling Carolyn, continued getting her voicemail. I placed a pillow in a convenient spot on the bed and then I slugged it over and over as hard as I could with my right hand. Afterward, I was breathing heavily and sweating like a pig. Then I did it again, using both hands this time, and this resulted only in making me feel like an idiot while causing even more sweat to ooze from every pore. I undressed and moved to plan B; I popped a Xanax and drank it down with whiskey number six. It took a long time to kick in, and I lay there waiting, trying in vain not to dwell on where in the hell my girlfriend was and with whom she was out doing it.

thirty-two

I SLEPT THROUGH THE night and woke to an empty bed. It was nine. I checked my phone. No missed calls, no text messages, nothing. Carolyn hadn't come home, hadn't even called. I leapt out of bed and flew head-first into a frenzy, knowing this time there'd be no pulling me away from fury's comforting arms. I dialed her number. It went straight to voicemail, forcing me to listen to her recorded voice, waiting for the beep.

"Where are you?" I screamed into the phone. Then I called right back. Again, the same thing. I started pacing and began to sweat, or maybe I was already sweating. I called Starbucks, though I knew she wasn't working, and they told me as much. I wanted to ask for the other girl, the one Carolyn had said she was out with, but I couldn't remember her name.

Nine twenty and already the apartment was a sweatbox, the trains passing every four or five minutes, not a cloud in the sky, and the sun pouring in. There wasn't a damn thing I could do but wait, so that's what I did, watching the clock, every passing minute feeling like ten. By the time it reached eleven I felt as though an entire day had passed.

I resumed pacing, the creaking floorboards accentuating the misery in the room, sounding like cackling laughs, mocking me. I was starving but couldn't eat, feeling nauseated and distraught. I dropped face-first into the bed, then screamed as loudly and for as long as I could into the pillow. Then I stood and punched it repeatedly, which was apparently becoming a habit, a throwback to my salad days when I'd hit the heavy bag hanging in my room to rid myself of youthful frustrations. A train roared by and I yelled "fuck." Then, five minutes later, at exactly 11:23, Carolyn sauntered in. She looked tired, her face sallow and somewhat puffy. Her hair was a mess and she was still wearing her Starbucks uniform—black pants and shirt while the straps of her green apron hung lifelessly from her purse. I couldn't decide if the sight of her brought relief or more rage.

"You're kidding me, right?" I asked.

"I'm not fighting with you right now."

"Where in the hell were you?"

"I told you where I was."

"Bullshit, Carolyn. Why didn't you call?"

"I did, right after you hung up on me. I called you right back and you didn't answer. I was going to tell you I was staying at Holly's."

Holly, the name I couldn't remember.

"Well then why in the hell didn't you tell me that on the phone?"

"I was going to."

"Bullshit. You said, 'I'll talk to you later then.' That's what you said. Then I hung up."

"Yeah, and then I called right back to tell you."

"Oh you bitch, you didn't even leave a message."

"You're so romantic, the way you talk to me sometimes."

"Fuck you."

"No thank you," she said in a snotty, superior voice. I snatched the pillow from off the bed and hurled it at her as hard as I could, which of course did nothing but piss us both off even further, her because of the indicative display of violence, me because I wanted the damn thing to hit her with the weight and force of a television set.

"Where did you stay last night?" I asked.

She shook her head, undressed, slipped into a pair of black shorts. She brushed her teeth and crawled into bed, but not before grabbing Thomas and holding him in her arms. I glared at her the entire time. Thomas tried wrestling free and when she wouldn't let go he hissed at her. My first thought—irrational or not—was that he smelled somebody else's scent on her and, whether or not that was the case, I felt a rush of pride toward him. She let him go and he jumped off the bed.

"Are you going to keep staring at me like that?" she asked.

"I asked you a question."

"Stratton, I'm tired and hung over. Can we please talk about this later?"

"Where were you?"

"Ugh," she said and shook her head.

"Carolyn, I swear to god, if you cheated on me I'm going to explode."

"I didn't cheat on you!" she screamed, bolting upright. "I told you, I stayed at Holly's. Now let me friggin' sleep, okay? If you *need* me to account for every stupid minute of last night, then I will, just let me sleep first. I feel awful."

"Right, Carolyn. Do you have any idea what I've gone through worrying about where in the hell you were?"

"Of course, it's always about you, Stratton. Maybe if you stopped thinking about yourself all the time, you might actually trust me for once and wouldn't have to worry so friggin' much. Now leave me the hell alone and let me sleep."

"Yeah, sure. Go ahead and sleep. Sleep away the whole goddamn day, for all I care."

"You're one to talk."

"Blow me," I said.

"No thanks," she replied in the same shitty tone as she had before.

I sat at the desk and bore into her with my eyes while yearning to flip over the entire bed with her still in it. Despite the fight, she seemed to fall asleep almost immediately, and even that—that she was able to sleep at a time I knew I'd never be able to—pissed me off.

I sat for twenty minutes, until I was certain she had in fact entered dreamland, and then I tiptoed across the apartment and sorted through the clothes she'd worn the night before, separating her panties from the pile. I held them a few inches from my face, scrutinizing them closely even though I wasn't exactly sure what I was looking for. The white crusty residue that sometimes follows sex, or maybe a load of somebody else's cum that had seeped out of her on the walk home? Whatever it was, it wasn't there; I found nothing suspicious. Again, I wasn't sure if I was relieved or disappointed.

§ 2 §

Watching Carolyn sleep off her hangover only agitated me further, so I went to a café and read for a few hours until I had drained the coffee from my cup. When I stepped outside, the humidity almost knocked me back in. It took a second to catch my breath, and by the time I made it back I was a sweaty mess.

Carolyn was awake. She lay on her side, eyes open, holding a pillow in her arms. I didn't want to fight anymore and tried smiling, but instead flashed her the grin of the polite variety typically offered to passing strangers. I went to the bathroom. She was still watching me when I walked out, the bottom half of her face concealed by the pillow. Thomas weaved figure eights between my legs. I picked him up. Carolyn took a deep breath and tossed the pillow behind her, then rolled to her back and closed her eyes. She lifted her chin and took another deep breath, then arched her back and exhaled in a pleasurable moan. She had lost the shorts and was wearing a pair of black bikini string panties. She bent her legs, lifting her knees in the air, and then ever so slowly moved them apart. I wasn't sure what the hell was happening, and I held my breath until she had spread her legs as far as they would go. Then she placed her hands on her knees and slowly moved them up, taking the more desirable inner-thigh route. I felt Thomas against my shin and didn't realize I had dropped him.

I stepped toward the bed. My mouth was watering, and I wondered if this was some kind of game. I didn't really care if it was, for I wanted her then more than I ever had before. No, it was more than that. I *needed* her.

I slowly climbed on top of her and she stared into me with her bright green eyes; the world seemed to fade away as it always did when she looked at me. She cupped my face, kissed me tenderly and with love. I couldn't stop touching her, both of us filled with a desperate hunger that can only ever come after a big fight. Her body was taut, simple, and in this way it was perfect. She removed her panties herself and unbuttoned my jeans, pushing them down with her hands and then with her feet. Soft moans brushed against my chest and neck, my body nothing more than a mess of tingling nerves. I forgot about writing, forgot our troubles. Forgot everything. In this world a man must have success in at least one thing or perish. Something Bukowski once said. Well, I had all the success I needed then, and could go the rest of my life without writing another word as long as I had it.

Carolyn was sopping wet; I slid in easily. We held tightly to each other, kissing, touching, smelling, tasting.

"You're shaking," she whispered.

"I know."

She came almost immediately, and in the past I've always had trouble continuing on after the girl has reached climax. My problem is that I can never convince myself that the postcoital experience is an enjoyable one, as it almost never is for me, but I didn't have that problem then; if anything, I had to go slow to keep from finishing too soon, though it'd be too soon regardless of how long I lasted; I wanted it to last forever.

"I love you," she breathed into my ear, her hand caressing the side of my face.

"I love you, too."

I brought myself to the edge, slowed, then stopped. I had to pull out of her to keep from popping. She still moaned heavily, then raised her hips to me and when I reentered her she bit my neck and sent goose bumps trickling up my spine. She kept her eyes closed. I kept mine open to watch her, her lips twitching with sharp intakes of breath at each gentle thrust.

I lifted my body so that I could see myself going in and out of her. I couldn't watch without climaxing, without going to that white oblivion, and when it began I felt as though I were being pulled in. I shuddered, held my breath, and bit down on the pillow to stay anchored to the world to keep from being lost. And then it was over.

I stayed inside her, our faces inches apart, both of us slick with sweat and out of breath. She slid her hands up my back, ran her fingers through my hair. Maybe I was wrong, maybe Carolyn was still happy, still believed in me, hadn't found refuge in the arms of another. Perhaps the problems were only in my head, of my own creation. In that moment, I didn't really care, and I wished I could have stayed lost in it forever.

❦ 3 ❦

We lay around for hours before deciding to see a movie to escape the sickening railroad smell and the torrid heat. It was the first time we had gone since our very first date in December. I wanted to see a big-budget action film, but Carolyn wanted to see a romantic comedy. We saw the latter. It was a terrible film filled with the same tired clichés and gorgeous actors, devoid of originality and anything else beyond cheap laughs. But I could tell Carolyn liked it by the way she kept giggling and squeezing my hand.

It was eight o'clock when we exited. The streets were packed and the lights had come on though it was still early enough to see without them. The air remained thick and heavy and I was sweating again before we had walked twenty yards.

"So what did you think?" Carolyn asked, slipping her fingers into mine.

"Ugh," I said. "Movies like that are precisely why I hate romantic comedies. They're all completely full of shit."

"You think so?"

"Yes, of course. Things are never like that. They never tackle the hard issues, pretending that jealousy doesn't exist, and in the rare times they do, it's only ever parodied for the sake of cheap laughs. They never show relationships as they actually are. I mean, while that guy is on his stupid trip, his girlfriend is probably sleeping with her ex or taking it from behind by some stranger she met in a bar, but of course that never occurs to him," I said, and as easily as that, I had become defensive, but it wasn't entirely because of the movie. I suddenly realized that Carolyn's actions from the night before had lingered in my thoughts the entire day; I was still suspicious of where she had stayed and upset at the prospect of having been lied to.

"Jesus," she said with distaste, and I couldn't blame her, either.

"I could tell you liked it, though," I said, hearing the edge in my voice, and despite not wanting it there, I knew that Caroline had detected it also.

"Oh yeah, and why's that?"

"What do you mean? You kept laughing and gripping my hand and looking over at me during all the stupid funny parts."

She let go of my hand then and shook her head. "For your information, I didn't like it either, Stratton. I thought it was bad. I kept laughing because I was thrilled to be there with you, feeling your hand on my knee. God, why do you always do that?"

"Do what?" I asked, and the edge in my voice had grown sharper. I was tense, and perhaps I wanted to fight, for I had ignored the kind things she had actually said in order to focus on the one negative.

"Make shit up in your head and then convince yourself that it's true."

"Oh give me a break. I don't do that."

"You do it all the time! Always! And what's even worse is that if I really did like the movie, then you'd think it was some kind of slight toward you."

"Bullshit, Carolyn," I said. "I would not have."

"Yes, you would. Anytime somebody has a different opinion than you, you always think it's some kind of personal affront. It's maddening!"

We walked beneath the trees in silence, five minutes from home. At first I wasn't angry because she had caught me off guard by using a word like *affront*. But then I thought about it more and started to get pissed even while knowing I should let it go. What she had said was partly true—hell, maybe all of it was. But no, to hell with that, because I wasn't that way all the time and she was giving me far less credit than I deserved. To say otherwise was to completely disregard all the good qualities I believed I possessed.

"Yeah? And what about you?" I asked when we were two blocks from home.

She shook her head. Her eyes misted over and I knew that an angry, frustrated cry was on the way, which had the effect of frustrating me.

"Yet another thing you always do," she said, shaking her head.

"Great, another thing. Can't wait to hear this one. Enlighten me, darling."

"You always justify being an asshole by pointing out other people's flaws. Always, Stratton. And you're so friggin' judgmental about them, even faults that a person has no control over. Why don't you just deal with your own shit and leave other people alone."

"Right," I said as we made it back. "More bullshit. Since you seem so keen on spouting it, why don't you tell me where in the hell you really stayed last night?"

It was boiling inside the apartment, and the smell made me sick while my mind returned to the August months of my youth and to the raw stench of manure that, at times, grew so heavy I could hardly stand it.

Carolyn dropped her purse and sat on the bed. She shook her head. A tear slowly trickled down her cheek. I crossed the room and leaned against the desk.

"Everybody tries to make you happy, don't you see that?" she pleaded, lifting her hands and dropping them on her thighs while completely ignoring my question.

"Like hell," I said, in no mood to be criticized and upset that we could no longer make it through a day without fighting.

"Everyone does so much for you, but you're so goddamn busy feeling sorry for yourself that you never even realize it. Everyone! Gene. Me. Even Linda. But no, you hold on to your pride and your pity and keep on playing the victim card. Hold on to it all, Stratton. It seems to have gotten you this far."

"Right," I said. "The victim card. You have me figured out perfectly."

She shook her head again. Or maybe she had never stopped. "You only think of yourself. It's always you. You, you, you. You don't even listen to half the things I tell you. If it doesn't concern you, then you just glaze over and go someplace else."

"You're kidding me, right?"

"It's true!" she screamed. "Tell me, when is the last time you thought of anyone other than yourself? When? No, never mind. Tell me this: This one will be way better. When is my birthday?"

"What the hell are you talking about?"

"It's an easy goddamn question!" she screamed. "When is my birthday?"

"How should I know? You haven't had one since we've been together."

She shook her head; another tear fell from her eye. "Yes, I have. It was on Thursday, and I told you at least three different times since we've been together. Three times, Stratton," she said, holding up three fingers as though I might otherwise be confused. "I came home from work and just sat here waiting for you to surprise me with something, or at the very least to wish me a happy birthday. But you never did. You just lay in bed pitying yourself the whole friggin' day, and that's why I went out last night. To celebrate my birthday with friends, okay? I mean, you didn't even tell me that you loved me!"

"Why in the fuck didn't you remind me?" I roared.

"Because I shouldn't have had to!"

"Right, and then you go out and party all night without me. You know what? No, never mind. It's not worth it. I'm not going to sit here and listen to this shit," I said, and started toward the door.

"Fine, run away, then! That's what you always do!" she yelled, bawling now, her entire face scarlet and tear-streaked. Her nose was running and she kept sniffling.

I stopped a few feet short of the door. "Alright, I'll stay, then. Let's argue, darling. Let's have a good old-fashioned knock-down, drag-out affair."

"Why, Stratton? Why do you have to be such an asshole all the time?"

"Yes, I'm an asshole. An asshole who gave you a place to live when you had nowhere else to go."

"If I knew it would have been like this, then I would have never agreed to it!"

"Oh don't give me that bullshit! If it wasn't for me, then you'd probably be in some South Side whorehouse sucking cock for spare change. After Jimmy? If you let him fuck you, then who wouldn't you let?"

"Yes, go ahead, Stratton, tear me down if it makes you feel better. It's the only thing you can do because you know I'm right!"

"Fuck you!" I yelled, and as she sat crying, she buried her face in her hands and I felt myself tense, clenching my own hands into fists while feeling the urge to swing at her. I think I might have even cocked my arm, and then from out of nowhere, her words returned to me: *It's me we're talking about here. Cute and lovely little me. You shouldn't be mean to me. I'm your laaaady, remember?*

I dropped my head. Remembering those words had none of the pacifying effects one might assume; if anything, they made it worse, for I was well beyond reason and cheap sentimentality; I was, quite frankly, too goddamn mad. But what they did offer was a brief distraction, and during it I unclenched my hands and took a deep breath.

"I can't do this anymore," Carolyn said. She closed her eyes and shook her head. "I tried, but I just can't do it."

"Fine, Carolyn. Go ahead and leave, then."

With her eyes still shut, and in a voice so soft it was almost a whimper, she said, "You push everyone away, Stratton. Everyone. Even the people who love you. Always so preoccupied with what you don't have that you never realize just what you do."

And she was right, of course, about everything, but I didn't accept it then, and if I had, I'm certain I wouldn't have tolerated the sight of my own image in the looking glass. But I could have guessed at how it'd appear, and instead of opening my eyes and shattering the mirage built on a foundation of lies and deceit, and thus owning up to the truth—which, even then, still had the power to save me—I chose the alternative, and simply turned away. For I was craven, and preferred to be wrecked by praise than saved by criticism.

"Well fuck it then, Carolyn. I'll be the one who leaves," I said in a level voice that surprised even me. She kept her hands over her face and continued shaking her head. Not another word was spoken. I simply turned and left, just as I had done when I had confronted her about the letter, just as I had done at the restaurant downtown. I just left, quietly shutting the door behind me, and once outside, I was met by the darkening night and the late August wind blowing from the east, coming in from off the water.

❦ 4 ❧

I can't really recall what I was feeling then, but I assume I felt everything, every emotion, big and small, just as most experience over the course of a relationship, except in my case it all came during a ten-minute walk. I went right back to the same theater and bought with my last ten dollars a ticket to the film I had wanted to see in the first place. And then I sat and watched shit get blown up and torn to pieces.

For the first half hour or so I was somewhat numb and got into the movie while hardly thinking of Carolyn. But before the hour was up, the whole fight began replaying in my mind, and as it did, I felt a sharp pain in both hands from the white-knuckled grip I had on the armrests. Sometime during the second hour, I began to realize that Carolyn was right, about everything, and thus I accepted what a piece of shit I had truly been. My mind quickly turned to how I could fix the problem. Surely there had to be a solution. For twenty minutes, I believed there was. And then all of a sudden, I knew there wasn't, and I spent the last thirty minutes in deep despair and crushing remorse, which segued to full-blown panic by the time the movie ended.

I rushed out ahead of the crowd and bought flowers from the first store I passed. I speed-walked, then broke into a jog. I had the shakes again, and it was then I realized what had been happening: In some odd way I was racing through the five stages of grief at hyper-speed. During the first half hour, I wasn't numb; I hadn't thought of Carolyn because I was in denial.

Carolyn.

I sprinted the rest of the way back and rushed up the stairs and nearly shouldered through the door. But when I got inside I found the apartment empty. And by empty, what I really mean is abandoned. Carolyn's stuff was gone—her clothes, her television, her bags. Everything. I walked to the desk and went back to the door. Hanging on the hook beside it were Carolyn's keys. I lifted them away and, behind them, almost escaping notice, I found the ankle bracelet I had bought her for Christmas. She had finally taken it off, and thus left it behind.

I sat on the bed, placed my head in my hands. Then I dialed Carolyn's number. Straight to voicemail. In my sweetest voice, I left a message asking her to please call me back. And then, when I least expected it, something reached out from under the bed and grabbed ahold of the back of my ankle. I jumped and yelped in surprise. But it was only Thomas and his sandpapery tongue. I was confused as hell why he'd been left behind.

"Where's Mommy?" I asked, picking him up.

He looked at me with indifference, maybe pity. Pity in the eyes of a cat. I must be going crazy.

I called Carolyn's phone again. Again, straight to voicemail. I grabbed the bottle of Xanax and counted how many pills were left. I had seventeen. I silently congratulated myself for stockpiling them in the days I still had insurance. I took one and lay waiting for the pain to abate even though I knew it wouldn't. There weren't enough pills in the world to dull the brand of pain I was feeling. After fifteen minutes, I took a second pill and then pondered taking a third. I decided against it because I knew that I'd sleep through the ringer if Carolyn called. Instead I went upstairs and knocked at Gene's door.

"Did Carolyn come here?" I asked the second he opened it.

"You okay, kiddo? You look horrible."

"I've certainly been better, Gene. Have you seen her? Did she come up here before she left?'

"Afraid not. What's going on?"

I shook my head. "All her stuff is gone. I'm sorry, I need to go find her."

I raced back down and flew out into the night. Where, where would she go? I had no idea. Starbucks was closed. I didn't know where her friend lived. I called her phone again. Straight to voicemail. I headed west past the stadium, then started south. I walked all the way to the place she had lived with Jimmy. It took me an hour. I had convinced myself that Jimmy's moving away was part of an elaborate lie so Carolyn could still see him without raising suspicions, but when I got there, it was dark inside and obviously empty. I rang the buzzer anyway, and when nobody responded, I rang it again.

Nothing.

From there I walked to Starbucks, which stood dark and empty just like the apartment, and at two in the morning, I wasn't sure why I had expected otherwise. I checked my phone. No calls. I tried hers again. Nothing. Then I sat on the stoop. My heart was beating so fast that it scared me. Then I stood and walked home. It took another hour. I was dizzier than hell from the Xanax, and in its haze, it suddenly dawned on me that Carolyn wasn't going to call. She had had enough, just as Gene had promised, and with that realization came a whole heap of other thoughts I didn't feel up to dealing with. I took the third pill, which was the most I'd ever taken at once. Then I undressed and crawled into bed.

❦ 5 ❦

I woke early. The apartment was cool. Silence save the beating of my own heart. A pounding headache paired with a sickness for which there's no cure. An agony at dawn to top all the others and a weary wish that the day prior was nothing but a dream. But no, Carolyn's spot along the wall was as stark as the day I had moved in. I grabbed my phone. No missed calls. I lay back down with the phone still in my hand. When I woke again, it was a little after noon. I dialed her number. Instead of her voicemail, as I had expected, there was a standard greeting telling me that the number had been changed. I couldn't breathe, and my hands started shaking again. Or maybe they never stopped. I feared I might be having some sort of breakdown. I called Starbucks and asked for her by name.

"She doesn't work here anymore."

"What do you mean?"

"She came in and quit this morning."

"Do you know why?"

"Nope," the girl said. "I didn't talk to her."

I hung up and went to the bathroom, hunched over the toilet, and heaved though nothing came up. Then I pressed my cheek against the porcelain seat just as I had the first morning at Jeff's, months and months ago. Where was Carolyn's home? Somewhere in Iowa. Iowa is a big state. I couldn't remember the town. How in the hell could I not remember the name of the town Carolyn was from?

I went to the library and scanned through a list of every town and city in the state of Iowa, but not a single one was familiar. Then I searched by her last name. No results. Not a single result for the last name of Reyug in the entire state of Iowa. What else could I do? She didn't use email. Her number had been changed. I couldn't remember where she was from.

I left the library and navigated my way back to Starbucks. Maybe the person I had talked to had been instructed to tell me what she had and maybe Carolyn really was still there. When I arrived, I conjured up a smile and approached the counter. I could tell by the girl's Southern accent that she wasn't the one with whom I had spoken.

"Hi. I'm curious, is Carolyn Reyug working today?"

"Ya know, she was supposed to but she came in before we opened and quit, just like that," she said with a heavy Southern drawl.

"You're kidding me?"

"Well, no. I wish I was."

"Any idea why?"

"I'm sorry, I don't really know."

I nodded and felt tears well up again. I couldn't help it.

"I don't suppose Holly is working now?"

Confusion crossed her face.

"There's no one here by that name, I'm afraid."

I exhaled in a long, slow hiss, and as the air left my body, crushing defeat entered.

"Are you okay, sir?" she asked.

"No, I'm not," I said, shaking my head. "Not even close."

I left and started down the road that'd lead me back home, again, for the second time in twelve hours. Now there was truly nothing I could do. Out of options. Thanks for playin', pal, better luck next time. And who was Holly, if not somebody from Starbucks? I guess it didn't really matter.

I made it home. Silent. Empty. The same monument to bleakness as the day I moved in. I took the phone from my pocket. Nothing. It hadn't rung in two days. How many more days would pass until it would?

I took two Xanax and three shots of whiskey, then I moved the chair to the window and sat looking out while teetering between feeling angry and feeling sad. The dizziness hit twenty minutes later. Then I lay on my back and waited for sleep to take me someplace far away. I didn't care where, just as long as it was somewhere other than where I was.

❧ 6 ☙

Every time I woke, the pain was still there. Still there, waiting to be dealt with. I took more pills and fell back to sleep. When I couldn't sleep I thought of Carolyn, of how badly I wanted her here and how everything would be fine if I could just see that dreadful smile of hers again, if I could just stare into her beautiful green eyes. If only I could hear the way she'd laugh on the late nights when neither of us felt like sleeping, then everything would be just fine. That's all I wanted. The world to go back to the way it was. I wouldn't fuck it up again. I wouldn't.

On the third day, I was out of Xanax. Then there was nothing left to do but take the pain and regret and swallow it down like its own jagged little pill. Nothing to do but let it all come and hit me like the trains roaring past my window. Fuck those trains. Let them pass, let them come right through the wall, for all I care. What did it matter? It didn't. Carolyn was gone, and she wasn't coming back. It didn't matter at all.

thirty-three

YOU DON'T THINK I can do the shooting, do you? That since I've put it off this long, I'm just going to casually skim past? Perhaps I'll ignore it entirely, pretend it didn't happen? No, I won't, because I *can* tell it. I can and I will. Why? Because fuck you, that's why.

The fans were both on their highest setting. I couldn't hear a thing with them blowing on me. I was still hot, and with the stench of manure, it took forever to fall asleep. An hour, maybe longer. But I was exhausted from the long run earlier in the day and from the anxiety derived from worrying about my mother, and I eventually did fall asleep. It was deep and dream-filled. I don't think I woke once.

He came home late, or rather, early, considering it was dawn—sometime before six in the morning. He was blackout drunk and my mother had fallen asleep on the couch with the television on. He woke her by dousing her with a glass of cold water, and I can only assume the fight was on from there. If they yelled at each other, I didn't hear it, not then anyhow; nor do I know what was said or for how long they argued. But I do know that the fight escalated quickly when my father reached into the dining room china cabinet to retrieve a solid brass elephant statuette that must have weighed five pounds, and he hurled it across the room at my mother. He missed and instead shattered the window behind her. My eyes snapped open, but I stayed in bed because at first I thought I'd dreamt the loud noise. I strained to listen, faint hints of dawn breaking beyond my bedroom window. Both fans were still running, but aside from their incessant hum, the house was completely silent. It was silent because my father had retreated into the bedroom to get his gun while my mother dialed 911. It was something she had never done before despite the countless fights they had endured over the years. She somehow knew that this one was different, and she must have been scared. Very scared. And when my father returned with the gun in his hand, my mother screamed, loud and piercing, a scream that swept up and down my body like a flame. It was then that I threw the covers aside and leapt out of bed.

"You killed me first, Darla! You're a fucking whore and I hope you rot in hell!" he yelled as I opened my bedroom door.

My eyes found him first. He was sweating profusely. Strings of spit hung from his stubbly chin. His white T-shirt was filthy, covered with dirt and spilled beer and a slew of other stains I couldn't begin to guess at. The whites of his eyes were yellow. And then he lifted the gun. My mother was twenty feet away, and when I turned and found her, I realized she wasn't watching my father, but rather, she was looking straight at me. Our eyes met for a split second only, just enough time for some acknowledgment to pass between us—perhaps nothing more than a simple good-bye—before the gun went off. Her eyes were there, and then all of a sudden they weren't, but I had felt something. I'm still certain today that she had, too.

My mother crumpled straight down to the floor like a sackful of weights, coming to rest in an unnatural pose, her legs bent at odd angles beneath her. I rushed to my mother's side, but when I reached her she was already dead. I think I was screaming. I know I was crying. A siren whined in the distance and I looked up at my father. He stared at my mom for a moment without seeming to notice me, taking in the heaping mass she had become, and then he looked down at the gun as though feeling it in his hand for the first time while wondering how it had gotten there. And upon his face the drunken, confused gaze slowly drained away and turned grave, for he suddenly realized the true reality of what he had done. Without pause, he lifted the gun to his temple, squeezed his eyes tightly shut, and pulled the trigger. In the quiet room, there followed a resounding metallic click, for what he didn't know was that the gun held but a single bullet. A bullet he'd already used. And in defiance of this newfound logic, which, to him, must have been confounding, he continually pulled the trigger. And the gun continued to click. He finally gave up after about twenty of these. Then he shrugged once, dropped the gun on the floor, and walked outside and sat on the porch swing. The police arrived and I heard him say that he had just killed his wife. His voice was nonchalant, as though passing along the following day's forecast calling for rain.

There was blood everywhere. It just kept pouring out of her and I didn't think it would ever stop. I could smell it, metallic-like, a mixture of salt and rust filling my nose. The hollow-point did exactly the type of damage Jason's dad had said it would do. Most of my mother's face had caved in, and the bullet had triggered some synapse that made her jaw slowly open and close, open and close, open and close. I prayed it would stop, but it didn't. The back of her head was gone, and most of her brain had seeped out of the gaping hole onto the floor. I tried pushing it back in with my hand as though this might somehow help her. It squished between my fingers and I think I may have vomited then, and though I already knew that she was dead, it was at that exact moment that I fully accepted the truth of what that really meant. My mother was gone. She was never coming back.

I lifted her up and held her in my arms because I knew there was nothing else I could do. And so that's what I did, holding her tightly while rocking her back and forth and howling with tears, my right cheek pressed tightly against what remained of hers, continually telling her that I loved her. I'm sure the police eventually pulled me away, but I don't remember that happening, or much of anything else. I remember being taken to the police station and changing out of my blood-soaked shorts. I remember being asked a few questions. And at some point, hours later, my wrestling coach, Mr. Khoury—who was every bit of a father to me as my own, and maybe even more of one—came and picked me up. Everything else is lost.

I've thought about that night for twelve straight years, and while I can't always remember how my mother looked, I'll never forget the way her face collapsed or how the back of her head had simply vanished, leaving behind chunks of broken skull that clung to flaps of hair-covered skin. I'll never forget the spray of blood that hovered in the air above her like a misty cloud, or the way her brain came apart and left a trail on the floor behind her, and certainly not the way she had dropped, crumpling straight down and coming to rest in a busted heap. Those things I'm doomed to always remember. And all of it done by a bullet I myself had loaded earlier that very same day, the only bullet that was left. If only I had used them all up, or hadn't loaded the gun at all, or even something as simple as battling the heat without the fans so I could've heard them arguing sooner, then maybe she'd still be alive today. I had felt it in my bones that something would happen and yet I allowed myself to be talked out of it. And because of that, my mother was killed. That is the fact I must live with. But despite the result and of all the images that will forever haunt me, I'm left with one that will always soothe. My mother and I had shared a moment together, or rather, we had owned it, for when our eyes met, everything ceased to exist but us. Just the two of us, together, if only for the fraction of a second. At least we were given that much.

She had been having an affair for several months and was planning to leave my father. I don't know how he found out about it. Nobody ever figured it out, not even the police. The other man was an attorney she had met at the grocery store. He was tall and handsome with dark hair and eyes, a few years older than she. I sat watching from the back of the courtroom as he took the stand at the end of the trial, hating him with everything inside of me. And when the verdict was read—life imprisonment with the possibility of parole—I stole a gun from Jason's father's cabinet and went to the man's house, the attorney's, and snuck onto his property with every intention of killing him.

He lived twenty miles away in a home that sat on the shore of a small lake. His backyard sloped downward, and at the end of it, a long wooden dock jutted out into the water. I snuck back there and hid within a cluster of trees while gathering the courage to kill him, just shoot the son of a bitch and be done with it. I didn't care about the consequences. But after watching him sit with his arms crossed at the end of the dock, I realized he was crying. I had convinced myself that he'd been using my mother, wooing her with his wealth and position to add excitement to his life by having a casual fling, but after seeing how crushed he still was, how deflated he appeared, I suddenly realized that he really had loved my mother, and probably had every intention of marrying her just as they had talked about once the timing was right for her to leave my father, which, according to his word in court, was going to be that very week. The defense attorney threw everything he had at him, but the man never wavered, not that it would have mattered. My mother was, after all, dead, and my father's defense was that he was so intoxicated he couldn't recall the shooting—his blood alcohol level was .41, and toxicology results showed there was enough cocaine and heroin in his system to kill an elephant.

I sat in the bushes and watched the man for a while. At some point I started crying too, moved by an urge to go out there and sit with him so we could mourn together. I didn't, of course, and when I finally left I never saw him again. But I hold firmly to the belief that he loved my mother, and that she loved him back, for on that final day, she looked as happy as she had ever looked before, and if there's any solace to what followed, it's that in the last hours of her life, she had regained much of the vibrant sheen she'd lost along the way, and had fallen deeply in love, truly feeling happiness.

Sometime during the trial, my father's relatives tried contacting me. They even showed up in town, but whenever they arrived at a place I happened to be, I'd quietly sneak away unseen. To have allowed them into my life would have only served as a reminder of something I wanted to forget. I believed it was possible then. One of them, my father's brother, took the stand midway through the trial, and it was then I learned of my father's discharge from the military, and everything else from his past. The relatives hung around for several weeks and called dozens of times.

But when I never returned a single call, they eventually took the hint and quietly went away. I was happy they did. For all I know, they may have been good people, but I wasn't ready for them. Not then, anyhow.

I, too, testified against my father, being the only actual witness to the crime. I was terrified, feeling jittery as I sat straight as a board in the same suit I'd worn to my mother's funeral. I could see my father at the defendant's table in my peripheral vision, but I refused to look at him. And then the district attorney, who had a habit of pacing as he asked questions, passed the table, and my gaze was accidentally averted and I met my father's eyes for the first time since everything happened and for what would be the last time. He sat slumped, his face unshaven and hair disheveled, and he stared at me with such sorrow that you could tell he was a man who knew his life had come to a sudden end, and I have no doubt that he felt terrible regret for what he had done, which is, of course, what I had hoped for, his pain and agony. I took comfort in it. Then I quickly looked away and, in a shaky voice, answered the question that I'd been asked. I didn't look at my father again. There, in the courtroom, was the last time I ever saw him.

❦ 2 ❧

Two weeks after the shooting, for the first time since it had happened and for what would be the last time, I entered my parents' home. It had been cleaned, all the dishes removed from the various tables, ashtrays emptied, all the surfaces wiped and dusted. It was the same house, but everything familiar was gone, and in many ways the loss of a place is not unlike the loss of a person. The initial impact is less profound, but both vanish without notice or permission, leaving the self diminished. That's how I felt that day. Diminished. And in need of testimony of the life I had once lived there.

In the living room I stood in the spot my father had pulled the trigger. A chill ran up my spine. Then I stood in the very place my mother's life had ended. The carpet had been shampooed, the walls scrubbed. All the blood and the brains were gone. I ran my hands up the wall, then down it. I dropped to my knees. Where the baseboard met the carpet a spot of blood had been overlooked. It was dry, almost black. It didn't look like blood, but I knew that it was. I scraped it away with my thumb and some of it got stuck beneath my nail. I left it there, the very last thing of my mother.

I stood and studied the softball-size hole in the wall and could see the markings the police had made digging out the bullet. They needed it for evidence, though I figured it was superfluous since the evidence was already weighted enough in their favor. I ran my thumb along the hole's sharp edges, then stuck my finger into it. The bullet had lodged itself into a wooden stud. The perimeter had splintered, but the stud had held. For some reason I wished the cops had left it behind. And I wonder, as I sit writing these words this many years later, where that bullet is now, because the mad truth is that the bullet still exists somewhere.

The silence changed with each room. In the living room, I had encountered the heavy silence of pain and anguish that still lingered. But in the bedroom, the silence was an altogether different one, that of nostalgia, which had a voice of its own. I closed my eyes and could hear the thud of my fists against the heavy bag, the sound of my neighbor's radio that always blared when she lay by the pool and I lustily watched from my window, the smack of my lips against Emily Cole's—Emily, in sixth grade, the first girl I ever frenched. I would have never had the courage to kiss her myself, but luckily one of my friends had been there to urge us on, and even then I was scared shitless to do it. I had grown up in that room, and the essence of those events had persisted even though the door itself had been slammed shut on that particular childhood, and I knew that I was forever changed.

The windows were closed and the room was stifling. Otherwise it had remained untouched, the fans still aimed at my bed, the covers exactly as I had thrown them aside when I heard my mother's scream. The heavy bag still hung from the ceiling. I punched it a few times. It felt hard against my knuckles.

I opened drawers, looked through clothes. Then I studied all the wrestling brackets from tournaments I had won; they nearly covered every inch of all four walls. The month before, I had asked my mother where we'd hang all the future brackets I was sure to win. That had been my biggest concern then, where we'd hang the new brackets.

It didn't take long for the silences to become deafening, and when I fled the house, I didn't take anything with me. I left it all, even the pictures. Still today, I wish I had taken them. But I didn't, and I have no idea what happened to everything I left behind. I never asked.

A few weeks after the shooting I received my mother's death certificate. Date of birth: July 25, 1968, 3:47 P.M. Date of death: August 29, 2000. In the slot where the time was supposed to have been recorded, the coroner had simply written "At Dawn."

thirty-four

❦ 1 ❧

THE DAYS PASS. THEY'RE in no great hurry to pass but they pass all the
same. I write. I think of Carolyn. I sit in my quiet apartment and watch
the world in a rush beyond these walls, while within them little changes.
I sit and I wait for the trains and the vibrations. Sometimes Thomas sits
with me; sometimes he does not. We've become a family. Like the one
I was born into, it's not a perfect family. But it's a family all the same.

❦ 2 ❧

I had a great friend once, back in Ohio. A friend named Jason Daniels
who I lived with after my mother died. When I left for college I told
him and his family that I'd call with my contact information once I got
settled, but of course I never did. I knew that I wouldn't. When I left
that August day, it was the last time I saw or talked to any of them. I
left them all behind. I tried to leave *it* behind as well. The past. I should
have known better.

On my way out of town I stopped at my mother's grave for one last
visit. I had hoped to say good-bye, to tell her that I'd never forget her and
that I had felt her with me in March, when I stood covered in sweat in
the middle of the mat with twelve thousand people looking down at me,
my arms raised high, that I could hear her voice in the crowd and that I
could have never done it without her. "You're going to be my little state
champion someday," she had always said, and she was right, too. I *was* her

little state champion, if only she could have been there to see it. I wanted to say these things to her, but when I got to the grave I had a hard time not imagining what effect two years had had on her body, and I wasn't sure if I was supposed to look at the tombstone or the place I thought her face must be. In the end I didn't feel anything looking at either, and I merely told her that I loved her. Then I turned and walked away.

❧ 3 ❧

I didn't leave the apartment for two weeks. Then, in the middle of September, I couldn't take being pent-up any longer. I went for a long stroll. The summer heat had ended and the crisp autumn cool had taken the reins. I stopped and bought a cheap cigar and smoked it on my way to the water. It tasted terrible and gave me a headache almost immediately, but I stayed the course and sat in the sand smoking it till it was gone. Then I left and passed by the Lamplighter, the bar that had started it all. I thought about walking in, but didn't. I had beaten myself up enough already. It was time to move on.

I entered an Irish pub on Roscoe I'd never been to before. It was large, and the half-filled horseshoe-shaped bar was big enough to seat fifty people; around it, the Cubs game was being broadcast from fifteen or so televisions. I took an empty stool and ordered a Corona from an authentic and genial middle-aged Irishman with rosy cheeks and thinning hair and watched the game like everyone else. I lost interest quickly and then I just sat staring at my beer. I wasn't in the mood to drink and only occasionally sipped at the bottle to keep up appearances. And it was then that a familiar voice reached out to me from across the bar.

I went cold, and after taking a moment to compose myself, I slowly lifted my head. Sure enough, straight across from me with two other friends I recognized sat Jeff. He was dressed in a suit and tie as though he'd come straight from the office. He was laughing at something that had been said, and then he stopped and looked back up at the television.

It was obvious he had yet to see me. My first instinct was to simply stand and leave before he did.

I slammed the rest of my Corona. I had planned to slide off the stool but something kept me rooted there instead. I'm not exactly sure what. Perhaps some odd desire to make amends for one of many misdeeds I had done. Or maybe it was simply due to the sight of a familiar face during a time I felt most alone. I guess the reason is irrelevant, and when the bartender returned and asked in his thick brogue if he could get me another, I declined. "But I'm curious," I said. "How much is a shot of Johnny Walker Blue Label?"

"Ahh, drinkin' the good stuff, are we? A shot there of the Blue will run you forty."

I nodded. The Corona had left me with forty-six dollars in my wallet. "In that case, I'd like to order one and send it across the bar."

"Absolutely. And to whom will we be sending it?"

"To the man in the dark suit and yellow tie, please."

"With the slicked-back hair?"

"That's the one."

I reached into my wallet and laid two twenties on the bar. The Irishman swiped them away. "Coming right up," he said.

I took the rest of my cash—a five and a one—and left them for a tip. Then I watched the bartender uncork the bottle of Blue and carefully fill a shot glass to the brim with it. I'd be lying if I said I wasn't nervous, because I was. Part of me wanted to flee, even then, just make for the door and get the hell out of there. Another part, however—the part of me that still yearns to be a writer and bear witness to unpredictable scenes and situations out of curiosity alone—asserted itself and caused me to stay. I truly had no idea what to expect.

The bartender carried the shot over to Jeff and gently set it down in front of him so as not to spill any. Words were spoken. The bartender turned and pointed at me. Jeff glanced around him and our eyes met for the first time since December, when he had looked down at me with a blood-covered face from his apartment window. He took me in. His features immediately hardened, his eyes narrowing into tight little slits. I lifted my empty bottle to offer cheers, but Jeff made no reciprocation, nor did he make any move toward the shot. He finally looked away and spoke to the bartender, who promptly nodded, hefting his shoulders up and dropping them heavily in disappointment. The Irishman lifted the shot glass and turned. He seemed very uncomfortable as he crossed the bar and set it down in front of me.

"I'm sorry, sir," he said with genuine sadness. "But your friend has declined the drink in no uncertain terms. He's far from what we'd consider a gentleman in Ireland."

I shrugged. "It was worth a shot. And you never know unless you try, right?"

I'm not sure the bartender followed, but his affable nature insisted that he aimed to please, even if that meant agreeing to things he didn't fully understand.

I picked up the Blue and threw it back, sending forty dollars down the hatch. It tasted no different to me than a shot of five-dollar whiskey.

"Thank you," I said to the bartender, and then I stood and made for the door.

I took my time strolling along the city streets in no great hurry to return to my empty apartment. It was four o'clock, and the day had grown dark with the promise of rain.

I had a single letter waiting in the mailbox. It was from my father, addressed to Carolyn; it was the first to arrive since she had left. I placed it on the kitchen counter and went upstairs to Gene's, but it was Linda who answered the door, wearing nothing beneath a gray tee that fell to her knees while her face was puffy with sleep.

"Linda!" I said with great surprise.

"Hey you," she replied.

I reached in and hugged her tightly.

"Damn, it's great to see you!"

"Good to see you, too."

"So things are better?"

She nodded. "Things are good."

"Man, I'm happier than hell to hear it."

"Thank you. But how are you?"

"I'm doing alright, hanging in there. Just came up to say hello to Gene."

"Well, he's here, but he's sleeping. Want me to wake him up?"

"Nah, don't worry about it. It's nothing important."

I hugged her again and vowed to stop back later and then returned to the emptiness below. I grabbed my father's letter off the kitchen counter. The rain had started and I moved the chair in front of the window and propped my feet on the sill while keeping the letter in my lap. A cool wind pushed through, bringing with it the scent of the freshly fallen rain, and on the other side of the unshaded window, Lake Michigan stretched eastward, dusky looking and barely visible over the blank backsides of the buildings opposite, and further out, nothing more than a speck against the darkening sky, the small, green light of a faraway boat slowly flickered, dim one second, bright the next, like the soft whisper of a long-neglected dream one tries dismissing but never can quite forget.

The rain fell steadily and water dripped from the branches of the small oak. I watched them, drooping under the weight of the rain but continually shaking free and bouncing back up again with dogged determination, the leaves a verdant green, but with the fall chill and the shortening days, I could feel them ready to change color. Then, on the sill, something caught my eye reflecting in the light. I reached over and plucked away a piece of the rim of the glass I had shattered against the hole in the wall. I turned it over in my fingers, remembering the day I'd thrown it, a day when Carolyn was still here. Then I took a deep breath and chucked it out the window and continued watching the rain, feeling the wind on my face, the weight of the letter in my lap. Thomas jumped up and stared out with me, both of us silent, watching. Both waiting for the trains.

* * *

DECEMBER 24

What more can I say to put this mess to bed? Is that even a realistic goal—putting it all to bed—or am I merely creating more idealistic expectations, just as I had done with Carolyn? I'm assuming the latter.

Four months have gone by, and thus began a new season of wind and snow and cold that rages on even now. It doesn't let up. Four months since she left. I never did hear from her. I still don't know where she went.

The days passed. Most of the time I had trouble passing with them, but I got by. Somehow.

Call it resilience. I've gotten over worse, I suppose. Would I say I've *gotten over* anything? Maybe. Maybe not.

I miss her, though, and can still feel her here most nights. Everywhere another reminder, the bottle of shampoo in the shower I've yet to remove, the café I pass most days where we had first said "I love you" in front of the open fire and afterward had laughed so hard my stomach ached and coffee shot from her nose, the memory of having ice-skated at Millennium Park exactly one year ago tonight, after which I bought the ankle bracelet I gave her Christmas morning, the one she left behind. I guess I've grown sentimental. That's what love does to us. That's what losing love does, too. It makes us sentimental.

But I hope she'll remember me, as I know I will her, the way she'd growl when I was playful in the early-morning hours when she still slept and wanted to be left alone, or the way her heart seemed to break when we were unable to keep an adorable puppy with more fluff than body one lazy afternoon in a pet store. And then there were the late nights we'd whisper through the dark while drifting off to dream in each other's arms, the nights I reveled in having her near enough to touch. When I picture her, I see the way her eyes shone green after the spring rain had fallen, the asphalt glistening in the fading dusk as the sun dropped beneath the horizon while along the lake the skies lit up in orange and red with hints of blue and purple, everything darkening at day's last light, still and quiet. The good times. That's what I've chosen to hold on to.

And then there's Thomas, who now sits a single foot away, purring loudly while watching my hand work across the page. It took me a long time to figure it out. Carolyn once promised she'd never leave me alone, and she made good on that. She left me Thomas.

Over three hundred pages in and yet I'm still debating the true point of this letter. Maybe nothing more than a feeble attempt to put it all behind me and move on, some semblance of closure. We'll see if it works. I think part of the reason is to apologize to Carolyn, even while it's to you that I write. But truth can be a funny thing, often muddled and made more complicated than it really is. Just try asking somebody why they love you and you'll typically get a long list of qualities you may or may not possess. But the truth is much simpler than that. You love somebody because of how they make you feel. It's the true reason you love anything.

Linda has moved in with Gene. He emptied his storage room for her, and of course I was the one who helped carry it all out. Much of the junk found its way here, which I suppose was my own way of filling the void Carolyn left behind, albeit unsuccessfully. They both seem much happier now, and I'm happy for them even though it makes me miss Carolyn that much more, that Gene now has what I no longer do and that at the end of the day I return to an empty bed while they share theirs together. But good for them; I think they'll make it. And I'm happy for them both.

So much pain in this world. So much sadness and regret. I wonder how much of both it's possible to endure. I also wonder how much we bring upon our own selves, by our own means. Most of it, I should think.

So what's next for me? I haven't the slightest idea. Only in Hollywood do stories end conveniently wrapped in a neat little bow. I truly don't know, but if I could say just one thing to her now, it would be that I'm trying, Carolyn.

In the end, we are who we are, but I'm trying.

But enough of that. This is, after all, my love story, and I fervently believe there's enough love in this world for everyone, if only people would take the time to look for it. But of course, finding love is only half the battle, like writing the first draft of a long book; the work has only just begun. It had been my philosophy for a long time to do without the things I couldn't bear to lose. Though, truth be told, I never was very good at it. But I'm still here, still fighting the good fight even while not knowing just what that is half the time. And there is always hope. Always.

I don't know, Dad. Perhaps I've blamed you for too much, which is why I felt inclined to write so much now, the one and only reply you'll ever receive from me. I have no idea what the two of you shared in your letters, but this is the only wish of Carolyn's I'm still able to grant, this very long letter, an answer to the hundreds you've written me, only one of which I ever read, the only one I ever will. After everything had happened, there was a time when I was able to function, and I accomplished things I'll take to the grave being proud of, things I know that Mom would have been proud of, too. Maybe there will be more of them; maybe there won't. But I'm done peering over my shoulder. The more I try getting back the things I've lost along the way the more stuff keeps going out the window. For good or bad this is the life I've lived, and perhaps there's something to it, or will be in time. Who's to say? But at the very least, now you know. My side of the story.

The End